W9-ADO-592

PRAISE FOR

SORCERY OF THORNS

★ "An enthralling adventure replete with spellbinding characters, a slow-burning love story, and a world worth staying lost in."

—*Kirkus Reviews*, starred review

"*Sorcery of Thorns* is a bewitching gem, full of slow-burning romance, loyal friendships, and extraordinary world-building. I absolutely loved every moment of this story."

STEPHANIE GARBER,
#1 *New York Times* bestselling author of the Caraval series

"If you loved the Hogwarts Library, or the Great Library of the Clayr, you'll be right at home at Summershall. Tightly paced, hugely atmospheric, with a touch of wry humor, this book had me from its gothic beginning right to the perfect end."

—KATHERINE ARDEN,
author of *The Bear and the Nightingale*

"Brimming with twisty enchantment, Sorcery of Thorns is Margaret Rogerson at her most playfully addictive. The heir apparent to Diana Wynne Jones, no one can match her dark whimsy or joyous magic. This book is sheer delight."

—JESSICA CLUESS,
author of the Kingdom on Fire trilogy

"Like the grimoires that fill its pages, *Sorcery of Thorns* lives, breathes, and beckons you closer with each enchanting word. This is classic fantasy at its very best."

—JULIE C. DAO,
author of *Forest of a Thousand Lanterns*

SORCERY
OF
THORNS

Also by Margaret Rogerson

An Enchantment of Ravens

SORCERY
OF
THORNS

MARGARET ROGERSON

MARGARET K. McELDERRY BOOKS
New York   London   Toronto   Sydney   New Delhi

MARGARET K. McELDERRY BOOKS
An imprint of Simon & Schuster Children's Publishing Division
1230 Avenue of the Americas, New York, New York 10020

This book is a work of fiction. Any references to historical events, real people, or real places are used fictitiously. Other names, characters, places, and events are products of the author's imagination, and any resemblance to actual events or places or persons, living or dead, is entirely coincidental.

Text copyright © 2019 by Margaret Rogerson
Cover illustrations copyright © 2019 by Charlie Bowater
All rights reserved, including the right of reproduction in whole or in part in any form.

MARGARET K. McELDERRY BOOKS is a trademark of Simon & Schuster, Inc.
For information about special discounts for bulk purchases, please contact Simon & Schuster Special Sales at 1-866-506-1949 or business@simonandschuster.com.
The Simon & Schuster Speakers Bureau can bring authors to your live event. For more information or to book an event, contact the Simon & Schuster Speakers Bureau at 1-866-248-3049 or visit our website at www.simonspeakers.com.
Also available in a Margaret K. McElderry Books hardcover edition
Book design by Vikki Sheatsley
The text for this book was set in Sabon.
Map by Robert Lazaretti
Manufactured in the United States of America
First Margaret K. McElderry Books paperback edition June 2020
10 9 8 7 6 5 4 3 2 1
Library of Congress Cataloging-in-Publication Data
Names: Rogerson, Margaret, author.
Title: Sorcery of thorns / Margaret Rogerson.
Description: First edition. | New York : Margaret K. McElderry Books, [2019] | Summary: When apprentice librarian Elisabeth is implicated in sabotage that released the library's most dangerous grimoire, she becomes entangled in a centuries-old conspiracy that could mean the end of everything.
Identifiers: LCCN 2018037616 (print) | ISBN 9781481497619 (hardcover) | ISBN 9781481497626 (paperback) | ISBN 9781481497633 (eBook)
Subjects: | CYAC: Apprentices—Fiction. | Libraries—Fiction. | Magic—Fiction. | Foundlings—Fiction. | Fantasy.
Classification: LCC PZ7.1.R6635 Sor 2019 (print) | DDC [Fic]—dc23 LC record available at https://lccn.loc.gov/2018037616

For all the girls who found themselves in books.

ONE

NIGHT FELL AS death rode into the Great Library of Summershall. It arrived within a carriage. Elisabeth stood in the courtyard and watched the horses thunder wild-eyed through the gates, throwing froth from their mouths. High above, the last of the sunset blazed on the Great Library's tower windows, as if the rooms inside had been set on fire—but the light retreated swiftly, shrinking upward, drawing long fingers of shadow from the angels and gargoyles who guarded the library's rain-streaked parapets.

A gilt insignia shone upon the carriage's side as it rattled to a halt: a crossed quill and key, the symbol of the Collegium. Iron bars transformed the rear of the carriage into a prison cell. Though the night was cool, sweat slicked Elisabeth's palms.

"Scrivener," said the woman beside her. "Do you have your salt? Your gloves?"

Elisabeth patted the leather straps that crisscrossed her chest, feeling for the pouches they held, the canister of salt that hung at her hip. "Yes, Director." All she was missing was a sword. But she wouldn't earn that until she became a warden, after years of training at the Collegium. Few librarians made it that far. They either gave up, or they died.

"Good." The Director paused. She was a remote, elegant woman with ice-pale features and hair as red as flame. A scar ran from her left temple all the way to her jaw, puckering her cheek and pulling one corner of her mouth permanently to the side. Like Elisabeth, she wore leather straps over her chest, but she had on a warden's uniform beneath them instead of an apprentice's robes. Lamplight glinted off the brass buttons on her dark blue coat and shone from her polished boots. The sword belted at her side was slender and tapered, with garnets glittering on its pommel.

That sword was famous at Summershall. It was named Demonslayer, and the Director had used it to battle a Malefict when she was only nineteen years old. That was where she had gotten the scar, which was rumored to cause her excruciating agony whenever she spoke. Elisabeth doubted the accuracy of those rumors, but it was true that the Director chose her words carefully, and certainly never smiled.

"Remember," the Director went on at last, "if you hear a voice in your mind once we reach the vault, do not listen to what it says. This is a Class Eight, centuries old, and not to be trifled with. Since its creation, it has driven dozens of people mad. Are you ready?"

Elisabeth swallowed. The knot in her throat prevented her from answering. She could hardly believe the Director was speaking to her, much less that she had summoned her to help transport a delivery to the vault. Ordinarily such a responsibility fell far above the rank of apprentice librarian. Hope ricocheted through her like a bird trapped within a house, taking flight, falling, and taking flight again, exhausting itself for the promise of open skies far away. Terror flickered after it like a shadow.

She's giving me a chance to prove that I'm worth training as a warden, she thought. *If I fail, I will die. Then at least I'll have a use. They can bury me in the garden to feed the radishes.*

Wiping her sweaty palms on the sides of her robes, she nodded.

The Director set off across the courtyard, and Elisabeth followed. Gravel crunched beneath their heels. A foul stench clotted the air as they drew nearer, like waterlogged leather left to rot on the seashore. Elisabeth had grown up in the Great Library, surrounded by the ink-and-parchment smell of magical tomes, but this was far from what she was used to. The stench stung her eyes and stippled her arms with goose bumps. It was even making the horses nervous. They shied in their traces, scattering gravel as they ignored the driver's attempts to calm them down. In a way she envied them, for at least they didn't know what had ridden behind them all the way from the capital.

A pair of wardens leaped down from the front of the carriage, their hands planted on the hilts of their swords. Elisabeth forced herself not to shrink back when they glowered at her. Instead she straightened her spine and lifted her chin, endeavoring to match their stony expressions. She might never earn a blade, but at least she could appear brave enough to wield one.

The Director's key ring rattled, and the carriage's rear doors swung open with a shuddering groan. At first, in the gloom, the iron-lined cell appeared empty. Then Elisabeth made out an object on the floor: a flat, square, iron coffer, secured with more than a dozen locks. To a layperson, the precautions would have appeared absurd—but not for long. In the twilit silence, a single, reverberating thud issued from within the coffer, powerful enough to shake the carriage and rattle the doors on their hinges. One of the horses screamed.

"Quickly," the Director said. She took one of the coffer's handles, and Elisabeth seized the other. They hefted its weight between them and proceeded toward a door with an inscription carved atop it, the arching scroll clasped on either side by weeping angels. OFFICIUM ADUSQUE MORTEM, it read dimly, nearly obscured by shadow. The warden's motto. *Duty unto death*.

They entered a long stone corridor burnished by the jumping light of torches. The coffer's leaden weight already strained Elisabeth's arm. It did not move again, but its stillness failed to reassure her, for she suspected what it meant: the book within was listening. It was waiting.

Another warden stood guard beside the entrance to the vault. When he saw Elisabeth at the Director's side, his small eyes gleamed with loathing. This was Warden Finch. He was a grizzled man with short gray hair and a puffy face into which his features seemed to recede, like raisins in a bread pudding. Among the apprentices, he was infamous for the fact that his right hand was larger than the other, bulging with muscle, because he exercised it so often whipping them.

She squeezed the coffer's handle until her knuckles turned white, instinctively bracing herself for a blow, but Finch could do nothing to her in front of the Director. Muttering beneath his breath, he heaved on a chain. Inch by inch, the portcullis rose, lifting its sharp black teeth above their heads. Elisabeth stepped forward.

And the coffer *lurched*.

"Steady," the Director snapped, as both of them careened against the stone wall, barely keeping their balance. Elisabeth's stomach swooped. Her boot hung over the edge of a spiral stair that twisted vertiginously down into darkness.

The horrible truth dawned on her. The grimoire had wanted them to fall. She imagined the coffer tumbling down the stairs, striking the flagstones at the bottom, bursting open—and it would have been her fault—

The Director's hand clasped her shoulder. "It's all right, Scrivener. Nothing's happened. Grip the rail and keep going."

With an effort, Elisabeth turned away from Finch's condemning scowl. Down they went. A subterranean chill wafted up from below, smelling of cold rock and mildew, and of something less natural. The stone itself bled the malice of ancient things that had languished in darkness for centuries—consciousnesses that did not slumber, minds that did not dream. Muffled by thousands of pounds of earth, the silence was such that she heard only her own pulse pounding in her ears.

She had spent her childhood exploring the Great Library's myriad nooks and crannies, prying into its countless mysteries, but she had never been inside the vault. Its presence had lurked beneath the library her entire life like something unspeakable hiding under the bed.

This is my chance, she reminded herself. She could not be afraid.

They emerged into a chamber that resembled a cathedral's crypt. The walls, ceiling, and floor were all carved from the same gray stone. The ribbed pillars and vaulted ceilings had been crafted with artistry, even reverence. Statues of angels stood in niches along the walls, candles guttering at their feet. With sorrowful, shadowed eyes, they watched over the rows of iron shelves that formed aisles down the center of the vault. Unlike the bookcases in the upper portions of the library, these were welded in place. Chains secured the locked coffers, which slid between the shelves like drawers.

Elisabeth assured herself that it was her imagination conjuring up whispers from the coffers as they passed. A thick layer of dust coated the chains. Most of the coffers hadn't been disturbed in decades, and their inhabitants remained fast asleep. Yet the back of her neck still prickled as though she were being watched.

The Director guided her beyond the shelves, toward a cell with a table bolted to the floor at the center. A single oil lamp cast a jaundiced glow across its ink-stained surface. The coffer remained unsettlingly cooperative as they set it down beside four enormous gashes, like giant claw marks, that scarred the table's wood. Elisabeth's eyes darted to the gashes again and again. She knew what had made them. What happened when a grimoire got out of control.

Malefict.

"What precaution do we take first?" the Director asked, jolting Elisabeth from her thoughts. The test had begun.

"Salt," she answered, reaching for the canister at her hip. "Like iron, salt weakens demonic energies." Her hand trembled slightly as she shook out the crystals, forming a lopsided circle. Shame flushed her cheeks at the sight of its uneven edges. What if she wasn't ready, after all?

The barest hint of warmth softened the Director's severe face. "Do you know why I chose to keep you, Elisabeth?"

Elisabeth froze, the breath trapped in her chest. The Director had never addressed her by her given name—only her last name, Scrivener, or sometimes just "apprentice," depending on how much trouble she was in, which was often a fantastic amount. "No, Director," she said.

"Hmm. It was storming, I recall. The grimoires were restless that night. They were making so much noise that I barely heard the knock on the front doors." Elisabeth could easily picture the scene. Rain lashing against the windows, the tomes howling and sobbing and rattling beneath their restraints. "When I found you on the steps, and picked you up and brought you inside, I was certain you would cry. Instead, you looked around and began to laugh. You were not afraid. At that moment I knew I couldn't send you away to an orphanage. You belonged in the library, as much as any book."

Elisabeth had been told the story before, but only by her tutor, never the Director herself. Two words echoed through her mind with the vitality of a heartbeat: *you belonged*. They were words that she had waited sixteen years to hear, and desperately hoped were true.

In breathless silence, she watched the Director reach for her keys and select the largest one, ancient enough to have rusted almost beyond recognition. It was clear that for the Director, the time for sentiment had passed. Elisabeth contented herself with repeating the unspoken vow she had held close for nearly as long as she could remember. One day, she would become a warden, too. She would make the Director proud.

Salt cascaded onto the table as the coffer's lid creaked open. A stench of rotting leather rolled across the vault, so potent that she almost gagged.

A grimoire lay inside. It was a thick volume with disheveled, yellowing pages sandwiched between slabs of greasy black leather. It would have looked fairly ordinary, if not for the bulbous protrusions that bulged from the cover. They resembled giant warts, or bubbles on the surface of a pool of tar. Each was the size of a large marble, and there were dozens altogether, deforming nearly every inch of the leather's surface.

The Director pulled on a heavy pair of iron-lined gloves. Elisabeth hastened to follow her example. She bit the inside of her cheek as the Director lifted the book from the coffer and placed it within the circle of salt.

The instant the Director set it down, the protrusions split open. They weren't warts—they were eyes. Eyes of every color, bloodstained and rolling, the pupils dilating and contracting to pinpricks as the grimoire convulsed in the Director's hands. Gritting her teeth, she forced it open. Automatically, Elisabeth reached into the circle and clamped down the other side, feeling the leather twitch and heave through her gloves. Furious. Alive.

Those eyes were not sorcerous conjurations. They were real, plucked from human skulls long ago, sacrificed to create a volume powerful enough to contain the spells etched across its pages. According to history, most sacrifices had not been willing.

"The Book of Eyes," the Director said, perfectly calm. "It contains spells that allow sorcerers to reach into the minds of others, read their thoughts, and even control their actions. Fortunately, only a handful of sorcerers in the entire kingdom have ever been granted permission to read it."

"Why would they want to?" Elisabeth burst out, before she could stop herself. The answer was obvious. Sorcerers were evil by nature, corrupted by the demonic magic they wielded. If it weren't for the Reforms, which had made it illegal for sorcerers to bind books with human parts, grimoires like the Book of Eyes wouldn't be so exceptionally rare. No doubt sorcerers had attempted to replicate it over the years, but the spells couldn't be written down using ordinary materials. The sorcery's power would instantly reduce the ink and parchment to ashes.

To her surprise, the Director took her question seriously, though she was no longer looking at Elisabeth. Instead she focused on turning the pages, inspecting them for any damage they might have sustained during the journey. "There may come a time when spells like these are necessary, no matter how foul. We have a great responsibility to our kingdom, Scrivener. If this grimoire were destroyed, its spells would be lost forever. It's the only one of its kind."

"Yes, Director." That, she understood. Wardens both protected grimoires from the world, and protected the world from them.

She braced herself as the Director paused, leaning down to examine a stain on one of the pages. Transferring high-class grimoires came at a risk, since any accidental damage could provoke their transformation into a Malefict. They needed to be inspected carefully before their interment in the vault. Elisabeth felt certain that several of the eyes, peering out from beneath the cover, were aimed directly at her—and that they glittered with cunning.

Somehow, she knew she shouldn't meet their gaze. Hoping to distract herself, she glanced aside to the pages. Some of the sentences were written in Austermeerish or the Old Tongue. But others were scrawled in Enochian, the language of sorcerers, made up of strange, jagged runes that shimmered on the parchment like smoldering embers. It was a language one could only learn by consorting with demons. Merely looking at the runes made her temples throb.

"Apprentice . . ."

The whisper slithered against her mind, as alien and unexpected as the cold, slimy touch of a fish beneath the water of a pond. Elisabeth jerked and looked up. If the Director heard the voice, too, she showed no sign.

"Apprentice, I see you. . . ."

Elisabeth's breath caught. She did as the Director had instructed and tried to ignore the voice, but it was impossible to concentrate on anything else with so many eyes watching her, agleam with sinister intelligence.

"Look at me . . . look . . ."

Slowly but surely, as if drawn by an invisible force, Elisabeth's gaze began to travel downward.

"There," said the Director. Her voice sounded dim and distorted, like she was speaking from underwater. "We are finished. Scrivener?"

When Elisabeth didn't answer, the Director slammed the grimoire shut, cutting its voice off midwhisper. Elisabeth's senses rushed back. She sucked in a breath, her face burning with humiliation. The eyes bulged furiously, darting between her and the Director.

"Well done," the Director said. "You held out much longer than I expected."

"It almost had me," Elisabeth whispered. How could the Director congratulate her? A clammy sweat clung to her skin, and in the vault's chill, she began to shiver.

"Yes. That was what I wished to show you tonight. You have a way with grimoires, an affinity for them that I have never seen in an apprentice before. But despite that, you still have much to learn. You want to become a warden, do you not?"

Spoken in front of the Director, witnessed by the angel statues lining the walls, Elisabeth's soft reply possessed the quality of a confession. "It's all I've ever wanted."

"Just remember that there are many paths open to you." The scar's distortion gave the Director's mouth an almost rueful cast. "Be certain, before you choose, that the life of a warden is what you truly desire."

Elisabeth nodded, not trusting herself to speak. If she had passed the test, she didn't understand why the Director would advise her to consider forsaking her dream. Perhaps she had shown herself in some other way to be unready, unprepared. In that case, she would simply have to try harder. She had a year left before she turned seventeen and became eligible for training at the Collegium—time she could use to prove herself beyond a doubt, and earn the Director's approval. She only hoped it would be enough.

Together, they wrestled the grimoire back into the coffer. As soon as it touched the salt, it ceased struggling. The eyes rolled upward, showing crescents of milky white before they sagged shut. The slam of the lid shattered the vault's sepulchral quiet. The coffer wouldn't be opened again for years, perhaps decades. It was secure. It posed a threat no longer.

But she couldn't banish the sound of its voice from her thoughts, or the feeling that she hadn't seen the last of the Book of Eyes—and it had not seen the last of her.

TWO

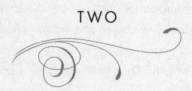

ELISABETH SAT BACK, admiring the view from her desk. She had been assigned to transfers on the third floor, a vantage from which she could see all the way across the library's atrium. Sunlight streamed in through the rose window high above the front doors, casting prisms of ruby, sapphire, and emerald across the circular balconies' bronze rails. Bookcases soared upward toward a vaulted ceiling six stories above, rising around the atrium like the layers of a wedding cake or the tiers of a coliseum. Murmurs filled the echoing space, punctuated by the occasional cough or snore. Most of those sounds did not belong to the blue-robed librarians striding to and fro across the atrium's tiles. They came from the grimoires, muttering on the shelves.

When she breathed in, the sweetness of parchment and leather filled her lungs. Motes of dust hung suspended in the sunbeams, perfectly still, like flakes of gold leaf trapped in resin. And teetering stacks of paperwork threatened to spill from her desk at any moment, burying her in a landslide of neglected transfer requests.

Reluctantly, she wrested her attention toward the imposing

piles. The Great Library of Summershall was one of six Great Libraries in the kingdom. It was a full three day's journey from its closest neighbors, which were spaced evenly apart in a circle around Austermeer, with the Inkroads connecting them to the capital at the center like the spokes of a wheel. Transferring grimoires between them could be a delicate task. Some volumes nurtured such a potent grudge toward each other that they couldn't be brought within miles of the same location without howling or bursting into flame. There was even a house-sized crater in the wilderness of the Wildmarch where two books had clashed over a matter of thaumaturgical doctrine.

As an apprentice, Elisabeth was entrusted with approving transfers for Classes One through Three. Grimoires were classed on a ten-point scale according to their level of risk, with anything Class Four and above requiring special confinement. Summershall itself held nothing above a Class Eight.

Closing her eyes, she reached for the paper on top of the stack. *Knockfeld*, she guessed, thinking of Summershall's neighbor to the northeast.

But when she turned the paper over, it was a request from the Royal Library. Unsurprising; that was where more than two-thirds of her transfers went. One day she might pack up her belongings and travel there, too. The Royal Library shared a grounds with the Collegium at the heart of the capital, and when she wasn't busy with her warden training, she would be able to wander its halls. In her imagination its corridors stretched on for miles, lined with books and passageways and hidden rooms that contained all the secrets of the universe.

But only if she earned the Director's approval. A week had passed since the night in the vault, and she hadn't come any closer to deciphering the Director's advice.

She still remembered the exact moment that she'd vowed to become a warden. She had been eight years old, and she had fled into the library's secret passageways in order to escape one of Master Hargrove's lectures. She hadn't been able to bear another hour of fidgeting on a stool in the stifling storeroom-turned-classroom, reciting declensions in the Old Tongue. Not on an afternoon when summer pounded its fists against the library's walls, thickening the air to the consistency of honey.

She recalled the way sweat had trickled down her spine as she crawled through the passage's cobwebs on her hands and knees. At least the passage was dark, away from the sun. The golden glow that filtered between the floorboards provided enough light to see by, and to avoid the skittering shapes of booklice as she disturbed their nests, sending them racing around in a panic. Some grew to the size of rats, engorged on enchanted parchment.

If only Master Hargrove had agreed to take her into town that day. It was just a five-minute walk down the hill through the orchard. The market would be bustling with people selling ribbons and apples and glazed custards, and travelers sometimes came in from outside Summershall to peddle their wares. She had once heard accordion music, and seen a dancing bear, and even watched a man demonstrate a lamp whose wick burned without oil. The books in her classroom hadn't been able to explain how the lamp worked, so she assumed it was magic, and therefore evil.

Perhaps that was why Master Hargrove didn't like taking her into town. If she happened to encounter a sorcerer outside the library's protection, he might steal her away. A young girl like her would no doubt make a convenient sacrifice for a demonic ritual.

Voices snapped Elisabeth back to attention. They were emanating from directly beneath her. One voice belonged to Master Hargrove, and the other to . . .

The Director.

Her heart leaped. She flattened herself against the floor-boards to peer through a knothole, the light that poured through it setting her tangled hair aglow. She couldn't see much: a slice of desk covered in papers, the corner of an unfamiliar office. The thought that it might belong to the Director sent her pulse racing with excitement.

"That makes for the third time this month," Hargrove was saying, "and I'm simply at my wit's end. The girl is half-wild. Vanishing off to who-knows-where, getting into every possible kind of trouble—just last week, she released an entire crate of live booklice in my bedchambers!"

Elisabeth barely stopped herself from shouting an objection through the knothole. She'd collected those booklice with the intention of studying them, not setting them free. Their loss had come as a tremendous blow.

But what Hargrove said next made her forget all about the lice.

"I simply have to question if it's the right decision, raising a child in a Great Library. I'm certain that whoever left her on our doorstep knew we are in the practice of taking on foundlings as our apprentices. But we do not accept those boys and girls until the age of thirteen. I hesitate to agree with Warden Finch on any matter, yet I do believe we ought to consider what he's been saying all along: that young Elisabeth might fare better in an orphanage."

While unsettling, this was nothing Elisabeth hadn't heard before. She endured the remarks knowing that the Director's will assured her place in the library. Why, she could not say. The

Director rarely spoke to her. She was as remote and untouchable as the moon, and equally as mysterious. To Elisabeth, the Director's decision to take her in possessed an almost mystical quality, like something out of a fairy tale. It could not be questioned or undone.

Holding her breath, she waited for the Director to counter Hargrove's suggestion. The skin on her arms tingled with the anticipation of hearing her speak.

Instead, the Director said, "I have wondered the same, Master Hargrove. Almost every day for the past eight years."

No—that couldn't be right. The blood slowed to a crawl in Elisabeth's veins. The pounding in her ears almost drowned out the rest.

"All those years ago, I did not consider the effect it might have on her to grow up isolated from other children her age. The youngest apprentices are still five years her elder. Has she displayed any interest in befriending them?"

"I'm afraid she's tried, with little success," Hargrove said. "Though she may not know it herself. Recently I overheard an apprentice explaining to her that ordinary children have mothers and fathers. Poor Elisabeth had no idea what he was talking about. She quite happily replied that she had plenty of books to keep her company."

The Director sighed. "Her attachment to the grimoires is . . ."

"Concerning? Yes, indeed. If she does not suffer from the lack of company, I fear it is because she sees grimoires as her friends in place of people."

"A dangerous way of thinking. But libraries are dangerous places. There is no getting around it."

"Too dangerous for Elisabeth, do you think?"

No, Elisabeth begged. She knew these weren't ordinary

books the Great Library kept. They whispered on the shelves and shuddered beneath iron chains. Some spat ink and threw tantrums; others sang to themselves in high, clear notes on windless nights, when starlight streamed through the library's barred windows like shafts of mercury. Others still were so dangerous they had to be stored in the underground vault, packed in salt. Not all of them were her friends. She understood that well.

But sending her away would be like placing a grimoire among inanimate books that didn't move or speak. The first time she had seen such a book, she had thought it was dead. She did not belong in an orphanage, whatever that was. In her mind's eye the place resembled a prison, gray and shrouded in damp mists, barred by a portcullis like the entrance to the vault. Terror squeezed her throat at the image.

"Do you know why the Great Libraries take in orphans, Master Hargrove?" the Director asked at last. "It is because they have no home, no family. No one to miss them if they die. I wonder, perhaps . . . if Scrivener has lasted this long, it is because the library wished it to be so. If her bond to this place is better left intact, for good or for ill."

"I hope you are not making a mistake, Director," Master Hargrove said gently.

"I do as well." The Director sounded weary. "For Scrivener's sake, and our own."

Elisabeth waited, ears straining, but the deliberation over her fate seemed to have concluded. Footsteps creaked below, and the office's door clicked shut.

She had been granted a reprieve—for now. How long would it last? With the foundations of her world left shaken, it seemed the rest of her life might come tumbling down at any moment. A single decision by the Director could send her away for good. She had never felt so uncertain, so helpless, so small.

It was then that she made her vow, crouched amid the dust and cobwebs, grasping for the only lifeline within reach. If the Director was not certain that the Great Library was the best place for Elisabeth, she would simply have to prove it. She would become a great and powerful warden, just like the Director. She would show everyone that she belonged until even Warden Finch could no longer deny her right.

Above all . . .

Above all, she would convince them that she wasn't a mistake.

"Elisabeth," a voice hissed in the present. "Elisabeth! Are you asleep?"

Startled, she jerked upright, the memory swirling away like water down a drain. She cast around until she found the source of the voice. A girl's face peered out from between two nearby bookcases, her braid flicking over her shoulder as she checked to make sure no one else was in sight. A pair of spectacles magnified her dark, clever eyes, and hastily scribbled notes marked the brown skin of her forearms, their ink peeking out from beneath her sleeves. Like Elisabeth, she wore a key on a chain around her neck, bright against her pale blue apprentice's robes.

As luck would have it, Elisabeth hadn't remained friendless forever. She had met Katrien Quillworthy the day they had both begun their apprenticeship at the age of thirteen. None of the other apprentices had wanted to share a room with Elisabeth, due to a rumor that she kept a box full of booklice underneath her bed. But Katrien had approached her for that very reason. "It had better be true," she had said. "I've been wanting to experiment with booklice ever since I heard about them. Apparently they're immune to sorcery—can you imagine the scientific implications?" They had been inseparable ever since.

Elisabeth covertly shoved her papers to the side. "Is something happening?" she whispered.

"I think you're the only person in Summershall who doesn't know what's happening. Including Hargrove, who's spent the entire morning in the privy."

"Warden Finch isn't getting demoted, is he?" she asked hopefully.

Katrien grinned. "I'm still working on that. I'm sure I'll find something incriminating on him eventually. When it happens, you'll be the first to know." Orchestrating Warden Finch's downfall had been her pet project for years. "No, it's a magister. He's just arrived for a trip to the vault."

Elisabeth nearly tumbled from her chair. She shot a look around before darting behind the bookcase next to Katrien, stooping low beside her. Katrien was so short that otherwise, all Elisabeth could see was the top of her head. "A magister? Are you certain?"

"Absolutely. I've never seen the wardens so tense."

Now that Elisabeth thought back, the signs from that morning were obvious. Wardens striding past with their jaws set and their hands clenching their swords. Apprentices forming clusters in the halls, whispering around every corner. Even the grimoires seemed more restless than usual.

A magister. Fear thrilled through her like a note shivering up and down the strings of a harp. "What does that have to do with us?" she asked. Neither of them had so much as seen a regular sorcerer. On the rare occasions that they visited Summershall, the wardens brought them in through a special door and ushered them straight into a reading room. She was certain a magister would be treated with even greater caution.

Katrien's eyes shone. "Stefan's made a bet with me that the magister has pointed ears and cloven hooves. He's wrong, naturally, but I have to find a way to prove it. I'm going to spy on the magister. And I need you to corroborate my account."

Elisabeth sucked in a breath. She glanced reflexively at her abandoned desk. "To do that, we'd have to go out of bounds."

"And Finch would have our heads on pikes if he caught us," Katrien finished. "But he won't. He doesn't know about the passageways."

For once, Finch wasn't Elisabeth's greatest concern. The Book of Eyes' bloodshot, bulging stare flashed through her mind. Any of those eyes could have previously belonged to someone like her or Katrien. "If the magister catches us," she said, "he'll do worse than put our heads on pikes."

"I doubt it. The Reforms made it illegal for sorcerers to kill people outside of self-defense. He'll just make our hair fall out, or cover us in boils." She wiggled her eyebrows enticingly. "Come on. This is a once-in-a-lifetime opportunity. For me, at least. When will I ever get to see a magister? How many chances will *I* have to experience magical boils?"

Katrien wanted to become an archivist, not a warden. Her job wouldn't involve dealing with sorcerers. Elisabeth's, on the other hand . . .

A spark blazed to life inside her breast. Katrien was right; this *was* an opportunity. The other night, she'd resolved to try harder to impress the Director. Wardens were not frightened of sorcerers, and the more she learned about their kind, the better prepared she would be.

"All right," she said, rising from her crouch. "They'll most likely take him to the eastern reading room. This way."

As she and Katrien wound through the shelves, Elisabeth shook off her lingering misgivings. She did try not to break the rules, but her efforts had a curious way of never working out. Just last month there had been the disaster with the refectory's chandelier—at least old Mistress Bellwether's nose looked mostly normal now. And the time she'd spilled strawberry jam all over . . . well. Best not to dwell on that memory.

When they reached the bust of Cornelius the Wise that Elisabeth used as a place marker, she cast around for a familiar crimson binding. She found it halfway up the shelf, its gold title too worn and flaked to read. The grimoire's pages rustled a drowsy greeting as she reached up and scratched it just so. A click came from inside the bookcase, like a lock engaging. Then the entire panel of shelves swung inward, revealing the dusty mouth of a passageway.

"I can't believe that doesn't work for anyone but you," Katrien said as they ducked inside. "I've tried scratching it dozens of times. Stefan, too."

Elisabeth shrugged. She didn't understand, either. She concentrated on trying not to sneeze as she led Katrien through the narrow, winding corridor, batting away the cobwebs that hung like spectral garlands from the rafters. The other end let out behind a tapestry in the reading room. They paused, listening, to make sure the room was empty before they fought their way out from behind the heavy fabric, coughing into their sleeves.

Apprentices were forbidden from entering the reading room, and Elisabeth was both relieved and disappointed to discover that the room appeared quite ordinary. It was a manly sort of space, with a great deal of polished wood and dark leather. A large mahogany desk sat in front of the window, and several leather armchairs encircled a crackling fireplace, whose logs popped and sent up a fountain of sparks when they entered, making her jump.

Katrien didn't waste any time. While Elisabeth looked around, she went straight to the desk and started rifling through the drawers. "For science," she explained, which was frequently what she said right before something exploded.

Elisabeth drifted toward the hearth. "What's that smell? It isn't the fire, is it?"

Katrien paused to waft some air toward her nose. "Pipe smoke?" she guessed.

No—it was something else. Sniffing industriously, Elisabeth tracked the smell to one of the armchairs. She inhaled above the cushion, only to recoil at once, her head spinning.

"Elisabeth! Are you all right?"

She sucked in gulps of fresh air, blinking away tears. The caustic odor clung to the back of her tongue thickly enough that she could almost taste it: a scorched, unnatural smell, like what she imagined burnt metal would smell like, if metal were able to burn.

"I think so," she wheezed.

Katrien opened her mouth to speak, then shot a look at the door. "Listen. They're coming."

Moving quickly, they squeezed behind the row of bookcases lined up against the wall. Katrien fit easily, but the space proved cramped for Elisabeth. At the age of fourteen, she had already been the tallest girl in Summershall. Two years later, she towered over most of the boys. She kept her arms rigid at her sides and breathed shallowly, hoping to appease the grimoires, who were muttering in disapproval at the intrusion.

Voices came from the hall, and the doorknob turned.

"Here you are, Magister Thorn," said a warden. "The Director will arrive shortly to escort you to the vault."

Her stomach somersaulted as a tall, hooded figure strode inside, his emerald-green cloak billowing around his heels. He crossed to the window and flicked the curtains open, then stood gazing out across the library's towers.

"What's happening?" Katrien breathed below her shoulder. "I can't see anything from down here."

Elisabeth's perspective consisted of a horizontal slice above the books' spines. She couldn't see much, either. Slowly, carefully, she inched sideways for a better angle. The tip of the magister's pale nose came into view. He had taken down his hood. His hair was pitch-black and wavy, longer than the men wore it in Summershall, shot through at the left temple with a vivid streak of silver. Another inch to the side, and . . .

He's hardly any older than we are, she thought in surprise. Both the silver streak and his title had prepared her for someone far older. Perhaps his appearance was deceiving. He might maintain the semblance of youth by bathing in the blood of virgins— she had once read something to that effect in a novel.

For Katrien's benefit, she gave a slight shake of her head. His hair was too thick for her to tell whether or not he had pointed ears. If he had hooves, the hem of his cloak concealed them.

She followed up the signal with another, more urgent shake of her head. The magister had turned in their direction, his gaze fixed on the shelves. His gray eyes were extraordinarily light in color, like quartz, and the look in them as they scanned the grimoires turned her blood to ice. She had never seen eyes so cruel.

She didn't share Katrien's confidence that if he found them, he wouldn't hurt them. She had grown up on tales of sorcery: armies raised from mass graves to fight on the behalf of kings, innocents sacrificed in gory rituals, children flayed as offerings to demons. And now she had been to the vault, and seen for herself the work of a sorcerer's hands.

As the magister drew nearer, Elisabeth found to her horror that she couldn't move. A grimoire had seized her robes between its pages. It growled around the mouthful of fabric, tugging like an angry terrier. The sorcerer's eyes narrowed, searching for the source of the noise. Desperately, she grabbed her robes and yanked, only for the grimoire to release it at the exact same time, throwing her against the shelves—

And the bookcase collapsed, taking her with it.

THREE

ELISABETH'S EARS RANG. She choked in a cloud of dust.
When her vision cleared, the magister was standing over her.
"What's this?" he asked.

Her fearful cry emerged as a croak. She flung herself away
from him, scrambling amid the pile of books and broken shelving. Half-blind with terror, it took her longer than it should have
to realize that she felt fine, with the exception of several highly
unmagical splinters. He hadn't cast a spell on her. Her scrabbling
slowed, then stilled. She looked over her shoulder.

And froze.

The sorcerer had sunk down onto one knee and clasped his
hands atop the other. Firelight played across his pale, angular
features. She tried to avert her eyes, but couldn't. As her heart
threw itself against her ribs, she wondered whether he was using
magic to lock her gaze in place, or whether she was simply too
terrified to look away. His every feature projected villainy, from
his dark, arching eyebrows to the sardonic twist of his mouth.

"Are you hurt?" he asked at last.

She said nothing.

"Can't you speak?"

If she didn't answer, he might hurt her to provoke a reaction. Trying her best, she managed another croaking sound. Amusement glittered in his eyes.

"I was warned I'd see some strange things in the countryside," he said, "but I admit, I didn't expect to find a feral librarian roaming the stacks."

Elisabeth possessed only the vaguest notion of what she must look like, aside from the parts of herself that she could see. Ink stained her fingernails, and dust streaked her robes. She couldn't remember the last time she had remembered to brush her hair, which stuck out in tangled chestnut-brown wisps. Her spirits lifted a cautious fraction. If she were dirty and homely enough, he might not find her worth his time or his magic.

"I didn't expect you to find me, either," she heard herself say. Then, horrified, she clapped a hand over her mouth.

"So you can speak. You'd just rather not speak to me?" He lifted an eyebrow when she nodded. "A wise precaution. We sorcerers are terribly wicked, after all. Prowling the wilds, stealing away maidens for our unholy rituals . . ."

Elisabeth didn't have time to react, because just then, a knock came on the door. "Everything all right in there, Magister? We heard a crash."

That deep, gravelly voice belonged to Warden Finch. Elisabeth reared back in alarm, protectively gripping her wrists. When Finch discovered her out of bounds—out of bounds and speaking to a magister—he wouldn't bother with the switch; he would cane her within an inch of her life. The welts would last for days.

The magister's gaze lingered on her for a moment, appraisingly, before he turned toward the door. "Perfectly all right," he replied. "I'd prefer not to be disturbed until the Director's ready to take me to the vault, if you don't mind. Sorcerer's business. Very private."

"Yes, Magister." Finch's reply sounded grudging, but his footsteps moved away from the door.

Too late, Elisabeth's foolishness sank in. She should have called out to Finch. She could think of several reasons why the magister might want to be alone with her in private, and a caning paled in comparison.

"Now," he said, turning back to her. "I suppose I should clean up this mess before someone blames it on me, which means you have to move." He unclasped his hands from his knee and offered her one. His fingers were long and slender, like a musician's.

She stared at them as though he had aimed a dagger at her chest.

"Go on," he said, growing impatient. "I'm not going to turn you into a salamander."

"You can do that?" she whispered. "Truly?"

"Of course." A wicked gleam entered his eyes. "But I only turn girls into salamanders on Tuesdays. Luckily for you, it's a Wednesday, which is the day I drink a goblet of orphan's blood for supper."

He looked entirely serious. He didn't seem to have noticed her robes, which labeled her an apprentice, and therefore an orphan by default.

Determined to distract him, she took his hand. She hadn't forgotten her mission for Katrien. When he pulled her up, she pretended to stumble, and landed with her fingers buried in his black-and-silver hair. He blinked at her in surprise. He was almost as tall as her, and their faces nearly touched. His lips parted as if to speak, but no sound came out.

Her breath quickened. With that startled expression on his face, he looked less like a sorcerer who bargained with demons and more like an ordinary young man. His hair was soft, the texture of silk. She didn't know why she would notice such a thing. Hastily, she snatched her hands from him and backed away.

To her dismay, he grinned. "Don't worry," he assured her, smoothing his tousled hair. "Young ladies have seized me in far more compromising locations. I understand the impulse can be overpowering."

Without waiting for her reaction, he turned to study the wreckage. After a moment of consideration, he raised his hand and spoke a string of words that left her ears buzzing and her head turned inside-out. Dazed, she realized that he was speaking Enochian. It was unlike any language she had heard before. She felt as though she should recognize the words, but the moment she tried to repeat them to herself, the syllables trickled from her mind, leaving only a raw, resounding silence, like the air after a deafening clap of thunder.

Her hearing returned with a susurrus of rustling paper. The pile of spilled grimoires had begun to stir. One by one, they lifted into the air, floating in front of the sorcerer's extended hand amid swirls of emerald light. They spun and flipped and shuffled, sorting themselves back into alphabetical order while behind them, the fallen bookcase righted itself with a labored creak. The broken shelves fused, whole again; the grimoires flew back to their original positions, a few reluctant stragglers switching places at the last second.

Magic, she thought. *That is what magic looks like.* And then, before she could stop herself, *It's beautiful.*

She would never dare give voice to such a thought aloud. The sentiment verged on betraying her oaths to the Great Library.

But a part of her rebelled against the idea that in order to be a good apprentice, she should close her eyes and pretend she hadn't seen. How could a warden defend against something they didn't understand? Surely it was better to face evil than cower from its presence, learning nothing.

Emerald sparks still danced across the tidied shelves. She stepped forward to touch the grimoires, and felt the magic skate across her skin, bright and tingling, as though she'd plunged her hands into a bucket of champagne. Surprisingly, the sensation wasn't painful. Nothing happened to her body—her hands didn't change color, or shrivel like a prune.

When she looked up, however, the sorcerer was staring at her as though she'd grown a second head. Clearly, he had expected her to be afraid.

"Where is the smell?" she asked, emboldened.

He appeared momentarily at a loss. "The what?"

"That smell—the one like burnt metal. That's sorcery, isn't it?"

"Ah." A line appeared between his dark brows. Perhaps she had overstepped. But then he went on, "Not exactly. It accompanies sorcery sometimes, if the spell is powerful enough. Technically it isn't the smell of magic, but a reaction when the substance of the Otherworld—that is, the demon realm—comes into contact with ours—"

"Like a chemical reaction?" Elisabeth asked.

He was looking at her even more strangely now. "Yes, precisely."

"Is there a name for it?"

"We call it aetherial combustion. But how did you—?"

He broke off as another knock came on the door. "We're ready for you, Magister Thorn," said the Director outside.

"Yes," he replied. "Yes, I—one moment."

He glanced back at Elisabeth, as though he half expected her to have vanished like a mirage the instant he turned away. His pale eyes bored into her. For a moment, it seemed he might do something more. Utter a parting word, or conjure a spell to punish her for her insolence. She squared her shoulders, bracing for the worst.

Then a shadow crossed his face, and his eyes shuttered. He pivoted on his heel and started for the door without speaking. A final reminder that he was a magister and she a lowly apprentice librarian, wholly beneath his notice.

She slipped back behind the shelves, breathless. A hand darted out and gripped hers.

"Elisabeth, you're absolutely mad!" Katrien hissed, materializing from the darkness. "I can't believe you touched him. I was poised to jump out and bludgeon him with a grimoire the entire time. Well? What's the report?"

Her nerves sang with exhilaration. She smiled, and then for some reason began to laugh. "No pointed ears," she gasped. "They're completely normal."

The reading room's door creaked open. Katrien clamped a hand over Elisabeth's mouth to smother her laughter. And not a moment too soon—the Director was waiting outside. She appeared as stern as always, her tumble of red hair gleaming like molten copper against the dark blue of her uniform. She glanced back into the room, and paused; after a moment of searching, her gaze unerringly found and held Elisabeth's through the shelves. Elisabeth went rigid, but the Director said nothing. One corner of her mouth twitched, tugging at the scar on her cheek. Then the door clicked shut, and she and the magister were gone.

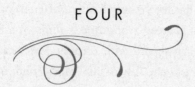

FOUR

THE MAGISTER'S VISIT marked the last exciting event of the season. Summer arrived in an onslaught of scorching heat. Soon afterward, an epidemic of Brittle-Spine left everyone exhausted and miserable, forced to massage the afflicted grimoires with foul-smelling ointment for weeks on end. Elisabeth was assigned to care for a Class Two called The Decrees of Bartholomew Trout, which developed a habit of wiggling provocatively every time it saw her coming. By the time the first autumn storm blew over Summershall, she never wanted to see another pot of ointment again. She was ready to collapse into bed and sleep for years.

Instead, she jolted awake in the dead of night, convinced she had heard a sound. Wind lashed the trees outside, howling through the eaves. Twigs pelted against the window in staccato bursts. The storm was loud, but she couldn't shake the feeling that she had woken for a different reason. She sat up in bed and threw off her quilt.

"Katrien?" she whispered.

Katrien rolled over, muttering in the throes of a dream. She didn't rouse even when Elisabeth reached across the space between their beds and shook her shoulder. "Blackmail him," she mumbled against her pillow, still dreaming.

Frowning, Elisabeth slipped out of bed. She lit a candle on the nightstand and glanced around, searching for anything amiss.

The room she shared with Katrien was located high in one of the library's towers. It was small and circular, with a narrow, castle-like window that let in drafts whenever the wind blew from the east. Everything looked exactly as it had when Elisabeth had gone to bed. Books lay open on the dresser and slumped in piles along the curved stone walls, and notes belonging to Katrien's latest experiment littered the rug. Elisabeth took care not to step on them as she crossed to the door and drifted into the hall, her candle enfolding her in a hazy glow. The library's thick walls deadened the wind's howling to a faraway murmur.

Barefoot, dressed in only her nightgown, she drifted down the stairs like a ghost. A few turns brought her to a forbidding oak door reinforced with strips of iron. This door separated the library from the living quarters, and it always remained locked. Prior to the age of thirteen, she hadn't been able to unlock it herself; she'd had to wait for a librarian to come past and usher her through. Now she possessed a greatkey, capable of unlocking the outer doors of any Great Library in the kingdom. She wore it around her neck at all times, even when sleeping or bathing, a tangible symbol of her oaths.

She lifted the key, then paused, running her fingertips across the door's rough surface. A memory flashed before her: the claw marks on the table in the vault, which had scored the wood as though it were butter.

No—that was impossible. Grimoires only transformed into

Maledicts if damaged. It was not something that would happen in the middle of the night, with no visitors and all the grimoires safely contained. Not with wardens patrolling the darkened halls, and the Great Library's colossal warning bell hanging undisturbed above their heads.

Resolving to banish her childish fears, she slipped through the door and locked it again behind her. The atrium's lamps had been dimmed for the night. Their light glimmered off the gilt letters on books' spines, reflected from the brass rails that connected the wheeled ladders to the tops of the shelves. Straining her ears, she detected nothing out of the ordinary. Thousands of grimoires slumbered peacefully around her, velvet ribbons fluttering from their pages as they snored. In a glass case nearby, a Class Four named Lord Fustian's *Florilegium* cleared its throat self-importantly, trying to get her attention. It needed to be complimented out loud at least once per day, or it would snap shut like a clam and refuse to open again for years.

She stole forward, holding her candle higher. *Nothing's wrong. Time to go back to bed.*

That was when it struck her—an eye-watering, unmistakable smell. The last few months fell away, and for a moment she stood in the reading room again, bending over the leather armchair. Her heart skipped a beat, then began pounding in her ears.

Aetherial combustion. Someone had performed sorcery in the library.

Quickly, she snuffed out her candle. A banging sound made her flinch. She waited until it happened again, quieter this time, almost like an echo. Now suspecting what it was, she snuck around a bookcase until the library's front doors came into view. They had been left open and were blowing in the wind.

Where were the wardens? She should have seen someone by

now, but the library seemed completely empty. Chill with dread, she made her way toward the doors. Though every shadow now possessed an ominous quality, stretching across the floorboards like fingers, she skirted around the shafts of moonlight, not wanting to be seen.

Pain exploded through her bare toe halfway across the atrium. She had stubbed it on something on the floor. Something cold and hard—something that shone in the dark—

A sword. And not just any sword—Demonslayer. Garnets glittered on its pommel in the gloom.

Numbly, Elisabeth picked it up. Touching it felt wrong. Demonslayer never left the Director's belt. She would only allow it out of her sight if . . .

With a stifled cry, Elisabeth rushed to the shape that lay slumped on the floor nearby. Red hair feathered by moonlight, a pale hand outflung. She gripped the shoulder and found it unresisting as she turned the body over. The Director's eyes stared sightlessly at the ceiling.

The floor yawned open beneath Elisabeth; the library spun in a dizzy whirl. This wasn't possible. It was a bad dream. Any moment now she would wake up in her bed, and everything would be back to normal. As she waited for this to happen, the seconds unspooling past, her stomach heaved. She stumbled away from the Director's body toward the doors, where she coughed up a sour string of bile. When she put out her hand to steady herself, her palm slipped against the door frame.

Blood, she thought automatically, but the substance coating her hand was something else—thicker, darker. Not blood—ink.

Elisabeth instantly knew what this meant. She wiped her hand on her nightgown and gripped Demonslayer's pommel in both hands, shaking too violently to hold it with only one. She stepped out into the night. The wind rushed over her, tangling her hair. At first she saw nothing, only the twinkling glow of a few lamps still lit down in Summershall. Their lights flickered as the orchard's trees thrashed in the wind. A high wrought iron fence stood around the library's gravel yard, its sharp finials spearing the restless sky like daggers, but the gate hung open, warped on its hinges, dripping with ink.

Then, in the distance, a hulking silhouette moved among the trees. Moonlight shone on its greasy surface. It limped toward the village with a rolling, ungainly gait, like a malformed bear clumsily attempting to walk on two legs. There was no mistaking what it was. A grimoire had escaped from the vault. Drawing upon the power of the sorcery between its pages, it had swelled into a gruesome monster of ink and leather.

Upon sighting a Malefict, Elisabeth was supposed to alert the nearest warden or, if that was impossible, race up the stairs to ring the Great Library's warning bell. The bell would call the wardens to arms and prompt the townspeople to evacuate into the shelter beneath the town hall. But there was no time. If Elisabeth turned back, the monster would reach Summershall before anyone even had a chance to rise from bed. Countless people would die in the streets. It would be a slaughter.

Officium adusque mortem. Duty unto death. She had passed beneath that inscription a thousand times. She might not be a warden yet, but she would never be able to call herself one if she turned away now. Protecting Summershall was her responsibility, even at the cost of her life.

Elisabeth flew through the gate and down the hill. The sharp gravel gave way to a soft, wet carpet of moss and fallen leaves that soaked the hem of her nightgown. She tripped over a root in her path, nearly losing her grip on the sword, but the Malefict didn't pause, only continued its lumbering advance in the opposite direction.

Now she was close enough to gag on its rotten stench. And to see how big it was, far larger than a man, with limbs as thick and gnarled as tree stumps. Paralyzing waves of fear crashed over her. Demonslayer grew heavy in her hands at last. She was no hero, just a girl in a nightgown who happened to be holding a sword. Was this the way the Director had felt, Elisabeth wondered, when she faced her first Malefict?

I don't have to beat it, she thought. If she could distract it for long enough, and make enough of a commotion doing so, she might save the town. *After all, disturbing the peace is what I'm good at. Most of the time, I do it without even trying.* Courage crept back to her, freeing her frozen limbs. She drew in a deep breath and shouted wordlessly into the night.

The wind tore her voice to shreds, but the monster finally lumbered to a halt. The oily black leather of its hide rippled as if reacting to a fly. After a long, considering pause, it turned to face her.

It was bulky and roughly man-shaped, but lopsided, crude, as if a child had fashioned it from a lump of clay. Dozens of bloodshot eyes bulged across every inch of its surface, ranging from the size of teacups to the size of dinner plates. Their pupils had shrunk to pinpricks, and all of them stared directly at Elisabeth. The library's most dangerous grimoire walked free. The Book of Eyes had returned.

After gazing at her for a moment, it wavered, torn between her and the town. Slowly, its eyes began to roll back in the direction of Summershall. It must not have seen her as a threat. Compared to all those people ahead, she wasn't worth bothering with. She needed to convince it otherwise.

She raised Demonslayer and charged, leaping over fallen branches, dodging between the trees. The Malefict's bulky form loomed above her, blocking out the moonlight. She held her breath against its nauseating stench. Several of its eyes swiveled to focus on her, their pupils enlarging in surprise, but that was all they had a chance to see before the blade swiped across them, spattering ink in an arc through the shadows.

The monster's roar shook the ground. Elisabeth kept running; she knew she couldn't face the Book of Eyes head-on. She plunged through the orchard and skidded to a crouch behind the mossy ruin of an old stone well, sucking in gasps of clean air.

Somehow, hiding from the monster was worse than facing it. She couldn't see what it was doing, which allowed her imagination to fill in the gaps. But she did determine, without a doubt, that it was looking for her. Though it moved with unnerving stealth, it was too large to pass between the trees without betraying its presence. Branches snapped here and there, and apples plopped to the ground with hollow smacks. The sounds gradually drew nearer. Elisabeth stopped panting; her lungs burned with the effort of holding her breath. An apple struck the well and burst, spattering her with sticky fragments.

"Apprentice . . . I'll find you . . . only a matter of time . . ."

The whisper caressed her mind like a flabby hand. She reeled, clutching her head.

"Better if you gave up now . . ."

The greasy suggestion swirled through her thoughts, compelling in its bloodless pragmatism. Her mission was impossible. Too hard. All she had to do was give in, put down the sword, and her suffering would be over. The Book of Eyes would make it quick.

The Book of Eyes was lying.

Gritting her teeth, Elisabeth looked up. The Malefict stood above her, but it hadn't seen her yet. Its eyes twisted in their sockets, moving independently of one another as they scanned the orchard. The ones she'd injured had closed up, weeping rivulets of ink like tears.

"*Apprentice . . .*"

Resisting the whispers was like treading water in sodden clothes, barely keeping her nose and mouth above the surface. She forced herself to stop holding her head and clenched her fingers around Demonslayer's grip. *Just a little longer*, she told herself. The monster shifted closer, and a yellow eye looked down. When it spotted her, its pupil dilated so hugely that the entire iris appeared black.

Now.

She thrust Demonslayer upward, piercing the eye. Ink cascaded down her arms and dripped onto the moss. The Malefict's bellow shuddered through the night. This time, as she scrambled away, she saw new lights winking on in the town below. More joined them with every second that passed, spreading from house to house like banked embers flaring back to life. Summershall was waking. Her plan was succeeding.

And her own time was running out.

An arm swept from the darkness, tossing her through the air like a rag doll. A bright shock of pain sparked through her as her shoulder clipped a tree trunk, sending her spinning through the damp grass. She tasted copper, and when she sat up, gasping for breath, her surroundings blurred in and out. A strap of her nightgown hung loose, torn and bloodied. The Malefict's dark shape towered over her.

It leaned closer. It had a lumpy head, but no face, no features aside from those countless bulging eyes. "*An odd girl, you are.*

Ahhh . . . there's something about you . . . a reason why you woke tonight, while the others slept. . . ."

The Director's sword lay in the grass. Elisabeth snatched it up and held it between them. The blade trembled.

"I could help you," the monster coaxed. *"I see the questions inside your head . . . so many questions, and so few answers . . . but I could tell you secrets—oh, such secrets, secrets you cannot imagine, secrets beyond your strangest dreams. . . ."*

As if caught in a whirlpool, her thoughts followed its whispers toward some lightless, hungry place—a place from which she knew her mind would not return. She swallowed thickly. Her hand found the key hanging against her chest, and she imagined the Director slamming the grimoire shut, cutting off the monster's voice. "You are lying," she declared.

Guttural laughter filled her head. Blindly, she lashed out. The monster heaved back, and Demonslayer whistled harmlessly through the air. Wood splintered behind her as she scrambled away. The Book of Eyes had struck the tree that had stood behind her a moment before, a blow that would have crushed her like a toy.

She fled, stumbling over fallen apples. Disoriented, she nearly smacked into a pale shape that stood between the trees. Something winged and white, with a sad, solemn face eroded by time. A marble angel.

Hope seized her. The statue marked a cache with supplies that could be used by wardens or townspeople during an emergency. She fumbled in the earthen hollow beneath the pedestal until her fingers bumped against a rain-slicked canister.

The Malefict's voice pursued her. *"I will tell you,"* it whispered, *"the truth of what happened to the Director. Is that a secret you would like to hear? Someone did this, you know . . . someone released me. . . ."*

Elisabeth's fingers froze as she fumbled the canister open.

"I could tell you who it was—apprentice!"

The air rippled with motion, but she reacted too slowly. Slimy leather closed in on her from all sides, capturing her in a squeezing, stinking grip. The monster had caught her. It raised her up, lifting her feet from the ground, surveying her with eyes so near she could see the hemorrhaged veins that traced through them like scarlet threads. The fist began to tighten. Elisabeth felt her ribs bend inward, and her breath escaped in a thin gasp.

This is not how it will end, she thought, struggling against the dark. She was to be a warden, keeper of books and words. She was their friend. Their steward. Their jailer. And if need be, their destroyer.

Her arm came free, and she flung the canister's contents into the air. The Malefict gave an agonized howl as a cloud of salt enveloped its body. Its grip loosened, and Elisabeth slid from its grasp to land with a sickening crack against the angel statue. She blinked away stars. For a moment she could not move, couldn't feel her limbs, and wondered if she had broken her back. Then the feeling in her fingers returned in a prickling wash of agony. Demonslayer's grip pressed against her skin. She hadn't let go.

Before the monster's whispers could sink their claws into her again, she rolled onto her side, where she found herself face to face with a giant, filmy blue eye. It was reddened and watering, quivering in pain as it attempted to remain open long enough to focus on her. Using the last of her strength, she dragged herself upright. She raised the Director's sword above the monster's body and drove it downward with all her strength, burying it to the hilt in the monster's greasy hide.

The eye's pupil expanded, then contracted. "*No*," the Malefict gurgled. "*No!*"

Gouts of ink bubbled from the wound. She clenched her jaw and twisted the blade. The monster heaved, throwing her aside. Demonslayer remained stuck fast in its body, far from her reach, but she no longer needed it. The eyes twitched wildly and then went still, rolling upward, the lids relaxing. As if aging in rapid time, the leather skin began to turn gray, then crack and peel. A cloudy film spread over the eyes. Chunks of its body collapsed inward, sending up fountains of fiery ashes. As she watched, the Malefict disintegrated on the wind.

She remembered what the Director had told her in the vault. This grimoire had been the only one of its kind. She had been responsible for it, and she had destroyed it. She knew she hadn't had a choice. But still she thought to herself, *What have I done?*

Ash swirled around her like snow. A brassy ringing filled the air. At last, far too late, the Great Library's bell had begun to ring.

FIVE

"THIS IS MADNESS. The girl has done nothing. You know she is innocent—"

"I do not know that, Master Hargrove," said Warden Finch. "Only two people handled the Book of Eyes when it arrived in Summershall. Now one of them is dead. Tell me, why was Scrivener out of bed when the Malefict broke free?"

Hargrove wheezed a disbelieving laugh. "Are you truly suggesting that Scrivener had something to do with this? That she *sabotaged* a Class Eight grimoire? Preposterous. What earthly reason would she have to do such a thing?"

"She was found out of bed, out of bounds, with the Director's sword."

"Which the Director left to her in her will, for heaven's sake! It belongs to Scrivener now—"

Elisabeth's eyelids fluttered. She lay beneath a thin, scratchy blanket in an unfamiliar bed. *Not a bed, a cot.* Her toes were cold; her feet stuck off the end. The stone wall she faced didn't belong to her room, and Finch and Hargrove's argument didn't make any sense.

"The Director's keys were missing from her key ring," Finch growled, "and we found them at the entrance to the vault. Someone took them. Scrivener was the only one there. The library had been secured for the evening—no one else could have gotten inside."

"I'm certain there's another explanation." She had never heard Hargrove so upset, even after the booklouse incident. Sunk halfway into a dream, she envisioned him gesticulating the way he did during his lectures, his fragile, age-spotted hands waving through the air as though he were conducting an orchestra. "We must investigate," he said, "speak to Scrivener, employ *logic* to understand what happened last night."

"I've already sent a report to the Magisterium. A priceless grimoire has been destroyed, and the sorcerers will want someone to answer for it. They'll get the truth from her, one way or another."

A long silence followed. "Please, I beg you to reconsider." Hargrove's voice sounded muffled, as if he had moved off, intimidated into backing away. "The Director trusted Scrivener, even loved her. We both know she wasn't one for sentiment. Surely that must count for something."

"It does. It tells me that the Director loved the wrong person, and the mistake killed her. You're dismissed, Hargrove."

"Warden Finch—"

"Director," Finch corrected. "If you've forgotten your place, Hargrove, I'm sure I can find you a new one."

Why is Finch calling himself the Director?

Elisabeth's memory flooded back as she fought her way

awake. Ashes. Bells. Wardens surrounding her with their swords drawn, Finch emerging from the group to seize her arm. He had dragged her downstairs and thrown her in this cell. She recalled the rage that had twisted his pockmarked face in the torchlight. And she remembered the wetness that had shone on his cheeks when he turned away.

At once, she regretted waking. Every inch of her body ached. Bruises throbbed on her arms and back, and whenever she breathed in, her ribs stabbed her lungs. But far worse than the pain was the rush of understanding that followed.

He blames me for what happened. She hadn't expected to be hailed as a hero—but this? *And if he's the Director now . . .*

Biting the inside of her cheek, she forced herself to sit up. She clutched the coarse blanket to her chest, finding that she was still dressed in her nightgown, crusted stiff with ink and stained with her own blood. Looking around, she found no sign of Hargrove, but Finch stood outside the bars of the cell door. Hard lines etched his features as he gazed down the corridor. A single torch blazed on the wall behind him, throwing his long, threatening shadow into the cell. She struggled to make sense of her final memory from last night. Why had his face been wet? It hadn't started raining.

The truth dawned on her. "You were in love with the Director," she realized aloud.

Her voice was little more than a thin scratching, but Finch swung around as though she'd hurled an insult. "Shut your mouth, girl."

"Please," she insisted. "I loved her, too. You must listen to me." The words came tumbling out as though a dam had broken inside her. "Someone else released the Book of Eyes last night. I came downstairs, and . . ."

As she began recounting the story in fits and starts, Finch's hand stole toward the hilt of his sword. He squeezed the leather grip until it creaked. Elisabeth stammered to a halt.

"Always telling tales," he said. His eyes shone like black beetles in the torchlight. "Always causing trouble. You expect me to believe you, after all the rules you've broken?"

"I'm telling the truth," she said, willing him to see the honesty on her face. "You can't send me away to the sorcerers. It was a sorcerer who did this."

"Why, pray tell, would a sorcerer free a grimoire, knowing it would be destroyed? Those spells are gone now. No chance of getting them back, and all the sorcerers are weaker for their loss."

He was right. There was no reason for a sorcerer to have done it. But she knew that what she had sensed had been real, and if he would only *believe* her . . .

"There was something wrong last night," she blurted, grasping at a memory. "There weren't any wardens on patrol aside from the Director. I didn't see anyone in the halls. It was a spell—it must have been. You can check the logs, ask the wardens. Someone else must have noticed."

"Lies and more lies." With satisfaction, he spat on the ground outside the cell.

Terror seized Elisabeth. She had the sense of wandering into a dark wood and suddenly realizing that she was lost with no hope of finding her way. Finch was never going to believe her, because he did not want to. Her guilt was the best gift he had ever received. The Director had chosen to love Elisabeth, not him, and finally he had an opportunity to punish her for it.

"An idiot, you are," he was saying. "Always thought so. Irena never believed me, claimed you had *promise*, but I knew you weren't worth the trouble of room and board, ever since you were a fat little babe, filling the library with your squalling."

Irena. That was the Director's name? She had died without Elisabeth even knowing it.

"I'm telling the truth," she whispered again. Her face prickled, hot with humiliation. "I smelled sorcery in the library. A smell like burnt metal. Aetherial combustion. I swear it."

His lip curled in a sneer. "And how would you know that smell?"

"I—last spring, when—" She cut herself off, feeling ill. If she explained that she'd snuck into the reading room and spoken to a magister, she would only make things worse. She looked down and shook her head. "I just know," she finished weakly.

"Read it in a grimoire, no doubt," he growled. "One you shouldn't have been reading, filling your head with the words of demons. Are you consorting with demons, girl? Have you begun dabbling in sorcery—is that how you know?"

She retreated in bed until her back thumped against the wall. "No!" she cried. How could he accuse her of such a thing? She had sworn her oaths, just like him. If she broke them by attempting sorcery, she would never become a warden, never be permitted to set foot in a Great Library again.

"We'll find out soon enough." He turned away, lifting the torch from the wall. "I've heard what the Magisterium does to traitors. Their interrogations are worse than torture. When they're finished with you, girl, you won't be fit to sweep the library's floors." The light began to recede, taking his shadow with it.

Elisabeth scrambled free of the blanket and stumbled to the cell door, gripping the bars. "Stop calling me girl," she called after him. "I'm an apprentice!"

There came a dreadful pause. "Are you, now?" Finch asked, his voice ugly, full of relish.

His torch bobbed away, leaving her in darkness. Slowly, she reached for the key around her neck, the key she hadn't taken off in the three and a half years since the Director had given it to her, and grasped only emptiness.

There was nothing there.

Elisabeth's days blurred together. The Great Library's dungeon lay deep underground, far from any glimpse of sunlight, and she was alone. She rested on her cot listening to the scufflings of rats and booklice, grateful for their company. Without them a thick, suffocating silence descended over her cell, tormenting her with strange imaginings.

Finch didn't visit her again; neither did Master Hargrove. At regular intervals, torchlight flooded the corridor and a warden came to shove a tray of food beneath the cell door. Less often, he unlocked the door and replaced the waste bucket in the corner. It was always the same warden who did this. She tried pleading with him the first few times, but he didn't listen. The looks he gave her were proof enough that he believed whatever Warden Finch—*the Director*—had told him.

That I am a traitor, she thought, *and a murderer.*

Despair dulled her mind. Grief lapped at her in a ceaseless tide. She had never guessed that the Director loved her. Certainly not enough to leave her Demonslayer, her most prized possession. Elisabeth wished she could carry that knowledge back in time and do everything differently. She finally had proof that the Director had believed in her all along, but it had come too late, and at far too great a cost.

As the days crept past and her tears ran dry, she obsessively combed through the attack in her head, trying to piece together exactly what had happened. It was difficult for her to imagine the Directer being taken by surprise, but every piece of evidence pointed to the fact that a sorcerer had ambushed her. He'd stolen her keys and gone down to the vault, then freed the Book of Eyes. No one had interrupted him, because he'd used a spell to—what?

To trap the rest of the library in an enchanted sleep. That was what the Book of Eyes had meant, when it had told her that she'd woken while everyone else slept. Katrien was ordinarily a light sleeper, and yet even a firm shake hadn't roused her. Meanwhile the sorcerer had needed the Director awake, alone, so that he could take her keys. . . .

But how had he gotten inside the library in the first place? All of its locks were made of solid iron, impossible to open with magic.

It didn't matter. He had found a way. And now Elisabeth was to be given over to the sorcerers, any one of whom could be the saboteur, waiting for the chance to eliminate a loose end. No justice awaited her at the Magisterium. Only death.

She laughed—a strange, unpleasant sound that she barely recognized as her own. The warden had just arrived to deliver her daily meal, and he gave her a wary look as he pushed the tray beneath the door. *He thinks I have gone mad.* As darkness returned to her cell, seeping in from the corners like water over the deck of a sinking ship, she wondered whether he was right. It seemed that it was the rest of the world that had gone mad, not her—but if she was the only one who thought so, could she truly call herself sane?

The bruises on her arms, glimpsed every so often in the torchlight, faded from deep purple to a sickly, mottled yellow. A week passed in the world above. Her routine never varied, until one day, after the portcullis ground upward with a shriek of iron against stone, two pairs of boots echoed down the corridor instead of only one.

Elisabeth knew what this meant: the sorcerers had come for her at last.

SIX

LIGHT AND NOISE assaulted Elisabeth. She squeezed her eyes shut against the glare, deafened by the pounding of boots as wardens marched her through the hall. Finch gripped one of her shoulders so tightly that her bones ground together. After so long underground, she felt less like a human being and more like some small creature torn from its den by a hawk's talons, fearful and flinching, confused by every sound. An ill-fitting dress pinched her ribs and flapped around her calves, foreign after years of wearing a comfortable robe. No doubt it was the longest one they had been able to find, and it was still a good six inches too short for her tall frame.

Somewhere nearby, a familiar voice called out to her. "Katrien!" she called back, her own voice ragged with disuse. She glanced around wildly until Katrien pressed into view, struggling to squeeze between two wardens. There were shadows beneath her eyes, and strands stuck out from her unraveling braid.

Elisabeth's chest constricted. "You shouldn't be here," she croaked.

"I tried to visit you, but the wardens wouldn't let me," Katrien panted, barely seeming to hear. A warden thrust an arm in front of her, trying to force her back, but she ducked under it and continued her pursuit. "Then I organized a distraction—we disguised Stefan as a senior librarian and had him run through the archives with his trousers off—but one of the wardens still wouldn't leave his post, and I couldn't sneak past him."

Even dizzy with fear, Elisabeth sobbed out a laugh.

"We wouldn't have given up," Katrien insisted. "A few more days, and I would have figured out a way to get you out. I swear it."

"I know," Elisabeth said. She reached for Katrien's hand, but at that moment Finch shoved her toward the door. Their finger-tips brushed before the wardens tore them apart, and she had the horrible feeling that that was the last time she and Katrien would ever touch.

"I'll—I'll come back," Elisabeth shouted over her shoulder. She didn't believe that was true. "I'll write letters." She was almost certain she wouldn't be able to do that, either. "Katrien," she said, as Finch shoved her out the door. "Katrien, please don't forget me."

"I won't. Don't forget me, either. Elisabeth—"

The door slammed shut. Elisabeth staggered, blinking spots from her eyes. She stood in the courtyard. Sodden autumn clouds filled the sky, but the natural light still pounded against her head like a hammer against an anvil. When her vision adjusted, she saw that she had emerged from the same door through which she and the Director had taken the Book of Eyes, with its inscription at the top, which now more closely resembled an accusation.

Why did I survive, and the Director did not?

A hoof raked through gravel, drawing her attention away.

Two enormous black horses stood before Elisabeth, champing at their bits, and behind them, a coach waited. Emerald curtains hung in its windows, and its wood was carved with an elaborate design of twining thorns. The artisan had taken particular care to render the thorns in lifelike detail; she could almost feel the stab of their cruel points from where she stood.

A shadow swept across the courtyard. The wind picked up, scattering loose leaves across the ground with a dry, hissing rattle. Desperately, she glanced around until her gaze settled on one of the courtyard's many statues: a towering marble angel with a sword clasped against its chest. Ivy twined up its robes, forming natural handholds. She knew from experience that she could shimmy atop it in seconds if she didn't mind skinning a knee. With luck, she'd be off across the rooftops before the sorcerer could catch her. She sucked in a breath and bolted, her boots spraying gravel in every direction.

A whiff of burning metal scalded her lungs, and then the sound of cracking, crumbling stone filled the air. She skidded to a halt in front of the statue. It had begun to move.

Marble ground against marble as it opened its featureless eyes and raised its head. With a serene expression, it drew the sword from its scabbard and unfurled its wings above the courtyard. Emerald sparks danced over the edges of its pinions as the feathers spread apart, almost translucent in the morning light. Then the sword lowered, pointing directly at Elisabeth. The angel's placid face gazed down at her without mercy.

She stumbled back, only to find that the entire courtyard had come alive. The hooded men in the alcoves above her head turned shadowed faces in her direction. Gargoyles stretched, testing their claws against the edges of the roof. Even the angels who clasped the scroll over the door looked down at her, their gazes pitiless and cold. Elisabeth choked down a scream. Now she understood why Finch hadn't bothered to bind her hands. There was no escaping a sorcerer.

She took another step back, and another, until a shadow fell across her: the shadow of a man. She hadn't heard him exit the carriage. Frost crept through her veins, freezing her in place.

"Elisabeth Scrivener," said the shadow's owner. "My name is Nathaniel Thorn. I've come to escort you to Brassbridge for your questioning, and I don't recommend trying to run. Attempting to escape will only prove your guilt to the Chancellor."

She spun around. It was *him*. The emerald cloak billowed at his heels, and the wind tangled his dark, silver-streaked hair. His gray eyes were just as pale and piercing as she remembered, but if he recognized her in return, he showed no sign. A faint, bitter smile tugged at one corner of his mouth.

She took a step back. Of course. He must be the real culprit. Why else would a magister embark upon this lowly errand? It would certainly be convenient for the saboteur if she never reached Brassbridge, the sole witness to his crime vanished by an accident along the way.

"You're afraid of me," he observed.

A tremor ran through her, but she stood her ground. If she didn't reveal that she suspected him, she might survive long enough to escape. "You're a sorcerer," she rasped, feeling that was answer enough. And then she asked, hoping to distract him, "Who is the Chancellor?"

His eyes narrowed. "If you're going to play the fool, you'll need to do a better job than that."

"I'm not playing." Her nails dug into her palms. "Who is the Chancellor?"

"That word truly doesn't mean anything to you?"

She shook her head. He leaned in for a closer look, his pale eyes searching her face. She waited for something to happen: a bolt of pain meant to force a confession, or an alien presence clawing through her thoughts in search of the truth. Behind him, statues bent their heads together as if they were discussing her fate. She even heard them whispering, in grinding voices of earth and stone. A long moment passed, but the sorcerer only exhaled a single, humorless laugh and withdrew. Relief poured through her.

"Chancellor Ashcroft is the second most powerful person in the kingdom. He's the current head of the Magisterium." He paused. "You do know what the Magisterium is?"

"It's the sorcerers' government. I'm to be taken there." *If you don't kill me first.* Clad in only the threadbare, too-short dress, she had never felt more defenseless. "The journey to the city takes three days," she ventured, struck by an idea. "I don't have any of my things."

The magister, Nathaniel, glanced at the door. "Ah, yes. I'd nearly forgotten. One moment." Bowing his head, he murmured an incantation. The Enochian words sizzled when they struck the air, like grease spattered on a hot stove.

Elisabeth tensed, uncertain what he meant to do. Prepared for the worst, she nearly missed the curious whistling sound that came from above. A shadow appeared on the ground beside her, rapidly growing larger. She leaped aside as a sizable object came plummeting from the sky and landed with a thud on the gravel.

The object was her own trunk. She gaped at Nathaniel, then rushed to the trunk and flipped its latches open. The inside contained several dresses she hadn't worn since she'd turned thirteen, neatly folded. Her rarely used hairbrush. Nightclothes.

Stockings. No apprentice's robes, but then, she hadn't expected those. As the spell dissipated, an emerald glow shimmered over the trunk's contents.

"Why are you looking at me like that?" he inquired.

"You used a demonic incantation to pack my stockings!"

He raised an eyebrow. "You're right, that doesn't sound like something a proper evil sorcerer would do. Next time, I won't fold them."

She didn't have a chance to dig deeper inside the trunk without arousing suspicion. She had hoped for an opportunity to fetch her belongings herself. She doubted that Nathaniel had included anything she could arm herself with, certainly not Demonslayer, but there might be something of use. She would have to take a closer look later, in private.

She straightened, and the blood rushed from her head. She staggered, overcome by a wave of dizziness. The dungeon had left her body weak.

A hand caught her elbow. "Steady, miss," said a soft voice beside her.

She turned to find a servant standing there, supporting her, and realized this must be the coachman, though somehow she hadn't seen him until now. He was a young man dressed in old-fashioned livery, his hair meticulously powdered white. He appeared to be around Nathaniel's age, and he was slight of build and quite short—not as short as Katrien, but still a good deal shorter than Elisabeth. In all other respects he was unusually forgettable. *What an unremarkable person*, she thought, and then frowned. She never thought of anyone as unremarkable. Where had that come from?

There was something strange about this servant. Try as she might, she couldn't seem to describe anything else about him, not even the color of his eyes, though she stood less than an arm's length away.

"Excuse me," he said in his courteous, whispering voice. "Shall I take your trunk?"

She nodded dumbly. When he bent to lift her trunk, she reached out, feeling as though she should help. He was so slender, he looked likely to hurt himself.

"Don't worry about Silas," Nathaniel said. "He's stronger than he looks." His tone held the air of a private joke.

Was Nathaniel mocking him? She inspected the servant's face for any sign of discomfort, but found none. Instead, he wore a faint smile. Where Nathaniel's smile was villainous, this boy's smile belonged to a saint. Elisabeth wondered why she had only just noticed how beautiful he was, almost ethereal, as though he were spun from frost or alabaster in place of flesh and blood. She had never seen anyone so beautiful, never known it was possible; a lump formed in her throat simply looking at him.

As if he sensed her attention, the servant looked up and met her eyes. And her breath caught on a scream.

His eyes are yellow. He isn't human. He's—

The observation vanished like a candle snuffing out. *Yes, he truly is an unremarkable person*, she thought, watching the servant return to her side.

"May I help you into the carriage, miss?" he asked.

She nodded and took his gloved hand. She trusted him, though she didn't know why. Strange; she could have sworn—sworn there was something. . . .

"Is Nathaniel cruel to you?" she asked under her breath. She could not imagine what it would be like to be a sorcerer's servant, forced to witness depravities day in and day out.

"No, miss. Never. I am essential to him, you see." As he

assisted her up the steps, he lowered his voice even further. "No doubt you have heard that sorcerers bargain away their lives to demons in exchange for their power."

Elisabeth frowned, but Nathaniel spoke before she could wrap her head around the servant's words.

"Make yourself comfortable, Miss Scrivener. We have a long journey ahead of us. The sooner we get started, the faster I can get back to tormenting widows and scandalizing the elderly with my nefarious black arts."

She bolted inside, requiring no further encouragement. The interior of the coach was as opulent as its exterior, full of deep green velvet and glossy woodwork. She had never ridden in a carriage before. Her closest experience was sitting in the back of a wagon on the road down to Summershall, holding a chicken on her lap.

She pressed herself into the corner, folding up her legs to fit the space, waiting for Nathaniel to follow. Would he sit beside her, or across from her? Perhaps he planned to amuse himself at her expense before he killed her. She tensed when the carriage dipped beneath someone's weight. But the door closed, leaving her inside, dry-mouthed and alone.

Hooves clattered, and the coach swayed into motion. To distract herself from the queasy churning of her stomach, she tugged the curtains open. Nathaniel's spell was wearing off the courtyard outside. She watched the angel sheath its sword and sink back into its original position, closing its eyes as though falling asleep. The gargoyles yawned, blinked, tucked their faces beneath their tails. Everywhere faces settled, pinions furled; the hooded men turned away and clasped their hands in silent prayer. She released a held breath when the last statue went still, returning the courtyard to lifeless stone, as if its occupants had never moved, never spoken, never opened their marble eyes.

The courtyard slid past, and the gates fell behind them. As they passed the orchard and picked up speed, a muffled conversation carried through the wall. Elisabeth inspected the window, then slipped open its latch, hoping to overhear something useful. Nathaniel's voice wafted in on a trickle of fresh air.

"I do wish you would stop bringing up demons in public," he was saying.

The servant's soft voice answered, barely audible above the clopping of the horses' hooves. "I can't help myself, master. It's in my nature."

"Well, your nature vexes me."

"My sincerest apologies. Would you like me to change?"

"Not now," Nathaniel said. "You'll spook the horses, and frankly, I have no idea how to drive a carriage."

Elisabeth's brow wrinkled. Spook the horses? What was he talking about?

"You truly should learn how to do things for yourself, master," the servant replied. "It would be useful if you could tie your own cravat, for example, or for once manage to put your cloak on the right side out—"

"Yes, yes, I know. Just try to behave more normally around the girl. It wouldn't do for her to find out." Nathaniel paused. "Is that window open?"

She jerked away as a swirl of green light twined around the latch and forced the window shut, cutting off their conversation. She could try again later, but she suspected the latch would remain stuck fast for the remainder of the journey.

The little she had overheard filled her with dread. It sounded as though the servant was Nathaniel's accomplice in the scheme to kill her. Before the coach stopped for the night, she needed to formulate a plan. Planning had always been Katrien's strength, not hers. But if she failed to escape, she would die, and if she died, she would never bring the Director's murderer to justice.

Desperate for inspiration, she looked out the window again, only to confront a view she didn't recognize: sheep grazing on a hill, surrounded by woodland. She sought and found the Great Library beyond the trees, nestled amid a patchwork of farms, its brooding towers looming above the countryside amid wreaths of gray cloud. She had gazed out of those towers her entire life, dreaming of her future far away. Doubtless she had gazed at this very road, understanding the landscape as a bird might, now finding it strange and unfamiliar from the ground.

She pressed her forehead against the glass, swallowing back the ache in her throat. This was the farthest she had ever been from Summershall. After so long dreaming, it seemed cruel beyond measure that she was to receive her first and very likely last taste of the world as a captive, a traitor to everything she held dear.

The carriage swung around a bend in the road, and Summershall's rooftops vanished behind the hill. Soon the trees closed in, and the Great Library, too, was gone.

SEVEN

THE COACH JOSTLED, shaking Elisabeth awake. She sat up, wincing at the crick in her neck, then froze, every sense on the alert. She heard only insects singing—no hooves clattering, no wheels rattling over the road. The coach had come to a stop. It was dark out, but lamplight shone disorientingly through the crack in the curtains. Peering between them, she found that they'd drawn up outside an old stone inn.

The door's latch turned. She slumped back into the position from which she'd just awoken, her mind racing. Through her eyelashes, she watched Nathaniel lean inside, his face a pale blur in the dark. The wind had left his hair tousled, its silver streak agleam.

"I hope you haven't died in here, Miss Scrivener," he said.

She didn't move. She barely allowed herself to breathe.

"It would be rather inconvenient for me if you did," he went on. "There would be all sorts of tedious meetings, an inquest, an accusation or two of murder . . . Miss Scrivener?"

Elisabeth still did not move.

Nathaniel heaved a sigh and climbed into the carriage. Her pulse pounded as he drew nearer, carrying with him the smell of night air and sorcery. What she planned to do was dangerous. But she had no choice—or at least, she had no better one.

When he reached for her shoulder, she came to life. He wasn't wearing gloves, and when her teeth sank into his hand, he shouted. In a flash she was outside the carriage and running. The lights of the inn juddered up and down as she sprinted toward the road. They winked out of sight when she skidded down the embankment on the opposite side, and for a terrible moment, tumbling over rocks, she saw nothing: only blackness lay ahead. Then she struck the bottom with a splash. Water flooded her stockings, accompanied by the stench of mud and rotten weeds. She had landed in a ditch. Beyond, she made out a gloomy tangle of branches—a thicket.

She plunged inside. Twigs lashed her face, and leaves snagged in her hair. Her heart seized as something clamped down on her shoulder, but it was only another branch, disturbed by her passage. She half expected the trees to come alive around her; for their roots to uncoil from the earth like snakes and wrap around her ankles. But there was no sign of pursuit. No sign, in fact, of anything else living at all.

If there were animals in these woods—birds, squirrels—they had all fallen silent, leaving her alone with the sounds of her harsh breathing and her crashing progress through the brush. At first the silence didn't trouble her, not so late at night. Then she thought, *Where have the crickets gone?*

She burst into a clearing and stumbled to a halt. Nathaniel's servant, Silas, stood in front of her. His hands were folded behind his back, and he wore a slight, apologetic smile. Not a single white strand had escaped the ribbon that tied his hair. He was so pale that he resembled a ghost against the shadowed trees.

Terror clutched her throat with strangling fingers. "How did you get here?" she asked, her voice a thread in the dark. She should have seen him chasing her. At the very least, she should have heard him. It was as though he had appeared from thin air.

"All good servants have their secrets," he replied, "which are better left unspoken, lest they spoil the illusion so dear to the master and his guests. Come." He extended a gloved hand. "It's cold outside, and dark. A warm bed awaits you at the inn."

He was right. Elisabeth suddenly felt foolish for running through the woods at this hour. She couldn't even recall why she had fled. She took a step toward him, then balked, darting a look around. Why did she trust Silas? She didn't know him. He was going to help Nathaniel—

"Please, miss," he said quietly. "It's for the best. Dreadful things roam the shadows while the human world sleeps. I wouldn't like to see you harmed."

Concern and sorrow transformed his features into those of an angel, easing her fears. No one so beautiful, so full of sadness, could have anything but her best interests at heart. She stepped forward as though hypnotized. "What sort of dreadful things?" she whispered.

Without any effort, Silas lifted her into his arms. "It is better if you do not know," he murmured, almost too softly for her to hear.

She gazed up at his face in wonder. The moon shone silver overhead, the black branches laced beneath it like fingers clasped in prayer. Frosted by its glow, Silas looked as though he were spun from moonlight himself. He carried her between the silent trees, over the ditch, and back across the road.

When they reached the inn's yard, a boy was leading Nathaniel's horses toward the stable. The nearest horse pinned back its ears and flared its nostrils. A shrill whinny split the night.

The sense of peace fell from Elisabeth at once, like a heavy blanket flung from her body. She sucked in a breath. "Let me down!" she said, struggling in Silas's arms.

What had happened just now? She had tried to run—she knew that. But how had she gotten so dirty? She couldn't have made it far before Silas had caught her. Her last memory was of reaching the road, and after that . . . she must have struck her head in the scuffle.

Nathaniel jumped down from the carriage. "My god, she bit me," he said to Silas in disbelief. "I think she broke the skin."

Elisabeth hoped so. "That's what you get for drinking orphan's blood!" she shouted. The stable boy stopped and stared.

Unexpectedly, Nathaniel began to laugh. "You impossible menace," he said. "I suppose it's my fault for assuming you were harmless." He shook his hand. "By the Otherworld, this stings. I'll be lucky if I haven't contracted a disease. Silas? Make sure her room has a lock. A good one."

Elisabeth's struggling subsided as Silas carried her toward the inn. He *was* stronger than he looked, and she needed to save her energy, which was fading rapidly—more rapidly than she'd expected, even after the dungeon. Nathaniel watched her, but she couldn't make out his expression in the dark.

Silas set her down inside the door. To her relief, the inn bustled with activity. The Inkroads were the best-kept roads in Austermeer, maintained by the Collegium, and heavily traveled. Lamplight glowed against the whitewashed walls, upon which the shadows of patrons stretched and laughed and raised their glasses. Her stomach growled at the smell of cooking sausages, greasy and laden with spices. A wave of hunger left her light-headed.

A maid hurried past them, but she didn't so much as glance in their direction. No one in the busy inn seemed to have noticed Elisabeth looming there, dripping ditch water on the rug, or Silas standing silently beside her.

Before she could call for help, Silas steered her toward the stairs. "This way. Our rooms have been arranged." He placed a steadying hand on her back when she tripped. "Careful. I fear Master Thorn would not forgive me if I let you fall."

She had no choice but to obey. Her head felt stuffed with cotton wool. The noise of the inn's crowd throbbed in her temples like a second pulse: cheers and laughter, the clattering of cutlery. Upstairs, Silas led her down the hall, toward a door at the end. As he unlocked it, she noticed that he had on the same white gloves as that morning. But there wasn't a speck of dirt upon them, even though he'd spent all day handling the carriage's reins.

"Wait," she said, when he turned to leave. "Silas, I . . ."

He paused. "Yes?"

Her head pounded. There was something important she'd forgotten. Something she needed to know. "What color are your eyes?" she asked.

"They are brown, miss," he said softly, and she believed him.

The lock clicked behind her. At once, the pounding in her skull improved. The room was small and warm, with a fire crackling in the hearth and a braided rug whose colorful patterns reminded her painfully of the quilt on her bed at home. First she tested the window and found it wouldn't open. Then she yanked on the doorknob, to no success. Temporarily out of options, she peeled off her dress and sodden stockings, which she laid out on the hot stones to dry. Despite the warmth, she'd begun shivering.

She was busy reviving herself by the fire, trying to decide what to do next, when green light flared in the corner of the room. She leaped up, seized a poker from the hearth, and flung it in the light's direction. The poker bounced off with a thud. It was not Nathaniel who had materialized there, but merely her trunk, now sporting a new dent on top.

Her weariness forgotten, she rushed to the trunk and flung it open, rummaging around for anything useful. Dresses and stockings went flying across the room. Her hairbrush skidded beneath the bed. She had nearly reached the bottom, and resigned herself to a lost cause, when instead of encountering another layer of linen or cotton, her fingertips brushed leather.

Warm leather, imbued with a life of its own.

A thrill ran through her. Cautiously, she lifted the object from the bottom of her trunk. It was a grimoire, an unusually thick and heavy volume bound in glossy burgundy leather. Gilt lettering shone across its spine: A Lexicon of the Sorcerous Arts. Without hesitation, she pressed her nose to its pages and inhaled deeply. The edges of the paper had worn velvet-soft with age, and possessed a warm, sweet scent, like custard.

"How have you gotten here?" she asked, now assured of the grimoire's friendliness. Ill-natured grimoires tended to smell musty or sour. "You're as far from home as I am."

The Lexicon's pages whispered as though trying to answer. She turned it over and found a numeral *I* stamped on the back cover. Class One grimoires were typically reference works or compendiums. They couldn't speak to people directly like a Class Seven or higher, or even make vocalizations, an ability that most grimoires demonstrated beginning at Class Two.

The cover nudged her hand. Puzzled, she let go, and a scrap of paper slipped out from between the pages. She lifted it with a frown.

Elisabeth, the note read in a familiar messy scrawl, *if you've found this, then I was right, and the sorcerer has spelled your trunk to his carriage. I've hidden this grimoire inside in case it can help you prepare for whatever lies ahead. Never forget that knowledge is your greatest weapon. The more knowledge the better, so you can hit the sorcerer over the head with it and give him a concussion. That's why I chose such a big one.*

I would tell you to remain brave, but I don't have to. You're already the bravest person I know. I promise we'll see each other again.

—K

P.S.: Don't ask how I managed to smuggle the grimoire out of bounds. I didn't get caught, which is the important part.

Tears stung Elisabeth's eyes. Katrien made it sound like a small matter, but she could lose her apprenticeship if she were found to have stolen a grimoire. She had risked a great deal to sneak it out of the library. No doubt she had known how much it would lift Elisabeth's spirits to hold a piece of home.

Elisabeth ran thoughtful fingers over the Lexicon's cover, wondering where Katrien would begin. Surely there was something inside that could tell her more about Nathaniel. The more she knew about him, the better equipped she would be to fight back.

She held the grimoire aloft. "Do you have a section on magisters, please?" she inquired. It was always wise to be polite to books, whether or not they could hear you.

The Lexicon folded open in her hands. A golden glow kindled within the pages, bathing her face in light. The pages ruffled as if stirred by a breeze. They moved faster and faster, flipping on their own, until they reached a point about halfway through. Then they halted with a flourish and graciously smoothed aside. A red velvet ribbon slid into place, marking the spot. The glow faded to a burnished gleam, like candlelight shining from polished bronze.

The Magisterial Houses of the Kingdom of Austermeer, read the section heading at the top. And then, beneath that:

Of all the sorcerous families, none are so powerful as those descended from the great sorcerers granted the title of "Magister" by King Alfred during the Golden Age of Sorcery, as a reward for the miraculous feats they performed for the crown. It was these first magisters who founded the Magisterium in the early sixteenth century. The organization, which began as a private occult society, later developed into a governing council from whom a Chancellor of Magic is elected every thirteen years. . . .

Elisabeth skipped onward, skimming the paragraphs until a familiar name caught her eye.

House Ashcroft, elevated to prominence by Cornelius Ashcroft, also known as Cornelius the Wise, is celebrated for its participation in a number of public works that have shaped the landscape of present-day Austermeer. Cornelius Ashcroft laid down the Inkroads and transported thousands of tons of limestone for the construction of the Great Libraries in 1523, while his successor, Cornelius II, raised Brassbridge's famous Bridge of Saints from the waters of the Gloaming River in a single day.

Meanwhile House Thorn is known for the darkest of all magics—necromancy—with which the house's founder, Baltasar Thorn, repelled the Founderlander invasion of 1510 using an army of dead soldiers raised to fight for King Alfred. Though necromancy is classified as a forbidden art as of the Reforms of

1672, concessions exist for its use during wartime. The might of House Thorn is credited with the kingdom's continued independence from its neighbors, who have not threatened Austermeerish soil since the War of Bones.

She stopped reading. Her skin crawled. Tales of the War of Bones had given her nightmares as a child. It did not seem possible that all its horrors were the work of a single man, Nathaniel's ancestor. She was in worse danger than she had realized.

The grimoire stirred beneath her hands. Without prompting, it flipped to a different section. She only had time to read the chapter heading, *Demonic Servants and Their Summoning,* before a knock sounded on the door. She froze, consumed by the urge to pretend she wasn't there. Slowly, stealthily, she closed the grimoire and set it aside.

"I know you're awake, Miss Scrivener," Nathaniel said through the door. "I heard you talking to yourself in there."

Elisabeth bit her lip. If she didn't answer, he might break into her room by force. "I was talking to a book," she replied.

"Somehow I'm not in the least surprised. Well, I've brought you dinner if you promise not to bite me again. Or throw anything at me, for that matter."

She glanced at the poker.

"Yes, we heard you all the way from downstairs. The owner made me leave an extra deposit. I'm fairly certain she thinks you're up here knocking holes in the walls." He paused. "You aren't, are you? Because I'm afraid you won't be able to tunnel your way to freedom before morning, no matter how hard you try."

An evasive silence seemed like the best response, but just then, her body's needs betrayed her. Her stomach gave a dizzying twist of hunger, accompanied by a noisy growl. She could barely think for the smell of sausages drifting through the door.

Why had Nathaniel brought her dinner? Perhaps he had poisoned the food. More likely, he was attempting to lull her into a false sense of security before they reached a remote area, where he could kill her and dispose of her body more easily. It didn't make sense that he would murder her in an inn, surrounded by potential witnesses. In fact, he had practically admitted as much inside the coach.

Better to accept the food, and keep up her strength, than starve and grow too weak to fight.

"One moment," she said, stealing toward the door. Carefully, she tested the doorknob. It was unlocked. She wrenched it open in a sudden rush of courage, only to promptly slam it shut again in Nathaniel's face. She had recalled, too late, that she was wearing only her shift.

"I'm not decent," she explained, hugging her arms to her chest.

"That's all right," he replied. "I hardly ever am, myself."

The split-second glimpse of him standing in the hall was seared into her mind. He wore a white undershirt, open at the throat, the sleeves rolled up to his elbows. The light of the hallway's sconces had revealed a long, cruel scar twisting across the inside of his left forearm. Riding outside all day had left his cheeks flushed and his lips reddened, which gave him a startlingly debauched look, enhanced by his disheveled hair and cynical, penetrating gaze. The effect was such that she almost hadn't noticed the tray in his hands.

No, he hadn't looked decent at all. How much of her had he seen in return? Those gray eyes seemed to miss nothing.

After a moment, he sighed. "I'll set the tray on the floor. You can take it once I've left. And don't try to run—Silas is guarding the stairs. The door will lock with magic when you're finished."

A jingle of silverware and crockery followed his instructions. She waited until she heard his footsteps move away, and then cracked the door open again. Through the narrow space, she inspected the tray, which was laden with dark bread and herb-freckled cheese. And there—sausages. They did not seem to be a trap. She crouched down, pushing the door open wider.

Nathaniel had almost reached the end of the hallway. Watching him, she made out the sore-looking bite mark on the skin of his right hand. Proof that he could be hurt like an ordinary man. He might have killed the Director, but he wasn't invincible. As long as Elisabeth lived, she still stood a chance.

She gathered her courage. "Nathaniel," she said.

His stride slowed, then stopped. He tilted his head, waiting.

"I'm—" She swallowed as her voice gave out, and tried again. "I'm sorry that I bit you."

He turned. His gaze flicked over her, casually appraising the way she reached out and clutched the edge of the tray, as if someone might try to snatch it away from her. His eyes lingered on the fading bruises that marked her arms from the battle with the Malefict. As the moment spun on, she had the uncomfortable feeling of being turned inside out and inspected like an empty pocket. "Are you?" he asked at last.

Unconvincingly, she nodded.

"I see you haven't had much practice lying," he said, still scrutinizing her. "You're awful at it. Even if you weren't, that tactic wouldn't work on me."

"What tactic?"

"Pretending to be meek and obedient in the hopes I'll let my guard down in time for your next escape attempt. You've already proven yourself to be an agent of chaos. I'm not about to forget it. Is there anything else before I go?"

Heat flooded Elisabeth's cheeks. The tray's edges bit into her fingers. It had been foolish of her to imagine that she could trick him. But if he were willing to answer questions, at least she could take the opportunity to learn more. "How old are you?" she asked.

"Eighteen."

She sat back in surprise. "Truly?"

"I haven't sacrificed virgins for my perfect cheekbones, if that's what you mean. Virgins, in general, have fewer magical properties than people tend to assume."

Elisabeth tried not to look too relieved by that information. "It's only that you're young to be a magister," she ventured.

His face grew unreadable. Then he smiled in a way that sent a chill down her spine. "The explanation is simple. Everyone standing between myself and the title is dead. Does that satisfy your curiosity, Miss Scrivener?"

She found, suddenly, that it had. She didn't want to know what could put an expression like that on a boy's face, as though his eyes were carved from ice, and his heart had turned to stone. She no longer wished to face the person who had murdered the Director in cold blood. Looking down, she nodded.

Nathaniel made to leave, then paused. "Before I go, can I ask you something in return?"

Staring at her supper, she waited to hear what the question was.

"Why did you grab my hair that day in Summershall?" he asked. "I know you didn't do it by accident, but I can't for the life of me come up with a rational explanation."

Her stomach unknotted in relief. She had expected him to ask something terrible. Distantly, she thought, *So he does remember me from the reading room, after all.*

"I was finding out whether you had pointed ears," she said.

He paused, considering her answer. "I see," he said, with a serious expression. "Good night, Miss Scrivener." He strode around the corner.

Elisabeth wasted no time dragging the tray inside. She was so hungry that she set upon her dinner on the floor, devouring it with her hands. She barely noticed in between bites that someone, somewhere else in the inn, was laughing.

EIGHT

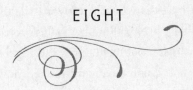

AUSTERMEER'S COUNTRYSIDE FLOWED past the coach's window. They passed farms, and rolling wildflower meadows, and wooded hills tinged gold with autumn color. Mist pooled in the hollows between the valleys, and sometimes stretched fingers across the road. As the afternoon shadows deepened, the coach clattered into the Blackwald, the great forest that slashed through the kingdom like the stroke of a knife. Everything grew dark and damp. Here and there among the undergrowth stood shocking white stands of birch trees, like specters floating among the black gowns of a funeral party. Gazing out at the gently falling leaves, the thick carpets of ferns, the occasional deer bolting into places unseen, Elisabeth was enveloped by a pall of dread, as though the mist had seeped inside the coach and surrounded her.

Nathaniel would make the attempt here, she was certain. When he reached the city without her, he could claim she'd run and vanished among the trees. In a place like this, no one would find a girl's body. No one would even bother looking.

Escape felt increasingly hopeless. She had tried again last night, but after breaking her room's window and climbing down the roof, Silas had been waiting for her in the inn's garden. Strangely, she didn't remember the rest. She must have been overcome by exhaustion. Afterward she'd had an unsettling dream of being back in Summershall's orchard, digging the emergency salt canister out from under the angel statue. But this time the statue had come alive, and looked down at her with vivid yellow eyes.

A nudge against her hand interrupted her thoughts. Frowning, she tore her gaze from the forest to the grimoire on her lap. This was the third time it had bumped her with its cover, like a dog begging for attention.

"What is it?" she asked, and the Lexicon gave another, more insistent nudge, until she loosened her grip and it flipped itself open with an eager flutter.

It had opened to the same section as last night, *Demonic Servants and Their Summoning*. Elisabeth shuddered. Illustrations from books flashed through her mind: drawings of pentagrams and bleeding maidens, of demons with horns and snouts and tails feasting on entrails like ropes of sausage. But the Lexicon wanted her to read this for a reason. Steeling herself, she bent over the pages.

Relatively little is known about demons even within the sorcerous community, it told her beneath the heading, *in part due to the danger of conversing with demons, who are notorious deceivers, and will seize any chance to betray their masters. For once a bargain with a demon is struck, it is in the demon's best interest to see its master dead; thus it may secure another bargain with a new master, and maximize the amount of human life that it receives in payment.*

Demons populate a realm known as the Otherworld, a plane adjacent to our own, which is the source of all magical energy. Without the connection established by a demonic bargain, humans cannot draw energy from the Otherworld. Therefore sorcery's very existence is contingent upon the summoning and servitude of demons—a regrettable, but necessary, evil. It is both a blessing and a curse that demons crave mortal life above all else, and are therefore eager to treat with humans. . . .

Could this be Nathaniel's weakness? She grasped in vain at the thought. Her head felt muddy, as though she had been reading for hours instead of only seconds. The grimoire nudged her hand again, and she realized she'd been staring off into space. Determinedly, she rubbed her eyes and continued reading.

The Otherworld teems with hordes of lesser demons: imps, fiends, goblins, and the like, which are not difficult to summon; but they do not make reliable servants, for they are little more intelligent than common beasts. Being the province of criminals and unskilled dabblers, lesser demons are illegal to summon as of the Reforms. True sorcerers seek only the service of highborn demons, which for all their danger may be bound to the conditions of their summoning, and therefore compelled to obey the orders given to them by their masters.

"Where on earth is Nathaniel's demon?" Elisabeth murmured. It seemed odd for him to travel without it. She briefly had the sensation of teetering on the edge of a revelation, but the epiphany leaked from her mind like sand, leaving only a tinny ringing in her ears.

Further speculation on the nature of demons and the Otherworld exists, the Lexicon continued on the next page, *but by and large the sources are highly inconsistent—if not fabricated outright—and their value dismissed by contemporary scholarship. The most notorious example of these is the Codex Daemonicus, by Aldous Prendergast, written in 1513, once held in high esteem but now believed to be nothing more than the ramblings of a madman. Prendergast was declared insane by his own friend, Cornelius the Wise, for his claims that he entered the Otherworld and discovered a terrible secret, which he concealed within his manuscript in the form of a cipher—*

"Miss Scrivener?"

Elisabeth flinched and slammed the grimoire shut. She had been concentrating so hard on reading that she hadn't noticed the coach had come to a halt.

"We've reached our stop for the evening," Nathaniel went on, opening the door wider. "It's best not to travel in this forest after dark." His eyes tracked her as she set the Lexicon aside, but he didn't comment on its presence.

When Silas helped her out of the coach, she tensed. The coach had pulled off the road into a forest clearing. Stars glittered above, and the trees clustered close around them, dark and watchful, breathing mist. They were far from any sign of civilization, even an inn.

This was the place. It had to be. Her hands curled into fists as Nathaniel stepped away into the meadow, casting around on the ground as though searching for something. A place to bury her body? She shot a look over her shoulder, only to find Silas standing close behind her. Though he kept his gaze politely lowered, she felt the weight of his attention.

"There are no buildings in the Blackwald," he said, as though he had been reading her mind. "The moss folk do not take kindly to intrusions on their territory. While few of them remain, they can still prove dangerous when the mood strikes them."

Elisabeth's breath caught. She had read stories about the

moss folk, and had always hoped to see one, but Master Hargrove had assured her that the spirits of the forest were all long dead—if they had ever existed to begin with.

"Don't let Silas frighten you," Nathaniel put in. "As long as we take care not to disturb the land when we make camp, and stay out of the trees, they won't bother us."

He paused, looking down. Then he knelt and placed a hand on the ground. She saw his lips move in the dark, and felt a snap of magic in the air. The spell that followed wasn't anything like what she expected. Emerald light unfolded around him into the shape of two tents, which swelled with bedrolls and unrolled lengths of fine green silk down their sides. Nathaniel stood to examine his handiwork. Afterward, he gestured toward the farthest tent. "That one's yours."

She stiffened in surprise. "You're giving me my own tent?"

He looked around, eyebrows raised. A lock of silver-streaked hair had fallen over his forehead. "Why, would you prefer to share one? I wouldn't have expected it of you, Scrivener, but I suppose some species do bite each other as a prelude to courtship."

Heat flooded her cheeks. "That's not what I meant."

After a moment of studying her, his grin faded. "Yes, I'm giving you your own tent. Just remember what I told you about running. Silas will keep watch tonight, and I assure you, he's a great deal harder to get past than a locked door."

Why give her a tent if he only meant to kill her? This had to be a trick. She remained awake long after she crawled inside, alert and listening. She didn't take off her boots. Hours passed, but a fire continued to crackle, and the murmured tones of Nathaniel and Silas's conversation carried through the canvas walls. Though she couldn't make out any words, the ebb and flow of their exchange reminded her more of two old friends than a master and servant. Occasionally Nathaniel would say something, and very softly, Silas would laugh.

Finally, the conversation ceased. She waited for an hour or so longer—long enough for the fire's embers to fade to a dull red glow against the canvas. Then, unable to stand the tension any longer, she crawled out of her bedroll and poked her head through the tent's flap. The air smelled of pine and wood smoke, and crickets sang a silvery chorus in the night. Silas was nowhere to be seen. Bent at the waist, she took a step outside. And stopped.

"Out for an evening stroll, Scrivener?"

Nathaniel was still awake. He sat on a fallen log near the edge of the forest, his chin resting on his clasped hands, facing the trees. The embers smoldering behind him cast his face into shadow. He didn't turn, but she knew he would cast a spell the instant she tried to flee.

She had a choice. She could run from her fate, or she could face it head on. After a moment of stillness, she picked her way through the wildflowers, feeling strangely as though she were trapped in a dream.

"Do you not sleep?" she asked as she drew near.

"Very little," he replied. "But that's particular to me, not sorcerers in general." As he spoke, he didn't look away from the trees. She followed his gaze, and froze.

A shape moved within the ferns and pale thin birches, picked out by moonlight. A spirit of the wood. It was stooped over, collecting objects from the ground. A curtain of mossy hair hung from its head, and a pair of antlers crowned its brow. Its skin was chalk-white and cracked, like birch bark, and its long, crooked arms hung to its knees, ending in knotted, twiglike claws. A chill shivered up and down Elisabeth's arms. Slowly, she stepped forward and sank down on the opposite end of the log.

Nathaniel spared her a glance. "You aren't afraid of it," he observed, almost a question.

She shook her head, unable to tear her gaze from the forest. "I've always wanted to see the moss folk. I knew they were real, even though everyone told me differently."

The fire at Nathaniel's back etched the lines of his jaw and cheekbones, but didn't reach the hollows of his eyes. "Most people grow out of fairy stories," he said. "Why did you carry on believing, when the rest of the world did not?"

She wasn't sure how to answer. To her, his question made little sense—or if it did, it wasn't a kind of sense she wished to understand. "What is the point of life if you don't believe in anything?" she asked instead.

He gave her a long look, his half-hidden expression indecipherable. She wondered why he had been sitting here watching the moss spirit, alone, for so long.

Movement caught her eye. As they'd spoken, the spirit had raised something small—an acorn—to inspect it in the moonlight. That was what it had been collecting, and surely it had found many, but there seemed to be something special about this acorn in particular. Using its gnarled claws, it raked aside the covering of leaves on the ground and scooped out a hole from the loam. It buried the acorn and mounded the leaves back on top. A sigh stirred through the forest at that exact moment, a breeze that rushed forth from the heart of the wood and swept over Elisabeth, combing through her hair.

The stories claimed that the moss folk were stewards of the forest. They tended to its trees and creatures, watched over them from birth to death. They had a magic of their own.

"Why are there so few of them left?" she asked, pierced by a sorrow she couldn't explain.

For a moment, she thought he wasn't going to answer. Then he said, "Do you know of my ancestor, Baltasar Thorn?"

She nodded, hoping her goose bumps weren't visible in the firelight. The embers popped and snapped.

"At the beginning of the sixteenth century, the Blackwald covered half of Austermeer. This was a wild country. It was ruled as much by the forest as it was by men."

But not any longer, she finished. "What did he do?"

"It was the necromantic ritual he performed during the War of Bones. To grant life, even a semblance of it, one must take life, trade it like currency. Unsurprisingly, raising thousands of soldiers from the grave took a great deal. The life came from the land itself. His magic left two-thirds of the Blackwald dead and dying in a single night. The moss folk are tied to the earth— those that survived were stricken like blighted trees." Nathaniel paused. He added in a dry tone, "Baltasar, of course, received a title."

Elisabeth's fingernails dug into the wood of the log beneath her, soft and spongy with decay. Now that she looked more closely at the moss spirit she saw that one of its knees was swollen and disfigured, like a canker on the trunk of an oak.

"I suppose you must be proud," she said. "It's the reason why you're a magister."

"Is that what you think I'm doing?" He sounded amused. "Meditating fondly on my ancestor's deeds?"

"I don't know. I hope not. No one should take pleasure from such a thing." *Not even someone like you.*

Perhaps his supply of mockery wasn't as infinite as she assumed. He only gazed into the forest a moment longer, then stood. "It's late." He nodded at the spirit. "You're lucky to have seen one. A hundred years from now, they'll all be gone."

He brought his fingers to his lips. Before she could stop him, a whistle broke the stillness.

The spirit jerked toward the sound like a startled deer. In the gloom she saw two blue-green eyes, glowing incandescently, like fox fire. Withered lips pulled back from sharp, gnarled, brown teeth, and then the spirit had vanished, leaving only a patch of trembling ferns where it had once stood.

"You don't know that for certain," Elisabeth said. But her voice sounded tentative in the dark. Looking at the empty hill, where magic had once walked and now was gone, she could almost imagine that he was right.

"I never did answer your question." He set off toward his tent. "If you don't believe in anything," he said over his shoulder, "then you have a great deal less to lose."

When they reached Brassbridge the next evening, Elisabeth was still alive, and faced the troubling possibility that she had been wrong about Nathaniel Thorn. Alone with her questions, she gazed out the window as the sunset's light poured over the city, transforming the river into a ribbon of molten gold.

Even from afar, her first glimpse of the capital had taken her breath away. Brassbridge sprawled on an unimaginably large scale along the winding bank of the river. The city's peaked slate rooftops formed an endless maze, their chimneys trickling threads of smoke toward a ruddy sky. Above them loomed the somber edifices of cathedrals and academies, their spires topped with bronze figures that blazed like torches against the darkening rooftops, flaming ever brighter as the shadows deepened. She sought the Collegium and the Royal Library among the clutter of towers, but she couldn't tell any of the grand buildings apart.

Soon the horses' hooves clashed over a bridge's cobblestones, and the river slid beneath them, stinking of fish and algae. Statues flashed past the windows, their hooded silhouettes ominous against the glowering clouds.

Doubt gnawed at Elisabeth's thoughts, intensifying as the sun sank beneath the statues' bowed heads. Last night in the Blackwald, Nathaniel hadn't tried to kill her. He hadn't so much as touched her. Had he intended to hurt her, he almost certainly would have done so by now. But if *he* wasn't the sorcerer who sabotaged the library, that meant—

The clamor of traffic intensified as the coach's door swung open. Nathaniel clambered inside amid a swirl of emerald silk. He flashed Elisabeth a grin, pulling the door shut as he took a seat in the opposite corner.

"Best if I don't show myself," he explained. "I don't want to inflame the public. They go absolutely mad in the presence of celebrity, you see, and I'd prefer them not to storm the carriage. There are only so many propositions of marriage a man can bear."

Elisabeth stared at him, nonplussed. "Aren't they afraid of you?"

Nathaniel leaned toward the window, using his reflection to fix his disheveled hair. "This may come as a shock, but most people don't think sorcerers are evil." He gestured toward the city. "Welcome to the modern world, Scrivener."

Elisabeth looked out. Wrought iron lamps cast an orange glow over the bridge's sidewalk. A group of soot-smudged children ran parallel to Nathaniel's coach, pointing and shouting. A woman selling pastries attempted to hail them, nearly overturning her tray in excitement. They clearly recognized the coach with its thorns and emerald curtains. Recognized it, and were not afraid.

The truth, astonishing though it was, began to sink in. "All those things you said, about drinking blood and turning people into salamanders . . ."

Nathaniel propped his elbow on the door and covered his mouth with his hand. His eyes shone with suppressed amusement.

Shock swept over her. "You were teasing me!"

"To be fair, I didn't think you would actually believe I drank orphan's blood. Are all librarians like you, or is it only the feral ones who have been raised by booklice?"

Elisabeth wanted to object, but she suspected he had a point. Almost everything she knew, she had learned either from Master Hargrove, who hadn't traveled farther than the privy in over a half a century, or from books, many of which were hundreds of years out of date. The rest—stories told to her by the senior librarians, their details so frightening that she behaved as a good apprentice ought and ceased asking about sorcerers altogether. Now she wondered how many of those stories had been lies. Her teeth ground at the betrayal.

"Why did you come to fetch me from Summershall?" she demanded, rounding suddenly on Nathaniel. "Why you, and not anyone else?"

The ferocity in her voice took him aback. His grin disappeared, and the sparkle left his eyes, leaving them as cold and gray as doused embers. "When the report arrived at the Magisterium, I recognized your name."

"How? I never told you my name."

"The Director did." Seeing her expression, he explained, "I wanted to know the name of the girl who almost murdered me with a bookcase. It seemed wise, in case I ever crossed paths with you again."

"Did the Director say anything else about me?"

"No." Then, after a pause, "I'm sorry."

A lump closed Elisabeth's throat. She turned back to the view. As she watched the sky deepen to indigo, a sick feeling of despair pooled in her stomach. Soon the journey would reach its end, and she did not know what, or who, awaited her there. She could no longer put a face to the Director's killer.

In the dark, her first impression of the city's streets was an imposing one. Buildings nearly as high as her Great Library reared from the fog, candlelight wavering through their windowpanes. She had never seen so many structures in one place, nor even a fraction of the people. As their coach wove through the traffic, pedestrians bustled past: men with walking sticks and top hats, and women wearing high-collared dresses trimmed in lace. They carried shopping parcels, hurrying across the street and climbing in and out of carriages with a sense of urgency that seemed foreign to Elisabeth, accustomed to the sleepy rhythm of country life. Everything was painted by the hazy glow of the lamps, which Nathaniel informed her did not run on magic, as she'd assumed, but rather an invention called gaslight.

The carriage finally rolled to a stop on a narrow, gloomy side street. Numbly, she followed Nathaniel outside. The fog enveloped her boots and eddied around the hem of her dress. The nearest streetlamp had gone out, submerging them in shadow. There were no other people in sight.

"This is the lodging house where the Magisterium has arranged for you to stay," Nathaniel said. "I may see you briefly at your hearing tomorrow, but otherwise, you're rid of me from here onward."

Elisabeth gazed up at the lodging house in silence. Once it had been a dignified brick building. Now its forbidding walls were blackened with soot, and bars had been affixed to its windows, the metal leaving rusty streaks down the brick. She folded her arms across her stomach to suppress a shiver.

"Odd," he went on, speaking to himself. "There's supposed to be someone waiting for us—but no matter, I can take you to the door. . . ." Without looking, he offered her his arm.

Elisabeth barely saw the gesture. She was still staring up at the lodging house. It reminded her of the orphanage she had imagined as a child, the grim place where she would be cast away, unwanted and forgotten. "You're going to leave me here?" The words forced themselves out, sounding small.

Nathaniel hesitated, his expression wiped clean. A heartbeat passed. He looked young and very pale in the dark. Then he stepped forward, motioning for Elisabeth to follow.

"Don't tell me you've succumbed to my charms," he said over his shoulder. "I assure you, no good will come of a passionate affair between us. You, a small-town country librarian, me, the kingdom's most eligible bachelor—you needn't scoff, Scrivener. It's true—go out on the street and ask anyone. I'm quite famous."

But Elisabeth hadn't scoffed. The sound that had escaped her had been a stifled cry of alarm. In a nearby alley, behind the extinguished streetlamp, a group of figures stood watching them: hulking and shining-eyed, their breath steaming in the night. She blinked, and they were gone—but she was certain she hadn't imagined them.

She opened her mouth to warn Nathaniel, who was by now several paces ahead. But before she could make another sound, a rough grip seized her around the waist and yanked her toward the alley. A hand crushed her mouth, and the cold point of a knife appeared at her throat.

NINE

THE HAND CLAMPED over Elisabeth's mouth reeked of sweat. When she tried to bite it, her teeth couldn't find purchase against the man's palm. The taste of his skin filled her mouth: bitter and metallic, like dirty coins. She threw herself against his hold in a panic, only for the blade to press more firmly against her throat. She fell still, rattled by her own helplessness. He dragged her a scuffling step backward. Then another.

She didn't know what awaited her in the alley, but she suspected it was far worse than this man and his knife.

Nathaniel paused with his foot on the lodging house's bottom step. "Scriv—" he began as he turned, only to fall silent, calmly taking in the scene. "For heaven's sake," he said. "What is all this about?"

Her captor must have smirked, because his breath wafted foully over her cheek.

"What do you want?" Nathaniel persisted. "Money?" He glanced between the knife, Elisabeth, and the man restraining her, whereupon he made a face at what he saw. "No, let me guess. A wart remedy? If I were you, I suppose I would be equally desperate."

He didn't seem impelled by any sense of urgency. But as he spoke, he discreetly flicked together his thumb and middle finger, the motion almost hidden by the folds of his cloak. A single green spark flew from his fingertips. Nothing else happened.

"Can't cast a spell on my knife." The man's coarse voice vibrated against Elisabeth's back. He sounded pleased with himself. "It's pure iron. Made sure of that."

"Well, you can't blame me for trying." Nathaniel's gaze drifted toward the alleyway, casually, then back to them. "The alternative causes such a mess. Blood is impossible to get out of silk, and I can't tell you how many times my servant has had to wash questionable stains from this cloak."

A soft, resigned sigh came from very close nearby. Her captor flinched and yanked her around toward the source, but no one was there: only a dim expanse of empty street, littered with discarded newspapers.

"I'm afraid I've lost count," said Silas's whispering voice directly behind them. The ghost of a breath fluttered Elisabeth's hair.

Her captor spun again, but once more, he was met with nothing. Elisabeth felt his heart pounding through his shirt. The blade trembled in his slippery grip. An image floated to the surface of her mind, like a drowned, ghostly flower rising from a deep pool: Silas standing in a dark wood, his hands folded behind his back. But that hadn't actually happened, had it? She had seen it in a dream.

"Stay back," the man warned. "If you make a move, I'll cut her. Don't matter to me whether she lives or dies. And I'm not alone, neither—"

"You never did explain to me what some of those stains were, master," Silas said.

"Best if I leave that to your imagination," Nathaniel replied.

"Where the bloody hell are you?" her captor roared, and then his roar turned into a scream. Both the knife and the hand fell away at once, and Elisabeth stumbled forward; but Nathaniel was there, and he caught her before she fell.

She gagged and spat on the ground, desperate to rid the man's taste from her mouth. "There are more," she gasped, "more men, in the alley."

"I'm truly sorry to have to tell you this, for both our sakes," Nathaniel said, "but those are not men."

As if in agreement, a growl shuddered through the dark. A shadow detached itself from the mouth of the alley and prowled into the glow cast by the faraway streetlamps. The light delineated a long, snarling muzzle, much too large to belong to a dog. Slit-shaped nostrils flared as they scented the air. Steam gusted from them on the exhale. A pair of horns emerged next, curved and frontward-pointed. Mist flowed over black scales, shifting as powerful muscles bunched beneath them. Not a man—and not an animal, either.

"They are demons," she whispered.

"Lesser demons. Fiends." Nathaniel glanced behind them. "Highly illegal to summon, in part because they'll do practically anything for the promise of a . . . oh, never mind."

"The promise of a what?"

Nathaniel winced. "A meal. That charming gentleman with the knife probably told them they'd get to eat you."

Given what she knew about demons, Elisabeth wasn't surprised. As the fiend came fully into view, ribs strained against its starved-looking sides. Vertebrae bulged from its spine like knuckles. It resembled a huge, gaunt hound that had been skinned and armored in scales.

Before she could reply, two more of the creatures prowled into sight, cutting her and Nathaniel off from the route that led past the lodging house. Their breath fogged the air, and their narrow eyes shone red. Whinnies rang out as the horses spooked, but the fiends' attention didn't waver, fixed hungrily on Elisabeth.

Silently, Nathaniel nodded toward the building. She caught his eye to signal that she'd understood. Together they moved backward toward the steps, matching each other's slow, deliberate movements. As they went, Nathaniel muttered an incantation. Emerald light spun out between his cupped hands, coiling like a rope.

"She's stringy," he insisted as the fiends advanced, speaking in a conversational tone. "A bit gamey. Do you see all that hair? There's practically nothing underneath it."

A snarl came from behind them, reverberating through Elisabeth's bones. Hot, fetid breath gusted across the back of her neck. They turned simultaneously to find a fourth fiend crouched on the stoop, blocking the door. Saliva hung in quivering strings from its jaw.

"Worth a try," Nathaniel said, and pulled Elisabeth toward him in a hard embrace.

The world exploded around them. A shower of brick, wood, and metal erupted outward, crashing down amid a billowing cloud of dust. She was aware of Nathaniel's heart thundering against her own, of the muscles of his shoulders pulling taut as he wrenched something back to him—a rope of emerald fire, a whip. He lashed out again, and this time she saw the whip strike the side of the building, which collapsed so quickly it seemed to turn into liquid, cascading downward in a waterfall of stone. A single high-pitched yelp sounded from beneath.

He released her body, but kept hold of her wrist, towing her through the wreckage. She couldn't tell where the fiends were buried. The silence was as thick and choking as the dust that filled the air, punctuated by the clatter of a brick tumbling to the ground as the debris settled.

"I need you to get inside the coach," Nathaniel explained, a snap of urgency breaking his composure at last. "They won't stay down for long. What are you doing?"

Elisabeth had tugged her arm from Nathaniel. She kicked aside a stray brick and snatched up a metal bar that had rolled free from the rubble. She clutched it and scowled at him. His eyes assessed her. A slight change came over his face, a recalculation.

"Very well, you unutterable menace," he said. "Help me hold them off." He nodded toward the driver's seat.

She climbed up first. Silas was nowhere to be seen. She seized the rail for balance as the coach shuddered, rolling forward a few precarious inches. The wheels creaked ominously against the brakes. Any moment now the horses were going to take off regardless of whether the carriage came with them. Judging by the sweat lathering their coats, that moment would be soon. She considered the incomprehensible tangle of reins.

Instead of springing up beside her, Nathaniel hesitated. He looked over his shoulder. Dust obscured the street behind them, but in one place an eddy stirred the cloud.

The moment she saw it, a fiend hurtled from the spot with a reverberating snarl. Nathaniel's whip cracked, meeting the demon in midair. Green fire curled around its neck, and a leisurely flick of his wrist sent it flying back into the wreckage.

The horses screamed, straining against their restraints. Nathaniel threw his whip aside, yanked on the brakes, and vaulted toward the coach as it lurched into immediate motion. He clung to the edge for a breath-stopping moment as the wheels jolted over loose bricks, throwing the vehicle to and fro like a ship on storm-tossed waves. Elisabeth stretched out a hand. He took it, and she pulled hard, lifting him into the air. Another yank, and his weight struck the bench beside her. Without waiting to see his reaction, she twisted around to face the rear. He took up the reins and snapped them. The horses straightened their course.

As the buildings slid past, the dust began to blow from the rubble in tatters. Shapes heaved themselves from the debris, and crimson eyes winked to life in the dark. She tightened her hold on the metal bar.

"I thought you didn't know how to drive a carriage," she shouted over the pounding of hooves.

"Nonsense," Nathaniel shouted back. "I'm a fast learner when properly motivated."

The coach veered around the corner onto another deserted street, its far wheels lifting from the ground with the force of the turn. They were picking up speed, fast, but the fiends had joined the chase. They streamed from the ruin, teeth bared, shaking dust from their horns. Elisabeth counted six, and felt a clutch of panic.

"Does this qualify as proper motivation?" she asked.

"That depends. How close are they?"

A fiend pulled away from the pack, gaining on them with startling speed. It drew up alongside the coach's rear wheels, sprinting like a greyhound, and angled its head, evaluating her with a glittering red gaze—calculating, she realized, the distance for a jump. The moment it gathered its haunches, she swung her makeshift weapon.

It connected with a crack. Her whole body shuddered at the impact, and flecks of drool spattered her face. Thrown off balance, the fiend clung to the side of the coach much as Nathaniel had a moment earlier, tearing the finely carved wood to splinters as it scrabbled for purchase. Each claw was as long as a man's finger, dirty and hooked. One swipe would tear her apart. The glaring eyes declared that it intended to do just that.

But the blow she'd landed had left a raw mark seared across its scaled muzzle. Saliva hissed and sizzled on the bar in her hands, evaporating like water thrown onto a hot saucepan. Her perspective shifted. The bar was made of iron.

Encouraged, she swung again, and felt a satisfying crunch. The fiend went limp. Its claws slid free. When it struck the ground, it tumbled end over end and lay struggling to rise, its wounded head sending up trickles of steam. The other fiends leaped over its body, their eyes locked on the coach.

She turned to Nathaniel, her weapon still steaming.

"That close," she said.

Nathaniel spared her a glance, and then another, followed by a third, before he wrenched his attention back ahead. "I am applying myself to the fullest," he assured her.

The coach swung around another bend. Someone screamed. A horse reared, struggling against its handler; a basket of cabbages spilled across the road. They had left the empty byways behind. As they careened down the street, dodging carts and wagons, Elisabeth had brief impressions of shocked faces flashing past in the gaslight. Pedestrians scrambled for the curb, fleeing from their path.

The first fiend rounded the corner behind them. It didn't

bother weaving through the traffic, but instead took a direct route, bounding over the displaced carts as if they were stones laid across a river. Coal and apples and kitchen utensils went flying. Bystanders fell back, shielding their heads with their arms, as the street disintegrated into chaos.

"Stop," she cried. "People are going to get hurt!"

"What do you propose I do? Raise a white flag? Ask the fiends nicely not to eat us?" A muscle worked in Nathaniel's jaw, betraying his own frustration.

"Use your magic!" she exclaimed, astonished that she had to be the one to suggest it.

For a wild moment he looked as though he might laugh. "Sorcery requires focus," he shot back instead. "Concentration. There are limits. I can't fling spells around while I—"

He swerved the carriage, narrowly avoiding a cart that hadn't moved out of their way quickly enough. The pony hitched to the cart shied from the hooves of Nathaniel's horses and crashed into a booth stacked with baskets of herring. The cobblestones vanished beneath a silvery flood of scales. Elisabeth ducked as the coach's wheels sent a stray fish spinning over their heads.

"I've seen you bring an entire courtyard of statues to life," she said. "You're a magister. These people are counting on you. Make a stand."

He conveyed to her with a single look that he found her difficult, irritating, and probably mad, but as they barreled toward a square, he pulled up on the reins and swung the coach around. She braced herself as the wheels jumped the curb. They dragged to a shuddering halt on the paving stones, drawn up beside the grand brick buildings that lined the square, a fountain interposed between themselves and the street.

As soon as the coach stopped moving, Elisabeth clambered from the driver's bench onto the flat wooden roof. From here she could see the entire path they had taken after turning onto the main street. She took in the confusion of toppled wagons, balking horses, scattered produce. Shouts carried on the night breeze, mingled with the shrill whinnies of the horses. Closer by, the handful of vendors near the fountain were hastening their efforts to pack up their carts. The pedestrians had seen the coach coming, and had already emptied the square. A few stragglers hurried up the steps of the nearby buildings, where they were swiftly pulled inside. Doors slammed. Faces pressed to windows. The air smelled of roasted chestnuts, and despite everything, Elisabeth's stomach growled.

Her eyes roved across the scene of chaos. At first she saw no hint of the fiends. Then a hunched, scaled back slinked between two abandoned wagons; a plume of steam rose from behind an overturned cart. She fixed her gaze on the spot until a fiend prowled into view, and her heart skipped at the sight of it. The left side of its head was burnt, its left eye a weeping ruin. It was the fiend she had struck from the coach.

"How hard are they to kill?" she asked, as Nathaniel climbed over the rail and joined her.

"That depends on your definition of killing." The wind ruffled his hair and teased his cloak. "Anything that comes from the Otherworld can't be slain in the mortal realm, just banished back home. Their spirits live on after their bodies are destroyed."

It felt dangerous to speak in the tense, expectant hush that had fallen over the square. Elisabeth noticed that someone had lost their hat, and it had blown into the water of the fountain. A lady's glove lay in the gutter. The fiends prowled nearer, winding sinuously between the carts. They had separated, advancing from six different directions.

She amended, "How many times do I have to hit them before they won't get back up again?"

Nathaniel's mouth twitched. "I think you'll get the hang of it, Scrivener. You aren't lacking in enthusiasm. Now—give me a moment. I need—fifteen seconds. Perhaps twenty."

He closed his eyes.

She had imagined sorcery to be immediate, like drawing a sword. Now, seeing the stillness of concentration that settled over Nathaniel's face, she wondered, for the first time, what it must be like to cast a spell. The effort that it required—not of the body, but of the mind.

He drew in a breath and began to speak without opening his eyes. The Enochian words fell jagged-edged from his lips, stinging the air. The wind intensified, whipping around him, flinging leaves and scraps of newspaper skyward, tousling the spray of the fountain. The hair stood up on Elisabeth's arms. His expression remained perfectly serene.

This was not like drawing a sword. It was like commanding an army. Becoming a god.

Above them, the sky darkened. Black clouds gathered, sweeping inward, funneling over the square in a boiling vortex. The air grew oppressive with moisture. The streetlamps dimmed. A greenish glow bloomed deep within the clouds, drenching everything in the uncanny twilight that preceded a storm.

Whatever Nathaniel was doing, the fiends weren't going to give him fifteen seconds. The moment he began his incantation, the fiend with the ruined eye sprang forward. It snarled at the others, issuing a command. The two fiends on either side of it leaped toward the square, their muscles bunching with powerful strides that carried them toward the coach at an impossible speed. Their tongues lolled from their mouths, crimson and steaming.

Elisabeth shook her windblown hair out of her face and raised the bar over her shoulder. The seething rotation of the clouds matched the sick turbulence in her stomach.

Teeth flashed. She swung. A crack split the night, and a burst of emerald fire scorched her vision.

As the spots cleared, she discovered that she was still standing. Both fiends lay on the ground in front of the coach. The first one was sprawled with its neck bent at an unnatural angle. She had done that. But something else had happened to the second. It lay in a tangled heap, its burnt flesh popping and sizzling like meat on a spit.

Nathaniel extended his hand. Emerald lightning forked down from the clouds, flashed once, twice, with a sharp crack and an echoing rumble that shook the ground and rattled the windows—and when it faded, another fiend lay cooked on the ground. Sparks danced between Nathaniel's fingers. He turned to strike the next fiend.

It was the leader, the one with the ruined eye. While Elisabeth and Nathaniel were busy with the others, it had prowled over to an overturned cart on the street. Now it stood there, watching them in silence, its lips skinned back from its teeth.

Lightning rippled through the clouds, spiderwebbing outward in a maze of jagged filaments. Power coursed around Nathaniel, ready to answer his call. But he didn't act.

He was staring at the fiend's front foot, resting on the cart, the cart that was pressed against a boy's chest, who had been trapped there when the cart toppled over. The boy appeared younger than Elisabeth, his slack, unconscious face tipped to the side. A knot of people looked on from some distance away, clustered against a building that hadn't let them inside. A woman near the front of the crowd was screaming; two young men held her back. All three of them had the same ginger hair as the boy beneath the cart.

"I can't," Nathaniel said. His lips barely moved, as if he were in a trance. "Not without hitting him, too."

Elisabeth reacted instinctively, readying herself to jump down from the coach. "I'll lure it away," she said.

He caught her arm. "That's exactly what the fiend wants," he snapped. "To draw you out on your own so you'll make an easier target. Don't be an idiot, Scrivener."

She looked at the boy, who would die if they did nothing, and back to Nathaniel. *Don't be an idiot.* "Is that what you call it?" she asked.

Something unidentifiable passed across his face. He let go.

Elisabeth's boots struck the paving stones. She advanced on the fiend across the empty square, newspapers blowing past in the wind. She weighed the iron bar in her hands. The fiend bared its teeth wider, giving her an inhuman grin. Its claws flexed, pushing the cart harder against the trapped boy. It wouldn't move until the last possible second.

Lightning cracked behind her, illuminating the street in a wash of green. Elisabeth didn't take her eyes from the demon.

A raindrop spattered the ground at her feet. She broke into a run, feeling the bar become an extension of her arm. Everything moved quickly after that. Fangs, claws, snarls. The bone-jarring impact of her weapon glancing off a horn, a bright ribbon of pain tearing down her shoulder. With each breath, she inhaled the stink of carrion and brimstone. She concentrated all her effort on pacing backward as she deflected the fiend's blows, pulling it away from the unconscious boy.

The rain began to fall in earnest, sheeting across the square, running into Elisabeth's eyes and blurring her vision. Another flash of lightning transformed her circling opponent into a stark etching of light and shadow. A second flash, a third. Had Nathaniel missed the other fiends? There should have only been two of them left. As she spun, searching, she saw more silhouettes creeping toward her, their eyes shining like embers through the curtain of rain. Too many of them to count. In her horror, she faltered.

There was no pain—but suddenly the world turned sideways, and the paving stones rose to meet her, cold and wet and grimy, slamming the air from her lungs. The bar skidded out of reach. She struggled to breathe, feeling as though a vise had clamped around her chest.

A lightning bolt split the air so close by that for a stunned moment she was certain it had struck her. Then the steaming body of the leader collapsed at her side, the light dimming from its single red eye.

"Steady on, Scrivener." Arms lifted her from the ground, gathering her onto Nathaniel's lap.

"The boy," she croaked.

"His family has him," Nathaniel said. "Don't worry. He'll be fine."

But we won't be. There were too many fiends. They were surrounded. She gazed up at Nathaniel's gray eyes, wondering if his face was the last thing she would ever see. Rain dripped from his nose and clung to his dark eyelashes. This close, she thought that his eyes did not look as cruel as she had once imagined. She had been so frightened of him before that she hadn't spared much thought for how handsome he was, which now seemed like a terrible waste.

Nathaniel's brow furrowed, as though he saw something in Elisabeth's expression that troubled him. He looked away, squinting against the downpour. "Silas?" he asked.

"Yes, master?" The servant's voice was little more than a whisper in the storm.

Somehow, Elisabeth had forgotten about Silas. She struggled to keep her eyes open. And there he was—impeccably dressed, balanced effortlessly on the edge of a rooftop high above them. He gazed down at the scene with detached, pitiless interest. The pounding rain left his slender form untouched.

How did he get all the way up there?

Shadows advanced from every side. They loomed at the corners of Elisabeth's vision, permeating the fog with their carrion stench.

"We could use some help down here," Nathaniel said, "whenever you're finished admiring the view."

Silas smiled. "With pleasure, master." He removed first his right glove, then his left, and neatly slipped them both into his pocket. Then he stepped from the edge of the rooftop, out over a four-story drop.

Elisabeth couldn't see him after that. Her eyes sagged shut on the sliver of now-empty sky as all around her there came a chorus of yelps, and crunches, and howls, punctuated every now and again by the sound of something limp and heavy being flung against a wall. All of that came from far away. Her thoughts had stuck on a single image: the sight of Silas's hands when he'd taken off his gloves.

He didn't have fingernails. He had claws.

"Elisabeth?" Nathaniel asked, and the sound of her name chased her into the dark.

TEN

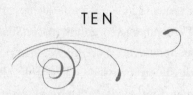

ELISABETH WOKE SURROUNDED by sunlight. Though she had no idea where she was, a peaceful sense of well-being enveloped her. Silken sheets whispered against her bare skin as she stirred. When she turned her head, her bright, blurry environment resolved itself into a bedroom. The walls were papered with a pattern of lilacs, and the delicate furniture looked as though it might break if someone accidentally leaned on it too hard, which Elisabeth supposed meant that it was expensive.

She wasn't alone in the room. Porcelain chimed soothingly nearby. She listened for a moment, then sat up in bed, a down comforter tumbling from her shoulders. Puzzled, she inspected herself. She had on her spare nightgown, and a bandage had been neatly applied to her arm. Not only that—someone had bathed her and brushed her hair.

Her head throbbed. A light touch revealed a knot on her scalp, sore beneath her fingertips. Perhaps that explained why she couldn't remember a thing. Across the room, Silas stood with his back to her, presently in the act of lifting the lid from a sugar tin. He was dressed, as usual, in his emerald livery, and appeared to be making her a cup of tea.

"Where am I?" she asked.

"You are in a guest room of my master's house," Silas replied. "We thought it safest to convey you here after the attack."

The attack. Her gaze fixed on his spotless white gloves, and her blood turned to ice.

Last night came rushing back: the snarls and the chaos, the lightning and the rain, and along with it her memories of the journey to Brassbridge, the ones he had somehow suppressed. She now clearly remembered the way he had caught her in the woods outside the inn; how he had made her forget that his eyes were yellow, not once but many times. Whenever she had drawn close to understanding what he was, he had turned her thoughts away.

"You're a demon," she said. Her voice sounded clumsy in the delicate room, too loud, out of place among the lilacs and fine china.

Silas tilted his head, acknowledging the obvious. "Do you take sugar in your tea, miss?"

Elisabeth didn't answer. She slid to the opposite side of the bed, as far away as she could get, and seized a chamberstick from the bedside table. It was heavy, fashioned from solid silver. "I know what you are," she warned. "You can't make me forget again."

He stirred the tea one last time and fastidiously placed the spoon on a folded cloth. "As it happens, you're correct. You have a surprising resistance to my influence; I doubt I could have continued much longer."

"What do you mean, your influence?" she demanded. "What did you do to me? And why?"

Silas turned. He merely looked at her, trembling and clutching a chamberstick, a single startled reflex away from hurling it at his head. After a few seconds of meaningful silence, Elisabeth was forced to admit that he had a point.

"Humans," he sighed. "Such excitable creatures. At least you didn't scream, and I thank you for it. Some demons enjoy the sound of mortals shrieking and pleading for their lives, but I have never possessed a taste for melodrama, unless it is safely confined to the opera." His eyes moved to the chamberstick. "That won't do you any good, by the way."

Slowly, Elisabeth lowered it to the bedspread. She watched Silas cross the room. When he set the tray down beside her, she flinched, but he withdrew without touching her, standing with his hands politely folded behind his back. It was the same way he'd stood in the thicket. She wondered if he was trying to make himself look less threatening, which was such a peculiar thought that she bleated out a laugh.

"What is it?" he inquired.

"I didn't know that demons could make themselves look like us. I expected . . ." She wasn't sure what she had expected. Horns and scales, like a fiend. She certainly hadn't expected him to be *beautiful*. "Something else," she finished.

A shadow of a smile crossed his face. His hair wasn't powdered, as she had first assumed. Everything about him was the flawless white of marble, down to the long pale lashes that shaded his sulfurous eyes. "Highborn demons such as I are able to change our shape according to our masters' wishes. In society I appear as a white cat, but when at home or running errands, Master Thorn prefers me in this form. Otherwise I am, as you say, 'something else.'"

A chill passed over Elisabeth. The Lexicon's words of warning came back to her. The grimoire had made it sound as though merely speaking to a demon was dangerous. But after everything Nathaniel had done to bring her to the city safely, she didn't think he would leave her alone with Silas if he posed a threat. She recalled the night in the Blackwald, remembering the quiet sound of Silas's laughter, the way the two of them had joked like old friends.

"Please." Silas's voice interrupted her uneasy thoughts. "Won't you drink your tea?"

She hesitated before she reached for the teacup. Steam wreathed her face as she took a cautious sip, aware of Silas's expectant gaze. Her eyes widened in surprise. "It's good." In fact, it was the best cup of tea she'd ever tasted in her life. Not what she had expected, considering that it had been made by a—

She set the cup down with a clatter, sloshing hot liquid over her fingers. The heat and the steam had brought back a sudden, visceral memory of the man holding a hand over her mouth, his breath damp on her cheek. Then the way he had simply been *gone*, as if he had vanished into thin air. What had Silas done to him?

"I killed him, miss," the demon said softly. "He would have done the same to you, and you wouldn't have been his first victim. I smelled it on him—so much death. No wonder the fiends were willing to follow him."

She made a strangled sound. "You can read my thoughts?"

"Not precisely."

"Then how . . . ?"

"I've spent hundreds of years observing humankind during my service to the Thorn family. I don't wish to insult you, but you are not complicated beings."

She shuddered, staring at her hands, at the too-perfect cup

of tea, wondering what else he could tell about her simply by looking.

"Are you feeling unwell? Perhaps you should get more rest."

She shook her head, not meeting his eyes. "I've rested enough."

"In that case, I have news that may ease your mind." He lifted a newspaper from the nightstand and passed it to her. She took it warily, glancing at his gloves, but she couldn't see any evidence of his claws. "The attempt on your life has already reached the morning papers."

Elisabeth almost did a double take. The headline on the front page read SUSPECT . . . OR HERO? and was accompanied by a sketch of Nathaniel and herself standing on top of the coach as fiends closed in around them. Nathaniel's lightning slashed through the crosshatched sky, and the artist had taken the liberty of replacing her iron bar with a sword. Her eyes flicked back to the headline. "This is about *me?*"

Silas inclined his head.

Incredulous, she began skimming the article. *The young woman, identified by an anonymous source as one Miss Elisabeth Scrivener, demonstrated uncommon courage and vigor in holding off her demonic attackers, going so far as to save the life of a helpless bystander. . . . She is believed to have arrived in Brassbridge as a suspect in the acts of sabotage on the Great Libraries, though we must question the Magisterium's wisdom in naming her a suspect when this vicious attempt on her life suggests the precise opposite. It is clear that the true culprit hoped to silence her using any means possible. . . .*

Elisabeth's cheeks flamed as the article went on to speak glowingly of *reports from our trusted sources* that she had single-handedly defeated a *rampaging Malefict before it imperiled the lives of innocents in the quaint village of Summershall.*

Then, annoyingly, it devoted a subsequent column to *Magister Nathaniel Thorn, Austermeer's Most Eligible Bachelor—When Will He Select a Bride?*

Something nagged at her, and she went back to the beginning to reread the first several sentences. "Wait a moment," she realized aloud. "This says *acts* of sabotage."

Silas reached toward her. She tensed, but he only flicked to the second page. Scanning through the article's continuation, her breath stopped.

"There was an attack on the Great Library of Knockfeld?" Her lips moved as she raced through the cramped text. "'Another Class Eight Malefict . . . three wardens dead, including the Director . . . first labeled a tragic accident, now believed to be connected to the incident in Summershall.' This happened two weeks before the Book of Eyes!" She looked up at Silas. "Why would any of this ease my mind?"

"Last night has altered your circumstances considerably. Your hearing has been called off in the midst of the public outcry incited by the press. Once you are well enough for a carriage ride, Master Thorn has been instructed to bring you directly to the Chancellor."

She sat in disbelief, inhaling the paper's scent of cheap ink and newsprint. Her head felt empty, ringing with Silas's words. "Why does the Chancellor want to see me?" she asked.

"I was not told." Something like pity shaded the demon's alabaster features. "Perhaps you might consider getting dressed. I can assist you, if you wish. I have taken the liberty of altering today's selection."

Elisabeth frowned. Her best dress hung from a hook on the wardrobe, lengthened with fashionable panels of silk. Now, it looked like it would fit. Silas had done that himself? She touched her neatly brushed hair, recalling her earlier observation that someone had bathed her and changed her clothes. When realization struck, she recoiled. "Did you undress me?"

"Yes. I have decades of experience—" Reading her horror, he raised a placating hand. "I apologize. I have no interest in human bodies. Not in any carnal sense. I forget, at times . . . I should have said so earlier."

Elisabeth was not to be taken for a fool. "I've read what demons do to people. You torture us, spill our blood, devour our entrails. The entrails of maidens, especially."

Silas's lips tightened. "Lesser demons eat human flesh. They are base creatures with vulgar appetites."

"And you are so different?"

His lips thinned further. Against all odds, offense shone in his yellow eyes, and when he spoke, the edges of his courteous, whispered consonants were slightly clipped. "Highborn demons consume nothing but the life force of mortals, and even then, only once we have bargained for it. We care for nothing else."

She sat back, her heart pounding. Slowly, she calmed. Silas seemed to be telling the truth. He wasn't attempting to disguise the fact that he was evil, only clarifying the nature of his misdeeds. Strangely, that made her feel that she could trust him, in this matter at least.

She thought of the silver streak in Nathaniel's hair, so unusual to see in a boy of eighteen. *How much of his life have you taken?* she wondered.

"Enough of it," Silas said, almost too quietly for her to hear. "Now, if you are certain you don't require assistance . . ."

"No thank you," she said hurriedly. "I can get ready without any help."

His raised eyebrows informed her that had his doubts, but he bowed politely out the door all the same, leaving Elisabeth alone with a thousand questions and a cooling cup of tea.

When she opened the door fifteen minutes later, Silas was nowhere in sight. She poked her head out of the room and peered down the hallway. While she had never spent much time in a real house, this one seemed enormous compared to the homes in Summershall. The hallway marched on for a considerable length, set with dark wood paneling and an astonishing number of doors. For some reason all the curtains were drawn, reducing the sunny day to a twilit gloom.

She crept outside and drifted down the hall. Though grand, the house possessed an air of abandonment. She didn't see any servants, demonic or otherwise, and the air was so still that the methodical ticking of a grandfather clock somewhere deep within the manor seemed to reverberate through the soles of her boots like a heartbeat. Everything smelled faintly of aetherial combustion, as if magic had soaked into the building's very foundations.

After several twists through the labyrinthine halls, the odor intensified. She turned this way and that, sniffing the air, and finally determined that the smell was seeping out from beneath one closed door in particular: a door whose panels were covered in soft snowdrifts of dust, the wood around the ornate knob scored with scratches, as though someone's hand had slipped repeatedly while trying to unlock it.

Elisabeth wavered. She was not going to touch a sinister-looking door in a sorcerer's home. But perhaps . . .

Holding her breath, she bent and brought her eye level with the keyhole. The room was dark inside. She leaned forward.

"Miss Scrivener," said Silas's soft voice, directly behind her.

She flung herself around, striking the wall with enough force to rattle her teeth. How did Silas move so silently? He had done the same thing to the man last night, right before he killed him.

Silas's expression was remote, as though graven in marble, but he spoke as courteously as ever. "I did not mean to startle you, but I'm afraid that room is best left alone."

"What's inside it?" Elisabeth's mouth had gone dry as bone.

"You would not wish to see. This way, please."

He guided her back the way she had come, and then down a broad, curving stair, huge and carpeted in velvet, which swept all the way to the foyer two floors beneath. Unlit chandeliers hung above her head, their crystals twinkling in the dimness, and her footsteps echoed on the checkered marble floor. The grandness of it brought to mind a deserted fairy-tale castle. Her imagination peeled away the dreary pall of abandonment, replaced it with light and laughter and music, and she wondered why the house was kept this way, when it could be such a beautiful place.

"Master Thorn will join us shortly," Silas said. Then he added, "You may look around, if you like."

Without permission, Elisabeth had already crossed the foyer and picked up a candlestick made of solid crystal. Guiltily, she set it down. As she did so, Nathaniel's gray eyes reflected across its facets, multiplied by the dozen, and she gasped—but when she whirled around, no one stood behind her. The crystal had reflected a portrait hanging on the wall. And the man in the portrait was too old to be Nathaniel, though he bore a close resemblance, down to the silver streak that ran through his black hair. His smile, on the other hand . . . it was warm and kind and open, far happier than any smile she had ever seen on Nathaniel's face.

"My master's father, Alistair Thorn," Silas provided. "I served him in his time."

He's dead, she realized with a jolt. *He must be.* Suddenly, she found it uncomfortable looking into his eyes. Her gaze strayed to the white cat the artist had painted on Alistair's lap. It was a dainty, long-haired creature, captured in the act of grooming its paw.

The air stirred, and Silas stood beside her, studying the next portrait over, which depicted a blond woman in a lilac gown. This time Elisabeth recognized something of Nathaniel in her expression, the way her eyes sparkled with the suppressed laughter of an unspoken joke. On her face it looked welcoming instead of mocking, illuminated by love.

Silas said, "His mother, Charlotte."

Wistfulness tugged on Elisabeth's heart. "She's beautiful."

"She was."

Elisabeth glanced at Silas, lips parted around an apology, but he was expressionless, still gazing at the portraits. She instantly felt foolish for almost apologizing to a demon—a being who had not loved any of them, for demons could not feel love, or compassion, or loss.

Silently, he gestured to the third and final portrait.

Elisabeth stepped forward and examined it closely. The painting was of a boy, perhaps seven years of age, pale and grave, with a dark collar buttoned high around his neck. He looked so serious. Perhaps that came with being the heir to the Thorn legacy. Had he known the stories about Baltasar even then? It felt strange to think of Nathaniel as a child. An innocent.

"So he wasn't born with the silver in his hair," she said finally, looking to Silas.

"No, he wasn't. The silver is the mark of our bargain. Every sorcerer possesses one, unique to the demon that serves them. But this portrait isn't of Master Thorn. It's of his younger brother,

Maximilian. He passed away a year after it was painted."

Elisabeth stepped back. The hair stood up on her arms. The house felt like a mausoleum, its cold, empty halls full of ghosts. Nathaniel's entire family was gone. The Lexicon's words returned to her: *For once a bargain with a demon is struck, it is in the demon's best interest to see its master dead. . . .*

"What happened to them all?" she whispered, not certain this time if she really wanted to know the answer.

Silas had gone still. It took him a moment to reply, and when he did, his whispering voice floated through the foyer like mist. "Charlotte and Maximilian perished together in an accident. A senseless tragedy for a sorcerer's wife and son. I know what you are thinking—I was nowhere near them when the accident occurred. Alistair followed only a few months later, and I was there, that time. It proved . . . a difficult year for my master."

"You killed him," Elisabeth said. "Alistair."

Silas's reply came as a breath, barely louder than the distant ticking of the grandfather clock. "Yes."

"Nathaniel knows?"

"He does."

Elisabeth grappled with this information. "And he still—he still decided to—"

"He bound me to his service directly after it happened. He was only twelve years of age. The ritual was surely frightening for him, but of course, he already knew me well." Silas drifted toward a blank spot on the paneling, where there was an empty spot left for one final portrait. He lifted his gloved hand and lightly touched the wall. "I was there when Master Thorn came into the world, you see. I heard him speak his first words, and watched him take his first steps. And I will be there when Master Thorn dies," he said, "one way or another."

Elisabeth took another step back, almost colliding with a coatrack. Nathaniel had told her that everyone else in line for his title was gone, but she hadn't expected anything like this. Certainly not that he had been completely alone in the world at only twelve years old, bargaining away his life to the demon who had killed his father. The demon who would one day kill him.

A step creaked. Elisabeth turned. Nathaniel was coming down the stairs, one hand in his pocket, the other skimming along the banister. He looked striking in an expensively tailored suit, the cut of the green brocade waistcoat accentuating his strong shoulders and narrow waist. She stared, trying to reconcile his careless poise with what she had just learned. He returned her gaze evenly, an eyebrow lifted as though in challenge.

When he reached the bottom, Silas went to him at once. With the silent efficiency of a professional valet, he went about making minute adjustments to Nathaniel's clothes: fixing his cuffs, straightening his collar, tweaking the fall of his jacket. Then, with a slight frown, he undid Nathaniel's cravat and whisked it from his neck.

"Does it need to be so tight?" Nathaniel objected as Silas retied the cravat in a complicated series of knots, his gloved fingers moving with nimble certainty over the fabric.

Silas could easily throttle him with that, Elisabeth thought, astonished. Yet Nathaniel appeared completely relaxed, trusting of his servant's ministrations, as if he had a murderous demon's hands at his throat every day.

"I'm afraid so, if you wish to remain fashionable," Silas replied. "And we wouldn't want a repeat of the incident with Lady Gwendolyn."

Nathaniel scoffed. "How was I supposed to know tying it that way meant that I intended to proposition her? I have better things to do than learn secret signals with handkerchiefs and neckcloths."

"Had you listened to me, I would have told you, and spared you from getting champagne thrown in your face—though I heard several people say afterward that that was their favorite part of the dinner. There." He stood back, admiring his work.

Nathaniel automatically reached up to touch the cravat, then dropped his hand when Silas narrowed his yellow eyes in warning. With a lopsided grin, he strode across the hall toward Elisabeth, his boots rapping on the marble floor.

"Are you ready, Miss Scrivener?" he asked, offering her his arm.

Elisabeth's heart skipped a beat. She might have misjudged Nathaniel, but she had been right about one thing. A sorcerer did want her dead. And somewhere out there, he was waiting.

Chilled to the bone, she nodded and took his arm.

ELEVEN

THE COACH PASSED tall, grand houses of gray stone, stacked tightly alongside each other like books on a bookshelf. Bright blooms of foxglove and deadly nightshade spilled from their window boxes, and wrought iron fences bordered them in front, guarded by statues and gargoyles that turned their heads as the coach passed. Heraldic devices were carved upon the pediments above the front doors. Many of the houses were clearly centuries old, their elegant facades wrapped in a sense of untouchable wealth.

She watched a woman exit a carriage, jewels glittering on her ears. A small child opened the door for her, and Elisabeth assumed he was the woman's son until she dismissively handed him her shopping parcels. She saw the boy's eyes flash orange in the light before the door swung shut. Not a boy—a demon.

"Does this entire neighborhood belong to sorcerers?" she asked Nathaniel. Her stomach writhed like a nest of snakes. The saboteur could live in any one of these houses. He could be watching her even now.

"Almost exclusively," he replied. He was looking out the opposite window. "It's called Hemlock Park. Sorcerers like their privacy—our demons are a bit like dirty laundry, not a secret, but an aspect of our lives that commoners rarely see, and one that we prefer they don't think about too much. A lot of old blood around here, as you can probably tell. Sorcerous lineages that go back hundreds of years, like mine."

Curiosity snuck through her guard. "I thought all sorcerers belonged to old families. Aren't you born into it?"

"I suppose that's true in the sense that magic is an inheritance." Nathaniel spared her a glance. "Or rather, demons are. A highborn demon can only be summoned by someone who knows its Enochian name, and families pass those names down through the generations like heirlooms. But occasionally a dabbler with no magical heritage digs up the name of a notable demon in some obscure text and manages to summon it. They have to keep the demon in the family for a few decades before the old houses begin to consider them respectable."

Dabblers and criminals. That was how the Lexicon had referred to people who summoned lesser demons, like fiends. True sorcerers didn't stoop to that level.

Not unless they wanted to eliminate a witness, and blame the murder on someone else.

Disturbed, Elisabeth mulled this over as they passed a park full of ancient oaks and winding gravel paths, and then a patch of urban woodland that made her feel like she was back on the outskirts of the Blackwald. The coach turned onto a drive flanked by marble plinths. A matching pair of stone gryphons sat atop them, flicking their tails and sunning their mossy wings. Eventually a structure came into view beyond a hedge, first visible as a flash of light on the copper of a domed cupola.

"Oh," she breathed, pressing her face to the window. "It's a palace!"

She felt Nathaniel watching her. When he spoke, he sounded oddly reluctant to correct her. "No, just Ashcroft Manor."

But there was no "just" about the building they were heading toward, an immense white manor surrounded by lavish gardens. Its roofline of towers, domes, and elaborate cornices resembled the skyline of a miniature city, and the sunlight threw dazzling prisms from a glass-roofed conservatory attached to its side. The drive circled around a large fountain directly in front, and as they drew nearer she saw that the water lifted by itself, splashing in vortices that continually changed shape: first it formed a group of translucent maidens leaping into the air like ballet dancers, who merged into a rotating armillary sphere, which next split apart into a pair of rearing horses, their manes tossing droplets across the drive. A few of the droplets struck the coach's windows and clung to the glass, sparkling like diamonds.

"And Silas says *I'm* extravagant with my magic," Nathaniel muttered.

Elisabeth made an effort to stop gaping openmouthed as they neared the manor. A crowd of people stood scattered around the drive, but as far as she could tell, they weren't sorcerers or even servants. They all wore brown tweed jackets and had notebooks tucked under their arms, repeatedly consulting their pocket watches as if they were in a great hurry. When they heard the carriage approaching, they looked up with hungry, eager expressions, like dogs waiting for scraps to be thrown from the dinner table.

"Who are those people?" Elisabeth asked uneasily. "They look like they're waiting for us."

Nathaniel slid over to her side of the coach, looked out, and swore. "Chancellor Ashcroft's allowed the press onto his estate. I suppose there's no escaping them. Courage, Scrivener. It will all be over soon."

When Silas opened the door, a wave of sound immediately swamped the coach. No one spared Silas a glance; they focused on Elisabeth as she stepped outside, jostling between themselves for a better position near the front of the crowd.

"Miss Scrivener!" "Do you have a moment—" "I'm Mr. Feversham from the *Brassbridge Inquirer*—" "Over here, Miss Scrivener!" "Can you tell us how tall you are, Miss Scrivener?"

"Hello," she said bemusedly. All the men looked very similar. Never before had she seen so many mustaches together in one place. "I'm sorry—I have no idea." She had grown since the last time Katrien had measured her.

"Is it true that you defeated a Class Eight Malefict in Summershall?" one of the men asked, already scratching away frantically in his notebook.

"Yes, that's true."

"Completely on your own?"

She nodded. The man's eyes nearly popped from his head, so she added kindly, "Well, I had a sword."

Another tweed-clad reporter dodged through an opening. "I see you've been spending a great deal of time alone with Magister Thorn. Has he declared his intentions?"

"I wish he would," Elisabeth said. "He hardly makes sense half the time. Knowing his intentions would be helpful."

Nathaniel made a choking sound. "She doesn't mean it that way," he assured everyone, taking Elisabeth's arm. "She's a feral librarian, you see—raised by booklice, very tragic. . . ." He tugged her out of the crowd and up the manor's front steps.

The double doors were engraved with a baroque-style gryphon. A footman dressed in golden livery stood in front of them. Elisabeth eyed him suspiciously, but he didn't have strangely colored eyes, nor did he repel her thoughts the way Silas had while exerting his influence. He was a man, not a demon.

"The Chancellor will arrive momentarily," he said, and Nathaniel groaned.

"What?" she asked.

"Ashcroft enjoys making grand entrances. He's an insufferable show-off. The press can't get enough of him."

Elisabeth thought it was rather hypocritical for Nathaniel to complain about people making grand entrances when he himself had arrived at Summershall in a carriage carved all over with thorns, and had made every statue in the courtyard come alive and at least one of them wave a sword, but she decided to keep that to herself, because she had just caught a whiff of aetherial combustion.

She stumbled back as a thread of golden light zigzagged through the air in front of her, like a rip appearing in a piece of fabric. The doors to the manor rippled, distorted, as a man pushed a flap of air aside and stepped through, affording a glimpse of a warmly lit study behind him. Elisabeth blinked, trying to make sense of what she was seeing. It was as if the world had transformed into a scene painted onto a set of curtains, and this other room was what lay beyond them. The man—the Chancellor—let go of the air, or the curtain, or whatever it was, and the sliver of study closed up behind him. As quickly as it had broken, reality returned to normal.

Chancellor Ashcroft beamed, bowing to the reporters as they broke into applause. Though he was almost old enough to be Elisabeth's father, he was undeniably handsome. His brilliant smile revealed laugh lines around his eyes that gave him a look of mischievous good humor, and his thick, glossy blond hair didn't show a hint of gray. He wore a golden cloak over a pearl-white suit, with an embroidered gold waistcoat on underneath.

"It's so good to see you, Nathaniel," he said. "And you must be Miss Scrivener. I am Oberon Ashcroft, the Chancellor of Magic. What a pleasure to meet you."

He took her hand and kissed it. All the words flew out of Elisabeth's head like a flock of startled pigeons. No one had ever kissed her before, even on her hand. When Ashcroft straightened again, she saw that while his right eye was bright blue, the left was a deep, gleaming crimson that caught the light like a ruby. Remembering what Silas had told her, she guessed that the crimson eye was his demonic mark.

"Miss Scrivener, I must apologize for the danger you encountered last night. I never imagined that such a thing could happen—fiends, running wild through the streets—but that's no excuse for failing to ensure your safety while you were under the Magisterium's protection."

"Don't you mean its custody?" she asked. A few of the reporters gasped, and Elisabeth froze, feeling a stirring of panic.

But Ashcroft didn't look angry. Instead, he gave her a rueful smile. "No—you're quite right. The Magisterium made a mistake, and it would be distasteful of me to pretend otherwise. How are you coping?"

His concern took her aback. "I . . ."

"You've been through a terrible ordeal. Accused of a crime you didn't commit, imprisoned, attacked by demons, and of course the loss of your Director, Irena. She was a remarkable woman. I had the pleasure of meeting her some years ago."

Suddenly, Elisabeth's eyes prickled with unshed tears. "I am well," she said, squaring her shoulders, willing the tears to retreat. This was the first time anyone had suggested to her that she had a right to grieve the Director's death, rather than accusing her of being responsible for it. Ashcroft even knew the Director by name. "I just want whoever killed her to be caught."

"Yes." He looked at her gravely. "Yes, I understand. Excuse me for a moment . . ." He turned to the reporters. "I called this press meeting to make a brief announcement. Following the events of last night, and having reviewed certain discrepancies in the official report from Summershall, Miss Elisabeth Scrivener is no longer a suspect in our investigation." Shock jolted through Elisabeth. "She is, instead, to be commended by the Magisterium for her brave actions in Summershall, which saved countless lives. The loss of a Class Eight grimoire is devastating to Austermeerish magic, but Miss Scrivener made the best choice available to her in a critical situation, and she performed to the highest possible standard. I will be personally sending a letter of recommendation to the Collegium, advising the preceptors to consider her for warden's training when she completes her apprenticeship."

Elisabeth swayed on her feet. A hand steadied her, a light, unexpected touch between her shoulders. Nathaniel stood at her side, gazing straight ahead.

"As you know," Ashcroft was saying, "the Great Libraries were built by my ancestor, Cornelius, so my commitment to bringing the saboteur to justice is far more than just a professional concern. . . ."

Elisabeth found that she could no longer follow the words. Her heart felt like it had grown too large for the confines of her ribs. She tried to keep her posture straight, desperate to look worthy of the Chancellor's praises, while privately, shamefully, another part of her wanted to hide. She had never known that hope could hurt so badly, like blood rushing back to a deadened limb.

She was grateful when afterward, as the reporters dispersed, Ashcroft drew Nathaniel aside to speak to him alone. She studied the gryphons on the door, pretending she couldn't hear snatches of their conversation through the sound of carriage wheels crunching on gravel.

"Before you leave," Ashcroft was saying in a low voice, "I wanted to thank you for what you did for Miss Scrivener." He paused. "Ah. I see. You haven't told her, have you?"

Nathaniel's reply was indistinct. What were they talking about? If only she could see their faces. The footman came past carrying her trunk, and she moved out of the way. When she looked up, Nathaniel was nowhere to be seen. Glancing around wildly, she saw him stepping briskly toward the coach, his emerald cloak billowing at his heels.

"Nathaniel!" she called out, as he began to climb into the coach. He flinched at the sound of her voice. Then he angled his face, waiting.

"You were going to leave without saying good-bye," she said.

"Good-bye, Scrivener," he said promptly, without looking at her. "It truly was a pleasure, aside from the time you bit me. Try not to knock over any of the Chancellor's bookcases."

Elisabeth had a strange feeling in her chest, like a soft piece of parchment being torn, just a little. She might never see Nathaniel again. She still didn't have his measure, but they had fought together last night—saved lives together—and surely that counted for something. Surely it was enough for him to want to shake her hand, or at least look her in the eye before he left.

She wished she had something better to say. But she couldn't think of anything, so she only said, "Good-bye."

Nathaniel hesitated for a long moment. Silas, sitting in the driver's seat, passed a glance between the two of them, as though he could see something between herself and Nathaniel that she could not. Then Nathaniel nodded, in a formal sort of way, and climbed inside and shut the door. Silas flicked the reins. The coach began to move.

So that's it, she thought.

She watched the coach grow smaller as it traveled along the drive, the sun shining from its lacquered roof, feeling a loss she couldn't explain.

TWELVE

"MISS SCRIVENER?"

Elisabeth started and looked up. Ashcroft stood beside her, and Nathaniel's coach was out of sight. She received the impression that the Chancellor had been speaking to her for some time now, but she hadn't heard a single word. She stammered out an apology, followed by a series of disjointed thank-yous for everything he had said during the speech, none of which seemed to make very much sense even to her own ears.

His expression softened. "Don't worry about any of that. Why don't you come inside?"

She followed him into the manor, and her eyes widened in wonderment. All the chandeliers were lit, throwing a liquid shine from the polished marble and gilded stuccowork. Mirrors in elaborate gold frames reflected the light from every angle. Servants in matching golden livery hurried to and fro, pausing to bow in their direction.

"You will be safe here," Ashcroft said. "The grounds are heavily warded; there hasn't been an intruder on the property in hundreds of years. In fact, in the seventeenth century, Ashcroft Manor even repelled an army."

With the manor's radiance shimmering across his blond hair and handsome features, the Chancellor resembled a hero from the pages of a storybook. Shyness gathered around Elisabeth like a layer of tulle, gauzy and unfamiliar. For once, she had to muster the courage to speak. "Sir, what was it that Nathaniel didn't tell me?"

"Ah. I see you overheard." A smile played about his mouth. "Well, he insisted on being the one to escort you from Summershall. It sounds as though you left quite the impression on him last spring—he was utterly convinced of your innocence. Nathaniel so rarely believes the best of people, I didn't have the heart to deny his request."

Surprise rendered her speechless. She glanced reflexively toward the windows, but the coach was long gone. Nathaniel had been concerned about her? That seemed impossible. He certainly hadn't shown any sign of it. Had he?

"Ah, Mr. Hob!" Ashcroft called out to a passing butler. "I see you've brought Miss Scrivener's things upstairs. Would you show her to her room?" He turned back to Elisabeth. "Miss Scrivener, I'm afraid my duties beckon. However, I would like to discuss the Summershall incident with you tomorrow. If there's any information you can give me—anything at all that you think might have caused the saboteur to target you last night—it would be of great help to our investigation."

She nodded, then hesitated as the butler led her toward the stairs. She did have information to give him; she was the only person who knew that the sabotage had been carried out by a sorcerer. Why not tell him now, rather than waiting until tomorrow? It would only take a moment. She paused on the bottom step, feeling dwarfed by the expanse of white marble and gilded banisters. "Sir?"

Ashcroft turned, his ruby eye catching the light of the chandeliers. He didn't look annoyed, only politely questioning, but her conviction faltered. Perhaps now wasn't the right time, after all—not with the butler and all the other servants listening.

"Where is your demonic servant?" she asked instead.

Ashcroft looked faintly surprised. "I keep her out of sight during the day, since demons upset my wife, Victoria. It's for the best. Lorelei has always served me faithfully, but one should never allow oneself to grow familiar with the creatures. It's best not to forget that they only obey us because they are bound to. Sorcerers have paid dearly for that mistake."

"Like Nathaniel's father," she said tentatively.

"Ah . . . well." His face clouded. "I don't know the full story. Only that there were certain . . ." He shook his head. "Alistair was a good man. He wasn't himself at the end. I wouldn't wish to speak ill of the dead."

Elisabeth turned his words over in her head as she followed the butler upstairs. What had Ashcroft meant to say before he'd trailed off?

She couldn't begin to fathom the bond between Nathaniel and Silas—how it was possible for Nathaniel to be so friendly with him not only knowing what he was, but after what he had done. And yet—Silas didn't seem to have ever hurt the younger Master Thorn. Why hadn't Silas taken advantage of the opportunity to harm him when he was only twelve years old, vulnerable and afraid?

She frowned, shoving the thoughts aside. She shouldn't waste time thinking about Nathaniel. It was none of her business if he wanted to risk his life trusting a demon.

"Your room, miss," the butler said, stopping outside a door. His voice was muddy-sounding, as if he had difficulty speaking. She looked up at him in surprise, and felt a twinge of unease. He was a huge man, solidly built, and considerably taller than even Elisabeth, which made him the tallest person she had ever seen. His suit fit oddly, and his gaze was curiously unfocused in a waxy face.

A rosy-cheeked servant bustled over, looking flustered. Fly-away strands of mousy brown hair wisped free from her bun. "Oh, good gracious, you're Miss Scrivener, aren't you? Come along, come along—I'm Hannah, dear, and I'm going to look after you while you're a guest here in the manor. Thank you, Mr. Hob."

Mr. Hob nodded and slumped off.

"Don't worry about old Mr. Hob," Hannah whispered, noticing Elisabeth's stare. "He had a fit some years ago that robbed him of most of his speech, but Master Ashcroft still hired him on when no one else would. A very decent thing to do, and Mr. Hob's as harmless as a fly, though he does sometimes give people a fright if they aren't used to him."

Shame flushed Elisabeth's cheeks. She resolved not to stare at the butler again, or to be afraid of him. Obediently, she followed Hannah into the room.

At first she couldn't conceive that this was a bedroom. She felt as though she had walked into an ice sculpture. Every-thing had been painted, upholstered, or embroidered in delicate shades of silver and white. A chandelier hung from the ceiling, reflected in the vanity mirror. The furniture was carved with elaborate flourishes and curlicues that reminded Elisabeth of the patterns that frost formed on windowpanes during Auster-meer's coldest months; the knobs were made of solid crystal.

Most astonishingly of all, a sapphire gown had been laid across the bed, waiting for her. Amid all of the wintry colors, its deep, lustrous blue stood out like a gem against snow.

"There must be a mistake," she said. Carefully, marvelingly, she touched the vanity table, half expecting it to vanish like an illusion in an enchanted castle. Next she eyed the gown askance, feeling as though it too might disappear if she looked at it directly. "That dress doesn't belong to me. I've never worn clothing so fine."

"Nonsense. Master Ashcroft is entertaining company tonight, and you will be expected to look presentable. Just be grateful we were able to find something close to your size, miss. There was such a fuss this morning, such a terrible fuss. Fortunately Lady Victoria's niece is traveling abroad, and she's an awfully tall young woman as well. We were able to borrow a few pieces of her wardrobe and make adjustments in the nick of time."

Elisabeth's attention had snagged on a single word. "Company?" she asked.

"You cannot expect such a great man to spend every evening at his leisure. Several members of Parliament, and their wives, are joining him for dinner."

Her pulse quickened. "Are they sorcerers?"

Hannah gave her an odd look. "No, dear. Master Ashcroft's guests are from the *Parliament*, not the Magisterium—and a good thing, too. I haven't the nerves for all those demons. I know they're necessary, but they're such unnatural creatures." She shuddered, and didn't notice the way Elisabeth relaxed. "Now, let's get this old dress off you. . . . Just look at that scratch on your shoulder, you poor girl. . . ."

An eternity later, Elisabeth had been groomed within an

inch of her life. Her skin felt tender from Hannah's scrubbing, and the long, hot bath in the claw-foot tub had left her fingertips as wrinkled as dried apricots. Her scalp alternately stung and throbbed from the torture Hannah had inflicted upon it with a comb. She smelled faintly, and unsettlingly, of gardenias.

Piles of sapphire silk rustled around her body as Hannah fastened the gown in place. It was beautiful, but it had a great deal of extra fabric; Elisabeth felt as though she were swimming in her own miniature sea. Then Hannah began to lace the corset up the back, and Elisabeth's breath hitched.

"I cannot breathe," she said, scrabbling at her chest.

Hannah firmly took her hands and set them aside. "It's the fashion, miss."

Elisabeth was deeply alarmed by the idea that not breathing was fashionable. "What if I have to run," she said, "or fight something?"

"In the master's house?" Hannah sounded shocked. "I know you've had some dreadful experiences lately, dear, but it's best if you keep such thoughts to yourself. That kind of talk is quite irregular for a young lady. Why, just look at you."

She wheeled Elisabeth around to face the mirror. Elisabeth stared at the girl reflected there, barely recognizing herself. Her hair cascaded over her shoulders in smooth, glossy chestnut waves, and she was cleaner than she had ever been before in her life. Her blue eyes contrasted vividly against her pink, scrubbed cheeks. While she had never possessed much in the way of curves, the sapphire gown made her figure look proud and statuesque. *Just like the Director,* she thought, with a tightness in her throat. Even the gown's color reminded her of a warden's uniform. She didn't understand why it was irregular to talk about fighting— not when she looked the way she did.

"How lovely," Hannah sighed. "The blue brings out your eyes, doesn't it?"

Elisabeth smoothed her hands wonderingly over the dress's silky fabric.

"I daresay it's time to bring you down for dinner. Don't worry, I'll take you there. It's awfully easy to get lost in this house—oh, dear, don't trip! Just lift the gown up a bit if you have to. . . ."

Twilight now painted the grounds in shades of indigo and violet, but inside the manor remained as bright as day. Perfume wafted through the halls, mingling with the fragrance of lilies arranged in vases on every table. When Hannah ushered Elisabeth into the dining room, its dazzle made spots bloom across her vision. Light shone from everything: the silver utensils, the jewels shivering like giant raindrops on the ladies' ears, the rims of champagne glasses as guests turned to see who had just entered.

Ashcroft was deep in conversation on the other side of the room, but a beautiful, frail-looking woman rushed over to Elisabeth and introduced herself as Ashcroft's wife, Victoria. Her auburn curls were piled atop her head in an intricate sweep, and she had a habit of self-consciously touching the string of pearls around her neck, as if to reassure herself that it was still there. With her light, nervous movements and glistening silver gown, she reminded Elisabeth of the dove that had nested in the stonework outside her and Katrien's room one spring, warbling anxiously whenever one of them stuck their head outside.

"I'm afraid Oberon can't get away from Lord and Lady Ingram," she said, smiling warmly. "Why don't I take you around and introduce you to some people before we take a seat? Everyone's so excited to have a look at you. They've read all about you in the papers."

Elisabeth spent the next several minutes being paraded around the room, learning the names of various important-looking people and attempting to curtsy at them, with mixed results. Eventually she gave up and explained that curtsying had not been included in her lectures at the Great Library, a statement that was, for some reason, met with peals of laughter. She smiled along, realizing they thought she'd made a joke.

Soon Ashcroft rang a fork against his glass. Silence fell as he stepped to the head of the table, and a servant pressed a champagne flute into Elisabeth's hand. She listened raptly as the Chancellor proceeded to give a speech on progress, comparing the new advances in coal, steam power, and natural gas to sorcery. "Like magic," he said, "technology frightens those to whom its inner workings remain a mystery, but for the sake of advancement, humanity must embrace change with open arms. I have always believed that sorcerers only hinder ourselves by living apart from commoners and conducting our affairs in secrecy. I consider it my goal as Chancellor to bring sorcery out of darkness, and into the light."

Gasps rang out as a golden radiance filled the room, far brighter than the candles. The sprays of lilies arranged across the tables had begun to glow, each delicate stamen blazing incandescently, bathing the guests' faces in a twinkling, ethereal light.

Ashcroft spoke over the applause. "To progress," he said, raising his glass.

Elisabeth copied the other guests and took a tentative sip of the champagne. It tasted sourer than she expected, but its bubbles fizzed down her throat and fanned embers in her stomach. She smiled and clapped, swept along on a bright tide of happiness that lasted through the dinner. Servants came in with trays of a fragrant green soup and white fish floating in an herb sauce, followed by platters of glazed pheasant and venison on beds of asparagus. She had never eaten anything so sublime. She polished off her seconds and was working her way through thirds—"I suppose you *are* very tall, dear," said Lady Ingram charitably—when someone mentioned Nathaniel's name near the head of the table. Elisabeth stopped chewing to listen.

"He must consider marriage promptly, of course, for the sake of Austermeer," one of the politicians was booming emphatically, slurred with drink. "Yes, yes, he is only eighteen—but Her Majesty the Queen is growing apprehensive. What if we were to have another war, and no Thorn to strike fear into the hearts of our enemies?" He banged his fist on the table, making the silverware rattle.

"Lord Kicklighter, we are hardly in danger of a war," someone else put in.

Lord Kicklighter's mustache quivered indignantly. "A nation is always in danger of a war! If not now, then in fifty years! And if Magister Thorn fails to produce an heir, what then? We haven't the population to defend ourselves against Founderland."

Elisabeth frowned and turned to Lady Ingram. "That man is speaking of Nathaniel as though he's livestock."

Lady Ingram sniffed. "Men like Magister Thorn have a responsibility to marry, especially now that he has no surviving relatives," she replied. "Baltasar Thorn's grimoire of necromancy will only open for those of his line, which means that Nathaniel is presently the only sorcerer who can read it. His complete disinterest in courtship has put everyone in government on edge."

"Unsavory, in my opinion," another man was muttering. "To resort to undead hordes in place of good Austermeerish men—"

"—yet it is a *last* resort, you understand, and it has kept the peace since the War of Bones—"

"But what about what happened to poor Alistair? Surely his fate is a sign that necromancy is a relic of the middle ages, not a weapon for the modern era." A flurry of scandalized murmuring followed this pronouncement.

"Such a tragedy, the loss of the younger brother," a woman sighed from the other end of the table. "We do not even know if Magister Thorn possesses an *interest* in ladies. He has never danced with a girl at the Royal Ball. If only Maximilian were still alive, there would be less of a fuss about carrying on the family name."

Elisabeth gritted her teeth. "But—"

Another woman, Lady Childress, had been watching Elisabeth keenly for some time now. "You call him by his first name, dear," she interrupted. "That's quite familiar." At once, every head turned in Elisabeth's direction.

She had never felt self-conscious about her height before, but now she wished she were shorter, so that she wasn't within view of every guest seated up and down the table. She didn't know what she was supposed to say. She had not been aware that there was a rule against referring to a person one's own age by their first name. Truthfully, she'd thought Nathaniel called her "Scrivener" because he didn't like her. She had the curdling realization that if she aired any of those realizations out loud, they'd all think she was an idiot.

"Does he possess an interest in young ladies, then, Miss Scrivener?" Lady Childress prompted.

"I do not know," Elisabeth replied, bristling. "He hasn't told me. I suppose that means it isn't any of my business."

The arrival of the desserts allowed everyone to pretend

that they hadn't heard Elisabeth's remark. She frowned as she accepted a heaping plateful of plum dumplings. Nathaniel's cynical air was beginning to make more sense. She didn't like to imagine how it must feel to have the private details of one's life under constant scrutiny, knowing every facet of your existence was gossiped about at dinner parties across Austermeer.

She was grateful when Ashcroft steered the conversation away to a discussion about steam power, which she didn't understand but found deeply fascinating. As her good mood returned, she polished off a custard and a pair of plum dumplings. Before she knew it everyone was leaving, tottering a bit and smelling strongly of liquor while the servants helped them back into their coats. Elisabeth had had two glasses of champagne herself, and the manor wore a glittery sheen, as if tinsel had been draped around the windows and chandeliers.

She followed the guests to the foyer, but no one was paying attention to her any longer. Ashcroft stood outside, trying to extricate his digits from Lord Kicklighter's enthusiastic handshake, and Victoria was deep in conversation with Lady Childress. Hannah was supposed to come collect her, yet the servant was nowhere in sight. A nearby clock indicated that it was almost one thirty in the morning. After a few minutes of waiting, Elisabeth caught a glimpse of Hannah's wispy bonnet bobbing down a hallway. She hurried after it, certain she would get lost in the manor if left to her own devices.

Hannah had a considerable head start, and Elisabeth soon discovered that she couldn't run on the slick floors while wearing satin slippers. After a few turns, she lost sight of her quarry and found herself stranded in an unfamiliar hallway. The manor's grandeur enfolded her in a shimmering world of marble, gold, and mirror-glass. With the champagne glowing inside her stomach like a newborn star, she felt as though she had wandered into a dream.

She paused to examine a filigreed sconce dripping with candle wax, then to trail her fingers over the features of a marble bust. The statue's subject had been young and handsome, and she found herself wondering what Nathaniel was doing at that very moment. Was he alone in his cheerless mausoleum of a house, unable to sleep, with only a demon for company? Perhaps she would see him again one day when she was a warden. But if she did, they wouldn't be able to talk about the time they'd fought off the fiends or watched the moss spirit in the Blackwald. They would exchange a handful of perfunctory words as she escorted him to a reading room, no better than strangers.

A strain of music reached her ears, and she snatched her hand from the bust. Somewhere nearby, someone had begun to sing. The sound unspooled through the halls like a silver thread, achingly beautiful, its melody wordless and strange. It lodged a hook in Elisabeth's heart, somehow seeming to express precisely the emotion of inarticulate longing that filled her. Helpless to resist its pull, she set off in search of the source, drifting past parlors, a ballroom, a conservatory brimming with palms and orchids.

Finally, she stepped into a music room. An elegant woman stood beside a pianoforte, her face shadowed, turning a lily between her slender, lace-gloved fingers. Elisabeth hadn't seen her at the dinner. She would have remembered. The woman had a fall of gleaming black hair that reached her waist, and she was dressed in an exquisite black gown against which her pale, perfect skin looked as white as candle wax. She stopped singing when Elisabeth entered; her fingers stilled, and the lily dropped to the carpet, forgotten.

"Hello, darling," she said in a musical voice, stepping into the light. "I wondered how long it would take you to find me."

Elisabeth's response died upon her lips as the woman's scarlet, smiling mouth gave way to scarlet, unsmiling eyes.

She wasn't a woman. She was a demon.

THIRTEEN

"HOW CHARMING YOU look." The demon came forward and draped her wrists over Elisabeth's shoulders, her eyes shimmering crimson in the candlelight. Her inhuman beauty was at once alluring and uninviting, like a sculpture made of ice. "Then again," she went on, "it isn't difficult for mortals to look charming. You are all so delicate, so endearingly soft and fragile, like kittens. Won't you come with me?"

A familiar sensation of woozy calm descended over Elisabeth. Her eyes drooped, suddenly heavy, and she fell into the demon's cold arms. But though she no longer had control over her body, her thoughts remained clear. The desire to give in and trust didn't overpower her as it had before. For some reason, the demon's influence wasn't working as it should.

What was it Silas had said? She had resisted him. Perhaps she was resisting now.

The demon didn't seem to notice anything amiss. She smiled and brushed a lock of hair away from Elisabeth's cheek as if she were a doll. Then she took Elisabeth's hand in hers, frigid as death beneath the glove's rough lace. "What a sweet girl you are," she said, and led her out of the music room, back into the hall.

Elisabeth caught glimpses of herself in the mirrors they passed: ripples of sapphire silk and chestnut waves, her own face as blank as a mannequin as she walked at the demon's side. Her panic was muffled and far away, an intruder pounding on the door in some hidden recess of her mind. Oddly, she was grateful for it, because the lack of fear allowed her to think. She guessed this was Ashcroft's servant, Lorelei. The color of her eyes was identical to the Chancellor's mismatched red one. But what did she want? Where were they going?

They traveled deeper into the manor, hand in hand. Lorelei took her through a salon, where Hannah stood polishing the silver with a dreamy expression, humming to herself—snatches of the same song Lorelei had been singing moments ago, slightly out of tune. She didn't so much as glance in their direction.

Several turns later, they reached a polished oak door. Firelight flickered on the parquet underneath. Lorelei entered without knocking, revealing the same study that Ashcroft had stepped out from earlier that day, when he'd appeared from thin air in front of everyone.

A fire crackled in the hearth on one side of the room. On the other, a great arched window looked out over a black ocean of trees, beyond which lay the glittering lights of the city. Ashcroft sat at a desk opposite the door. Not merely sitting, but staring down at a grimoire, his hands braced on either side of it, gripping the desk's edges. His gaze was unfocused, and his arms shook with tension. An ominous pressure filled the air. The grimoire floated above the desk, its pages drifting weightlessly, as though it hung suspended in water. The other grimoires in the shelves along the walls whispered and rustled uneasily.

Lorelei lowered Elisabeth onto a divan. As soon as she touched the cushions, she went boneless. One of her legs slid off to hang at an awkward angle, but she was powerless to move it. She felt like a puppet whose strings had been cut.

"Master," Lorelei said.

Ashcroft sucked in a harsh breath, surfacing from his trance. He stared in their direction uncomprehendingly, his brow creased. Then he blinked, coming back to himself. He unfastened his cloak and swept it over the grimoire, hiding it from view. Elisabeth's ears popped as the pressure in the room returned to normal.

"What is this? Has something happened to Miss Scrivener?" He crossed the room in a few quick strides and took Elisabeth's wrist, pressing his thumb to her pulse. Then he frowned at Lorelei, perplexed. "You've glamoured her. My orders . . ."

"Were not to harm her. I thought we should have a talk, master."

"Don't be upset," Ashcroft said. "Everything has worked out quite perfectly."

"You could have told me what you were planning!" Her voice lowered to a hiss. "You invited all those humans to come watch! Those reporters!"

"My dear, you know how I prefer to conduct my affairs. The more publicly I go about my business, the less room there is for speculation."

Lorelei paced over to the window and drew the curtains. "It isn't just the reporters. You've involved that sorcerer, Thorn. I don't like it. His servant has a reputation."

"Don't we all?"

"You don't understand. I grew up hearing stories about Silas in the Otherworld. Can you imagine what it takes for a being to become notorious in *our* realm?" She wrapped her arms around herself and smoothed her hands over her bare skin. She stood staring at the curtains, as though she could still see out into the night, far across the city. "You shouldn't court the attention of one such as him."

"He might be fearsome, but he isn't omniscient. I made sure our helpers remained out of sight."

Lorelei didn't reply. Ashcroft crossed to the study's cabinet and poured himself a drink from a crystal decanter. He sat down on an armchair across from Elisabeth and thoughtfully swirled his glass. He studied her face for a moment, then took a sip.

Elisabeth knew she wasn't supposed to be hearing any of this as she lay glassy-eyed and compliant on the divan. They spoke as though she weren't even in the room. And something, she was beginning to realize, was terribly wrong.

Ashcroft leaned back and crossed one ankle over the opposite knee, his glass loose in one hand. "Better Nathaniel than someone else from the Magisterium," he went on finally. "If the girl saw something she shouldn't, don't you imagine that a different sorcerer might have spelled the evidence from her long before she reached Brassbridge? But Nathaniel—I knew he wouldn't harm her. I must say, I was quite relieved when he stepped forward with a solution to that particular challenge." He took a sip. "Otherwise, I would have had to resort to more drastic measures. And you know how much I hate getting my hands dirty."

Elisabeth's mind spun sickeningly. Her instincts screamed at her to run, to fight, but she couldn't so much as twitch her little finger.

"You should have sent more fiends, master. You should have

ended this instead of drawing it out. Now you can no longer kill her. There are too many humans involved."

"The intention," said Ashcroft, "was never to kill her. I merely required an excuse to bring her here. We have only just begun, Lorelei. Whatever mistake occurred in Summershall, I can't afford to make it again. There must be no more surviving witnesses."

"Then what are we to do with *her*?" Lorelei spat.

"Who's to say she's a witness? She may have seen nothing."

"Even if that is true, she will prove a liability."

Ashcroft stood. "I know how to deal with her. Lay her out on the floor, please, Lorelei. As if she's taken a fall. Make it look convincing. Then leave us and fetch Hannah."

The demon's cold hands curled under Elisabeth's armpits. "You are infuriating, master," she murmured.

"Ah, but that is precisely why my life tastes so exceptional to you demons." He raised the crystal glass, reflecting prisms across his handsome face, and winked. "The bolder and brighter the spirit, the finer the vintage."

Elisabeth's cheek pressed against the wool carpet. Now she could only see an expanse of patterned fibers awash in the ruddy glow of the hearth. Thoughts circled in her head like vultures, bleak and inescapable, as Lorelei arranged her boneless limbs: Ashcroft was the saboteur. He had killed the Director. He had sent the fiends. He was responsible for it all. Nothing seemed real—not the roughness of the carpet against her cheek, nor the warmth of the fireplace soaking her gown. A chill settled deep inside her. Earlier that day, she had come within seconds of sealing her own fate by telling Ashcroft what she knew.

Lorelei's steps receded. A moment later, a gentle touch alit on Elisabeth's shoulder. She flinched—a real flinch, a physical reaction. The glamour was wearing off.

"Miss Scrivener?" Ashcroft asked softly. "Miss Scrivener, can you hear me?"

She wanted nothing more than to fly upright, to defend herself, to scream loud enough to rouse the entire manor, but her only hope of survival was to play along. She raised herself on her elbows, her hair hanging in a curtain around her face. The sour burn of champagne crept up her throat, and her stomach roiled.

"Do you remember anything? Are you hurt? Allow me to help you."

"I don't . . ." Elisabeth shook her head, keeping her face downcast as Ashcroft assisted her upright. She stumbled over a wrinkle in the carpet.

"Careful, now. You've taken quite the fall. Hannah"—the door opened—"could you return Miss Scrivener to her room? She seems to have had an accident."

"Oh, Miss Scrivener!" Hannah exclaimed.

A flurry of conversation followed, most of which Elisabeth did not hear, her head pounding numbly with horror. Ashcroft had never intended for the fiends to kill her. He had expected her and Nathaniel to fight them off, and for the event to reach the papers. He had engineered the entire thing so that he would have an excuse to call off the Magisterium's questioning and bring Elisabeth here, to his manor, as his guest.

As his prisoner.

"Yes," Ashcroft was saying, "she entered the study and simply collapsed—I've no idea what she was doing wandering around the manor. . . ."

"Oh, sir, I'm so terribly sorry! I'm afraid that must be my fault! I looked for her everywhere—"

"Please don't blame yourself," Ashcroft said kindly. "I will call for a physician first thing in the morning. Rest assured that Miss Scrivener will receive nothing but the finest care."

The next day, Elisabeth sat staring at the silver molding on the bedroom's wall as the physician's stethoscope pressed against her chest. She had spent the last twenty minutes breathing in and out according to his instructions, allowing him to peer into her mouth, eyes, and ears, and sitting still as he probed her neck and underarms, muttering indistinctly about glands.

While she waited, she clung grimly to hope. Ashcroft didn't know that she had overheard everything last night. All she needed was a moment alone with the physician, and she could explain the situation and get help. But Hannah, who had fussed over her all morning, refused to leave her side. She sat on the plush white love seat beside the bed, wringing her hands. Mr. Hob stood near the door, waiting to show the physician back downstairs.

Elisabeth couldn't trust anyone except the physician. If Hannah was any indication, the servants held their employer in high esteem. At best, she wouldn't believe Elisabeth; at worst, she'd go directly to Ashcroft. And if she did, Elisabeth would be doomed.

"Hmmm," the physician said as he removed the stethoscope's ivory trumpet. He jotted something down in his notebook, frowning.

She wouldn't be surprised if her heartbeat sounded abnormal. She could barely sit still, and she hadn't slept. The reflection in the vanity's mirror showed that she was as pale as a ghost, with dark circles beneath her eyes.

"And you say that you grew up in a library," the physician went on. "Interesting. Do you read many books, Miss Scrivener? Novels?"

"Yes, of course. As many as I can. Doesn't everyone?"

"Hmmm. Just as I thought." He scribbled another note. "An excess of novel reading, combined with the excitement of the past few days . . ."

She failed to see how any of this was relevant. "May I speak to you alone?" she asked.

"Of course, Miss Scrivener," he replied, in a mild, indulgent tone that raised her hackles. But at least he dismissed Hannah and Mr. Hob from the room. "What is it you would like to speak to me about?"

Elisabeth took a deep breath, waiting until the door clicked shut. Then she launched into an explanation immediately, racing through the details of the aetherial combustion in Summershall, the attempt on her life the night before last, and what she had witnessed in Ashcroft's study. She spoke in a forceful undertone, aware that Hannah might attempt to eavesdrop on the other side of the door. "So you see," she finished, "you must notify someone at once—someone who isn't involved with the Magisterium, in case any of the other sorcerers are loyal to the Chancellor. Anyone at the Collegium would do, or even the Queen."

The physician had dutifully taken notes the entire time. "I see," he said, adding one final flourish. "And how long have you believed the Chancellor to be responsible?"

"I don't *believe* he is responsible. I know he is." Elisabeth sat up straighter. "What are you writing?" Among the physician's scribbled notes, she had made out the word "delusions."

He snapped the notebook shut. "I know all of this must be very frightening for you, but try not to agitate yourself. Excitement will only worsen the inflammation."

She stared. "The—what?"

"The inflammation of your brain, Miss Scrivener," he explained patiently. "It is quite common among women who read novels." Before Elisabeth could think of a reply to this baffling remark, he called Hannah back into the room, who looked pinched with worry. "Please tell the Chancellor that I prescribe a strict period of bed rest for the patient," he said to her. "It is clear that this is a classic case of hysteria. Miss Scrivener should exert herself as little as possible. Once the swelling in her brain subsides, her mind may return to normal."

"*May* return?" Hannah gasped.

"I regret to say that sometimes these cases are chronic, even incurable. I understand that she is a foundling, staying here as a ward of Chancellor Ashcroft? Allow me to write down a recommendation for Leadgate Hospital. I am closely acquainted with the principal physician. If Miss Scrivener fails to recover, the Chancellor need only send a letter—"

Elisabeth's blood pounded hot with anger. She had listened for long enough. This physician was just like Warden Finch, just like Ashcroft: a man who thought he could do whatever he liked to her because he happened to be in a greater position of power. But he was wrong.

When he stood, she gripped his arm with enough force to halt him in his tracks. He tried in vain to pull away, then gaped at her as though seeing her for the first time, his mouth opening and closing like a startled fish. She tugged him close. No match for her strength, he lost his balance and nearly toppled face-first onto the bed.

"Listen to me," she said, in a low, fierce murmur too quiet for Hannah to hear. "I didn't grow up in an ordinary library. I grew up in a Great Library. You may scoff at books, but you have never seen a real book in your entire life, and you should count yourself lucky, because you wouldn't survive a moment alone with one." She tightened her fingers until he gasped. "You must go to the Collegium at once. The Chancellor said that he's only just begun. Whatever he is planning, more people will die. Do you understand? You must . . . you must . . ."

The physician had paled. "Miss Scrivener?" he prompted.

Elisabeth let go of him and pointed at the mirror. Or rather, at Mr. Hob's reflection—for although the butler stood outside in the hallway, the mirror made it possible to see him around the corner, waiting. Only he was no longer a butler, or even a man.

"Look," she whispered.

Mr. Hob's suit was the sole feature that remained unchanged. But now it hung on a gaunt, slumped, inhuman frame. His complexion had turned a sickly shade of lavender, and his skin looked grotesquely melted, gobbets of flesh dangling from his cheeks and chin like drips of tallow. His ears were pointed on the ends; his purple hands were clawed. Worst of all were his eyes, unnaturally huge and round and pale, like saucers. They shone in the shadows of the hall, a pair of glazed moons gazing back at her.

Glancing uncertainly between Elisabeth and the physician, Hannah opened the door the rest of the way. Mr. Hob didn't react. He stood silently, unblinkingly, with his horrible shining eyes, as everyone else stared at him.

"You see," Elisabeth whispered. "He is a demon. Some kind of goblin, or an imp."

There came a long pause. Then, the tension shattered. The physician cleared his throat and leaped away, skirting quickly toward the door, as if Elisabeth might lunge out of bed and attack him. As if *she* were the demon, not Mr. Hob.

"As I was saying," he said to Hannah, "please give my recommendation to the Chancellor at the earliest opportunity." He shoved a piece of paper into her hand. "This is obviously a very serious case. Leadgate has state-of-the-art facilities. . . ."

He didn't appear the slightest bit distressed by Mr. Hob as the butler led him out of sight. His voice receded down the hallway, extolling the virtues of ice water baths for the "mentally disturbed." Elisabeth sat stunned and shaking as his reaction sank in. None of them had been able to see Mr. Hob's true form except for her.

The mirror framed her reflection, alone. Trembling beneath a thin nightgown, the blood drained from her face, Elisabeth had to admit that she looked every inch the girl the physician claimed her to be. And she was trapped in Ashcroft Manor more certainly than she had been imprisoned in the Great Library's dungeon, at the mercy of her greatest enemy.

FOURTEEN

OVER THE NEXT few days, Chancellor Ashcroft treated Elisabeth with nothing but solicitous concern. She was confined to her room during the mornings and evenings, but for a brief time in the afternoons, Hannah dressed her and brought her down to the conservatory for some fresh air. There she rested under Hannah's supervision in a cushioned wicker armchair, with a blanket over her legs, breathing in the humid, earthy sweetness of plants and flowers. A riot of blossoms and lacy ferns enveloped her, their exotic petals dripping with moisture. This would have formed the very image of paradise, had she not also been surrounded by demons.

Now that she had seen Mr. Hob's real form, she saw demons everywhere. They scuttled to and fro on errands. They swept leaves from the flagstones, watered the pots, and pruned the flowers. Most were less imposing than Mr. Hob: smaller, their skin scaled instead of wattled. Some had sharp teeth, and others long, pointed ears. All of them were dressed incongruously in Ashcroft's golden livery. Guests often strolled along the paths, but they never spared the demons a second glance. To them, the creatures appeared as nothing more than ordinary servants. And the demons likewise ignored the guests, going dutifully about their tasks.

It was not the demons themselves that frightened Elisabeth, but rather the question of how Ashcroft had gotten so many to obey him. They were clearly lesser demons, not highborn demons like Silas and Lorelei. What had he promised them? What offer could possibly be tempting enough that they were willing to don uniforms and serve him? The possibilities were too horrifying to imagine.

She waited breathlessly for a chance to speak to someone, anyone, from outside the manor, but none of the guests ventured close enough for her to warn them. They observed her from a distance, as if she were one of the Chancellor's rare hothouse specimens: a carnivorous pitcher plant, or a poisonous oleander.

That afternoon, she forced herself not to flinch as a demon crept closer with a pair of shears and began trimming a palm behind her. Its skin was bright red in color, and its eyes were pitch black from edge to edge. Hannah hummed obliviously, tugging a needle through her embroidering hoop. The tune was lilting and odd—another one of Lorelei's melodies.

Whispers caught Elisabeth's attention. A group of girls her own age stood peering around a splashing indoor fountain, dressed in silk and lace. She could only imagine what she looked like to them, sitting stock-still, darting tense glances at a servant.

"What a pity," one of them said. "It was so kind of Chancellor Ashcroft to take her in. I hear she is quite mad."

"No!" exclaimed another, clutching her parasol.

"Oh, yes. Apparently she assaulted a physician. She nearly knocked him to the floor, according to Father. Her state of derangement results in beastly strength."

"I'm not surprised. She's enormous! Have you ever seen a girl so tall?"

The first said archly, "I might have once, in a traveling fair."

"I heard from Lady Ingram," yet another put in, "that she behaved strangely at the dinner the other night. She spoke little, and when she did, she was rude and appeared to have never been taught any manners. The warning signs were there from the start, said Lady Ingram."

Anger boiled up inside Elisabeth, threatening to spill over. She didn't hate easily, but she found in that moment that she hated Lady Ingram, hated these girls—how could they be so cruel and speak of manners in the very same breath?

A girl gasped. "Do you see how she's glaring at us?"

"Quickly, run—"

Elisabeth's fury drained away as they fled out of sight, their dresses' ribbons flouncing through the palm fronds. This, she had just realized, was yet another element of Ashcroft's plan.

Horribly, it made a great deal of sense. The more he displayed her in public, the more his guests could gossip about her, becoming increasingly convinced of her madness. Meanwhile, they saw for themselves that he was sparing no expense to keep her comfortable and well. Just as he placed an illusion on his servants, he wove a greater deception around himself, all without expending a single drop of magic. Even if Elisabeth did manage to speak to someone, they would only see her attempts to seek help as further evidence of her derangement.

She saw no way out of the trap he had built for her. Escape wasn't an option. If she attempted to run, he would know that she suspected him, and the game would come to an end. She would lose any chance she had left to expose him, however small. Her only choice was to play along.

Somewhere outside the conservatory, a clock chimed the hour.

"Come along, dear," Hannah said, rising from her chair. "It's time for your daily visit with the Chancellor. What a kind man, to take such a personal interest in your recovery. I do hope you appreciate everything he's doing for you."

Elisabeth bit her tongue as she followed Hannah out of the conservatory. If only Hannah knew his true purpose for summoning her to his study every day. Dread closed in on her with every step she took into the manor's shining, mirrored halls. By the time she reached the study, her insides were in knots. She struggled to control her expression as the door swung open, revealing Ashcroft wiping his hands on a cloth.

"Good afternoon, Miss Scrivener. Why don't you come in?" Though he sounded as warm as ever, she glimpsed a spark of frustration dancing within his mismatched eyes. It was the only sign that these visits hadn't yet yielded the information he desired. "Hannah, would you bring us tea?"

At his welcoming gesture, Elisabeth stepped inside and sat rigidly on the sofa. She forced her eyes not to stray to the grimoire on Ashcroft's desk. He always covered it with his cloak before she entered, but she knew it was the same grimoire he'd been studying her first night in the manor. Its presence left a sour, musty taste on the back of her tongue. The way he was scrubbing at his hands suggested it was equally unpleasant to touch.

Ashcroft set the cloth aside and settled across from her in his favorite armchair. He looked so genuinely concerned that, despite everything, she could almost believe that some part of him cared about her. Then sunlight struck the depths of his ruby eye, and she remembered in a flash the way the Director's red hair had spilled across the floor.

"How are you feeling today?" he asked, with a gentleness that made her skin crawl.

"Much better, thank you." She swallowed, gathering her courage. "I think I might be ready to leave now."

Ashcroft's brow furrowed sympathetically. "Just a few more days, Miss Scrivener. The physician was most emphatic about the importance of bed rest."

She looked down, trying not to let her terror show. Luckily, the physician hadn't included what she'd told him in his notes. Ashcroft wouldn't bother with these meetings if he had.

A knock heralded Hannah's return with a tray of tea and iced cakes. Elisabeth made a show of nibbling on them, even though she could barely force their sweetness down. Her stomach lurched when the door clicked open again. This time, it wasn't Hannah. She had only a few seconds of warning before Lorelei's glamour wrapped around her like a warm, smothering blanket. Then Ashcroft leaned forward, folding his hands in front of his knees.

Every day, this was how the interrogation began.

"Now, Miss Scrivener," he said, "why don't we talk about the attack on Summershall again? Let's see if you remember any new details, shall we?"

He sounded as kind as he had a moment ago, but the good humor had drained from his expression. Elisabeth knew that she walked along a knife's edge. One slip, and he would find out that Lorelei's glamour wasn't working as it should, compelling her to tell the truth. A single lapse could spell death. She strove to keep her expression blank and her voice wooden, grateful for the glamour's numbing influence. Without it, she wouldn't be able to sit and face Ashcroft calmly. More importantly, she wouldn't be able to lie.

"Can you tell me why you woke up that night?" Ashcroft pressed. "Did you hear something? Sense something?"

He had already asked her that question many times. She took care to keep her answer the same. "A storm blew in. The wind was loud—it blew branches against my window."

He frowned, dissatisfied. "And when you got out of bed, did you feel any differently than normal?"

He wanted to know how she had evaded his sleeping spell. But even Elisabeth didn't have an answer to that question. Mechanically, she shook her head.

Ashcroft's jaw tightened. It was the first indication that his patience had limits, a reaction that left her ill. She didn't want to witness what he was capable of when he lost his temper.

A sound came from Lorelei in the corner, where she was applying rosin to the bow of a violin. Today she wore a crimson gown that matched her lips and eyes. It was so long that it spilled off the chair like a waterfall and formed a shimmering pool on the carpet, as though she sat in a puddle of blood. "The girl is hiding something from you, master," she said.

Ashcroft looked around. "Are you certain? Is that possible?"

The hair stood up on the back of Elisabeth's neck. She forced herself not to react, aware that she could betray herself with any movement.

"If she has a secret, the impulse to protect it may remain, even through a glamour. Most humans haven't the fortitude. But this girl is strong-willed. Her spirit burns as brightly as a flame." Lorelei glanced at Elisabeth beneath her eyelashes, a gesture so like Silas that goose bumps spread across her arms. "I do so wish I could taste it."

Ashcroft leaned back, steepling his fingers. "What do you propose I do?"

"Enter her mind. Take the memory from her by force, and destroy the rest."

"It's too early for that. She must be seen for a few more days before I get rid of her. If news of her fate reaches the papers, I will need witnesses to support the physician's diagnosis."

Lorelei gave a delicate shrug. "Very well, master. And you're certain her presence here isn't distracting you from your work?"

Ashcroft glanced at his desk, at the grimoire hidden beneath his cloak. Based on the way it had levitated that first night in the study, Elisabeth guessed it was a Class Five, or even a Class Six. Private ownership of grimoires Class Four and up had been made illegal by the Reforms. If Ashcroft was willing to keep something that dangerous in his home, the book had to be important.

He sagged back in his armchair, shadows etching deep lines across his face. "It's proving stubborn," he said, "but I'll have what I need before Harrows."

Elisabeth's pulse quickened. The Great Library of Harrows was located in the northeast corner of Austermeer, where the Blackwald met the mountains—the most remote possible location to store high-security grimoires. Descriptions she had read of the place painted it as a fortress built of black stone from the bones of the Elkenspine Mountains. Its unbreachable vault contained two of the kingdom's three Class Ten grimoires. Did he aim to attack it, like Summershall and Knockfeld?

Whatever his plans, the grimoire on his desk clearly played some essential role. And no matter the risk, she had to find out what it was.

Her chance arrived two days later, when Mr. Hob appeared in the doorway in the middle of her questioning. "A visitor," he announced in his deep, garbled voice. "Lord Kicklighter here to see you."

"With no word ahead?" Ashcroft's expression darkened. "I'll meet him in the salon. Lorelei, watch over Elisabeth." He strode from the room, and a moment later Lord Kicklighter's greeting boomed down the hall.

Elisabeth's mind raced. Judging by the length of Kicklighter's handshake the other night, Ashcroft was going to be occupied for at least a few minutes. She felt Lorelei's bored gaze tickling over her. All she needed was to get the demon to leave the study for a few seconds. But she had nothing to work with. If only she were closer to the bookcases, she was certain she could manage to knock one over.

A decorative mirror on the wall afforded her a view of herself sitting on the couch. She looked drawn and pale, at odds with the extravagant amethyst gown Hannah had laced her into that morning. She was growing used to the way the expensive corsets squeezed her chest, but at tense moments like this, the garments still made her feel short of breath.

An idea struck her like lightning. She gasped loudly, drawing Lorelei's attention. Her hand flew to her breast. Then she rolled her eyes up into her head and collapsed onto the carpet with a lifeless *whump*, landing so hard that she rattled the teacups on the coffee table.

Silence. Elisabeth felt the weight of Lorelei's regard. Once she seemed to decide that Elisabeth wasn't faking it, she rose with a whisper of satin and stepped over Elisabeth's prone body on her way outside. As soon as she had gone, Elisabeth hiked up her skirts and scrambled to the desk. Bracing herself, she swept away Ashcroft's cloak.

The grimoire lay open beneath a length of iron chain

stretched along the valley of its spine, its pages filled with a slanted, spiky script. That was all she had a chance to observe before a wave of malevolence crashed against her, forcing her a step backward. A man's voice roared wordlessly within her mind, tearing at her in a maelstrom of anguish and fury.

She didn't have time to wonder whether she'd made a mistake. The edges of the room darkened; the grimoire's pages whipped as if the study's windows had been thrown open during a howling gale. She clenched her teeth and pushed against the grimoire's will, stretching out her hand, trembling with the effort. Sweat beaded her brow. Even the hands of the clock on the mantelpiece seemed to slow, like the air had turned to treacle. At last her fingertips brushed leather, and a confused, sickening rush of emotions thrummed through her body. Longing. Rage. Betrayal. She had never felt anything like it before. She swallowed thickly, wishing she had iron gloves to dampen the grimoire's psychic emanations.

"I'm not your enemy," she forced out. "I'm here as a prisoner of Chancellor Ashcroft. I intend to stop him, if I can."

At once the man's voice fell silent, and the pressure in the air disappeared. Elisabeth fell forward, catching herself on the desk, her muscles quivering from the strain. The grimoire now lay quiescent. Her desperate guess had proved correct—its malice and fury had been meant for Ashcroft, not for her.

"What does he want from you?" she murmured. Carefully, she lifted it from the desk.

Its cover was bound in strange scaled leather, crimson in color, which reminded her unsettlingly of the imps in the conservatory. A five-pointed pentagram was emblazoned on the front. Age had faded the title, but the words remained legible: *The Codex Daemonicus.*

Her heart skipped a beat. She had read this grimoire's title before, and not long ago. Where had she seen it? In Nathaniel's coach, traveling through the Blackwald . . .

I'll have what I need before Harrows, Ashcroft had said. Whatever he needed, it sounded as though he would find it in this book. She wracked her memory, trying to recall why the Lexicon had mentioned this volume. It had been in the chapter about demons. All she could remember was that it supposedly contained the ravings of a mad sorcerer, who claimed to have hidden some kind of secret inside—

Footsteps clipped down the hall. Breathless, Elisabeth snatched Ashcroft's cloak and yanked it back over the grimoire. Hoping that its psychic screams had been audible only to her, she scrambled across the room and threw herself back on the floor, arranging her limbs as closely to their original position as she could manage.

She wasn't a moment too soon. A shadow fell over her just seconds later, and then an acidic smell seared her nostrils, zinging through every nerve in her body. She shot upright, strangling back a shout, only for Lorelei to catch her in an unyielding grip, a suggestion of claws pricking through the lace of her gloves. The demon held a crystal vial full of what appeared to be salt.

"There, there," she soothed, her tone cloyingly sweet. "You're all right. It was just smelling salts, darling. You had a little spell, but it's over now."

"Give her to me," Ashcroft said. "This farce has gone on long enough. It's time."

Lorelei let go of her and stepped back. Before Elisabeth could react, Ashcroft seized her and spun her around. His expression was terrible to behold. It was as though he had spent all of his kindly charm putting up with Lord Kicklighter, and he had none left to maintain the act.

His patience with her had reached an end. Now, she was about to meet the monster beneath the man.

"Listen to me, girl," he said, and shook her until her teeth rattled, "you *will* tell me what you know." And then he splayed his palm over her forehead, and Elisabeth's thoughts exploded outward like a newborn star.

The study vanished; everything went pitch black except for her and Ashcroft and sharp-edged silver fragments that hung glinting in the darkness around them. Familiar images flowed over the surfaces of the fragments in silent flashes of color and movement. They were her own memories, floating in a void like the shards of a shattered mirror. Each one showed a different scene. The Director's red hair shining in the torchlight. Warden Finch raising his switch. Katrien's laughing face.

Though Elisabeth still dimly felt the Chancellor's brutal grip on her arm, in this place, he stood apart from her. He turned, taking in the fragmented memories, and then raised his hand. The shards began to spin around them in a glittering cyclone, blurring together to show him not just isolated fragments out of order, but whole memories, Elisabeth's life flowing past on a shimmering river of glass. Distorted sounds echoed through the void: laughter, whispers, screams. Her stomach clenched as she saw herself as a little girl bounding through the orchard toward Summershall, her brown hair flying out behind her, Master Hargrove struggling to keep up. These were *her* memories. They were not for Ashcroft to see.

"Show me what you've been hiding," the Chancellor commanded. His cruel, hollow voice rang from every direction.

The bright summer afternoon faded away, replaced by a ghostly image of Elisabeth descending the Great Library's stairs in her nightgown, a candle raised high. She felt his magic drawing the memory out of her, a force as inexorable as the undertow of a tide, and panic squeezed her lungs. She could feel the memory, hear it, smell it. She watched as Memory-Elisabeth unlocked the door and stood gazing wide-eyed into the dark. Any second now she would notice the aetherial combustion, proof that a sorcerer had committed the crime.

Elisabeth had to stop it. But she couldn't resist the pull of Ashcroft's sorcery. She sensed that if she fought him, her memories would shatter into a thousand pieces, gone forever. He would destroy her mind—her very life—if he had to. She needed to show him *something*.

So she reached deep inside herself, where her most precious memories were hidden, and found something that she could give.

"Do you know why I chose to keep you, Elisabeth?" the Director asked.

Elisabeth's breath caught. The memory had sped forward to the moment that she had found the Director's body. They were the same words from the vault, but this time whispered from the Director's dying lips, last words meant for Elisabeth alone. She had succeeded in blurring the two memories together. And it felt real, because to her it *was* real. Grief and longing speared her heart like an arrow. She had never expected to hear the Director's voice again.

"It was storming, I recall." The halting words fell from the Director's cracked lips. "The grimoires were restless that night. . . ."

Gazing up at the memory, Ashcroft frowned.

"The Great Library had claimed you."

Ashcroft shook his head in disgust and turned away. He gestured, and the shards began to disintegrate, crashing like a sheet of water toward the floor.

"No!" Elisabeth shouted. Too late, she remembered what

Lorelei had said two days ago. *Take the memory from her by force, and destroy the rest.*

"You belonged here. . . ."

Reality flooded back in a tempest of color and sound. Someone was screaming. Elisabeth's throat was raw. All of her was raw, and she tasted salt, and copper, and the world stank of singed metal.

Ashcroft's voice coasted above her agony like a ship on a calm sea. "She knew nothing. That memory she hid from us—it was just a sentimental trifle. Important to her, perhaps, but not to us. Fetch Mr. Hob. The arrangements have been made." His voice receded, or perhaps that was her getting farther away, tumbling down into some dark place from which there was no return. "She will be sent to Leadgate tonight."

FIFTEEN

OUTSIDE THE COACH'S windows, the night hung in
tatters. Greasy clouds cloaked the city, bleached by the
full moon, which shone like a silver coin lost in a dirty gutter. Elisabeth hadn't seen this part of Brassbridge when she and
Nathaniel rode in last week, aside from a dismal smear of factory
smoke on the horizon. The old brick buildings were blackened
with soot, and the coach's wheels splashed through foul-looking
puddles. A clammy chill permeated the air. Somewhere nearby, a
bell tolled mournfully in the dark.

She sat slumped forward, shivering uncontrollably. Disjointed thoughts filled her head like broken glass, and agony
lanced through her skull every time the coach bounced over a
rut in the road, whiting out her vision.

My name is Elisabeth Scrivener. I am from Summershall.
Chancellor Ashcroft is my enemy. I must expose him. . . .

She recited the words over and over again in her head until
they began to feel real. One by one, she pulled the jagged edges
of her memories together. The spell Ashcroft had used on her

should have destroyed her mind, leaving her an empty shell—but it had not succeeded. She was still herself. Even the pain only served to remind her that she was alive, and had a purpose.

A tall, serrated metal fence flashed past the window. The coach began to slow. It jostled to a halt outside a wrought iron gate, beyond which squatted the edifice of Leadgate Hospital. The hospital was a long, rectangular building with a hint of classical architecture in its pillared front and domed chapel, but these flourishes only served to emphasize the institutional bleakness of the rest. It loomed above the surrounding squalor and misery like something out of a nightmare. She knew instinctively that it was a place of suffering, not healing. A place where unwanted people, like her, were made to disappear.

Guards opened the gates to admit them, and the carriage crawled up the drive. Elisabeth pressed her face to the window. A party awaited them at the hospital's doors: a stout, hard-faced woman in a starched pinafore, flanked by two male attendants in matching white uniforms. When the coach halted again, one of the attendants opened the door. Mist slopped inside the carriage like spilled porridge.

"Come on out, dear," the matron coaxed. She spoke to Elisabeth as one might a small child. "Come nicely, and you'll be given a nice, hot supper by the fire. You'd like that, wouldn't you? Stew, and bread, and pudding with raisins—as much of it as you want. I'm Matron Leach, and I'll be a good friend to you here."

Elisabeth stumbled out, keeping her eyes downcast. She watched through a curtain of hair as one of the men circled around her, approaching her from behind with a bundle of leather straps and buckles. Her stomach lurched when she realized what they were: restraints, not just for her wrists, but for her ankles, too. With an effort, she forced herself not to panic.

She waited until the man was almost upon her. Then she spun, teeth bared, and kneed him savagely between the legs. She felt a stab of guilt as he groaned and crumpled to the ground, but it didn't last long; she was already off, Matron Leach shouting behind her.

She bolted across the hospital's grounds like a deer flushed from a thicket, her long legs carrying her faster than the men could keep chase. The thin grass gave way to a poorly tended garden lined with overgrown hedges and half-dead trees. She skidded to a halt amid a slush of fallen leaves. If she kept running, she would just go in a circle around the hospital. The fence that surrounded the grounds was too tall to climb, and topped with barbed metal finials.

But the shouts behind her were drawing nearer. She had to make a decision.

Her heart pounded in the roof of her mouth as she clawed her way beneath the nearest hedge. Roots and branches scraped her hands raw, and the sickly smell of rotting blossoms filled her nostrils. She raked the leaves up behind her to provide extra cover, and snatched her arms back inside as a man's boots pelted past, spraying dirt and leaves in her face. Inspired, she scooped up handfuls of earth and rubbed them over herself until she couldn't tell her limbs apart from the thick roots that twisted across the ground.

Minutes crept by. Lanterns bobbed through the dark, and calls rang out at intervals. Men peered into the hedges and thrashed the vegetation with cudgels, but she remained perfectly still, even when one of the cudgels dealt a bruising blow across her shin. Gooseflesh stippled her arms as the night grew colder, but she dared not so much as shiver.

"That's enough, boys," said one of the attendants at last.

"Wherever she's hiding, she's trapped here as sure as a rat in a bucket. We'll see if she's still alive come morning, and then we'll have our fun with her."

Laughter met this unpleasant pronouncement. Elisabeth watched them trail away toward the hospital. When the last man vanished inside, she scrambled from the hedge, shaking from head to toe. But just as quickly, she ducked back out of sight.

She was not alone in the yard. A shape lumbered through the dark some distance away, bent low to the ground. She thought it was another attendant, until she saw that it was sniffing the grass. It was following the path that she had taken from the coach, creeping along a meandering route toward her hiding spot. And when it straightened, its huge, round, shining eyes caught the light like mirrors.

It was Mr. Hob. He had caught her scent, and he was coming for her.

A door banged from the direction of the hospital. Elisabeth sucked in a breath and threw herself around the hedge, flattening her back against a tree. Someone had come outside and begun picking their way toward the gardens. Peering through the leaves, Elisabeth determined that this person wasn't part of the search party. She wore a uniform similar to the matron's, but she was just a girl, not much older than Elisabeth, with chapped hands and a round, unhappy face, holding a shaded lantern to her chest.

"Hello?" the girl called softly. "Are you there?"

Glancing in the opposite direction, Elisabeth found that Mr. Hob was now clambering along the ground on all fours, no longer pretending to be human. Elisabeth stared between them, fiercely willing the girl to be silent. But she didn't see the danger she was in, and spoke again into the dark.

"I know you're hiding. I've come to help you." She fished around in her pocket and brought up a lump of something wrapped in a handkerchief. "I've got some bread. It isn't much, but it's all I could get past the matron. She was lying when she said she'd give you stew and pudding—she says that to all the patients who come here."

Mr. Hob broke into a loping run, his eyes fixed on the girl. Elisabeth launched herself from the hedge in an explosion of leaves and reached her first, seizing the girl's wrist, yanking her along in the opposite direction. The bread tumbled to the ground.

"Do you have any salt," Elisabeth asked, "or iron?" She didn't recognize the sound of her own voice. It came out as a horrid croak.

"I—I don't—please don't hurt me!" the girl cried. Her weight dragged on Elisabeth's arm. If they didn't run faster, Mr. Hob would catch them.

Panic clutched at Elisabeth's chest. She realized what she must look like: smeared with dirt, her hair long and tangled and full of leaves, her dry lips cracked and bleeding. No wonder the girl was afraid. "What's your name?" she asked.

"Mercy," the girl stammered out, stumbling over the uneven ground.

"My name is Elisabeth. I'm trying to save your life. I'm going to ask you to do something, and then you'll believe me, but you have to promise not to scream."

Mercy nodded, her eyes wide and fearful—likely hoping that if she played along, Elisabeth wouldn't harm her.

"Look behind you," Elisabeth said. Then she clapped a grubby hand over Mercy's mouth, muffling her cry.

"*What is that?*" she wailed, when Elisabeth let go of her. "Why is it *chasing us?*"

So Elisabeth's hunch had been correct. The moment Mr. Hob started sniffing the ground and running on all fours, whatever illusion Ashcroft had cast on him was no longer convincing enough to disguise him. "He's a demon. I think he's a goblin. Is there a way out of this place?"

Small, panicked noises came from Mercy's throat before she was able to answer. "A back gate. For the workers who keep the grounds. That way." She pointed. "What—?"

"Run faster," Elisabeth said grimly. "And give me your lantern."

She didn't dare pause to look over her shoulder as they hurtled toward the back gate. It was tucked away behind a sagging, moss-roofed outbuilding, set beneath an arbor overgrown with ivy. The closer they drew, the louder Mr. Hob's wheezing breath rasped at their heels. Mercy fumbled through her pockets and produced a key. As she went for the gate, Elisabeth whirled around, swinging the lantern with all her strength.

Time froze in the space between one heartbeat and the next. Mr. Hob was upon her, his wattled face a hideous landscape of wobbling flesh. His eyes were so large, so pale, that she saw two miniature versions of herself reflected within them.

Then glass shattered as the lantern slammed against his shoulder. Oil splashed, and with an eager crackle, fire bloomed across the front of his ill-fitting suit. The heat scorched Elisabeth's skin; crying out, she dropped the lantern. Mr. Hob staggered backward and stared uncomprehendingly at the licks of blue flame rippling across his chest. Finally, it occurred to him to shrug off his jacket. He smacked the remaining fire out with a clumsy hand.

"Mercy," Elisabeth implored.

"I'm trying! I'm almost . . ." Mercy's key scraped against

the lock. Her hands shook violently, missing again and again. Meanwhile Mr. Hob advanced on them, his jacket smoking on the ground behind him. He took a step forward. Another. And then the lock clicked, and the gate clanged open, shedding flakes of rust.

Elisabeth shoved Mercy through first, then darted after. When she shoved the gate closed behind them, it wouldn't close all the way—it had jammed on something yielding. Mr. Hob's hand. He stared at them unblinkingly through the iron bars as his purple skin began to bubble and steam. Elisabeth threw her weight against the gate, muscles straining against Mr. Hob's resistance. The soles of her boots scraped across the pavement. He was too strong.

From beside her, there came an unexpected shout. A stone flew through the air and crushed Mr. Hob's knuckles with a wet, nauseating crunch. He snatched his hand back, and the gate rang out as it slammed shut. The latch fell into place automatically.

Elisabeth stumbled away and traded a wide-eyed look with Mercy, who clearly couldn't believe what she had just done. Mr. Hob stood there, watching them, as if unsure what to do next.

"We're safe now," Elisabeth whispered. "He can't get past the iron. And I don't think he's smart enough to figure out another way around."

Mercy didn't answer, too busy shuddering and taking gulps of air, her hands braced on her thighs. Elisabeth looked around. The gate had let them out in an alleyway behind a row of narrow, dreary brick buildings. Their curtains were closed, and there weren't any lights on inside. "Come on," she said, taking Mercy's arm. She led her out of sight of Mr. Hob and sat her down on an overturned crate.

"What did he want?" Mercy asked through her fingers.

Elisabeth hesitated. She could explain everything. She could ask Mercy to help her—to testify against Ashcroft. But who would believe her? She now understood that the world wasn't kind to young women, especially when they behaved in ways men didn't like, and spoke truths that men weren't ready to hear. No one would listen to Mercy, just as no one had listened to her.

She crouched in front of the other girl, coming to a decision. "Listen. It was me the demon wanted, not you. Wait until the coach leaves, and then you can return to the hospital. Mr. Hob— the demon—he won't come back for you." She closed her eyes and took a breath. "When people ask what happened, tell them I attacked you, and you had no choice but to help me escape. Say that a man chased us, a human man, dressed as a butler. Don't mention anything strange about him. And tell them that I was . . . that I was like a wild animal. That I didn't even know my own name."

She suspected that it wouldn't matter to Ashcroft whether she was rotting in Leadgate Hospital or starving on the streets. As long as he believed her mind had been destroyed, and he appeared to have done his best to help the poor, hysterical girl in his care, he would let the matter drop in favor of focusing on his plans.

"But you saved my life," Mercy protested.

"I'm the reason your life was in danger in the first place. Trust me. It's better this way." Elisabeth wrapped her arms around herself, wondering how much she could reveal. "You don't want to cross the man that demon serves," she settled on at last. "If he thinks you know something you shouldn't, he won't hesitate to hurt you."

Mercy nodded. To Elisabeth's dismay, she didn't look surprised. For her, men who wanted to hurt girls was simply the natural order of things.

"I'm glad you've gotten away from Leadgate." Mercy lifted her gaze and met Elisabeth's eyes with her own, sad brown ones. "You can't imagine what kind of place it is. Wealthy people pay money to come gawp at the patients here—to sympathize with the plight of the unfortunates, or some such rubbish. Sometimes . . . sometimes they pay for other things, too. The matron makes good money off it. Speaking of which—here." She reached into her pocket and pressed something hard and cold into Elisabeth's palm. A coin.

Elisabeth struggled to find words around the lump in her throat. She couldn't think of what to say, so instead she pulled Mercy into a tight embrace.

Mercy laughed, surprised. "Now I'll look dirty enough to say you attacked me."

"Thank you," Elisabeth whispered. She gave Mercy one last squeeze, and then let go and ran before the tears prickling the backs of her eyes had a chance to spill over.

She dodged past piles of rubbish and plunged down a steep cobblestone avenue. This time of night, the streets were all but empty. She doubted it was necessary to run, but every time she slowed she saw Warden Finch sneering at her, or a man's hands full of leather straps, or the Chancellor's charming smile. She paused at a corner to be sick, and then kept going. She didn't stop until she was forced to: she reached a promenade looking out over the river, and caught herself against the rail.

The sleeping city looked like an illusion spun from fairy lights. Pointed spires reared glittering into shadow, the statues atop them cutting shapes from the stars. Columns of gold shimmered on the black water beneath. Nearby the Bridge of Saints flickered with gaslight, its somber statues like a procession of mourners crossing the river, memorializing the passing of some long-dead king. The wind tangled her hair, smelling of soot and algae and the wild, endless expanse of night sky.

She stared across the shining city, ancient, impossibly vast, and wondered how all that light and beauty could exist side by side with so much darkness. She had never felt smaller or more insignificant. But finally, for the first time in weeks, she was free.

SIXTEEN

"THERE MUST BE some mistake," Elisabeth said to the freckled boy behind the counter. "Master Hargrove has known me my entire life. He wouldn't send this reply."

The paper shook between her fingers. The terse message read only, *We have no record of an apprentice named Elisabeth Scrivener at the Great Library of Summershall*. Underneath, in lieu of a signature, someone had stamped the Collegium's crossed key and quill. That meant the letter had been written by a warden, even though she had addressed it to Hargrove.

The clerk looked sympathetic, but his eyes kept darting nervously to the glass front of the post office. "I'm sorry, miss. I don't know what to tell you."

The paper blurred as she attempted to focus. This was wrong. Surely she was—she was—

"It's Finch, the new Director," she heard herself say. "He must have intercepted my letter. He's stripped me from the records. . . ."

Someone cleared his throat nearby. Elisabeth glanced over her shoulder in time to see the well-dressed gentleman in line behind her whisper something to his wife, both of them eyeing Elisabeth with a combination of disapproval and unease.

She looked back at the clerk and saw herself through his pitying gaze. She had been sleeping on the streets for the past few days. Her hair was tangled, her clothes dirty. Worst of all, her urgent attempts to contact the Great Library of Summershall were beginning to resemble the actions of a madwoman. An unfamiliar feeling of shame burned inside her stomach.

"Please," she said, the words rasping through her sore throat. "Can you give me directions to Hemlock Park? I know someone who lives there."

The clerk wetted his lips, glancing between her and the waiting couple. She could tell he didn't believe her. "Could I post a letter for you instead, miss?"

Elisabeth had used all of Mercy's money sending the first letter. She couldn't pay for a second. Suddenly, the shame overwhelmed her. She mumbled an apology and ducked past the staring couple, pressing a hand to her mouth as she fled from the post office. As soon as she reached the street, she doubled over in a coughing fit. Pedestrians gave her a wide berth, shooting her troubled looks. With a trembling hand, she folded the letter and slipped it into her pocket.

Her fever was getting worse. Yesterday morning, after sleeping huddled up and shivering in a doorway, she had woken with a cough. Today she felt so disoriented that she'd barely found her way back to the post office.

Her heel slipped on something slimy as she started down the sidewalk. A wet newspaper, pasted to the gutter. She peeled it free and held its translucent headline to the light, even though she had already read the article a dozen times since her escape from Leadgate. THIRD ATTACK ON A GREAT LIBRARY—FETTERING

IN FLAMES, the front page proclaimed. Beneath that there was an illustration of a spiny, deformed monstrosity—the paper's interpretation of a Malefict—howling in front of an inferno. The article went on to say that there had been at least two dozen casualties in the village, some lives claimed by the Class Nine Malefict, others by the blaze. The number made her head spin. Traders from Fettering occasionally stopped by Summershall's market. She might have met some of the people who had died.

Near the end, there was a quote from Chancellor Ashcroft: *"At this time we believe the saboteur is a foreign agent working to undermine the strength of Austermeerish magic. The Magisterium will stop at nothing to apprehend the culprit and restore order to our great kingdom."*

The paper crumpled in her hand. The attack had happened while she was trapped in his manor. He had lied to reporters while she lay in bed.

She was running out of time to stop him.

Yet the letter's response had left her unmoored. Weeks ago she wouldn't have bothered with the letter; she would have charged straight to the Collegium and pounded on the front doors until someone answered. Now she knew that if she did that, she would be turned away, or worse. She had counted on arming herself with Master Hargrove's good word to prove that she was someone worth listening to. The anticipation of holding his response—of being vindicated at last—was what had kept her going through the long, cold nights and the gnawing ache of hunger. Now she had nothing.

No . . . not nothing. She still had Nathaniel. But days of searching hadn't led her any closer to Hemlock Park. The city was huge; she felt as though she could remain lost within it forever, growing ever more invisible to the people passing by, until she faded away to a shadow. No one had proven willing to help her. Few were even willing to look at her.

She didn't know if Nathaniel would be any different. But of everyone in Brassbridge, he was the only person she could trust.

A glimpse of a short, slim boy passing through the crowd yanked Elisabeth to a halt. She stood frozen on the sidewalk as people flowed around her. It didn't seem possible. Either her fever was causing her to hallucinate, or Silas had appeared as though she had summoned him out of thin air by thinking his master's name. Could she be mistaken?

She whirled around, searching for another sign of him across the street. Her gaze latched onto a slight figure stepping neatly through the afternoon bustle. The young man wasn't wearing Silas's green livery, but instead a finely tailored suit, a cravat tied impeccably around his pale neck. But his hair—pure white, held back with a ribbon—could belong to no one else. He was not a hallucination. He was real.

She hesitated, wavering, and then rushed across the street, the dismayed shout of a carriage driver chasing in her wake. She scanned the crowd once she reached the sidewalk, but Silas was no longer in sight. She hurried along in the direction he had been heading, peering into the windows of shops as she passed. Her own dirty reflection stared back at her, pinched and desperate, her blue eyes bright with fever. She broke into a jog, trying to ignore the fire that roared in her lungs as she urged her body to move faster.

There. A flash of white hair ahead, turning onto a side street. She hastened after him, barely noticing that the buildings around her had grown dilapidated, the traffic thinner, its carriages replaced by carts filled with junk and wilted produce. Crooked eaves hung over the narrow avenue, strung with unused laundry lines. The damp, dark corners stank of urine. Silas stuck out like a sore thumb in his expensive suit, but no one spared him a second glance. The same wasn't true for Elisabeth.

"Where are you going in such a hurry, little miss?"

Her heart tripped. She kept her gaze fixed straight ahead, as though she hadn't noticed the man's leering face in the periphery of her vision. But he didn't give up, as she'd hoped. A boot crunched broken glass behind her, and multiple shapes detached from the shade of a nearby building.

"I said, where are you going? Maybe we can help."

"Give us a smile for our trouble, eh?" another man suggested.

Silas was too far ahead, a shape glimpsed behind a passing cart. Elisabeth tried to call out. Though she only made a hoarse, pathetic sound, he paused and began to turn, a yellow eye flashing in the light.

She couldn't tell whether he had truly heard her, or whether the reaction was a coincidence. She didn't have time to find out. "Silas," she whispered. And then she ran.

Pavement scuffed beneath her heels. When the men moved to cut her off, she dodged from the main street and into an alley, stumbling over crates and sodden drifts of newspapers. Rats fled squealing toward a branching alleyway, and she followed them, hoping they knew the best place to hide. As the deep shadows enveloped her, her boots skidded on something slippery. A putrid stench hung in the air, and puddles of fluid shone on the cobblestones, covered in floating scum. She had wandered into the rear of a butcher's shop. Her breath came in labored, agonizing rasps.

"This way!" a voice called. The men were close on her heels.

Elisabeth staggered to the end of the alley and around the

corner, only to draw up short at a dead end. The building that backed up against this alley looked abandoned. Its windows had been bricked over, and the door, once painted black, was badly peeling and secured with a padlock. She jerked at the doorknob, but the padlock held.

Footsteps splashed through the puddles. There was no use trying to be quiet; her pursuers would notice the adjoining alley any moment now. Fueled by terror, she dug her fingers into one of the wooden boards that crisscrossed the door and yanked with all her might, staggering backward when it wrenched free with a metallic squeal of protest. The board had come loose in her hands. Bent, rusty nails protruded from the ends.

She armed herself not a moment too soon. A man appeared at the mouth of the alley, his trousers spattered with congealed blood. His hair was closely shorn, and scabs covered his gaunt cheeks. Revulsion twisted Elisabeth's gut at the look in his eyes.

He grinned. "There you are, little miss. How about that smile?"

"Stay back," she warned. "I'll hurt you."

He didn't listen. With a yellow-toothed grin still fixed on his face, he took a step forward. Elisabeth braced herself and swung. The board struck his shoulder and lodged there, stuck fast. He howled, falling to his knees, reaching for the makeshift weapon. When she tore it back out, the nails made a horrible squelch. An arc of blood spattered the brick wall.

Shocked, she stumbled backward until her shoulder blades struck the door. She had slain a Malefict and battled demons, but this was different. He was a person. No matter how evil he was, he wouldn't disintegrate into ashes or return to the Otherworld if he died. His moans of pain throbbed sickeningly in her ears.

Officium adusque mortem. Was it her duty to fight him, even risk killing him, if escaping his clutches meant saving many more lives?

"Over here, you idiots!" the man snarled, clamping his hand over his wet, torn sleeve as he shoved himself upright, using the wall for support. Blood bubbled over his fingers as he glared at Elisabeth. "And be careful! She's found herself a weapon."

There came no reply from the butcher's lot.

"Did you hear me?"

The alley was silent as a tomb.

"Stop fooling around!" he snapped.

There came a faint splashing sound from around the corner. And then a soft, courteous voice said, "Do not judge your friends too harshly. I fear they are indisposed."

"Is this some sort of joke?" He limped back for a look. All the color drained from his slack face. "What—what *are* you?" he stammered.

"That is a difficult question to answer," the whispering voice replied. "I am an ancient thing, you see. I have brought about the fall of empires and attended the deathbeds of kings. Nations now lost to time once fought wars over the secret of my true name." He sighed. "But presently, I am inconvenienced. My day's plans didn't include traipsing down a squalid alleyway to dispatch a handful of second-rate criminals. Not in a clean suit, and certainly not in a new pair of shoes."

The man's eyes bulged from his head. He tried to run, but that was a mistake. Elisabeth didn't see what happened after he fled past the corner, out of sight. She only heard a choked-off scream, followed by a silence so thick it made her ears ring.

She slid down the door, the stained board clattering to the ground. A cough seized her body and shook her like a rabbit in the jaws of a hound. She blinked back tears as Silas stepped into view. He looked just as he had on the street, except for a spatter of blood on his face. He flicked a handkerchief from his breast pocket and dabbed the blood away, then examined the soiled handkerchief, pursed his lips, and cast it aside.

"Miss Scrivener," he said, giving her a minute bow.

"Silas," she gasped. "I'm so glad to see you."

"Curious. That is not what people usually say to me at a time like this."

"What do they usually say?"

"Generally they cry, or wet themselves." He studied her. "What are you doing here? Master Thorn and I assumed you would be back in Summershall by now."

Elisabeth didn't have the energy to explain Ashcroft and Leadgate. She was no longer certain that the tears in her eyes had to do with how hard she had been coughing. She knew she shouldn't be this relieved to see Silas—that he was evil, a murderer, a warden's worst enemy. But he didn't pretend to be anything other than a monster. In that way, he was more honorable than most of the people she had met since leaving Summershall.

"Did you kill those men?" she asked.

"When one calls upon a demon, one must be prepared for death to follow."

"I didn't . . ."

"You spoke my name. You wished for me to save you."

"You could have let him run," she said. When he said nothing, only looked at her, she added, "I suppose you will tell me they were bad men, like last time."

"Would that make you feel better, miss?"

She felt a dull twinge of horror upon realizing that it would. And once a person began to think that way, she wasn't certain how they ever managed to stop. A shiver ran through her.

"Don't say it," she whispered. "Silas—I've seen such terrible things. I've . . ."

He knelt in front of her. He reached for her, and she flinched, but he only placed a bare hand on her forehead, his touch so cold that it burned. "You aren't well," he said softly. "How long have you had this fever?"

When she didn't reply, unsure, he began to unbutton his jacket. She shook her head as he moved to tuck it around her. "I'll get your clothes dirty," she protested.

"It matters not, miss. Up you come."

He lifted her from the ground as easily as he had the last time. Elisabeth wondered if this meant she was finished starving, running, sleeping in the rain; perhaps she could stop fighting, just for a little while. She turned her face against his chest as he carried her away. "You're a proper monster, Silas," she murmured, caught halfway in a dream. "I'm glad of it."

If he replied, she didn't hear him. She floated through the world as if set adrift in a lifeboat on a gently rocking sea. The next thing she knew, Silas was saying, "Stay awake, Miss Scrivener. Just a little while longer. We're almost there."

She realized, foggily, that Silas had loaded her into a carriage, perhaps some time ago. Her head lolled. She blinked and the street came into focus beyond the windows, the grand houses of Hemlock Park rolling past.

Her eyelids sagged, and her gaze fell upon Silas's hands, resting folded on his lap. The claws that tipped his long, white fingers were exquisitely clean and manicured—and sharp enough to slit a person's throat. When he saw her looking, his lips thinned. He slipped his gloves back on, whereupon all evidence of the claws disappeared.

Soon Nathaniel's manor loomed into view. It had been

constructed at the intersection of two angled streets, giving it a curious wedge shape. With its profusion of gargoyles, carvings, and pointed stone finials, it resembled a castle squashed down into a brooding, five-story triangle. When the carriage came to a stop, Silas lifted her out. She watched him pay the driver in befuddled fascination. How curious it was to watch someone treat him like a gentleman, not a demon or even a servant, the driver tipping his hat in respect.

The manor's front door had six knockers, each in a different size, shape, and metal. As Silas opened the door, he struck the plate second from the top. Though it was made of solid verdigris-flecked copper, it made no sound; instead, a bell rang deep within the house. Elisabeth guessed that each knocker corresponded to a floor, with the sixth and lowest belonging to the cellar. Silas caught her up in his arms again, and brought her inside.

Footfalls pounded upstairs. Nathaniel appeared on the landing, taking the steps two at a time. Elisabeth stared. He wore only a pair of comfortable trousers and a loose white shirt, which billowed out around him as he tore barefoot down the stairs. His black hair was such a mess that the silver streak almost wasn't visible. She had never imagined him like this, unguarded, *normal,* but of course he couldn't spend his entire life wearing a magister's cloak and a cynical smile. Underneath it all, he was still a boy of eighteen.

Silas helped Elisabeth into one of the leather armchairs in the foyer. She was as limp and weak as she had been under Lorelei's influence, the last of her strength spent defending herself in the alley.

"Silas!" Nathaniel exclaimed. "Do you have my—augh! What is *that*?"

"That is Elisabeth Scrivener, master."

Nathaniel stiffened, taking in the sight of her. Emotions flashed across his face too quickly to follow. For a moment, shock prevailed. His gaze skipped over her bruised skin and filthy clothes. Then he withdrew inward, his expression hardening.

"This is a surprise," he observed in a clipped tone, descending the rest of the stairs at a measured pace. "Why is she here? I thought I told you that I—" He cut himself off with a quick glance back at Elisabeth, his lips pressed to a thin line.

"She requires a place to stay," Silas said.

"And you thought it would be an excellent idea to bring her here, of all places?"

"Look at her. She is ill. She has nowhere else to go. When I found her, she was being pursued by criminals."

Nathaniel's eyes widened, but he recovered quickly. "I suppose next you'll be rescuing orphans and helping elderly widows across the street. This is absurd." His knuckles had turned white on the banister. "Since when do you care about the welfare of a human being?"

"I am not the one who cares," Silas said softly.

"What is that supposed to mean?"

"You care about her, master, more than I have seen you care about anything in years. Don't attempt to deny it," he added when Nathaniel opened his mouth. "There is no other reason why you should wish so fervently for her to leave."

Elisabeth didn't understand what Silas was saying, but something terrible happened to Nathaniel's expression. He seemed to realize it, and looked away. "This is a wretched idea," he bit out, "and you should know that better than anyone."

"I do know better than anyone." Silas crossed the foyer to stand before him. "Better than you, certainly. And thus I can say with confidence that isolating yourself in this house isn't going to spare you from your family's legacy. It will only drive you to ruin."

Nathaniel's face twisted. "I could order you to take her away."

For a moment, Silas didn't reply. When he did, he spoke in a whisper. "Yes. According to the terms of our bargain I must obey any command that you give me, no matter how much I dislike it, or how greatly I disagree."

Nathaniel stepped forward. With his far greater height he towered over Silas, who looked very slight, almost insubstantial in only his shirtsleeves. Silas lowered his eyes deferentially. Though Elisabeth discerned no other shift in his expression or posture, Silas at once looked so ancient, so dangerous, and so chillingly polite that a shiver crawled down her spine. But Nathaniel didn't seem the least bit afraid.

"Silas," he began.

Silas looked up through his lashes. "Something is happening," he interrupted. "Something of consequence. I sense it in the fabric between worlds, rippling outward, casting its influence far in every direction, and Miss Scrivener has stood in its way like a stone. Her life is unlike any other that I have seen. Even marked by shadow, it burns so fiercely that it is blinding. But she isn't invincible, master. No human is. If you don't help her, this threat will eventually claim her."

"What are you talking about? What threat?"

"I know not." Silas's gaze flicked over to Elisabeth. "But she might."

Nathaniel stood still, his chest rising and falling silently, but with impassioned force, as if he had just run a marathon and was trying not to show that he was out of breath. The color was high in his cheeks. "Fine. She can stay." He pivoted on his heel, waving a hand. "Since this was your idea, you take care of her. I'll be in my study."

Elisabeth watched as he stalked away into the dark labyrinth of the manor, back straight and features set—as his stride hitched, and he almost looked back at her. But he did not. That was the last thing she remembered before the dark claimed her, and she drifted away once more.

SEVENTEEN

ELISABETH STIRRED AGAINST the bed's soft sheets. She lay for a moment with her mind as empty as a summer sky, pleasantly adrift, and then jolted awake all at once, her nerves sparking with energy. She sat up and threw off the covers. The motion disturbed something nearby, which jingled.

A silver breakfast service had been laid out on the bed beside her, glinting in the morning sunlight. Tempting aromas of melted butter and hot sausage wafted from beneath the covered dishes. Saliva flooded her mouth, and her stomach growled. Perhaps stopping Ashcroft could wait a few more minutes.

She reached for the silverware arranged atop a folded napkin, then hesitated. She had vague memories of being washed and tended to before being lulled to sleep by the soothing motions of a comb gliding through her hair. Blood rushed to her cheeks, but she resolved to thank Silas in spite of her embarrassment. He had been far gentler with her than Hannah, and by now she was certain that when he'd expressed his lack of interest in human bodies, he had been telling her the truth.

As she tore into breakfast, she tried to make sense of her current state. The time of day suggested that she had slept for almost twenty-four hours. Her fever had broken. She was in the lilac room again, like last time. A black silk dressing gown enveloped her, almost exactly the right length for her tall frame, which she suspected meant it belonged to Nathaniel. It smelled of expensive soap and a curious scent she could only identify, rather disconcertedly, as *boy*—which didn't seem as though it should be a good smell, but was.

A realization sank in: all of her possessions were gone. She didn't even have clean clothes. The only item in the room that belonged to her was the letter from Summershall, still folded, resting discreetly on the nightstand. Silas must have retrieved it from her pocket. How was she supposed to fight the Chancellor when he had so much, and she so little?

A knock came on the door. "I'm awake," Elisabeth said around a mouthful of pastry. She expected Silas, but instead Nathaniel strode in, fully dressed this time, armored in a tempest of emerald silk. Before she could get in another word, he paced to the window and braced his hands on the sill. He didn't seem to want to look at her. In fact, he seemed to want to say whatever it was he'd come here to say and then vacate the room as quickly as possible.

Elisabeth finished chewing, and swallowed. The pastry lodged dry in her throat.

"I should have known you'd go charging headlong into trouble at the earliest opportunity, you complete terror," Nathaniel said to the window. His words came out in a rush, as though he'd been rehearsing them in the mirror. "It appears that even the Chancellor wasn't up to the task of keeping you out of danger. Why aren't you in Summershall? Never mind. We'll contact the Collegium, and they'll arrange a coach for you." He tensed, angling his face. "What is that?"

Elisabeth had approached him with the letter from Summershall. Reluctantly, he took the paper. Their fingertips brushed, and she noted in surprise that he had calluses on his hand. She retreated, folding her arms tightly across her stomach, suddenly conscious that she was wearing Nathaniel's clothes with little else on underneath.

His brow furrowed as he read the letter once, twice, his gray eyes eventually lifting to hers, uncomfortably piercing in their intensity. "I don't understand."

"The new Director doesn't want me back. He's struck me from the records." She sank down on the end of the bed. "And I have more to tell you."

"Is it about the threat Silas mentioned?"

"I think so. You might want to sit down."

Nathaniel raised his eyebrows, but he compromised by leaning against the wall beside the window. Elisabeth opened her mouth, then hesitated and squeezed her eyes shut. The words formed knots inside her chest. It was harder to begin than she'd expected. She had been betrayed too many times, by so many different people. What if she was wrong about Nathaniel, and she couldn't trust him, either?

"You don't have to tell me if you don't want to." Her eyes flew open. Nathaniel was contemplating her with an unreadable expression. "It's all right," he said. "I know . . ." He considered his next words. "I know what it feels like to have things you can't say. To anyone."

A torrent of relief flowed through Elisabeth. *He isn't the Chancellor. He isn't like the physician, or Warden Finch.* Helplessly, hoarsely, she began to laugh. Hysterical sounds wrenched from her body, bordering on sobs, and tears gathered at the corners of her eyes. She tried to stop, but that only made it worse; her laughter turned into panicked gasps.

She expected Nathaniel to stare like everyone else had, as though she'd gone mad, for even she felt that she had gone mad, but instead the way he looked at her was—was—it was like turning a corner and unexpectedly meeting her own gaze in a mirror, in the split second that her startled eyes belonged to a stranger. A shock ran through her. Somehow, he did understand. She looked away, at last able to breathe until she calmed. He said nothing, only waited.

"I *must* tell you," she said finally, curling her hands into fists. "This is too important. Someone has to know aside from me." She took another deep breath. "It started that first night, with the Book of Eyes, when I came downstairs and smelled aetherial combustion. . . ."

The longer she spoke, the more a weight lifted from her shoulders. Until now, she hadn't realized how punishing it had been to keep all of those secrets—to be the only person who knew about Ashcroft, constantly aware that if something happened to her, the truth would vanish forever.

Nathaniel listened intently, never interrupting, his expression darkening the further she progressed. When she reached the part about the spell Ashcroft had used on her, a shadow fell across the room. At first she thought the sun had passed behind a cloud. Then she saw the emerald sparks dancing around Nathaniel's fingers as the room plunged further and further into a midnight gloom.

She broke off. "What—?"

Nathaniel had been so focused on her that he hadn't noticed

his own reaction. He glanced around, and went pale. The darkness retreated.

"Sorry," he forced out. "I didn't . . ." He struggled to compose himself. Then he said evenly, "What the Chancellor did to you—that spell—you shouldn't have been able to recover from it. And you shouldn't have been able to see through his illusions, either, or resist his servant's glamour. It sounds like you have some kind of resistance to demonic influence—which would explain quite a lot, actually, about everything that's happened to you since the Book of Eyes." He raked a hand through his hair, distracted. "But it's strange. I've never heard of anyone . . . never mind. Go on. Why on earth are you smiling?"

Elisabeth wasn't sure. The sun was shining through the window again. The silver streak in Nathaniel's hair was sticking straight up, and he clearly hadn't noticed. And he believed her. Finally. He believed every word. Looking down at her knees, she continued.

"So you see," she finished at last, "I must go to the Collegium straightaway and tell them everything I've learned. I think Ashcroft will strike the Great Library of Fairwater next, then Harrows. He's moving in a circle around the kingdom, sabotaging each Great Library in order. Perhaps he's saving the Royal Library for last. But the attack on Harrows is special to him for some reason."

Nathaniel's eyes narrowed. "The defenses at Harrows should be impenetrable. It's more secure than the Royal Library."

"His ancestor built the Great Libraries. He might know a secret way inside." She bit her lip. "And there are two Class Ten grimoires in its vault. If he succeeds—"

Nathaniel straightened. "I see your point."

"You don't seem surprised by anything I've told you," Elisabeth said tentatively. "You've known Ashcroft for a long time, but you still believe me."

He looked out the window again, the angle concealing his face. "I have spent the past day thinking of every possible thing that might have happened to you, and every person who might conceivably be responsible for it. I've moved past the point of surprise. And besides," he added quickly, bitterly, before she could comment, "I make a point of never underestimating what a sorcerer can do. No matter how good, or kind, or trustworthy they seem—I've seen what they're capable of with my own eyes."

The lines of his shoulder and back were tense. To him, this was obviously a personal matter. "You're speaking about your father," she said quietly, as all the comments people had made about Alistair began to come together.

Nathaniel stiffened. Silence reigned for a long moment. Then he said, in a clear attempt to change the subject, "You didn't trust me before. What changed your mind?"

Elisabeth picked at the dressing gown's hem. "I was afraid of you at first. Now I understand that you helped me. And I believe . . ."

He turned and raised an inquiring eyebrow.

"I believe there is kindness in you," she blurted out. "Even though you try to pretend otherwise."

The eyebrow lifted higher. "So you're hoping I might help you expose Ashcroft?"

"Yes," she said.

"Why?"

"It's the right thing to do."

He barked out a disbelieving laugh. It sounded almost pained, as though someone had struck him. "Tell me, do you have any evidence? A motive? Ashcroft is the most powerful man in the kingdom, and his reputation is as spotless as the Queen's linens. Everyone adores him."

"I know he's studying the Codex Daemonicus. Whatever's inside it will explain his plans."

"Sorcerers have studied the Codex for centuries and found nothing of worth." He shook his head. "You could bring your allegations to the Collegium, to the Queen herself, and no one would believe you. Ashcroft had you declared insane. He has a diagnosis from a physician and, by the sound of it, dozens of witnesses from high society." Elisabeth's hands twisted the dressing gown. Nathaniel went on relentlessly, "It would be your word, a disgraced apprentice librarian's, against the opinions of the most respected people in Austermeer."

"But if you came with me, and told them—"

"I have nothing to tell. I could swear to your honesty for days, but the fact remains that I witnessed none of what you've told me firsthand. Everyone would see me lavishing attention on you, and after that debacle with the press they'd just assume that I . . ." He ran a hand through his hair again, more roughly this time.

"That you what?"

He grimaced. "A word of advice, Scrivener. Whatever Ashcroft is doing, let it go. He's finished with you—you're safe now. I'll find a way to straighten out the matter with Summershall and then you can return home to your innocent country life."

"No." Elisabeth thrust herself up from the end of the bed. "I won't go back until I've stopped him."

Nathaniel's face hardened. "Sometimes people die," he bit out, "and there's nothing you can do to stop it."

"I will save them."

"You will join them," he snapped.

Fury surged through Elisabeth. It swelled in her heart, crackled over her skin, fizzed up the roots of her hair. She advanced on Nathaniel until their noses almost touched. "That is better than doing nothing!" she shouted.

For a moment he made no reply. They stood glaring at each other, matched in height. His breath stirred against her face. When he finally spoke, he struggled to keep his voice level. "You've been attacked, violated, tormented, left on the streets to starve. The odds you face are impossible. If you continue down this path, you'll die. Why won't you just give up?"

She stared. Was that a thing people did—just gave up? When there was so much in the world to love, to fight for? "I cannot," she said fiercely. "I never will."

Nathaniel's lips parted to deliver a retort that never came. Her gaze flicked to his mouth, and that was all it took for the air between them to change. Heat flushed her face at the realization of how close they were standing; Nathaniel's eyes widened, his pupils dark.

He took an abrupt step back. Then he pivoted and seized the edge of the door. Recovering quickly, Elisabeth caught it before he could slam it shut between them.

"What did Silas mean, when he said you cared about me?" she challenged.

A fall of hair hid Nathaniel's face from view, showing only the line of his jaw. "You of all people should know better than to make a habit of listening to demons."

He was right. What would the Director think if she saw Elisabeth now, willingly accepting refuge in the house of a sorcerer and his demon? Her fingers loosened in shock. The door tugged from her grasp, but Nathaniel didn't slam it, as she expected— it swung shut with a quiet click. As his footsteps faded, she slumped against the inside of the door and dug her knuckles against her eyes. She tried to rub the ghostly image of the Director from her mind.

It used to be so easy to tell right from wrong. Wardens followed a simple code: protect the kingdom from demonic influences, and never involve themselves in sorcery. But what was she supposed to do when the code turned against itself? Had she not accepted Silas's help, she might have died, and any hope of unmasking Ashcroft would have been lost along with her. Surely it was her duty to seek justice, no matter the cost.

Confusion roiled within her like a sickness. Perhaps having such thoughts meant she wasn't fit to be a warden. Even so, she refused to turn back. She needed to find a copy of the Codex. She had to find out what Ashcroft was after. And there was no better place to start than in a sorcerer's home.

EIGHTEEN

EMERALD LIGHT SPILLED through the crack beneath the door, illuminating the dust and prints on the floorboards. Outside in the hallway, Elisabeth shifted from foot to foot. She had spent hours exploring the manor. After poking her head into countless unused rooms, their furniture covered in sheets, she had encountered this one tucked away in a corner of the first floor. Nathaniel had been shut up inside it doing some sort of magic all day: occasionally she heard him move about or mutter an incantation. She had waited all afternoon, but he hadn't once emerged. Her patience was beginning to fade.

A glance down the hall confirmed that the house was as empty as ever. Aside from Silas, who seemed to be out, she hadn't encountered any servants. She gathered her courage and knocked.

"I thought you weren't going to be back until supper," Nathaniel said conversationally. "Well, hurry up and come in. I could use your opinion on . . ." He turned as the door swung open, his expression souring. "Scrivener."

Elisabeth didn't answer, too busy staring openmouthed at

their surroundings. The door had opened not on a room, but on a forest. Nathaniel stood in the middle of a mossy clearing, the ground dappled by jade-colored shafts of light that speared through the colossal pines. Butterflies as large as dinner plates clustered on the trunks, fanning their iridescent turquoise wings, and liquid notes of birdsong trilled through the air. The forest seemed to go on forever, its depths cloaked in swirling mist that occasionally parted to reveal hints of dark, distant hillsides and splashing white streams.

Elisabeth's spirits soared as she stepped through the doorway, passing from one world into another. She breathed in the scent of crushed moss and pine sap, and raised a hand to let the green light filter through her fingers.

Nathaniel watched her for a moment, silently. Then his mouth twisted into a bitter smile. "Don't get too excited. None of this is real. See? It's just an illusion I'm working on for the Royal Ball."

He waved a hand, and the scenery blurred like a runny watercolor painting turned over onto its side. She blinked, watching the ferns dissolve into wisps of green mist; the butterflies winked out of existence liked popped soap bubbles. Soon the last tree vanished, and instead of a forest, she stood inside the entrance to a study.

But this room was nothing like Ashcroft's study—nothing like any room she had ever been in before. It was wondrous. There was hardly a path to step through without knocking something over. Papers tumbled from every surface, pinned down here and there by odd bronze and glass instruments. A jeweled globe glittered in one corner on a brass stand, and the articulated skeleton of a large bird hung on wires above Nathaniel's head. The ceiling tunneled upward five stories, ending in a skylight that admitted bright shafts of sunshine. And on the shelves, winding around and around, reachable only by ladders . . .

Elisabeth lit up. "Grimoires," she breathed, even more delighted than before.

Nathaniel's expression grew odd. "You like this place?"

"Of course I do. It has books in it."

He just stood there, not trying to stop her, so Elisabeth clambered up the nearest ladder. She had spotted a familiar title on the shelf, winking its gilt for attention. When she reached for it, it squirmed free of its neighbors and dropped eagerly into her hand.

"I knew you had to be here somewhere!" she said to the Lexicon. She hadn't seen it since the ride into Brassbridge. "I can't believe he stole you."

The grimoire gave a guilty rustle. She looked over her shoulder at the marvelous, sparkling chaos of the study. From this vantage point she could see emerald flames dancing in the hearth, and overtop it a glass cauldron sending wisps of purple vapor up the chimney. There weren't any skulls, or severed crow's feet, or vials of blood. In fact, the study seemed . . . friendly. With a thoughtful frown, she turned back to the Lexicon. "I suppose you're better off here than with Ashcroft," she admitted.

"What do you want?" asked Nathaniel behind her. "I assume there's a reason you're inflicting yourself upon me."

She tucked the Lexicon beneath her arm. "I'd like to ask a favor."

He turned away and began rifling through the papers on his desk, appearing to accomplish nothing in particular aside from creating a bigger mess. "I thought I made myself clear this morning. I'm not going to help you get yourself killed."

"I just want to borrow some books."

"And this suspiciously sudden impulse has nothing whatsoever to do with Ashcroft?"

Elisabeth spotted some fragile glass instruments arranged on a table nearby. She climbed back down the ladder and drifted toward them. "What are these?" she inquired. "They look breakable."

"Don't touch those," Nathaniel said hastily. "No—don't touch that, either," he added, as she changed course and headed for the jeweled globe instead. When she ignored him, he threw his hands up in surrender. "Fine! Have it your way, you absolute terror. You can borrow as many grimoires as you want, as long as you keep your hands off everything else. That's the rule."

She beamed. He stared at her for a moment, and then snapped his gaze back to his desk.

"What is it?"

"You need some new clothes," he said, pretending to read one of the papers. She knew he was pretending, because the paper was upside down. "I'm going to run out of pajamas at this rate. I'll set Silas to the task—he loves that sort of thing. Prepare to be fashionable, Scrivener, because he'll accept nothing less."

Elisabeth reddened. She had forgotten she was still wearing Nathaniel's dressing gown. She tried to push away the memory of his dark eyes and parted lips, only inches away from her own. "The way you talk about Silas . . . you really trust him, don't you?"

For some reason, Nathaniel laughed. "With my life."

It took her a moment to grasp his answer's double meaning, and when she did, her heart fell. It was easy to forget that he had bargained away his life in exchange for Silas's service. How much of it? She couldn't bring herself to ask.

She shook off her troubled thoughts and bent herself to the task ahead. As Nathaniel resumed his work, she climbed the study's ladders, plucking out any grimoire that looked promising.

The light shifted and deepened, slanting through the skylight at a steep angle. Hours passed, but Elisabeth barely took note. She was back where she belonged, surrounded by the whisperings and rustlings of pages; the sweet, musty smell of books. Occasionally she looked down to see what Nathaniel was up to, and found him examining conjured butterflies and flowers beneath the lenses of a queer-looking magnifying device. He never once looked at her in return. But every once in a while, when her back was turned, she could have sworn she felt his gaze settle upon her, as tentative as the brush of a butterfly's wing.

Late in the afternoon, she staggered out of the study with such a prodigious stack of grimoires that she had to tilt her head to see around them. Climbing three flights of stairs to her bedroom didn't seem wise. Instead, she hauled the books into a room she had discovered during her exploration: a tiny parlor tucked into a warm, sunny crevice of the manor, its plump armchairs arranged around a fireplace in which someone had left a bouquet of dried lavender, the flowers now brown and brittle with age. She set the grimoires down on the coffee table, sneezing in the cloud of dust that puffed from its surface.

A review of the Lexicon had led her to focus on Aldous Prendergast, the author of the Codex Daemonicus. The books she'd selected to start with were all Class One and Two grimoires with sections on sixteenth-century history. One of them looked especially promising: Lady Primrose's Complete Handbook of Historical Personages, New and Revised Edition, which kept emitting delicate, ladylike scoffs at the dusty table, and refused to open for her until she went back and borrowed a pair of kidskin gloves from Nathaniel.

By nightfall, however, the grimoires had yielded disappointingly little information. She'd read that Prendergast had devoted his life to the study of demons and the Otherworld. He was obsessive about his work, even going so far as to claim that he had traveled to the Otherworld, which appeared to be the beginning of his falling out with Cornelius. The two were close friends before Prendergast wrote the Codex. Soon afterward, Cornelius had him declared mad and locked him away in a tower, where he died after lapsing into some sort of comatose state. It was not lost on Elisabeth that Ashcroft had attempted to get rid of her in much the same way. No wonder the volume's psychic howls had raged with fury and betrayal.

But none of the grimoires contained what she really needed: a clue as to what sort of secret Prendergast might have hidden inside the Codex—or, barring that, where she could find a copy of it to study.

Frustrated, she set the last grimoire aside and looked out the windows. It was almost too dark to continue reading. A bluish gloom had descended over the parlor, and the traffic had grown thinner outside. Her thoughts churned away as a carriage rattled past, shiny with rain, bright yellow leaves pasted to its roof. Thus far, the attacks on the Great Libraries had occurred about two weeks apart. That meant she had barely over a week left to expose Ashcroft before he attacked the Great Library of Fairwater, and less than a month until he targeted Harrows. She had barely begun, and already she was running out of time.

"Miss Scrivener?" She jumped. Silas stood at the entrance to the room, holding a silver tray. "I have taken the liberty of bringing your supper, unless you would prefer to move to the dining room."

Elisabeth hurried to clear a spot on the coffee table, ignoring Lady Primrose's indignant huffs of protest. "This is fine. Thank you." She watched Silas set the tray down. Earlier, she had ventured into the kitchen and seen no one. "Do you cook all the food here yourself?"

"Yes, miss." Silas lit the oil lamp in the corner, then went to draw the curtains. It was strange to see him perform such mundane tasks. His pale, slender form looked ethereal in the twilight, barely human. "I have served Master Thorn in every capacity these past six years."

I'm even eating meals made by a demon, she thought in dismay. Nevertheless, she owed Silas her life. It didn't seem right that he should wait on her hand and foot. "Would you . . . would you like to join me?"

He paused, head tilted. "Do you wish me to?"

Elisabeth hesitated, unsure what to say.

He considered her through his lashes. "I do not eat human food, miss—not without a reason. To me, it tastes of nothing but ash and dust." He tugged the curtains shut. Before they closed, she noticed that his breath didn't fog the glass. "But I will dine with you, if you wish."

Had she offended him? It was always so difficult to tell. "In that case, I won't trouble you."

He nodded and made to leave.

"It's very good," she blurted out. "I've never eaten this well except in Ashcroft Manor, and I'd prefer to forget about that. You're an excellent cook, though I have no idea how you manage it, if you can't taste anything."

Silas drew up short. She winced, hearing the clumsy words over again, but he didn't look insulted by her blundering praise. If anything, a hint of satisfaction showed on his alabaster features. He nodded again, more deeply this time, and vanished into the shadows of the hall.

. . .

The next day she entered the parlor with a second stack of books to find that in her absence every inch of it had been dusted and polished, the rug beaten, the sheets removed from the remaining furniture; the windows' diamond-shaped panes sparkled between the mullions. A sweet aroma hung about the room, which Elisabeth traced to the new bouquet of lavender in the hearth. Even Lady Primrose found nothing to criticize, and resorted to a few noncommittal sniffs before she reluctantly fell silent.

Elisabeth passed another unsuccessful afternoon reading. Two days stretched into three, and she found herself no closer to an answer. At times her attention wandered while she climbed through the rafters of Nathaniel's study, and she paused to watch him add an ingredient to the glass cauldron, which was still sending up purple smoke, or conjure a flock of hummingbirds that darted around him in iridescent flashes of viridian. The light sifting down from above outlined his shoulders and feathered his unruly hair. Sometimes, when the sun grew hot, he took off his waistcoat and rolled up his sleeves. Then she saw the cruel scar that wound around the inside of his right forearm, starker here than in the dim hallway of the inn.

He continued to ignore her, but it was not, Elisabeth found to her surprise, an unfriendly feeling silence. It was a great deal like being back in Summershall, companionably going about her business with other librarians doing the same nearby. She didn't want to examine that thought too closely, for it seemed wrong that a sorcerer's study should feel so curiously like home.

Clothes arrived courtesy of Silas, a parade of silk dresses in shades of cerulean, rose, and striped cream. After trying them on and wondering at the novelty of having clothes that didn't show her entire ankles, Elisabeth guiltily moved the blue dress to the back of her wardrobe. The color no longer reminded her of a warden's uniform, but instead of her time spent as a prisoner in Ashcroft Manor. She had had nightmares of it since, her memories of the past several weeks blurring together into phantasmagorical horrors—lying helplessly in the thrall of Lorelei's glamour while Ashcroft struck the Director down in front of her, or while a uniformed attendant tightened leather straps around her legs, Mr. Hob standing unblinkingly nearby. She woke from these dreams sweating in terror, and took hours to fall back asleep afterward.

Her breakthrough occurred on the third evening of her research, and it happened entirely by accident. She was taking notes in the parlor when a fight broke out between Lady Primrose and a Class Two named Throckmorton's Peerage, who had been spitting wads of ink at the other grimoires on and off all afternoon. Finally, Lady Primrose's nerves reached their limits. The parlor briefly transformed into a dervish of flying dust and flapping pages; then Throckmorton shunted itself beneath a cabinet, desperate to get as far away from the vengeful Lady Primrose as possible, who was emitting a high, thin shriek, like a teakettle.

"I can't say I feel sorry for you," Elisabeth said sternly, crouching on her hands and knees to haul Throckmorton back out like a misbehaving cat. "You should know better than to tease another grimoire."

Then she saw it: the flash of a metal object wedged behind the cabinet, the sunlight striking it just so. Whatever it was, it looked as though it had slid down and become lost, trapped against the wall. Elisabeth reached for it, and instantly snatched her fingers back in shock. The object was freezing cold to the touch. She wrapped her hand in her skirt and tried again, this time carefully lifting the object into view.

It was a small hand mirror, its ornate silver frame elaborately scrolled and swirled. But it wasn't an ordinary mirror. Icicles hung from the edges of the frame, and a layer of frost clouded the glass. When Elisabeth peered closer, she saw no hint of her own reflection. Ghostly, unfamiliar images flowed across the mirror's surface, moving beneath the frost.

First the mirror showed her an empty salon in an unfamiliar house, its colors reduced to pale suggestions by the ice. She sucked in a breath when a child ran laughing across the salon, pursued by a nursemaid. Then the image swirled, replaced by an office in which a man sat signing papers, and again, showing her a drawing room in which one woman played the piano while another embroidered nearby. Elisabeth stared, entranced. Those were real people. Judging by the angle, she was seeing through the mirrors of their rooms.

She held the mirror close to her face. Every time she exhaled, her breath fogged the ice, and soon a clear spot melted away at the center, bringing forth a flush of color from the images. The tinkling notes of the piano filled the parlor, as if it were being played behind a shut door in Nathaniel's house just a few rooms away. A lonely ache filled Elisabeth's chest.

"I wish you would show me someone I knew," she whispered to the glass. "I wish," she said, "that you would show me my friend Katrien."

The piano music stopped. The woman frowned and looked up, directly at Elisabeth. Her eyes widened, and she flew from the stool with a shriek. Elisabeth didn't witness the rest. She was still processing the fact that the woman had been able to see her when the image swirled again. This time, it looked into her own room in Summershall.

Her room—and Katrien's. Katrien sat on her bed, flipping through scribbled sheaves of notes. Crumpled pieces of paper covered Elisabeth's old quilt and gathered around the edges of the room like snowdrifts. Some of them sat on the dresser, against the mirror, written in a deliberately illegible scrawl. Katrien was clearly up to something.

Elisabeth's throat tightened. The mirror shook in her hand. She hadn't expected it to obey her request. If the Collegium found out that she had used a magical artifact, she would never be permitted back inside a Great Library. Not only that, she didn't know how the mirror worked, or where it drew its magic from—it could be dangerous to use. She should put it back where she'd found it and never touch it again.

But this was Katrien—truly Katrien, right in front of her. And she didn't have the strength to turn away.

"Katrien," she whispered.

Katrien sat bolt upright, then spun around. "Elisabeth!" she exclaimed, rushing to the dresser, her face filling the mirror. "What's happening? Are you a prisoner?" She paused to take in Elisabeth's surroundings. "Where *are* you?"

"I have so much to tell you. Wait! Don't go!"

"I'm not going anywhere! But, Elisabeth, you're fading—you've gone transparent—"

The frost was creeping back in. She breathed on the mirror again, but it was no use. This time, the frost didn't recede. As she scrambled for a solution, a different idea occurred to her. In the Great Library, Katrien had access to resources that Elisabeth did not.

"I need your help," she said into the rapidly diminishing circle. "I don't have time to explain, but it's important."

"Anything," Katrien said grimly.

"There's a grimoire called the Codex Daemonicus. I think it's a Class Five or Six. I need to find out where I can locate a copy—"

The last section of frost crystallized into place, and the mirror's surface turned milky white. Elisabeth had no way of knowing whether Katrien had heard her. She sat back, squeezing her eyes shut against frustrated tears.

She kept the mirror close for the rest of the day, hidden beneath the armchair's cushions, checking it periodically. But its magic seemed to have been exhausted. It showed her nothing, only a blank white oval. She lay awake in bed that night, watching a strip of moonlight travel across the ceiling, wondering what to do. The mirror sat on the covers beside her, its icy chill raising goose bumps on her bare arms. Katrien at once seemed close enough to touch and farther away than ever before.

Perhaps I should go to Nathaniel, she thought. *He'll know if there's a way to restore its magic.*

She dismissed the idea at once. Nathaniel seemed willing to tolerate her efforts to expose Ashcroft, but only under the condition that she didn't involve him in any way. He might take the mirror from her, especially if it turned out to be dangerous, or if he feared that she would break it. Better to wait and see if the magic returned on its own.

Nathaniel . . . she still didn't understand him. He wasn't being unkind to her, but he obviously didn't welcome her presence, either. Her arrival had disturbed him for some reason—his argument with Silas had made that clear enough. They never shared meals together, and he only spoke to her when absolutely necessary. When they weren't in his study, he avoided her completely.

Perhaps he didn't want to encourage her. He might not be interested in women, as the ladies had suggested during the dinner at Ashcroft Manor, or he could be like Katrien, who possessed no interest in romantic matters whatsoever. Either might explain why he'd never courted. But she hadn't mistaken the way his eyes had darkened the other morning, or the tension that had suffused the air between them.

She flipped over beneath the covers, restless. She imagined padding down the hallway in her nightgown and knocking on Nathaniel's bedroom door. She pictured him answering in the dark, his hair tousled with sleep, his nightshirt unlaced down the front. When she finally drifted off to sleep, it was to the memory of how soft his hair had felt in Summershall, and the callused brush of his fingers when he'd touched her hand.

When she awoke the next morning, the first thing she did was sit up and seize the mirror, her hair falling around it in a tangled curtain. The magic was back. Images moved beneath the frost again. But before she could invoke Katrien, a knock came on the door. She shoved the mirror beneath the blankets, holding her breath.

Silas slipped inside with breakfast. His yellow eyes traced over her, but if he sensed anything amiss, he said nothing. Elisabeth thanked him hurriedly as he brought the tray over, and upon realizing that her thank-you had sounded rather peculiar, seized a pastry and stuffed it whole into her mouth. Nothing about this performance seemed to surprise him, as he bowed and departed without comment. She waited several long moments after he had gone, certain that his senses were far keener than a human's. Then she scrambled to retrieve the mirror, ignoring the bite of its frozen metal.

"Show me Katrien," she commanded, and breathed against the glass.

The mirror swirled. Katrien was sprawled facedown on her

bed, partially burrowed into the crumpled balls of paper. After Elisabeth had said her name several times, she snorted awake and rolled straight onto the ground. Elisabeth winced at the thump she made on the rug.

"Are you all right?" she asked.

Katrien stumbled over to the mirror, squinting in the morning light. "I was going to ask you the same question, but I see you're eating breakfast in bed."

"I'm safe, for now." Elisabeth hesitated. "Katrien, you look . . ."

Pale. Overworked. Exhausted. She cursed herself for not noticing it the other day. The bags beneath Katrien's eyes and the grayish pallor to her brown complexion spoke of far more than just one night's worth of lost sleep.

Her friend glanced over her shoulder at the door, and paused for a moment as if making sure no one was outside. "Director Finch has been running the place like a prison," she confessed, lowering her voice. "The wardens perform random room inspections every few days. He's doubled the amount of work apprentices have to do, and we get thrown in the dungeon if we don't finish it." She rubbed her wrist, where Elisabeth glimpsed the swollen marks of a switch. "If you think I look bad, you should see Stefan. But don't worry. This won't last for much longer."

"What do you mean?"

"I'd tell you, but I'm worried we'll run out of time again. Trust me. I have the situation under control." She leaned closer. "So, I managed to have a look at the records last night."

Elisabeth sat up straighter. "Did you find it?"

Katrien nodded. "There were only two copies of the Codex Daemonicus ever written. One went missing hundreds of years ago, and the other is shelved somewhere in the Royal Library."

"So Ashcroft must have the missing copy. . . ." She trailed

off, thinking hard. She had found out from Silas that the Royal Library was one of the spired buildings overlooking the river, a short walk from Hemlock Park.

"Elisabeth," Katrien said.

She looked up to find the frost creeping back across the mirror, swallowing up Katrien's face. Elisabeth's heart leaped to her throat. "Only sorcerers are allowed into the Royal Library," she said rapidly. "And scholars, if they receive permission from the Collegium—but they have to have credentials. I need to find a way in."

"That's easy enough," Katrien replied. "Get a job there as a servant."

"But they'll never let a servant study a grimoire."

"Of course they won't *let* you. You realize what you have to do, don't you?"

Elisabeth shook her head, but her mouth had gone dry. Truthfully, she knew what Katrien was going to tell her, and she didn't want to hear it.

"I know you don't like it, but there's no other way." Her friend's voice was fading quickly. "You have to find out where the Codex is shelved in the Royal Library. You have to get in there," she said, "and then you have to steal it."

NINETEEN

FINDING A JOB at the Royal Library proved less challenging than Elisabeth had anticipated. As it turned out, a maidservant had quit just that morning after a giant booklouse skittered up her leg, and the Royal Library was in need of an immediate replacement. Elisabeth demonstrated to the steward that she would be an ideal candidate by lifting up one end of a cabinet in his office, uncovering a booklouse underneath, and stomping on it, much to the delight of a young apprentice who happened to be passing by. She then sat down opposite the steward's desk and answered a number of job-related questions, such as how quickly she could run, and whether she strongly valued keeping all ten of her fingers. The steward seemed impressed that she found all of his questions perfectly reasonable. Most people, he explained, walked straight out the door.

"But this is a library," she replied in surprise. "What do they expect—that the books *won't* try to bite off their fingers?"

After her interview with the steward, she had to meet with the Deputy Director, Mistress Petronella Wick.

Elisabeth had never heard of a Deputy Director, but she gathered that the Royal Library was large enough to need one. She instantly understood upon entering the office that she was in the presence of an exceedingly important person. Mistress Wick wore the indigo robes of a decorated senior librarian, clasped high about her throat with a golden key and quill. Her hair had turned silver with age, but that didn't diminish the elegance of her artfully piled braids. She had dark brown skin against which her white eyes appeared almost opalescent, and her posture was so impeccable that Elisabeth felt her own gangliness fill the room like a third presence. She was certain Mistress Wick could sense it, though she was clearly blind.

"You may be wondering why you have been brought before me," said Mistress Wick without preamble. "Here in the Royal Library, even the position of maidservant is a great responsibility. We cannot let just anyone enter our halls."

"Yes, Mistress Wick," Elisabeth said, sitting petrified in front of the desk.

"It is also a dangerous job. During my time as Deputy Director, several servants have been killed. Others have lost limbs, or senses, or even their minds. So I must ask—why do you wish to work in a Great Library, of all places?"

"Because I . . ." Elisabeth swallowed, and decided to be as honest as she could. "Because I belong here," she blurted out. "Because there's something I must find, and I can only find it here, among the books."

"What is it you wish to find?"

This time, she spoke without hesitation. "The truth."

Mistress Wick sat silently for a long time. Long enough that Elisabeth grew certain she would be turned away. She felt as though her very soul were being examined; as though Mistress

Wick could sense her true intentions for coming here, and at any moment would summon a warden to arrest her on the spot. But then the Deputy Director rose from her chair and said, "Very well. Come with me. Before you begin your training, you must visit the armory."

They exited the offices and walked together down a pillared hallway, their footsteps echoing from the vaulted ceiling high above. Reinforced glass cases were set into alcoves along the walls, casting strange, differently colored glows across the flagstones. The cases did not contain grimoires. Instead, they held magical artifacts: a skull radiating emerald light, a chalice filled with a draught of night sky, a sword whose pommel was twined with morning glories, the flowers blooming, dying, and blooming again as Elisabeth watched, their fallen petals crumbling away to nothing. She forced herself not to slow down, mindful of Mistress Wick's hand resting on her shoulder. But when she passed the next case, she drew up short in surprise.

Inside it was a frozen mirror, the icicles so long that they had merged and formed a translucent pedestal. Frost crystals swirled around the mirror as though a blizzard howled behind the case's glass.

"We are in the Hall of Forbidden Arts," Mistress Wick explained. "Every artifact in this place was banned a hundred and fifty years ago by the Reforms. They are relics of an era past, preserved to remind us of what once was." She moved toward the case, holding out her hand. She traced her fingers across the plaque. After a moment, Elisabeth realized she was reading the engraved letters by touch. "This is a scrying mirror," she said, drawing her hand away, "created by the sorcerers of old, with which one can gaze through all the mirrors of this world. It is believed to be the last of its kind. The rest were confiscated and destroyed, and no one knows how to make them any longer."

Elisabeth inched closer. "Is the mirror dangerous?"

"Knowledge always has the potential to be dangerous. It is a more powerful weapon than any sword or spell."

"But the mirror is magical. Sorcery." Elisabeth knew she shouldn't say more, but she yearned for answers, not only about the mirror, but about the change taking place within her heart. "Shouldn't that automatically make it evil?"

Mistress Wick sharply turned her head, and she immediately regretted asking. Yet the Deputy Director only placed her hand on Elisabeth's shoulder and ushered her away, moving with such surety that it was obvious she could navigate the hall on her own. Elisabeth was the one being guided through this dangerous place, not the other way around.

"Some would say so," Mistress Wick said. "But there is always more than one way to see the world. Those who claim otherwise would have you dwell forever in the dark."

The armory lay at the far end of the Hall of Forbidden Arts, guarded by two statues who held their spears crossed in front of its ironbound doors. Mistress Wick flashed them her Collegium pin, and they lifted their spears away. The doors groaned open without a touch.

Elisabeth stared in amazement. Beams of sunlight fell from high upon cloaks and swords and canisters, and even upon archaic suits of armor that stood at attention along the pillars, their metal polished to a high shine. A line of statues arrayed along the back appeared to have been used for weapons practice; they had chunks missing here and there, and weary expressions frozen onto their faces. Only one person was in the room. A boy stood at a trestle table near the center, spooning piles of salt onto the centers of scraps of fabric. The completed product formed small round bundles, like coin purses, tied shut with twine. He looked up as they entered and offered Elisabeth a friendly smile.

"Good afternoon, Parsifal," said Mistress Wick. "Elisabeth, Junior Librarian Parsifal will make sure you are outfitted for duty."

"Hullo," said Parsifal. Elisabeth liked him at once. He looked about nineteen, his pale blue robes belted over a plump stomach. He had a pleasant face, and a short thatch of blond hair that stuck up in places.

After Mistress Wick left, he bustled around the armory fetching items and laying them out for her on an empty section of the table: a leather belt, covered in loops and pouches, and a hooded white wool cloak, which was stamped on the back with a key and quill, and lined on the inside with a thin layer of chain mail.

"I had no idea I would be able to wear something like this," she said, reverently touching the cloak.

"Even servants have their own uniforms here," Parsifal replied proudly. "Though of course, it's mostly out of necessity. If you're going to work in the Royal Library, you need to be wearing iron—especially these days, with everything that's going on. Now, these are called salt rounds," he said, demonstrating how to hang the salt bundles on her belt, and how the thin fabric burst when flung against the flagstones, releasing an explosion of salt into the air. "If you ever run into trouble, using them should buy you enough time to run and alert a warden."

"Do I get a greatkey as well?" she asked hopefully, glancing at the two keys on Parsifal's key ring. Librarians earned the second when they graduated from apprentice to junior librarian.

He gave her an apologetic look. "Afraid not. Security reasons, and all that. You'll have to knock on the staff door at the beginning of your shift, and someone will let you in. . . ." He frowned thoughtfully, looking past her. "Say, is that your cat?"

Elisabeth turned, confused. A fluffy white cat sat on the floor behind her, staring up at them with yellow eyes. It was quite small for a fully grown cat; it could be a kitten, she thought, or perhaps it was just dainty. And strange . . . those yellow eyes looked terribly familiar. . . .

Her heart skipped a beat. "Yes," she choked out, seeing no other option. "That is—my cat."

"It's all right," Parsifal assured her. "Cats are always welcome in the Royal Library. They catch booklice, and they know to stay away from the grimoires. Having a cat with you might even help keep you safe, since they're so talented at sensing magic." To her horror, he went over to Silas and picked him up, holding him aloft at eye level. "What a lovely cat you are! Are you a boy, or a girl?"

"He's a boy," Elisabeth said hastily, when Parsifal appeared to be about to duck his head and check. "His name is—er—it's"—she gulped—"Sir Fluffington."

Dangling from Parsifal's hands, Silas gave her a look of extreme reproach.

Parsifal beamed. "Lovely," he repeated. "Well, you can have him back." He passed Silas over. "I'll show you around a bit, though don't worry about learning your way just yet. You'll have plenty of time to do that during training. First off, this is the Northeast Wing, where all the offices are. . . ."

Elisabeth hung back as Parsifal chattered away, staring aghast at the demon in her arms. His nose and the pads on his paws contrasted pinkly with his snowy fur. He was very fluffy. She felt an alarming urge to press her face against his belly, as though he were truly a cat and not an ancient, immortal being.

"Did Nathaniel send you to make sure I didn't get into trouble?" she whispered. Silas gave her a slow blink, which seemed to mean "yes." She scowled. "I'm not going to get caught by Ashcroft. I went sixteen years without seeing a sorcerer in Summershall—I'm not about to run into one here. And in any case, I'll be wearing a hood."

"Mew," said Silas. Even his meow was adorable. Elisabeth shuddered and put him down. He trotted after them, swishing his plumy tail.

Parsifal led her through the remainder of the Northeast Wing, past the reading rooms, and into the central atrium, which could have fit the entire Great Library of Summershall inside. It was a colossal octagonal space from which the four wings branched off beneath arches embellished with bronze scrolls and angels. The domed roof was made of stained glass, deep blue and spangled with constellations. Gracefully sculpted marble stairways ascended to the upper levels, where the shelves rose higher and higher until they grew lost in the dome's indigo-tinted haze. Librarians bustled across the checkered marble floor, their status differentiated not only by the number of keys on their key ring, but also by the shade of their robes, ranging from light to dark blue.

While Parsifal chattered on, she shut her eyes, letting the echoing, papery murmurings of the grimoires wash over her. She hadn't realized how badly she'd missed being in a Great Library until now—like something deep inside her, misaligned since leaving Summershall, had shifted back into its proper place. She was home.

She clung to the sensation as Parsifal showed her the statues that moved ladders on command, the tiled map of the library set into the center of the atrium's floor, and the pneumatic tubes hidden behind the bookshelves that carried messages across the building at lightning speed. While he did so, he explained what she could expect working alongside grimoires.

"You catch on awfully fast," he said, impressed. "It's too bad you aren't an orphan. Oh, that came out wrong. What I mean is, you would've made an excellent apprentice."

The compliment struck Elisabeth like a blow. For a moment she felt disoriented, as though she had been thrown outside her body. When people looked at her now, they didn't see an apprentice librarian, and certainly not a future warden. Perhaps they were right. After using a forbidden magical artifact and conspiring to steal from the Royal Library, even stopping Ashcroft might not be enough to earn her apprenticeship back. Was this shadow of her former life all she had left?

"Thank you," she said, gazing at the floor so Parsifal wouldn't see her expression.

Fortunately, he didn't notice anything wrong as he ushered her toward the entrance to the Northwest Wing. Foreboding prickled Elisabeth's skin as they drew near. The angelic figures carved around the archway had skulls beneath their hoods, and the entrance was cordoned off with a velvet rope. Beyond the rope, shadows engulfed the wing. A thick mist spilled across the floor, and low mutterings and whispers chased down the corridor, reverberating from the stone. They seemed to be coming from behind an iron gate that reared from the darkness, over a dozen feet tall, mist swirling around its edges. She dimly heard Parsifal explain that this wing contained the entrance to the vault.

"But what is that gate?" she asked.

"That's the entrance to the restricted archives. The grimoires inside there are almost dangerous enough for the vault, but not quite. Don't worry—you won't be assigned to the Northwest Wing. Now, if we hurry up the South Spire, we might be in time to see the wardens training on the grounds."

As they turned to go, Silas stared bright-eyed into the wing's shadows, and she wondered what he saw that she could not.

When Elisabeth got back to Nathaniel's house that night, she was so exhausted that she ate supper and fell directly into bed. Then she woke early the next morning and began the fifteen minute walk to the Royal Library through Hemlock Park, Silas trailing after her in the predawn gloom like a cat-shaped ghost. It wasn't likely that Ashcroft would happen to pass her in a carriage, but just in case, she stayed off the main street and took a circuitous route through hedged-in walking paths and a section of wooded park. She passed only servants plucking breakfast herbs from the backyard gardens, tossing out shovelfuls of soot, and emptying their households' chamber pots. She felt a squirm of guilty embarrassment upon realizing Silas must normally be responsible for those tasks—though truly, she couldn't picture him doing them.

The last leg of the walk took her past the Collegium's grounds. Horses poked their noses out of the stone stables, smelling sweetly of hay and warm bodies. A low-hanging mist silvered the lawn where wardens practiced swordplay. She tried to ignore the ache in her chest at the sight of the dormitories, decorated with gargoyles and ornate gables, where wardens lived when they began their training. Now that she had come to scrub the floors, her dream of joining them seemed as though it belonged to someone else.

Once she reached the servants' entrance of the Royal Library, she was instantly put to work by an old servant named Gertrude, who supervised her closely as she hauled a soapy bucket across the flagstone floor. Next she swept and dusted an unused reading room, and helped Gertrude carry out the rugs to be beaten. As the day stretched on, frustration simmered beneath her skin. She wouldn't get any closer to locating the Codex with Gertrude watching her like a hawk. The elderly servant even insisted on taking lunch with her, which eliminated all hope of Elisabeth seizing a chance to sneak off and check the catalogue.

But an opportunity arrived after lunch, when Elisabeth moved an armchair to sweep underneath it, and in doing so disturbed a nest of booklice. The lice went skittering in every direction, gray and chitinous, the young ones no larger than chicken eggs. Elisabeth let out a ferocious cry and began smacking them with her broom. When several fled toward the door, she at last sensed the taste of freedom.

"Slow down, girl!" Gertrude shouted, but Elisabeth pretended not to hear as she dashed around the corner, chasing the lice with her broom lofted like a javelin. Gertrude soon fell behind, wheezing. From there, Elisabeth only had to make a few more turns before she was out of sight.

She checked herself as she entered the atrium, reducing her speed to what she hoped was a purposeful-looking stride. She cut a path through the librarians and ducked behind a pillar. The catalogue room was set into the facet of the octagon opposite the Royal Library's front doors. All she had to do was sneak inside, go through the catalogue drawers, and find the card with the Codex's location. But when she peered around the pillar, her spirits plummeted.

The room bustled with activity. Librarians of every rank climbed ladders and consulted each other over desks, overseen by a bespectacled archivist. No one would look at her twice if she were wearing an apprentice's pale blue robes, but she was certain the archivist would notice her if she went up one of the ladders and started going through the tiny gilded drawers that covered every inch of the walls. And there weren't many places to hide in there, aside from beneath the desks and behind a few display cases containing grimoires.

She eyed the nearest display case. The grimoire inside looked familiar, and indeed, she recognized it from Summershall, where another copy was on display in the hall outside the reading room. It was an ostentatious-looking Class Four called Madame Bouchard's Harmonic Cantrips, its cover bracketed in gold and stitched with peacock feathers. Elisabeth's heart raced as a plan began to unfold within her mind. The only problem was that she couldn't do it alone.

A throaty growl drew her attention to the nearest section of bookcases. A marmalade-colored cat crouched there, fur standing on end, its tail lashing back and forth. Opposite it sat Silas, looking supremely unconcerned. As the other cat continued to yowl, he raised one of his dainty paws and licked it.

"Silas," Elisabeth hissed. She went over and scooped him up. The other cat bolted. "I need your help," she whispered, ignoring the strange look sent to her by a passing apprentice.

Silas gazed at her levelly.

"It's important," she tried.

His tail flicked, in a fashion that suggested he was feeling inconvenienced. She suspected he still hadn't gotten over the Sir Fluffington incident.

"If you leave me to my own devices," she told him, "I'm

likely to get into trouble, and I'm certain Nathaniel wouldn't appreciate that."

Silas's yellow eyes narrowed. Slowly, he blinked.

Elisabeth sagged in relief. "Good. Now, here's what I need you to do. . . ."

None of the librarians in the catalogue room paid any mind when, a few minutes later, a small white cat trotted inside. Not a soul reacted when he leaped onto one of the desks and minced across it. But they did pay attention when Silas launched himself at the glass display case, knocked it askew, and promptly streaked from the scene, looking for all the world like an ordinary cat that had gotten himself into unexpected trouble. Everyone froze as the case wobbled once—twice—then tumbled to the floor and shattered.

Madame Bouchard's Harmonic Cantrips seemed to have been waiting its entire life for this moment. It rose gloriously from the wreckage, unfurling a set of paper wings, which were a good seven or eight feet across. As the librarians shielded their heads from its flapping pinions, it spread its pages wide and unleashed a shrill, operatic wail. Desks trembled. Drawers rattled. The archivist's spectacles cracked. Librarians fled in every direction, covering their ears against the ear-splitting vibrato.

Elisabeth waited until the last librarian emptied out before she darted inside. She set her teeth against the noise—seeing that it possessed an audience, Madame Bouchard had launched into an aria—and glanced around at the drawers. The cataloguing system was different here than in Summershall, and there had to be thousands of drawers altogether. However, she swiftly determined that the drawers were divided into seven different columns, with bronze numerals fixed above them ranging from I to VII. Those had to represent grimoire classes, with classes

Eight through Ten omitted from the public catalogue.

She had previously estimated that the Codex was either a Class Five or a Class Six. She clambered up the ladder belonging to the Class Five section first, and found the drawer marked "Pe—Pi." After flipping through the cards and finding nothing, she checked the drawer labeled "Ci—Co," in case the grimoires were catalogued by title instead of author. When that proved unsuccessful, she moved to the Class Six section with her nerves shrieking nearly as loudly as Madame Bouchard. During the brief intervals in which the grimoire paused for breath, she heard shouts ringing across the atrium, rapidly drawing closer.

She found the Codex's card in the last drawer she checked, glanced at it, and slammed the drawer shut. As she leaped off the ladder, a warden came striding inside with a salt round at the ready and a length of iron chain. He stared at Elisabeth in bewilderment. She seized her broom and clutched it tightly.

"What are you doing in here?" he shouted over Madame Bouchard, who was now energetically practicing scales.

Elisabeth swept a bit of broken glass aside. "I'm cleaning up the mess, sir!" she shouted back.

A whirlwind of chaos ensued. The warden at last handed her off to an equally baffled librarian, who said, "Well, I must commend you for going above and beyond the call of duty, girl," and brought her back to Gertrude, who gave her a thorough scolding. But Elisabeth wasn't in any real trouble, for she could hardly be punished for sweeping a floor.

She spent the rest of the day meekly obeying Gertrude's commands. Under different circumstances she wouldn't have been able to wait to race back home and tell Katrien what she had done, as it was exactly the sort of story that her friend would love. But what she had seen on the catalogue card shadowed her mood like a dark cloud. She didn't want to tell Katrien about it; she didn't even want to think about it herself.

The Codex Daemonicus wasn't going to be easy to steal, because it was shelved in the restricted archives of the North-west Wing.

TWENTY

ELISABETH SLEPT POORLY that night, and had unsettling dreams. In them, she walked down the Northwest Wing's dark corridor, the gate looming larger and larger above her, stretching impossibly high. As she drew near, the gate creaked open of its own accord. A shape stood within the swirling mist beyond, waiting for her, its presence suffusing her with bone-deep horror. Before she made out who or what it was, she always jolted awake.

She wished she could speak to Katrien again, but the mirror's magic only renewed itself every twelve hours or so, and they had to save their brief conversations for important matters. They couldn't lie in bed and talk well into the night as they had in Summershall, bright-eyed and restless in the dark. As a last resort Elisabeth imagined she was back in their drafty tower room, snug beneath the familiar weight of her quilt, safe behind the library's thick stone walls, until she drifted once more.

It was no use. She had returned to the gate, and the ominous figure still awaited her. This time, when the gate swung open, it opened its mouth and screamed.

Elisabeth's eyes snapped open, her pulse racing. But the screams didn't fade. They ground against her skull, echoing ceaselessly from every direction. They hadn't happened in her dream—they were real.

She leaped from bed and belted on her salt rounds, then seized a poker and stumbled into the hall, where the screams grew louder. They came from the floor, the ceiling. They tore forth from the very walls. It was as though the house itself had begun howling in anguish.

A whiff of aetherial combustion drifted over her, and her stomach clenched with dread. Someone was performing sorcery. What if Ashcroft had spotted her in the Royal Library after all, and had traced her back here—and was now launching an attack on Nathaniel's house?

Without thinking, she headed for Nathaniel's room. He would know what to do. The screams throbbed painfully in her ears as she sprinted down the hallway, poker at the ready. She turned a corner and drew up short.

In the moonlight, something wet glimmered on the walls. She approached the wainscoting with hesitant steps and touched the substance. When she raised her hand, it gleamed crimson on her fingertips.

The walls were weeping blood.

Then she blinked, and everything returned to normal. The screaming ceased. The blood vanished from her fingers. Bewildered, she let the poker fall to her side. In the sudden quiet, she heard voices down the hall. They were coming from Nathaniel's bedroom.

"Master," Silas was saying. "Master, listen to me. It was only a dream."

"Silas!" This raw, tortured voice had to belong to Nathaniel, though it sounded little like him. "He's brought them back again, Mother and Maximilian—"

"Hush. You're awake now."

"He's alive, and he's going to—please, Silas, you must believe me—I saw him—"

"All is well, master. I am here. I will not let you come to harm."

Silence descended like a guillotine. Then, "Silas," Nathaniel gasped, as if he were drowning. "Help me."

Elisabeth felt as if there were a rope attached to her middle, towing her forward. She didn't will her steps to move, but she approached the room nonetheless, transfixed.

The door hung open. Nathaniel sat up in his nightshirt, tangled within a snarl of bedclothes, his hair in a wild state of disarray. His expression was terrible to behold: his pupils had swallowed up his eyes, and he stared as though he saw nothing around him. He was panting, and trembling; his nightshirt clung to his body with sweat. Silas sat on the side of the bed, angled away from Elisabeth, one knee drawn up to face Nathaniel. Though it had to be two or three in the morning, he was still dressed in his livery, aside from his hands, which were bare.

"Drink this," he said softly, reaching for a glass on the nightstand. When Nathaniel tried to grasp the glass and nearly spilled it, Silas guided it to his lips with the surety of many years of practice.

Nathaniel drank. When he finished, he squeezed his eyes shut and slumped back against the headboard. His face twisted as if he were trying to stop himself from weeping, and his hand sought Silas's and clasped it tightly.

Elisabeth suddenly felt that she had seen enough. She withdrew and retreated down the hall. But she lingered at the corner, stepping first in one direction and then another, torn with indecision, as though she were pacing the confines of a cage. She couldn't bring herself to go back to bed. She wouldn't be able to sleep, knowing Nathaniel was in such pain. Not after what she had heard, what he had said. She recalled the comments people had made about Alistair. Nathaniel had been having a nightmare, but was it only a nightmare, or something more?

After several long minutes, Silas appeared in the hall, and she realized that she had been waiting for him. He nodded at her without surprise—he had known she was there the whole time. She couldn't read anything in his expression.

"Will Nathaniel be all right?" she whispered.

"Master Thorn has taken medicine, and shall rest undisturbed until morning." That wasn't precisely an answer to the question she had asked, but before she could say so, he went on, "I would be obliged if you didn't mention tonight's events to my master. He feared this would happen. He has nightmares often. The draught will make him forget."

Oh, thought Elisabeth, and the world seemed to shift ever so slightly beneath her feet. "Is that why he didn't want me to stay here?"

"The answer is complicated—but yes, in part. His nightmares drove his father's human servants from the house long ago. They often cause him to lash out with his magic, as you saw, and he worries that in time, he might lose control in even worse ways."

"So he pushes people from him," she murmured, thinking aloud. "He doesn't let anyone get close." Her gaze drifted to the wall, then back to Silas. "It doesn't bother me. That is—I don't like getting woken up by the sound of screaming, and seeing blood drip down the walls, but I'm not upset by it, now that I know why it happens. I'm not afraid."

Silas considered her for a long moment. "Then perhaps you should speak to my master after all," he said finally. He turned. "Come with me. There is something I must give you. Something that, I regret to say, I have been keeping from you unjustly."

He led her downstairs to a sitting room—one of the many rooms in Nathaniel's house that she had peered into, but had never been inside. He didn't light any lamps, so Elisabeth could barely see. By all rights being alone in the dark with a demon should have frightened her, but she only had the strange thought that perhaps Silas was distressed, in his own way, and was not himself, for he always remembered to light the lamps. She felt her way to a couch and sat down. Silas's alabaster face and hands stood out, disembodied, as though his skin produced its own pale light.

A cabinet door opened and shut. He straightened with a long, slender bundle, which he held cautiously, as if it might burst into flame at any moment.

"This arrived from Summershall the day before I encountered you on the street," he said, holding it out to her. "There was no note, but it was posted by someone named Master Hargrove."

Elisabeth's heart gave a swift, painful throb, like a hammer striking an anvil. She took the bundle with trembling hands. There was only one thing it could be, and when she untied the twine and parted the fabric, the faintest whisper of moonlight glimmered across garnets and a liquid length of blade.

"I don't understand." She looked up at Silas. "Why didn't you give this to me earlier?"

His face was still as marble as he replied, "Iron is one of the few things capable of banishing a demon back to the Otherworld."

She hesitated. "And you thought I might use it against you? I suppose I can't blame you. I would have, once. Not to mention, its name is Demonslayer." She gazed helplessly at the sword. She still hadn't touched it. She couldn't bear to, for fear that it might reject her; that it might scald her as though she herself were a demon.

"Is something wrong, Miss Scrivener?"

"The Director left Demonslayer to me in her will, but I . . . I'm not sure I'm worthy of wielding it." A pressure built in her chest. "I no longer know what is right and what is wrong."

His hands settled over hers, cool and clawed, and gingerly brought them to rest against the sword. "Worry not, Miss Scrivener," he said in his whispering voice. "I can see your soul as clearly as a flame within a glass."

They sat there in silence for a time. Elisabeth remembered that day in the reading room, when the Director had spotted her behind the bookcase and almost smiled. She had been breaking the rules, but the Director hadn't minded. She had left her Demonslayer anyway. And she had not always been the Director—she had had a name, Irena, and she had been a girl once, too, and she'd had doubts and felt uncertain and made mistakes.

Somehow thinking about those things made Elisabeth feel as though she were losing the Director all over again, because she realized now that she had never truly known Irena, and would never get the chance. When a sob escaped her, Silas said nothing. He only passed her his handkerchief, and waited patiently for her to stop crying.

A long moment passed before she was able to speak. She dried her tears and blinked up at Silas. It struck her that he put up with a great deal from the humans in his care.

"Why did you fear my sword," she asked, "if you can't die in the mortal realm?"

A trace of a smile illuminated his beautiful features. "I fear not for myself. If I were banished, my loss would be an inconvenience for Master Thorn. It alarms me to imagine the state of his wardrobe. He would offend young ladies with his cravat."

She laughed, taken by surprise, but it was a painful laugh, for the truth was terribly sad. If something happened to Silas, Nathaniel would be well and truly alone. He'd lose the only family he had left.

"Silas—" She hesitated, then forged onward. "Will you tell me what happened to Alistair Thorn?"

"It is an unpleasant tale. Are you certain you wish to know?" She nodded.

"Very well." He turned and went to the fireplace, gazing at nothing she could discern, except perhaps the ashes. "You recall me telling you that Charlotte and Maximilian perished in an accident. That was the start of it all."

Elisabeth recalled what Nathaniel had said upstairs, terrible possibilities beginning to take shape in her mind. *He's brought them back again, Mother and Maximilian. . . .*

"Alistair was a kind man—a good one, if you will forgive the irony of a demon saying so, and a devoted husband and father. But after the accident, a change came over him. He began studying Baltasar's work day and night. Young Master Thorn grew lonely, and developed a habit of hiding in his father's study for company." Silas paused, as if considering whether to go on. "I shall get to the point. Two months after the deaths of his wife and younger son, Alistair exhumed their bodies and attempted to resurrect them via necromancy, here in this house. The ritual would not have raised them from the dead—not as themselves— but he had lost himself to grief, and would no longer listen to reason."

Ice flowed through Elisabeth's veins. "When you told me that you killed him . . ."

"Yes," Silas whispered. "We were distracted, Alistair and I, and the both of us failed to notice that Master Thorn had hidden himself behind the drapes. He had been there all morning, as quiet as a mouse. We understood that the spell might take Alistair's life, for it was a dark and terrible magic, but I knew when I glimpsed those eyes watching us through the curtains that it would take his son's as well. So I ended it at once, in the only way possible. Master Thorn saw everything: the bodies, the ritual, his father's death at my hands. He sees it still, when he closes his eyes to rest."

Elisabeth said nothing. The horror of it was too extreme. Her stricken thoughts jumped to the journey through the Blackwald, remembering how Nathaniel had stayed up, unable to sleep. How little she had understood.

"There is a lesson to be had from that night." Silas drew his gaze from the hearth and faced her again. He looked perfectly calm. "Alistair trusted me. He believed that I would never harm him, so he failed to command me not to. His trust was his undoing."

"No. He was right to trust you." Elisabeth's stomach twisted. How did Silas not understand? "Had he been in his right mind, he would have wanted you to stop him, no matter the cost. You saved Nathaniel's life."

"And what did I do next, Miss Scrivener?" he inquired.

"What do you mean?"

"When Master Thorn summoned me, while his father's body still lay warm on the floor, what did I do then?"

She had no answer.

"I took his life. Twenty years of it he bargained away to me, when he had scarcely seen the passing of half that number, and did not understand what he was giving, only that he did not want to be alone." He took a step forward. "And it will taste sweet once I have it, just as his father's before him, and the lives of his forebears stretching back three hundred years."

Elisabeth's hands tightened reflexively on Demonslayer. *Two decades.* "But how . . . how could you—?"

"I have devoured them all, Miss Scrivener." He took another step forward. His eyes were yellow slits. He did not look beautiful now. "Do not see compassion where there is none. Was it not to my advantage to save Master Thorn's life, so that I could claim a portion of it for myself?"

Silas was almost upon her. She raised Demonslayer between them and pointed it at his chest to halt his advance. Yet he took a third step forward nonetheless, and the blade pressed against his ribs, over his heart, if he had one. A smell of burnt flesh filled the air.

"Stop this!" she cried. "I don't want to hurt you. I can't. No matter what you've done, Nathaniel needs you."

"Yes," he whispered, as if she saw the truth at last. "You see, there is no absolution, no penance, for a creature such as I." His eyes shone bright with pain. "You could strike me down and the blow would only harm another."

She let the sword fall. Silas neatly stepped back and raised a hand to his chest. Some horrible light seemed to have gone out of him.

"I am a demon," he said. "You cannot see me as anything more."

Elisabeth shook from head to toe. She knew that if she tried to stand, her knees would give out beneath her. But it was not fear she felt. She did not know what this emotion was. Pity, perhaps, though she couldn't tell for whom, and anger and despair, tearing through her like a storm. She believed that Silas cared about Nathaniel; she had seen it as plainly as day. But how could someone care for another and still take so much from them?

Twenty years. If Nathaniel was fated to die young—in his early forties, perhaps—then with that much taken away, he might only have a handful of years left. Her chest squeezed at the thought, the air wrung from her lungs like water from a dishrag. She couldn't meet Silas's gaze any longer.

When she looked down, a gleam of metal caught her eye. Another object lay at the bottom of the wrappings, where it had been concealed beneath Demonslayer. Master Hargrove had sent her more than just a sword. Slowly, she set Demonslayer aside. She reached into the wrappings and lifted out a chain. She ducked her head and drew the chain over it, feeling the weight of her greatkey settle against her chest: cold, but not for long. Then she ran her fingers over the grooves, so familiar they were a part of herself, designed to open the outer doors of any Great Library in the kingdom.

"Silas," she said slowly. "If I got us inside the Royal Library after hours, would you be able to open the gate to the restricted archives?"

He paused. "There is a way."

She looked up at him, gripping the key. "Help me." The storm within her had stilled. "You've taken lives. Now help me save some."

He gazed down at her, beautiful again, an angel considering a mortal's petition from afar. "Is it that simple, Miss Scrivener?" he asked.

"It must be," she replied. "For it's the only thing to do."

TWENTY-ONE

A GREAT LIBRARY NEVER slept, even after all the people had gone to bed. Voices echoed through the atrium as Elisabeth crept along, keeping to the curve of the wall, where her white cloak blended in with the marble. Some of the grimoires snored, while their neighbors made disgruntled noises at them for snoring too loudly; others whispered, and laughed. One lone grimoire sang a piercing lament that soared high above the rest, a sound that lifted past the shafts of blue moonlight spilling through the starry dome, and rang unearthly in the firmament, like music played on a crystal glass.

Whenever a lantern bobbed into view, Elisabeth hid and waited until the warden had passed. The Royal Library was even more heavily patrolled at night than she had expected. She envied Silas, strolling along beside her as a cat. After one particularly close call—the warden came near enough that Elisabeth was able to see her green eyes, and count the number of buttons on her coat—Silas transformed back into a human, and caught her shoulder before she emerged from hiding.

"I must tell you something before we continue," he murmured. "The wardens wear too much iron for me to influence them. If they spot you, I cannot make them turn away and forget what they have seen."

She suspected she knew what he was getting at. "And if that happens, you'll leave me to face the consequences alone?"

He inclined his head, the faintest hint of regret etched across his brow.

"I understand," she whispered. "You owe your loyalty to Nathaniel, not to me."

As they moved on, Elisabeth wondered if her own proximity made Silas uncomfortable. She wore her greatkey, and there was also the thin layer of iron that lined her cloak. Demonslayer, slipped through her belt, formed a reassuring weight at her side. But if it did, he would have to tolerate it. She couldn't enter the archives unprotected.

They passed several more patrols before they reached the entrance to the Northwest Wing. The skeletal angels carved around the archway stared down at her, their eyes hollow pits, bronze skulls agleam, and the hair stood up on her arms as she imagined them turning their heads to watch her go by. But none of them moved. They didn't need to. Far worse things awaited her ahead.

She and Silas slipped past the velvet rope. Mist spilled over her boots and lapped at the hem of her cloak. It was thicker now than in the daytime, no doubt a magical emanation of one of the grimoires inside the archives. Silas, a cat again and only visible as a swirl of movement within the mist, headed toward the gate. Elisabeth forced herself not to take in its looming presence, still fresh from her dreams. Instead she focused on what Silas had instructed her to do before they'd set out. It was going to take both of them, working together, to sneak inside undetected.

She pressed herself into an alcove in the wall and waited for a warden to pass, his lantern floating eerily through the mist. Then she darted back out of hiding. They had about a minute until the next warden came by.

Silas already stood inside the archives, having squeezed between the gate's bars before transforming back into his human shape. She followed his gaze as he nodded upward. There, above the gate, some fifteen feet off the ground, hung an iron bell. She set her boots against the ironwork and began to climb.

She soon wished that she had brought a pair of gloves. Her sweaty palms found little purchase against the bars, which were already slick with moisture from the mist. It took her more than twice as long to scale the gate than she had estimated—long enough that the next patrol came walking past while she clung to the ironwork high above. She held her breath, her shoulders aching with the effort of remaining still, but the warden didn't look up. His silhouette faded into the mist.

Freeing a hand, she retrieved a wad of cotton and piece of twine from one of her belt pouches. She wrapped the cotton around the bell's clapper, and used her teeth to help tie it in place. When she was finished, she slid back down and landed with a bone-jarring impact on the flagstones. Silas reappeared opposite the bars. He had taken off his jacket and now used it to protect his hand from the iron as he turned a latch on the gate. It swung open silently on well-greased hinges.

"The gate is designed to open from within," he had explained earlier. "It is a fail-safe, so no one is able to get trapped inside if their key is taken from them. But there is, of course, a mechanism in place to alert the other wardens should such an event occur."

Above them, the bell swung frantically back and forth, but barely made a sound. Elisabeth's tampering had succeeded. She slipped inside, aware the most dangerous part was yet to come.

If their key is taken from them, Silas had said. Not if they *lost* their key, for no warden would be foolish enough to misplace their key ring.

The restricted archives stretched down a long corridor, lined on either side by towering bookshelves that rose from the mist and spanned upward into darkness. Lanterns hung from iron posts at regular intervals, creating a path down the center. She had the unsettling feeling that the lanterns were meant to keep people from getting lost, even though the hallway appeared to travel forward in a straight, unbroken line. Her gaze wandered to the shelves, then darted back ahead. Most of the grimoires were chained to the bookcases. But the most dangerous ones had their own displays, raised up on pedestals or locked away in cages. During her brief look she'd caught sight of a manuscript bound with stitched-together human skin, imprisoned inside a cage studded with spikes like a medieval torture device. Another had teeth embroidered along the edges of its cover, restrained by an iron bit shoved between its pages. All of them were silent, watching her. Waiting to see what she would do.

She turned to speak to Silas, but he was nowhere to be seen. He had vanished into thin air, leaving the gate open behind him. She shouldn't have been surprised, but his abandonment stung all the same. Perhaps he was trying to reinforce his message from the other night: that he was a demon, and not to be trusted.

It didn't matter, she told herself. She had only needed him to get inside. The rest, she could do on her own.

As soon as the gate clicked shut, the muttering began. Voices of every description crept and slithered and hopped along the corridor. Her skin crawled; she could almost feel the voices reaching from the mist and grasping at her like hands. She drew her iron-laced hood over her head, and the sounds faded to a distant, sinister mumbling.

She set out down the corridor, following the path of lamp-light through the center. The Codex's call number indicated that it was shelved about halfway down the archives. Now it was only a matter of finding it, removing it from the shelf, and sneaking back the way she had come. The hardest part would be climbing up the gate again to fix the bell after she escaped. She didn't know what to expect from the Codex—whether it would cooperate with her like the copy in Ashcroft's study, or whether it would fight her all the way out of the Royal Library.

Without warning, a tall, pale form rose from the floor nearby. Elisabeth whirled around, sweeping her cloak aside to grip Demonslayer's hilt. Nothing was there—only an eddy in the mist, and a display pedestal made of white stone. She had glimpsed the pedestal out of the corner of her eye and mistaken it for a person. Cursing herself, she turned back ahead.

And like a scene from her nightmares, Chancellor Ashcroft stood before her. He looked just the same as she had last seen him, but waxen, his handsome face devoid of expression, both the blue eye and the red one staring straight through her. His golden cloak seemed to be spun from lamplight and mist. With a choked-off cry, Elisabeth yanked Demonslayer from her belt and swung it through the air.

Ashcroft stepped out of range. The faintest of smiles tugged at his mouth. She swung once more, and again he retreated, her sword missing by a hair. That slight, taunting smile suggested that he knew precisely why she was here.

This time, she had no doubt that he would kill her. Even

armed with iron, she was no match for his magic. But he appeared content to toy with her first, and she wouldn't go down without a fight, not if there was even the slightest chance of stopping him. They moved through the archives in a silent dance: Elisabeth slicing the mist to ribbons, Ashcroft backing toward the shelves.

Then he failed to step quickly enough, and her sword slashed through him.

He dissolved into mist.

More figures emerged from the shadows, advancing toward her. Warden Finch. Lorelei. Mr. Hob. Even the man who had cornered her in the alley—and he wasn't the only dead person among them. The Director also rose from the mist, her spectral face grim with disappointment. They drew closer and closer, but Elisabeth didn't step back, even though the Director's expression made her stomach curdle. The figures weren't real. Whoever had conjured them, on the other hand—

"Whatever you are, you're showing me my fears," she declared, surprised by how steady her voice sounded. "You're trying to trap me, aren't you?"

She sheathed Demonslayer and turned. A large, ornate display cage stood directly behind her. Had she taken even one more step, away from the illusions, she would have run into it. As soon as she realized that, the figures subsided back into the mist.

A woman's pale, withered face gazed out at her from within the cage, mere inches away, floating in the darkness. Or it would have gazed at her, had the eyes not been stitched shut. And the face didn't belong to a person, at least not any longer: it had been sewn onto a grimoire's cover, which levitated opposite Elisabeth amid a swirl of vapor. A black ribbon twirled through the air around the grimoire, a silver needle gleaming on its end.

"*Smart girl.*" The grimoire spoke in a hissing, multitudinous voice: men, women, and children all speaking in chorus, each one as dry as sand whispering over bone. "*We've taken three wardens with that trick, now that we've convinced the Illusarium to help us. Too bad. Such an interesting face you have. Not beautiful, but bold.*"

The grimoire was unusually thick and heavily bound, filled with—*more faces*, Elisabeth thought in horror, as the binding creaked and the cover lifted, flipping past page after page of human faces, Enochian script simmering across them like freshly laid brands. At last it settled on an empty page and lovingly caressed the bare vellum with its needle.

"*We have room for you, if you ever change your mind.*"

"No, thank you," Elisabeth said, inching away.

"*Our stitches are neat. It would only hurt a little. . . .*"

Elisabeth squared her shoulders and wheeled around, mindful not to bump into the white stone pedestal she had seen earlier, situated just a few feet away from the cage. A plaque beneath the pedestal read THE ILLUSARIUM, CLASS VII, and atop it sat a glass sphere like a fortune-teller's crystal ball. So much mist poured from the sphere that she couldn't make out the shape within. If this grimoire possessed a voice, it chose to remain silent. Perhaps it could only communicate using its illusions.

She forced herself to keep walking and not look back, even though she could almost feel the first grimoire's needle scratching between her shoulder blades. When she drew near the section numbered on the catalogue card, her steps slowed, and her head tilted back. She swallowed.

A ladder ascended over three stories into the gloom, mist lapping at its bottom rungs. The call number suggested that the

Codex was at the top, where the lamplight barely reached. She steeled herself and placed her boot on the lowest rung, ignoring the spiteful jeers of the grimoires on the shelves. As she began her ascent, they rattled their chains with enough force to make the ladder bounce and tremble. Wads of ink flew past her into the dark.

Part of her expected to reach the top and find the Codex missing. It seemed that she had come too far, and faced too many trials, for any aspect of this mission to come easily to her. But when she finally hauled herself up to the final rung, the Codex's familiar scaled cover awaited her, encircled by chains. The secret to Ashcroft's plan, close enough to touch.

She reached for the chains, and then froze. Her joints locked; her muscles refused to obey. She had come here to steal from the Royal Library, but now that the moment was upon her, every fiber of her body revolted. Once she crossed this line, there was no going back. She imagined getting caught, having to face Parsifal and Mistress Wick, who had both treated her so kindly. Her heart burned with shame.

"Think of it as more of a rescue mission," Katrien had told her during their last, brief conversation through the mirror. "I'm sure the Codex would much rather be with you than with people who think it was written by a madman. Can you imagine what that would be like, knowing some sort of enormous secret and no one believing you?"

Yes, Elisabeth thought, with a wrench in her chest. For the Codex, this place must be as bad as Leadgate Hospital. Books, too, had hearts, though they were not the same as people's, and a book's heart could be broken: she had seen it happen before. Grimoires that refused to open, their voices gone silent, or whose ink faded and bled across the pages like tears.

The Codex looked as though no one had touched it in decades. Dust coated its chains, and a neglected case of Brittle-Spine had left its leather cracked and graying. It didn't stir at her arrival, as though the passage of time had reduced it to an ordinary book.

Just like that, she found she could move again. "I'm here to help you," she whispered. She gently unhooked its chains from the shelf. The other grimoires began rattling harder than ever, their nasty mutterings turning into desperate pleas as they watched their neighbor gain its freedom, but the Codex remained still, almost lifeless. It didn't resist her as she tucked it, chains and all, into a sack tied to her belt.

By the time she climbed back down the ladder, the grimoires had stopped rattling. A profound hush had fallen over the archives. No sinister voices whispered. No ominous figures appeared from the mist. The silence didn't feel hostile, but Elisabeth wasn't going to linger. As she strode quickly past the cage from earlier, the pale face inside rotated to watch her.

"It's been waiting a long time, that one," it whispered. *"So long since the Codex has known a kind touch, an open mind. But I see now that you are not the same as the other humans . . . you are different, somehow . . . yes, a true child of the library. . . ."*

Elisabeth's steps faltered. She wanted to listen to what the grimoire had to say. But right now, she didn't have time to chat with books.

A mixture of relief and regret flooded her as she slipped through the gate, leaving the archives behind. She waited until a patrol had passed, then shimmied up the gate to restore the bell, weighed down by the Codex's awkward bulk at her hip. The grimoire's words echoed in her mind as she turned to go. *A true child of the library.* What had it meant? How had it known?

The Book of Eyes had said there was something different about her, too.

She took one step toward the atrium. Before she could take a second, a hand shot from the mist and seized her cloak. With ruthless strength, it dragged her from the center of the hallway and into the same alcove she had hidden in before. But when the hand fell away, she didn't bolt or reach for Demonslayer. Silas stood in front of her, luminously pale, crouched between the hooded figures carved into the wall.

So he didn't abandon me after all, she thought in wonderment. *But where has he been?*

Before she could ask the question aloud, he held a finger to his lips. His yellow eyes flicked toward the hallway.

Lights shone through the mist. Wheels groaned as something heavy rolled along the corridor, accompanied by footsteps. The sounds swirled eerily, distorted by the stone and the mist, but they had to be coming from the direction of the vault. Elisabeth held her breath as the first warden emerged into view. She had a lantern in one hand, a drawn sword in the other. More wardens followed, a good dozen in all. Near the head of the procession strode Mistress Wick, elegant in her long indigo robes, and a man who could be none other than the Royal Library's Director. Medals decorated his blue coat. Gray hair fell loose to his shoulders, concealing some of the brutal scars that slashed across his face. Two fingers were missing from his hand, which rested on the hilt of an enormous broadsword.

"Are you certain this is wise, Marius?" asked Mistress Wick.

"No," the man replied grimly. "But we cannot take the risk."

Mistress Wick's brow furrowed. "If the saboteur's pattern continues, he is almost certain to strike Harrows. I can't help but feel we are playing into his hands."

"Be that as it may, there is no other vault in Austermeer that can contain the Chronicles of the Dead. The saboteur might decide to target the Royal Library at any time. And if he sets loose the Chronicles, every man, woman, and child in Brass-bridge will be dead by sunrise."

Elisabeth's skin prickled. She didn't recognize the title, but at Ashcroft's dinner, Lady Ingram had mentioned a grimoire written by Baltasar Thorn—a grimoire of necromancy. Only a handful of necromantic texts existed. Were they discussing the same one?

"It's true that Harrows is best prepared." Mistress Wick gazed sightlessly ahead. "And Director Hyde?"

"Hyde understands his duty. He accepts that he will die if he must, if it comes to that. If his sacrifice saves thousands."

The groaning and squeaking of the wheels drowned out their voices. A shape materialized from the darkness, sailing through the mist like a black ship skimming over ghostly waters. It was a cage, a great wheeled cage, which at first appeared to have nothing inside. Then the lamplight flowed through it, and Elisabeth made out an iron coffer hanging at the center, fixed there by a web of chains stretched taut from each of the cage's corners.

Her mouth went dry, and a cold finger drew down her spine. The shadow that fell upon the wall between the wardens didn't belong to a cage. Something else's shape rippled along the stone, stretching all the way to the ceiling many stories above, where it crooked sideways to flow across the ribbed arches overhead. Taloned fingers twitched above the wardens as though grasping for them, each claw as long as a sword. Though the shadow was too vast, too distorted by the masonry for Elisabeth to discern its features, something about its form seemed chillingly familiar.

A Class Ten. The way they spoke of the grimoire, it had to be. Even as a future warden, she had never expected to see one. Much less that she would stumble across a transfer in progress—the first of its kind in hundreds of years.

Soon, all three of the kingdom's Class Ten grimoires would be in the vault at Harrows.

TWENTY-TWO

ELISABETH DUNKED HER mop in the soapy bucket, then slopped it across the floor, pushing suds across the flagstones. Dirty water sloshed ahead, evicting booklice from their hiding places in the molding. She didn't have the energy to chase them. As she watched one fat louse skitter in a panicked circle, she paused to lean on the mop. Her eyelids drifted shut. Just one moment. One moment to rest her eyes . . .

"Good heavens, girl! What's gotten into you?"

Elisabeth jolted awake, her heart seizing as she saw a long shadow stretching up the wall. But she blinked, and it was only Gertrude, her fists resting on her hips.

"You aren't carrying on with some young man, are you? Well, let me tell you," Gertrude said, lifting the heavy bucket and hoisting it down the hallway for her in a rare display of kindness, "he isn't worth it. Not if he keeps you up at night and makes the rest of your life a misery. There you are, you silly girl."

Elisabeth nodded mechanically and resumed mopping. Her

limbs felt like they were made of lead. Grit and sand filled her eyes. If only Gertrude knew the truth.

By the time she'd gotten out of the Royal Library earlier that morning, the city's bells had been ringing the fifth hour, and the servants of Hemlock Park were already bustling about their work in the predawn dark. Though she had felt perfectly awake in the archives, her two nights of lost sleep came crashing down on the return journey. Her vision had begun to blur; her steps had weaved like a drunkard's. When she reached Nathaniel's house and stumbled on the threshold, she dimly recalled Silas lifting her and carrying her upstairs. He had helped her get ready for work while she dozed on her feet. Then, before she knew it, she was back at the library.

It had taken all her willpower not to skip work in favor of starting on the Codex. There was nothing more frustrating than spending her morning mopping floors, knowing that Ashcroft could make his next move at any moment. But she couldn't risk attracting attention. This was only her third day working at the Royal Library, and if she vanished right after the theft of a Class Six grimoire, Mistress Wick would take note. Better to spend her morning mopping floors than languishing in the dungeon.

So far, she hadn't noticed any signs that the Codex had been missed. No bells began ringing; no wardens came sprinting past. The morning crept by in a woolly haze of exhaustion.

At noon, Gertrude granted her an hour off and commanded her to take a nap, then return to work prepared to earn her pay. Elisabeth carried her lunch to a room that Parsifal had shown her in the South Spire. It looked out over the grounds, the broad swaths of green hemmed in by clumps of trees resplendent in shades of red and rusty orange. It was a crisp, sunny autumn day, and the wardens-in-training were out practicing drills. She cracked a window so that the distant sounds of shouting and swords clashing drifted in on the breeze. The trainees weren't much older than Elisabeth. Just weeks ago, she would have easily envisioned herself among them. Now she felt as though she were a ghost haunting her own body, gazing at her life through a dirty glass. She wasn't certain where she belonged—or, stranger still, what she even wanted. After knowing Nathaniel and Silas, could she truly declare magic her enemy, and go back to the way she had been before?

She was halfway through lunch, seated at a worktable in the corner, when Parsifal appeared in the doorway. "I thought you might be up here," he said. "Can I join you?"

When she nodded, he came over to look out the window. "I was too embarrassed to tell you the other day, but I used to come up here because the other apprentices bullied me. That's what happens when you have a name like Parsifal. I'd fantasize about how I'd be a warden one day and make them sorry."

She stopped chewing her apple. "You wanted to become a warden?"

"Don't look *too* surprised. Of course I did. Every apprentice wants to be one. Sometimes for the right reasons, but mostly because they fancy the idea of being in charge and thrashing other apprentices for a living."

"That isn't true," she protested, but then she thought of Warden Finch, and had to admit he had a point. "What made you change your mind?"

He shrugged. "I'm not sure. It's just that there's more to life than looking grim and stabbing things with swords, isn't there? There are other ways to make a difference." He stood there fiddling with his key ring, as if he were working up the courage to say something. As the seconds spun on, she began to feel uneasy.

"Elisabeth," he blurted out, "I know you told the steward your name is Elisabeth Cross. But are you . . . are you Elisabeth Scrivener, from the papers?"

The blood drained from Elisabeth's face. Her first name was so common, she thought she had been safe keeping it.

"I won't tell anyone," Parsifal hurried to add. "No one else knows. It's just that I kept thinking about it the other day, when I gave you the tour, and you knew far too much about grimoires for someone who'd never been inside a Great Library before. And you see, I'd been, ah, following your story in the news." His ears turned red. "I just—since you defeated a Class Eight Malefict, and all."

Elisabeth lurched upright. "Has there been anything else about me in the news?"

"No—nothing! That's why I wanted to . . . it was as though you completely vanished after the Chancellor's press release." He glanced over his shoulder. Then he lowered his voice. "Are you on some sort of secret mission for the Collegium? Have you been sent undercover?"

She stared.

"Right," he said knowingly, tapping the side of his nose. "You wouldn't be able to tell me if you were."

"That's correct," she said weakly, wondering how much trouble it was possible for a person to get into in one lifetime.

He glanced over his shoulder again. "Well—I have some information for you. I overheard two wardens talking this morning. Apparently, the saboteur struck the Royal Library last night."

"*What?*"

"He stole a Class Six grimoire while the wardens were performing a transfer from the vault. They've been keeping it quiet, because they don't want to send the press into a frenzy. But I thought you ought to be aware. For, you know"—he lowered his voice further—"your investigation."

"Thank you, Parsifal," she said. "Now, I should get back to— er—" She nodded toward the window, hoping Parsifal would use his imagination.

"Oh, yes, certainly! Is this a stakeout? Are you watching for someone? Right, you can't tell me. I shouldn't even be here. I'll just . . ." He inched toward the doorway. She nodded at him encouragingly and tapped the side of her nose. He hurried out of sight, looking thrilled.

Elisabeth blew out a breath and collapsed back into her chair. At least one good thing had come out of that. If the wardens believed the saboteur had stolen the Codex, they weren't likely to cast their suspicions toward a lowly maidservant. Perhaps after a few more days had passed, she could turn her full attention to Ashcroft without distractions. Now that the Chronicles of the Dead was on its way to Harrows, the need was more urgent than ever.

She barely recalled dragging herself home and up the stairs to her bedroom. The only detail that stood out to her was that she hadn't seen Nathaniel since his nightmare. He had remained shut inside his study all day yesterday, and judging by the emerald light that flickered beneath the door, he was still in there. She wondered if he had even left the room.

Upstairs, she lit a candle. She didn't change out of her servant's uniform, aware she might need the salt and iron on hand. Demonslayer went on the floor beside her, within reaching distance, but not close enough to appear threatening. She didn't want the Codex to perceive her as its enemy.

The grimoire waited under her bed, still inside the sack she had used to smuggle it from the Royal Library. She drew it out and placed it on her lap, feeling the heavy chains clink through the fabric. Seated on the floor, with her back against the mattress, she folded aside the burlap and unraveled the chain onto the carpet. The Codex lay inert and unresponsive. She drew in a fortifying breath, her hand suspended in the air.

"I'm a friend," she said, willing her intentions to pass down her arm, through her skin, as she placed her palm against the grimoire.

For a moment, nothing happened. No voice howled at her in rage and betrayal. No ominous pressure filled the room. All was silent. Then its pages stirred in an invisible breeze. Slowly, like an old man stretching and rising from sleep, the Codex unfolded itself into her hands.

Hope thrilled through her, followed by a quaver of apprehension. If Ashcroft had spent so much time studying this grimoire without success, why should she succeed where he had failed? Unlike him, she didn't have the slightest idea what Prendergast's secret might be about, and she knew next to nothing about codes and ciphers, either. Reaching this step had consumed so much of her attention that she hadn't had time to prepare for what came afterward.

She scanned the pages that had opened to her. The words swam in her vision, and she tried blinking away her exhaustion, only to discover that her eyes weren't at fault. It was the words that were moving, the ink bleeding in sluggish rivulets across the parchment. She flipped to a different section, past diagrams labeled with Enochian script, and found the same thing happening there, too. While the text itself was legible, the sentences had crawled completely out of order. Occasionally they aligned in such a way that a single paragraph became comprehensible:

The highborn demons hold their glittering court beneath a sunless sky. Once every fortnight they ride forth on horned white horses, clad in silks, to hunt beasts in the forests of the Otherworld with packs of baying fiends at their sides. The sound of a demonic hunting horn is not soon forgotten; for it is so beautiful, and so terrible, that it freezes the quarry of the hunt in place as if the prey has turned to stone. . . .

But the rest split apart before she could finish, the sentences meandering across the page like lines of marching ants. Frustrated, she turned to the scrying mirror and called for Katrien. When her friend's face appeared in the glass, she looked as tired as Elisabeth felt, ashen beneath the glass's patina of frost. They didn't have time to catch up. They raced through the likeliest possibilities as swiftly as they could, barely pausing for breath.

"The sentences might only fully align at a specific date and time," Elisabeth theorized, "like midnight on the winter solstice, or during certain conditions, like an eclipse."

"But Ashcroft's certain that he can crack it soon, isn't he? So if that's the case, either the phenomenon is due to happen sometime within the next two weeks, or—"

"Or the cipher has a different solution entirely," Elisabeth finished, glum.

"Take a second look at your research," Katrien urged. "There might be a clue that didn't seem relevant before. Do we even know for sure that Prendergast hid his secret as a cipher, or is that just an assumption people made without evidence? In the meantime, I'll see if I can find anything on my end."

As their time ran out, Elisabeth swallowed back the pitiful urge to beg Katrien not to go, watching her disappear beneath the ice. Loneliness pressed in, made worse by her fuzzy-headed exhaustion. She knew she should go to bed, but she was too tired to get up from the floor and wrap the Codex in its chain.

Instead she found herself idly turning pages, hypnotized by the crawling text. As the sentences strung themselves together, she read lavish, unsettling descriptions of what the demons ate at their feasts, or what they wore to their nocturnal, weeklong balls. Though the fragmented descriptions left her feeling more and more disturbed, she was unable to tear her eyes away.

Swans poisoned to death with nightshade are considered a particular delicacy at banquets. . . .

The most fashionable garment that evening was a gown made of silver moths, pinned alive to the fabric to preserve their luster. . . .

The candle burned lower on the nightstand. Her head nodded. Disjointed images swirled behind her eyelids: demons dancing in elaborate costumes, grinning as they feasted, tearing into flesh. The nightmarish fancies seemed to take hold of her and drag her downward, like the hands of sirens gripping a shipwrecked sailor, towing him into the deep and silent dark.

Abruptly, she woke up.

Or, she didn't wake up—for this had to be a dream.

She stood in some kind of old-fashioned workshop. Unfamiliar herbs hung in bundles from the rafters. Tallow candles flickered on every surface, spattering the stained floorboards with oily yellow wax. Bizarre items cluttered the shelves and the table in the center of the room: bird feathers, animal skulls, jars containing murky globs floating in vinegar. But that wasn't the part that convinced her she was dreaming. The room hung suspended in a void. The broken edges of its floorboards jutted out into a black abyss, and chunks of the ceiling had fallen inward, showing the same dark nothingness above.

No—not nothingness. The shining black substance reminded

her of something familiar. A rich, telltale scent of pigments filled the air. Ink.

"Who are you?" said a man's voice behind her, harsh with anger. "What are you doing here?"

Elisabeth spun around, her heart slamming against her ribs.

The man who stood there matched how she had always imagined a sorcerer would look before meeting Nathaniel and Ashcroft. Tall, gaunt, and sallow, with glittering obsidian eyes and a closely trimmed black beard that ended in a point at his chin. He wore flowing robes, and rings adorned each of his fingers, set with differently colored gems.

"Whoever you are, I refuse to tell you anything," he snapped. "I haven't spent hundreds of years trapped in this place for nothing."

Hundreds of years. He sounded serious. Now that she took in his expression, she saw that he wasn't angry, not entirely. Underneath the anger, he looked afraid, as though she had come to take something from him by force. His robes appeared old-fashioned, and so did everything else in the workshop, untouched by time for centuries.

Whatever this place was, it wasn't a dream. And neither was this man—this sorcerer. She glanced again at the inky void that surrounded them, her eyes widening as possibility dawned. Prendergast had hidden his secret *inside* the Codex.

She turned back to the sorcerer. "Are you Aldous Prendergast?"

That wasn't the right thing to say. His face darkened, and he crossed the distance between them in several quick strides. "How did you get here?" he demanded, seizing her shoulders. He shook her until her teeth rattled. "Answer me, girl!"

"I don't know! I was reading the Codex. I fell asleep."

"That is impossible," he snarled.

"A strange thing to say," she blurted out, "for someone who's over three hundred years old. That doesn't seem possible to me, either."

Prendergast's shoulders slumped. He let go of her shoulders and gripped the edge of the table, glaring. She found to her surprise that she wasn't the least bit afraid of him. He was so thin, she could easily push him off the end of the floor if he tried to harm her.

"What year is it?" he asked finally, directing his glare at a bottle filled with what appeared to be preserved rat tails.

Questions crowded against the back of her tongue, but she suspected he wouldn't bother answering any of them until she answered his first. "Eighteen twenty-four."

He digested her answer. "I'm not alive," he said after a long, fatalistic pause. "Not in any real sense."

Elisabeth recoiled. "Necromancy," she gasped, seeing his hollow cheeks and cadaverous figure anew.

"No, not necromancy, you idiot child," he snapped. "I am not a corpse. I left my physical body behind in the mortal realm, and anchored my mind to this—this—well, I don't imagine you would understand. You are no sorcerer, clearly, unless the standards have deteriorated significantly since my time. All you need to know is that I am trapped here by my own design. I cannot leave this place. And you should not have been able to visit me through the Codex—not without my permission."

She looked around. "Are we inside the Codex? An alternate dimension of some kind?"

His eyes narrowed. "So you do know your thaumaturgical theory."

Elisabeth decided not to tell him that she simply read a lot of novels.

"This is an artificial plane of existence," he went on grudgingly, "anchored to my grimoire, no bigger than the room surrounding us. To attempt to create a larger one would risk destabilizing the border between the mortal realm and the Otherworld."

"You truly have been there, then," she said. "To the Otherworld."

His eyes narrowed further. "Most people didn't believe me. They accused me of fabricating my studies."

"Aside from one man." She watched his expression closely. "A man who called himself your friend."

His face convulsed. "Who are you?" he rasped.

"My name is Elisabeth Scrivener. I am—I was—an apprentice librarian. But that isn't important. There is no cipher hidden inside the Codex, is there? *You* are the cipher. You hid yourself here to escape from Cornelius Ashcroft."

The color bled from Prendergast's fingers, still gripping the table.

"If you hadn't," she continued, the truth dawning on her as she spoke, "he would have used magic to read your memories, and whatever secret you're guarding, he would have taken it from you by force." Seeing his widened eyes, she explained, "His descendant tried to do the same thing to me."

Prendergast stared at her a moment longer, and then began to laugh. There was a high-pitched nervousness to his laughter that alarmed Elisabeth. She reminded herself that he had been trapped here for hundreds of years, alone, and she hadn't reacted so differently after being taken in by Nathaniel.

"You're lying," he said, once he had caught his breath. "I see it now. You are in league with the Ashcrofts. There is no other way you could know . . . that you would guess . . ."

"I'm not! I swear it."

"I know one thing for certain: Ashcrofts do not leave their victims intact." A feverish sheen glazed his eyes. "Can you even begin to imagine what drove me to choose an eternity of isolation over the attentions of my dear old friend? I left *everything* behind. My real body became a mindless, drooling husk. But that is what Cornelius would have done to me anyway when he finished tearing my mind apart. At least this way I was able to thwart him, the devil." Prendergast spoke with sudden ferocity. "He will never have it. And neither will you."

"Have *what*?"

Prendergast didn't answer. He spun and began to walk away, his robes billowing out around him, though there was nowhere he could go except deeper into the workshop, among the cluttered, sagging shelves.

"You may have outsmarted Cornelius," Elisabeth cried, hurrying after him, "but his descendant is after your secret now. He knows you're here, and he'll stop at nothing to find you."

Prendergast waved a thin hand, the gems on his fingers winking in the candlelight. "It doesn't matter. He will not be able to—"

"Get here, like I just did?"

He went still. "You're wasting your time."

"Listen to me," she urged. "I sought out your grimoire because he's been releasing Maleficts from the Great Libraries. Dozens of people have died. I need to find out why he's doing it, so I can bring proof to the Collegium. Otherwise, he'll never face justice."

Silence reigned. "So he's begun, has he," said Prendergast finally, weary. "He's trying to finish what Cornelius started."

"If you would only tell me what he's planning. I know that whatever it is, it hinges upon the Great Library of Harrows—"

Prendergast's voice lashed out like a whip. "Enough! Leave me be. It doesn't matter what he's planning, because"—he bent over, bracing his hands on his knees, and forced out the rest—"without me—he cannot succeed."

She hadn't come this far, stolen from the Royal Library, sought help from a demon, only to give up now. She strode up behind Prendergast and seized him by the arm. At her touch, his entire body shuddered, and he collapsed to his knees. Pain twisted his gaunt face.

Guilt overwhelmed Elisabeth. "Are you all right?"

But as soon as she spoke, she saw that whatever was going on, it wasn't limited to Prendergast. The candles sputtered, guttering in pools of wax. Darkness fell over the workshop. Then the floor heaved, a seismic convulsion that almost threw Elisabeth from her feet. Jars rolled from the table and shattered.

"The Codex Daemonicus," Prendergast gritted out. "Something is happening to the grimoire. You're in danger, girl. Your body is still in the mortal realm."

Her heart pounded in her throat. "How do I go back? I don't even know how I got here."

"Jump!" he snarled.

She didn't have time to think about his order—not with the world shaking apart around her. She sprinted toward the edge, gathering her strength, and hurled herself over the jagged ends of the floorboards, thinking, *This isn't real. It's only in my mind. I will not fall.*

But it felt like falling: tumbling end over end through the air until she had no sense of up or down, the bitter taste of ink filling her mouth, flooding her nose, choking her—

She woke with a gasp and a sense of impact, as though her soul had been slammed back into her body by force. She sat on the floor of her bedroom, dazed, with the Codex cradled on her lap.

The candle had gone out. Not because it had finished burning, but because she had slid sideways in her sleep and bumped her shoulder against the nightstand. This had knocked the candlestick over, drowning the flame. She counted herself lucky that the tipped candle hadn't started a fire. But she quickly changed her mind, because it had done something even worse.

Droplets of hot wax had splattered across the Codex's pages. As she watched, ink spread outward from the edges of the wax like a bloodstain, soaking through the paper, turning the pages black. She scrambled upright, flipping the grimoire onto the carpet. Overturned, its cover heaved and bulged as though something inside were trying to escape. Its moonlit shadow lengthened across the floor. Elisabeth tore a salt round from her belt, not a moment too soon, for the second she reacted, a thin, scaled hand stretched twitching across the floor and seized her ankle in its shriveled grasp.

The Codex had transformed into a Malefict.

TWENTY-THREE

ELISABETH TASTED SALT as the round exploded, filling the room with glittering particles, unexpectedly beautiful in the moonlight, like snow. The fingers loosened enough for her to wrench her ankle free. The Malefict answered with a ragged shriek. There came a confused flurry of movement, scaled limbs lashing out in every direction, and then the bedroom door tore straight from its hinges, letting in a spill of light from the sconces in the hall. A stooped, long-eared figure stood silhouetted in the doorway. Another shriek, and it flung itself around the corner.

She snatched Demonslayer from the floor and set off in pursuit, leaping over the splintered remains of the door. The Malefict sped down the hallway with a limping gait, the origin of its binding now clear. It resembled the imps from Ashcroft Manor, but its crimson scales were dusty and desiccated, and seams of stitching ran across its hide. Booklice had left its ears tattered. Patches of gold leaf clung to its body, dull and scabrous with age.

When it reached the stairs, it skittered down on all fours, its claws leaving gashes on the carpeting. At the bottom it careened into a table, sending a vase toppling to the marble tiles. Roses tumbled across the floor amid a cascade of water and broken porcelain. How long had there been fresh flowers in the foyer? Elisabeth hadn't noticed.

She dismissed the steps in favor of sliding down the rail, leaping into the fray while the Malefict scrambled to regain its footing on the slick tiles. She advanced on it slowly, Demonslayer held at the ready. It cowered away from her, clutching its emaciated hands to its chest, its ink-black eyes round and glistening. She suppressed a surge of pity as she cornered it against the wall. She wasn't about to underestimate its strength—not after what it had done to her door. An agitated Class Six was more than capable of overpowering a warden.

"What on earth is going on out here?"

Elisabeth froze at the sound of Nathaniel's voice coming from the hall. A moment later he stepped into the foyer's moonlight, fully dressed despite the hour. He stopped and leaned against the entryway, calmly evaluating the scene, as if he walked in on this sort of chaos daily.

Her stomach performed a strange maneuver. Her last memory of him, pale and trembling, reaching for Silas's hand, still felt recent enough to touch. Now that she had seen him that way, it seemed impossible for him to look so collected. So normal, as though nothing about him had changed. But then—nothing had. He had been hiding his pain from her all along. Not just her, but everyone save Silas, who alone had understood.

"Scrivener," he sighed. "I should have known it was you the moment I heard my great-grandmother's priceless antique vase hit the floor." He turned his assessing gaze to the Malefict. "And who's this? A friend of yours?"

The Codex bared a mouthful of fangs and produced an ear-splitting shriek. Above them, the chandelier trembled.

"Charmed," Nathaniel said. He turned back to Elisabeth. "If the two of you feel the need to destroy anything else, I've been meaning to get rid of Aunt Clothilde's tapestry for years. You'll know it when you see it. It's mauve."

Elisabeth opened her mouth several times before she could speak. "I need your help."

"What for? You look like you have the situation under control."

"Can you turn a Malefict back into a grimoire? With sorcery?"

"Possibly, assuming it's not too powerful." Nathaniel raised an eyebrow. "Why?"

She resisted the urge to grit her teeth. Nightmares aside, he was as infuriating as ever. "This grimoire is important evidence against Ashcroft." Pained, she admitted, "It's the only thing I have."

Both of his eyebrows shot up. "I *knew* you were up to something at the Royal Library. Theft, though? Really, Scrivener?"

Blood rushed hotly to her cheeks. Her grip on Demonslayer loosened. She sensed the mistake the moment she made it—she couldn't afford to become distracted—but she reacted a split second too late as the Malefict sprang into action, striking her aside and barreling past her guard. The next thing she knew, she lay sprawled on the floor, the air slammed from her lungs.

Don't let it escape, she thought desperately. If the Codex escaped, all would be lost.

The syllables of an incantation scorched the air. Emerald light swirled above her, reflecting on the wet tiles, limning the petals of the scattered roses. Elisabeth raised herself on one elbow, coughing, to see the Malefict frozen in midleap a mere hand-span from the windows. Nathaniel stood behind it, one arm outflung, so rigid with tension that a vein stood out in his neck. His hand shook with effort as his lips formed the words of the spell.

Slowly, surely, the Malefict began to fold inward on itself. The limbs curled, the head bowed, the scaled hide shrank inward. Its shape grew smaller and smaller. And then the light vanished, and the Codex dropped to the floor, intact, with a slam that resounded through the foyer.

Gingerly, Elisabeth scraped to her feet as Nathaniel doubled over, panting. He bit back a muffled groan, and she realized that she had asked far more of him than she'd imagined. She had felt confident Nathaniel could handle magic like this—Nathaniel, who brought stone to life and summoned storms—but in truth, she had never heard of a Malefict's condition being reversed. If it were easy, there would be no need for the Great Libraries or wardens.

"Nathaniel," she said. She stepped toward him, and collapsed.

Darkness swam before her eyes. Blood roared in her ears. Through the crashing waves of dizziness, she grew aware of someone holding her. She blinked rapidly, and the world filled back in. Nathaniel was touching her. His hands coursed over her sides, her arms, the contact at once impersonal and fraught with urgency. He was checking her body for injuries.

She didn't want him to stop. She had never been touched like this before. His hands left impressions across her skin like the trails of comets, urgent and tingling, her body yearning for more. A breathless ache filled her chest. The intensity of the sensation overwhelmed her.

"Where are you hurt? Can you tell me?" When she didn't

respond, Nathaniel cradled her face in his hands. "Elisabeth!"

The sound of her first name spoken in Nathaniel's voice, in that tone, finally jolted her to her senses. "I'm not hurt," she said. Her pulse raced beneath his fingertips. "I just stood up too quickly. I'm . . ."

"Exhausted," he finished when she trailed off, his gray eyes roving over her face. "When was the last time you slept?"

Three nights ago. She didn't say that out loud. Nathaniel's expression had already withdrawn. A muscle tensed in his jaw as he helped her stand and guided her to a chair. He looked sick, as though their shared touch had turned toxic, or the air was swirling from the room like water down a drain. Confusion pounded in Elisabeth's head. As her dizziness receded, her mind caught up. The explanation became clear: he thought this was his fault.

"Wait," she protested, but he had already stepped away.

"Silas," he said.

The moment Silas appeared in the shadows of the foyer, Nathaniel went to him. Elisabeth felt fine now, barely light-headed at all, but the tangle of emotions in her throat formed a knot so large she could barely breathe. Whatever was about to happen, she wished she could stop it, reverse time, give herself a chance to talk to Nathaniel first. Helplessly, she watched him lean over Silas and speak in a furious undertone.

"Why didn't you tell me I've been having nightmares? I'm not a child any longer. If I use sorcery while I'm asleep, *while there is someone else in the house*, I need to know about it! For heaven's sake, Silas, I could have hurt her!"

"Master," Silas said, quellingly.

"What was it this time?" Nathaniel went on, relentless. "Blood dripping from the walls, or corpses crawling along the hallway? Or perhaps it was my personal favorite, the apparition of Father staggering around with his throat cut. That one got rid of the butler in a hurry."

"They are illusions, master. Harmless."

"Don't." The word landed like a slap. "You know the magic that runs in my family's blood. You served Baltasar."

Silas inclined his head. "Therefore, I should think that my opinion—"

"I said, *don't*. Don't argue with me. Not about this." He added, expression cold, every inch a magister, "That's an order."

Silas's lips thinned. Then, impassively, he bowed.

Nathaniel dragged his hands through his hair and paced across the foyer. He wouldn't meet either of their eyes. "I'll locate alternative lodgings for you, Miss Scrivener," he said. "It shouldn't take more than a day or two. This arrangement was temporary from the start." With that, he headed for the stairs.

Elisabeth tried to understand how she had gone from "Elisabeth" to "Miss Scrivener" in a matter of seconds. The situation was tumbling away from her at horrifying speed, unraveling like a dropped spool of thread. She sensed that if she didn't intervene, she and Nathaniel would become strangers to each other, and she wouldn't be able to put things back the way they were before. She drew in an unsteady breath.

"I don't want another place to stay!" she shouted up the stairs.

Nathaniel took one more step and halted, his spine straight. He didn't turn around, as if he couldn't bear to face her.

"I like it here," she said, the truth surprising her as she spoke. "It almost feels like—like a home to me. I feel safe. I'm not afraid of you or your nightmares."

He laughed once, a bitter, humorless sound. "You barely

know me. You haven't seen what I can do, not truly. When that happens, I expect you'll change your mind."

She thought of that night in the Blackwald, when he had sat gazing through the forest at his ancestor's work, a wound hundreds of years old and still festering. Was that what he feared—that Baltasar's evil lived on inside himself? Every beat of her heart hurt, like a knife sliding between her ribs.

She lifted a rose from the floor. Its petals were damp, and the thorns pricked her fingers. A symbol of love and life and beauty, so unlikely to see in Nathaniel's empty, despairing manor, though in truth she hadn't thought of his house that way in quite some time. Now she understood that the roses had been for her. A sign of hope, struggling up through the ashes.

"Perhaps I haven't seen what you can do," she said. "But I've seen what you choose to do." She looked up. "Isn't that more important?"

The question slipped past Nathaniel's guard. He gripped the rail, off-balance. "I chose not to help you fight Ashcroft."

Her heart ached. She gazed at his shoulders, the line of his back, which expressed his unhappiness so plainly. "It isn't too late to change your mind."

Nathaniel bent and leaned his forehead on his arm. Silence reigned. The foyer stank of aetherial combustion, but beneath that, there was the faint scent of roses. "Fine," he said at last.

Joy rushed through Elisabeth like a gulp of champagne, but she didn't dare ask for too much at once. "I can stay?"

"Of course you can stay, you menace. It isn't as though I could stop you even if I wanted to." He paused again. She waited, breathless, for him to force out the rest. "And fine, I'll help you. Not for any noble reason," he added quickly, as her spirits soared. "I still think it's a lost cause. We're probably going to get ourselves killed." He resumed walking up the stairs. "But every man has his limits. If there's one thing I can't do, it's stand by and watch you demolish irreplaceable antiques."

Elisabeth was grinning from ear to ear. "Thank you!" she shouted after him.

Nathaniel waved dismissively from the top of the landing. But before he vanished around the corner, she saw him smiling, too.

TWENTY-FOUR

WHEN ELISABETH BROUGHT the scrying mirror to Nathaniel's study the next evening, he didn't seem surprised—even though, according to him, it had been lost for the better part of a century.

"It belonged to my Aunt Clothilde," he explained. "She died before I was born, but I always heard stories about how she used it to spy on her in-laws."

Elisabeth hesitated, remembering what Mistress Wick had told her the other day. "Wasn't that after the Reforms?"

"Yes, but you wouldn't believe the number of forbidden artifacts squirreled away in old homes like this one." He closed his eyes and ran his fingers over the mirror's edges, concentrating. "The Lovelaces found ambulatory torture devices in their cellar, including an iron maiden that chased them back upstairs, snapping open and shut like a mollusk. Personally, I won't even go into my basement. There are doors down there that haven't been opened since Baltasar built the place, and Silas tells me he had a bizarre obsession with puppets. . . . Ah." His eyes snapped open. "There we are."

She leaned over on the couch for a closer look. The glaze of frost had receded from the mirror's surface. According to Nathaniel, there was nothing wrong with it; its magic had only needed to be replenished after lying dormant for so many years. Now, she and Katrien should be able to talk for as long as they wanted.

A delighted laugh escaped her. She looked up to find Nathaniel watching her, his eyes intent, as though he had been studying her face like a painting. A shock ran through her body when their gazes locked. Everything shifted into sharp focus: the study's instruments glittering over his shoulder, the softness of his lips in the candlelight, the crystalline structure of his irises, infinitely complex up close.

For a heartbeat, it seemed as though something might happen. Then a shadow fell across his eyes. He cleared his throat and passed her the mirror. "Are you ready?" he asked.

Elisabeth bit back a rush of embarrassment, struggling not to let anything show on her face. Hopefully, he wouldn't notice that her cheeks had turned pink, or if he did, he would mistake the flush for excitement about Katrien.

"Yes, but I want to try something else first." She brought the mirror close to her nose, ignoring the jitters in her stomach. "Show me Ashcroft," she commanded.

Nathaniel tensed as the mirror's surface swirled. When it cleared, however, it didn't show an image. A pool of shimmering golden light filled the glass instead. Elisabeth frowned. She had never seen the mirror do anything like that before.

"I don't understand. Is he in a place with no mirrors nearby?"

"That's Ashcroft's magic." Nathaniel's tension had eased. "It looks as though he's cast protective wards on himself. They're intended to stop malicious rituals, but evidently they block scrying mirrors, too."

She blew out a breath, realizing she'd been holding it the entire time. "He prepares for everything. That was one thing I came to understand while trapped in his manor. It seemed too good to be true—being able to spy on him—but I had to try."

"Perhaps it's for the best," Nathaniel sympathized. "Imagine if we'd caught him in the privy. Or trimming his nose hairs. Or even—"

Elisabeth made a face. "Show me Katrien," she said to the mirror, before he could add anything else.

Her fingers tightened on the frame as the glass swirled again. She had prepared Katrien and Nathaniel for this moment as best she could, considering she'd only had a minute or so to speak with Katrien that morning, but now that the time had arrived for them to actually meet, she felt disturbingly queasy. For some reason, she didn't think she could bear it if her best friend ended up hating Nathaniel.

Katrien's face appeared in the mirror. She sat cross-legged on the floor, wrapped to the chin in an oversized quilt. Somehow, she managed to make the effect look threatening. Perhaps it was her gaze, dissecting Nathaniel like a laboratory specimen.

"Thorn," she intoned.

"Quillworthy," he replied.

A long pause elapsed, during which Elisabeth wondered if she might throw up. Finally, Katrien poked a brown hand from the quilt and pushed up her spectacles. The hand retreated back out of sight as though it had never existed. "I suppose you'll do," she said. "Now, what else do I need to know before we get started?"

Just like that, the awkwardness vanished. Elisabeth barely resisted leaping to her feet and cheering. She angled the mirror so Katrien could see both their faces. "To start with, Ashcroft is a couple of days late attacking the Great Library of Fairwater."

Katrien frowned. "Do you think that's because he hasn't made any progress on the Codex?"

"Exactly—he could be buying himself more time, because he isn't ready to move on to whatever he has planned for Harrows. . . ."

The three of them spoke well into the night, interrupted once by a random room inspection that left them scrambling to cancel the mirror's spell before a warden saw their disembodied faces hovering above Katrien's armoire, and a second time by Silas, who insisted on serving them a three-course dinner on the coffee table. Katrien watched Silas with keen interest, but thankfully said nothing.

They capped off the meeting by trying to get Nathaniel into the Codex. First they tried having him go alone—in order to establish a control, Katrien explained, but Elisabeth suspected she just wanted to watch Nathaniel struggle. Next they tried going together, linking their arms in the hopes Elisabeth could somehow pull him along with her. But every time, she simply materialized in the workshop dimension on her own. Prendergast grew so upset by her repeated arrivals that he began throwing jars full of severed fingers at her, at which point they decided to call it a night.

"Elisabeth," Katrien said, as they all got up and stretched. "Can I talk to you about something? In private."

Alarm jolted straight to Elisabeth's stomach. No doubt Katrien had noticed the way she had turned red every time Nathaniel took her arm. Did they truly need to talk about that?

As Nathaniel and Silas left the study, she sank back onto the couch, sandwiching her hands between her knees.

"Are you all right?" Katrien asked. "You look like you have indigestion. Anyway, I've been thinking about your resistance to magic. Where it might have come from, and so forth."

Elisabeth slumped into the pillows. She felt as though her organs were liquefying with relief. "Did you come up with any ideas?"

"Well," Katrien hedged, "there must be a reason why you're the only person who's been able to get inside the Codex, and it has to be related." She paused. "Do you remember that time you fell off the roof, and you didn't break anything?"

Elisabeth nodded, thinking back. She had been fourteen at the time, and had climbed two stories to avoid being seen by Warden Finch. "I got lucky."

"I don't think so. That fall should have hurt you, but you only walked away with a few bruises. Stefan swears you cracked one of the flagstones. Then there was the incident with the chandelier in the refectory—it practically landed on you. And the time you got strawberry jam all over—"

"I know!" Elisabeth interrupted, flushing. "I remember. But what does any of that have to do with me being able to get inside the Codex?"

Katrien gnawed on her lip. "You aren't just resistant to magic. You're also more physically resilient than a normal person. You've survived things that would have killed anyone else."

Elisabeth started to object, then remembered her battle with the Book of Eyes. The Malefict had squeezed her until she thought her lungs would pop, but as far as she knew, she hadn't so much as cracked a rib. In retrospect, that did seem strange.

"I was thinking about how those qualities might be connected," Katrien went on slowly, "and something occurred to me. Do you remember those experiments I did when we first met?"

"The ones with booklice?"

Katrien nodded. Her eyes grew slightly misty. "Fascinating creatures, booklice. They spend all day scurrying around in parchment dust, eating and breathing sorcery, but it doesn't harm them. They're gigantic, and hard to kill. I thought they were a different species at first, unrelated to normal booklice. But after studying them, I realized that wasn't the case. They start off normal when they hatch. It's the exposure to the grimoires that changes them."

For a moment, Elisabeth couldn't speak. Her head spun. She imagined herself as a baby, crawling between the shelves. As a little girl, sneaking through the passageways. She could hardly remember a time in her childhood when she wasn't covered from head to toe in dust. "Do you mean—are you saying I'm a *booklouse*?"

"The human version of one, at least," Katrien said. "As far as we know, you're the only person to have ever grown up in a Great Library. By the time most apprentices arrive at age thirteen, we must be too developed for any changes to occur. But you . . ."

Elisabeth felt as though she had been struck over the head with a grimoire. She had lived sixteen and a half years with a case of double vision, and suddenly, for the first time, the world had snapped into focus. This was why she had woken the night of the Book of Eyes' escape. This was why she had been able to resist Ashcroft, and why the volume in the archives had called her—what had it called her?

A true child of the library.

Ink and parchment flowed through her veins. The magic of

the Great Libraries lived in her very bones. They were a part of her, and she a part of them.

At the Royal Library that week, Elisabeth thought of little else. She went about her work as if lost in a dream, observing countless things she hadn't noticed before. Grimoires rustled on the shelves when she walked by, but remained still and silent for the librarians. Bookshelves creaked. Rare volumes tapped on their display cases to get her attention. Her route to and from the storage room took her past a Class Four that was infamous among the apprentices for its foul temper—they fled down the hallway, shrieking, as it spat wads of ink at their heels—but all she had to do was nod at it every morning, and it left her alone. In one particularly memorable incident, a section of shelving sprang open unprompted, knocking Gertrude from her feet in its eagerness to beckon Elisabeth toward a secret passageway.

But the longer she swept, scrubbed, and polished, the more the sparkling sense of wonder drained away, replaced by an emptiness that hollowed out a chasm in her chest. If she were never able to regain her standing with the Collegium, what was left for her in the world? Outside the Great Libraries, she felt like an animal in a menagerie—an oddity torn from its home and paraded through places it didn't belong. Every day, she tried to convince herself to quit so she could focus all her energy on Ashcroft. And every day, a wave of terror paralyzed her at the mere thought. The moment she set aside her uniform and stepped out the door, there might be no going back.

Gertrude tsked and sighed, still convinced that Elisabeth was preoccupied with a boy. In a way, Elisabeth was. Her lack of sleep now owed itself to late nights around the flickering green fire in Nathaniel's study. Cluttered with the results of their meetings, the room increasingly resembled the base of operations for a war. They had rearranged the furniture and tacked notes to the walls. But despite their efforts, Prendergast remained as uncooperative as ever, and they hadn't gotten any closer to uncovering Ashcroft's plans.

Today Elisabeth had been put to work cleaning the floor of the Observatory, whose blue-and-silver tiles gleamed like gemstones with every stroke of the mop. The room was designed for grimoires whose text could only be revealed by moonlight or starlight, or during certain planetary alignments. Astronomical devices whirred gently, off-limits to touch, particularly the enormous bronze armillary sphere that hung from the center of the Observatory's glass dome like a chandelier. When she strayed to the edge of the room and peered down, she discovered a dizzying bird's-eye view of the Collegium's grounds. All appeared quiet this afternoon, except for a single rider galloping toward the library, dressed in travel-stained Collegium livery.

She was almost finished when the Observatory's door creaked open. She looked up, expecting Gertrude with another task. Instead she caught a glimpse of a gold cloak entering the room.

"What would you like to speak to me about, Deputy Director?"

Shock numbed her at the sound of Ashcroft's voice, as though the floor had collapsed and plunged her into frigid water. She darted behind a pedestal, clutching the mop to her chest. Hiding there, frozen, she listened to the rustle of Mistress Wick's robes, willing her not to lead Ashcroft any nearer. No doubt the two of them believed the room to be empty.

Elisabeth's gaze strayed to the bucket of soapy water sitting a few feet away, and cold sparks danced over her skin. As long as Ashcroft didn't glance in the wrong direction . . .

"Just moments ago, we received news from a courier," Mistress Wick said. "I thought you should be the first to know that the Great Library of Fairwater has been sabotaged."

Elisabeth's breath halted. Turning, she peeked through the interlocking rings of the instrument atop the pedestal. The pair of them had stopped near the center of the room, where an array of mirrors reflected a concentrated beam of sunlight onto the tiles. Ashcroft stood partially inside it, the light slicing a stripe across his sleeve and winking brightly from something in his hand. He held a decorative walking stick, the gold handle carved into the shape of a gryphon's head.

"Oh, dear," he said. "I am so terribly sorry." Though he sounded genuine, amusement shone in his mismatched eyes. "Were there many casualties?"

"Four wardens and three civilians are dead, poisoned by the Malefict's miasma. Director Florentine survived, but she sustained a serious head injury. Reportedly, she cannot remember any details of the attack."

Ashcroft's lips curved into a satisfied smile. A head injury, or the effects of a spell? Elisabeth's stomach turned. If only Mistress Wick could see his expression.

As the two of them continued speaking, she remembered last night's meeting with Katrien and Nathaniel. By this point, they were almost certain that Ashcroft didn't leave Brassbridge when the attacks happened. Unless he knew an unheard-of spell powerful enough to transport himself halfway across the country, he couldn't possibly have carried out the attacks in person—not the one on Fettering, while he was interrogating Elisabeth every day in his study, and not this one, either; his clothes showed no signs of travel. Nathaniel's best guess was that he had to be working with another sorcerer as an accomplice.

Finally, Ashcroft turned to go. "I will return to the Magisterium at once," he was saying. "I assure you, we have our best sorcerers on the case."

"If I may speak bluntly, Chancellor, I fear your best sorcerers may not be up to the task. Thus far, only the Great Library of Harrows remains untouched. The saboteur has even targeted the Royal Library without consequences. . . ."

A shiver ran through Elisabeth as Ashcroft opened the door for Mistress Wick. Of course word of the Codex's disappearance had already reached him—the moment they'd attributed its theft to the saboteur, it had become part of the investigation. Would the Collegium have given him access to the Royal Library's records? And if so, would he bother taking a look at the new servants who had been hired?

Halfway out the door, he paused. His fingers thoughtfully caressed the carved gryphon's head. He turned to scan the Observatory, his ruby eye passing over the instruments. She tensed as his gaze neared the bucket, but he didn't appear to see it; his attention swept onward toward her hiding spot. She ducked out of sight, her heart pounding in the roof of her mouth. Even after the door clicked shut a moment later, she remained paralyzed for the better part of a minute before she dared look again.

Ashcroft had gone. She was alone.

That night, a solemn mood hung over the study. Nathaniel had spent all day working on his illusions for the Royal Ball, but the butterflies flapping incongruously around the room failed to lift Elisabeth's spirits. Over the past few days it had seemed more and more possible that Ashcroft had put his plans on hold, and that they might have extra weeks or even months to apprehend him. No one knew what to say to Elisabeth's news. Her painful decision not to return to the Royal Library had drawn a sympathetic look even from Silas.

She took a deep breath. The time had come to make an admission. "I don't think Prendergast is going to tell me anything about Ashcroft's goal. He still doesn't trust me. And if I'm the only person who's able to visit him, which seems likely, we can't use the Codex as evidence. We have nothing left to go on."

She looked around at their faces and saw the truth reflected there. The three of them believed everything she had told them, despite never having witnessed any sign of Prendergast for themselves. But to everyone else she would merely come across as a girl who had escaped from a mental hospital, making wild claims about a stolen book. They had reached a dead end. Gloom descended over the study, punctuated by a lash of rain against the windows.

Finally, Silas stood. "I shall fetch some tea."

Somehow, the tea helped. Elisabeth cradled her steaming cup, grateful for the warmth that spread from her stomach down to her toes. She offered Nathaniel a faint smile when he joined her by the fire. The rain had intensified to a steady drumming outside. Wind moaned through the eaves, and the fire hissed as droplets found their way down the chimney. The green glow of the flames turned Nathaniel's eyes the same color as the storm he had summoned on her first night in the city. He hesitated before speaking.

"I wanted you to know—in the end, if we aren't able to stop Ashcroft, I'm not going to abandon you afterward. I—"

He looked troubled, on the verge of some difficult confession. A bolt of nerves flashed through her, as though loosed by a crossbow, thudding straight to the pit of her stomach.

"I'll do everything in my power to restore your position with the Collegium," he finished, casting his gaze into the fire. "To make sure you're safe, in a place where Ashcroft will never find you. Knockfeld, perhaps, or Fairwater—somewhere that sorcerers don't often visit."

Elisabeth nodded, not trusting herself to speak. She didn't understand the disappointment that stung her eyes. He was offering her exactly what she wanted. It was just that she had thought, for a moment, that he might say something else.

"What do you think Silas and Katrien are talking about?" she asked, desperate to change the subject. The two had been deep in conversation for several minutes.

"My best guess is that they're plotting world domination." Nathaniel narrowed his eyes. "I don't think we should leave them alone together. It unsettles me."

"At least if they take over the world, we won't have to worry about Ashcroft any longer." She watched a butterfly land on top of the scrying mirror and fan its sapphire wings. No doubt Ashcroft would be at the Royal Ball, too. She wouldn't even be able to see Nathaniel's completed illusion. . . .

She sat up straighter. "Wait a moment. I've thought of something."

"Tempting as the prospect is," Nathaniel said, "we are not attempting world domination. It sounds fun in theory, but in reality it's a logistical nightmare. All those assassinations and so forth." At her blank look, he explained, "Silas used to tell me bedtime stories."

"I'm serious," she insisted. "I've had an idea. We may not have the evidence to make an official accusation against Ashcroft, but that doesn't mean we're helpless. We can still show everyone who he truly is."

"I don't follow."

"We confront him in public, at an event where all the important people in Brassbridge can see his reaction. He believes he destroyed my mind. And even before he used that magic on me, he had no idea that I overheard everything he said while I was under Lorelei's glamour."

She saw the moment that Nathaniel understood, because his expression went carefully neutral. "You want to take the offensive," he said slowly. "Reveal yourself to Ashcroft, and make a public accusation before he can regain control of the situation."

She nodded, leaning forward. "Everyone might think I'm raving mad at first, but there are too many suspicious coincidences to ignore. He won't be able to talk his way out of it. And with *you* by my side, accusing him along with me . . . think about it. Even if he tries to hurt us, he'll only prove—"

"No," Nathaniel interrupted. "Far too dangerous." He stood and briskly clapped his hands. "Meeting adjourned."

She grabbed his sleeve and yanked him back down before he could cast the spell to dismiss Katrien. "When is the Royal Ball? It's soon, isn't it?"

Nathaniel scowled.

"The ball is this weekend, Miss Scrivener," Silas provided. "Master Thorn, of course, is expected to attend, and his invitation includes a companion." When Nathaniel shot him a look of betrayal, he returned an angelic smile. "You did not order me to be silent, master."

Elisabeth ignored Nathaniel's sputtered protest. "Silas, would you be able to keep an eye on Ashcroft for us? Without him seeing you?"

He considered the question for a moment, then inclined his head. "I could follow him throughout the night, in case he attempts to retaliate. The Chancellor's servant, Lorelei, is not a significant threat to me. Nor are the lesser demons in his service."

A shiver ran down her spine as she recalled the way Lorelei had spoken about Silas in Ashcroft's study. "The Royal Ball would be a perfect opportunity," she said, turning back to Nathaniel. "And with Silas watching out for us, we would be far safer. Please," she added. "I know this is a last resort, but it could be our only chance to stop him."

"You might as well do it," Katrien said from the mirror. When all three of them looked at her, she shrugged. "Provoking the kingdom's most powerful sorcerer, turning Elisabeth loose in a ballroom . . . what could possibly go wrong?"

TWENTY-FIVE

PRESENTED WITH THE genuine article, Elisabeth conceded that it had, indeed, been foolish of her to mistake Ashcroft Manor for a palace. The real palace was so large that she couldn't see the entire building through the carriage's window. Instead she gaped at its towers upside down in the reflecting pool, which flashed past for an eternity, lit by votives floating on the water. She felt as though they had passed into a different world, leaving the city far behind. The drive up the lane clung to her like a spell—the trees sparkling with fairy lights, hedges trimmed into geometrical mazes, and fountains in the shape of swans and lions, everything veiled in the alluring shimmer of dusk.

But her bewitchment faded like a glamour as the coach slowed, joining the line of carriages pulling up at the front doors. The carriages stretched in a chain all the way around the reflecting pool, ejecting an endless stream of guests, who ascended the steps in candlelight. Soon, she would have to convince all of them of Ashcroft's guilt.

Her stomach lurched when the coach came to a full, final stop. A servant in the palace's rose-colored uniform opened the door, and Elisabeth accepted Nathaniel's hand, stepping down carefully in her tightly laced silk shoes. His severe expression faltered as his hand grazed the cape covering her gown.

"Scrivener," he said carefully, "I don't mean to be forward, but is that a—"

"A sword hidden underneath my dress? Yes, it is."

"I see. And how exactly is it—"

"I thought you didn't mean to be forward." She squeezed his arm. "Come on," she said, with a confidence she didn't feel. "Let's go."

Chandeliers glittered through the palace's windows, almost too dazzling to look at directly. She was aware of a number of curious looks being sent in her direction as they mounted the stairs, everyone eager to see the first companion Nathaniel had ever brought to the ball. Her heart pounded. If only they were attending as a real couple, about to pass the night dancing and laughing and sipping champagne.

At the top of the stairs, a pair of footmen ushered them inside. Slowly, she let go of Nathaniel. Pillars soared upward to a curved ceiling painted with moving clouds and cherubs. The gold-and-cream clouds drifted across the pastel blue sky, and the cherubs fanned their wings. The archway at the far end of the hall had to lead to the ballroom, its entrance sending down a curtain of golden leaves. Guests gasped in delight as they stepped through the illusion, vanishing into the room beyond.

A servant approached to take Elisabeth's cloak. She hesitated before she undid the ribbon tying the garment at her throat, feeling the silk glide through her fingers, the fur and velvet lift away. Afterward, she resisted the urge to fold her arms across her chest. The air chilled her bare skin as though she had shed a skin of armor.

Nathaniel glanced at her, and paused. He hadn't yet seen her in her gown. The chandeliers threw prisms over its ivory fabric, setting the ruched silk aglow with a silvery sheen. Golden leaves flowed across the bodice, clustered at the top to form a scalloped décolletage, and again at the gown's hem, where they floated atop a sheer layer of organza. Pearl earrings shivered against her neck like chips of ice.

Nathaniel had passed the ride to the palace in silence, his thoughts impossible to guess. Now his eyes widened; he looked lost. "Elisabeth," he said, his voice hoarse. "You look . . ."

"Marvelous," a man said, bustling over to shake Nathaniel's hand. With a sinking heart, Elisabeth recognized him as Lord Ingram from Ashcroft's dinner party. "Marvelous to see you, Magister Thorn. I just wanted to say, what excellent work on the illusions. When we heard you had been commissioned this year, we half expected to arrive and find the place decorated with skeletons!" He let out a braying laugh at his own joke. Nathaniel's jaw clenched, but Lord Ingram didn't notice. "And who is this lovely young lady?" He turned to Elisabeth, looking up, and then up some more, as he discovered that she was nearly a head taller than him.

"That is Miss Scrivener, dear," said Lady Ingram, arriving alongside her husband. "From the papers."

"Oh. *Oh*." Lord Ingram rocked back on his heels. "Miss Scrivener, I was under the impression you had been sent—well, that's hardly appropriate for me to—please excuse me." Lady Ingram was tugging him away, a frigid smile fixed on her face. He went without complaint, shooting troubled glances over his shoulder.

Elisabeth's heart sank further. Now that she looked, she saw signs of the rumors everywhere. Women paused to stare, then whisper to their partners, their lips molding around the word "hospital." No one else tried to approach her and Nathaniel as they made their way toward the ballroom. Gossip churned in their wake, hidden behind gloved hands and polite smiles.

"I'm ruining your reputation, aren't I?" she asked, watching the spectacle unfold.

"Don't worry," Nathaniel said. "I've been hard at work trying to ruin my reputation for years. Perhaps after this, influential families will stop trying to catapult their unwed daughters over my garden fence. Which actually did happen once. I had to fend her off with a trowel."

Elisabeth smiled, unable to resist his grin. But her smile faded as they neared the archway.

"Are you having second thoughts?" he asked.

She shook her head, trying to ignore the vise that closed on her lungs. It was too late to turn back. Even if it weren't, even if the ballroom teemed with Ashcroft's demons, she would still press on; she had no other choice.

As they passed through the curtain of leaves, wonder briefly overcame her fear. They stood in a great chamber overgrown by a forest glade. A flock of sapphire butterflies swirled around them, flashing like jewels, only to dart away toward the orchestra and scatter between the instruments. Ivy twined through the music stands, and wildflowers engulfed the refreshment tables. The enchanted scene was filled with people dressed in silk and fur and diamonds, laughing in amazement as leaves drifted down from the chandeliers.

But no amount of beauty could overcome the fact that somewhere within this grandeur, Ashcroft awaited them.

"Would you care for a drink, miss?"

Even before Elisabeth turned, she knew whom she would find standing beside her. Still, she almost started in surprise when she laid eyes on Silas: blond and brown-eyed, dressed in palace livery, holding a tray of champagne flutes. He looked thoroughly, resignedly human. She and Nathaniel made a show of selecting their glasses in order to buy themselves a few seconds.

"Thank you for doing this," Elisabeth whispered.

Silas sighed. "I assure you, I would not have agreed to the plan had this indignity been part of your original proposal. The livery is ill-fitting, and I would not wish to serve this detestable vintage even to a commoner. No offense intended, Miss Scrivener."

Elisabeth coughed, hiding a laugh. "None taken."

Demons weren't permitted inside the palace, but Nathaniel had been able to sneak Silas in that afternoon, illusion and all, when he'd arrived to enchant the ballroom. Silas had been keeping an eye on things ever since.

"Chancellor Ashcroft is on the other side of the room," he went on, "speaking to Lady Ingram. I believe he's preparing to make his way over. I will remain close." With that, he gave them a brief nod and blended back into the crowd.

Elisabeth's stomach twisted. She craned her neck, straining for any hint of Ashcroft, but even though her height allowed her to see far across the ballroom, there were too many guests blocking her view.

Nathaniel caught her hand. "This way. I've spotted a likely crowd. Prince Leopold is a sensitive type—he's bound to be sympathetic to what we have to say."

Her thoughts stuttered at the unexpected sensation of his

fingers twining with hers. She forced herself to focus. He was pulling her toward a group of people that included Lord Kicklighter, all of them bowing and scraping to a young man in a red military uniform.

"Is that him? The prince?"

Nathaniel nodded. "If you can believe it, I used to fancy him. Then he went and grew that mustache. Or he murdered a gerbil and attached it to his face. For the life of me, I can't tell which."

She glanced at him in surprise. "I didn't realize—then do you mean—"

"I like girls too, Scrivener." Amusement danced in Nathaniel's eyes. "I like both. If you're going to fantasize about my love life, I insist you do so accurately."

She frowned. "I am not fantasizing about your love life."

"Strange. This is unfamiliar territory. Young women are usually more than happy to devote a sizable portion of their brains to the task of contemplating my splendor."

"What about the ones who throw champagne in your face?"

"That only happened *once*, thank you very much, and there were extenuating—" Suddenly, his cheer vanished. "Never mind. Here he comes. Remember what we practiced."

"Nathaniel," Ashcroft said behind them. "Miss Scrivener. How excellent it is to see you."

His voice slid down Elisabeth's spine like a trickle of cold sweat. She braced herself, and turned. As soon as she met his eyes, the misery of her days in Ashcroft Manor came crashing back down on her in force. Her mouth went dry, and her hands shook. She had forgotten how handsome he was up close—how closely he resembled a storybook hero, with that golden hair and charming smile. Lady Ingram stood beside him, clearly wishing to get to the bottom of Elisabeth's reappearance as soon as possible. For a moment it was as though Elisabeth were back there, trapped with no possibility of escape.

A space discreetly formed in the crowd. The other guests carried on their own conversations, but Elisabeth felt the weight of their attention. For all that they appeared occupied, they were hanging on every word.

"We were all so worried when you disappeared from Leadgate Hospital," Ashcroft said. His eyes crinkled with concern—the same concern that had fooled her just weeks ago. "We feared you had been lost on the streets. Some areas of the city can be terribly dangerous for a young woman on her own."

"You're right," Nathaniel said. His gray eyes assessed Ashcroft's pearl-colored suit, and paused to take in his walking stick, which had the same gryphon's head handle from the Observatory. "She was in danger," he went on, his scornful gaze flicking back to Ashcroft's face. "But as it turns out, the criminals on the streets aren't half as bad as the ones living in mansions."

Ashcroft's smile hardened. Elisabeth might have imagined it: a flicker of uncertainty in his expression, a shadow of dawning realization.

"I hear you've made a miraculous recovery, Miss Scrivener," he said smoothly, turning back to her. "Is that true?"

Anyone could have bathed Elisabeth, dressed her, brushed her hair, and brought her to the Royal Ball, even if she had no mind left to speak of. She knew that was what Ashcroft was hoping, even expecting: that she was little more than a living doll, incapable of talking back. Now came the moment he would discover that despite all he had done to her, he had failed to break her. The thought filled her with resolve, like a molten blade plunged seething into water.

"I did not recover," she said. Gasps rang out around them. "I'm the same now as when you condemned me to Leadgate Hospital, on the recommendation of a physician who barely spoke to me. The only miracle is that I survived."

Ashcroft opened his mouth to reply, but she cut him off.

"It's shameful to call that place a hospital." She recalled Mercy's sorrowful face, and knew she wasn't the only girl who had remained voiceless for far too long. "The overseer, Matron Leach, accepts money from wealthy patrons who abuse the patients for pleasure. Or at least she did, before she turned herself in to the authorities this morning." That had been Silas's doing; he had returned in the early hours, sighing over the lower city's grime.

Lord Kicklighter's booming voice almost made her jump. "I say, Chancellor Ashcroft, is that not the same hospital that receives your funding?"

"I'll be sure to look into the matter." Ashcroft's smile had grown thinner, and his eyes had lost their genial warmth. "Bear in mind, these claims are coming from—"

"A young woman from whom you expected to profit?" Nathaniel inquired, with a savagery that startled Elisabeth. "Matron Leach produced documents connecting you to the scheme, after all. Or is there another, more pressing reason why you wanted Miss Scrivener out of sight, Chancellor? Perhaps you could enlighten us."

"I remember everything, Ashcroft," she added quietly. "Everything you did to me. Those afternoons in the study. The spell you used on me. The fiends."

Shock rippled outward. "My god," someone murmured, "did she say *fiends*?"

Ashcroft was no longer pretending to smile. "These allegations are absurd. Remember, everyone, that poor Miss Scrivener was diagnosed with hysteria by a licensed physician. She suffers from extreme anxiety. Delusions."

"I don't think I imagined the fiends," Elisabeth said. "They were in the papers."

In the crowd, someone gave a nervous laugh. People glanced between her and Nathaniel, then back to Ashcroft. The atmosphere had changed.

Elisabeth held her breath. They had practiced Nathaniel's next lines a hundred times.

"If truly you have nothing to hide," he said slowly, his gaze pinned on Ashcroft, "I'm certain we would all like to hear why you were so eager to silence a witness in the Great Library investigation. By now, it almost seems as though you don't want the saboteur to be found."

A hush fell as everyone waited for him to answer. In the newfound silence, Lord Kicklighter was conveying information to Prince Leopold in what he no doubt imagined was a whisper: "Yes, Leadgate Hospital. That's the one. The most disturbing accusations . . ."

When the orchestra started up with a flurry of violins, Ashcroft twitched. Several people took a step back from him. Lady Ingram seized her husband's arm and stalked off, her ramrod-stiff posture indicating that she wanted no part in this new, unexpected scandal.

"Excuse me," Ashcroft said briskly, offering everyone a forced imitation of his usual smile. "I have matters to attend to elsewhere." Then he turned and strode away.

Everyone watched him go, openmouthed. Guests parted to let him pass. Heads bent together, jewels sparkling, as the news of what had happened spread like wildfire across the ballroom. Horrified glances followed Ashcroft's departure. No one aside from Elisabeth and Nathaniel paid any attention to the palace servant who set aside his tray and, a moment later, tailed Ashcroft out the door.

The glitter of the chandeliers filled Elisabeth's vision. The bubbles in her champagne flute ticked against the glass, each one a miniature explosion beneath her fingertips. Suddenly the ballroom was too bright, too loud, too full of people, all of them turning in her direction.

"Miss Scrivener?" An unfamiliar man's face swam in front of her. Her hearing fluctuated strangely as he introduced himself as an official from the Magisterium. "If you would be available to make a statement—"

"Tomorrow," Nathaniel interrupted. He was scrutinizing Elisabeth, his eyes intent. A rush of gratitude overcame her when he took her arm. "Let's go somewhere quieter," he said.

Her memory seemed to skip. One moment he was steering her through the crowd, and the next he was supporting her in a hallway, allowing her to cling to him as her lungs rebelled. Each labored gulp of air slammed against her ribs like a punch. Black spots swarmed at the edges of her vision.

"It's over. Just breathe. Just breathe, Elisabeth."

She pressed her forehead against his shoulder, screwing her eyes shut. She was aware that she was gripping him so hard that it probably hurt, but she couldn't make herself stop. She felt as though she were dangling off the edge of a tower, and she would fall if she let go. "I'm sorry," she gasped.

"It's all right."

"I don't—I don't know why—"

"It's all right," he said again. He paused, and then added,

"When terrible things have happened to you, sometimes the promise of something good can be just as frightening."

She didn't know how long they stood there. Finally her shaking eased, and when she opened her eyes again, she found them standing in a hallway lined with windows and paintings. No people were in sight, aside from a servant passing with a tray at the end of the hall. Distant strains of music drifted in from the ballroom.

"How did you know what to do?" she croaked, turning back to Nathaniel.

His expression was unreadable. "Experience. I could barely leave the house for months after my father's death without having a similar attack."

She sucked in a breath. She realized that she was still gripping his coat, and forced her fingers to uncurl. "I'm sorry."

"I said it was all right."

"I meant for you. I'm sorry you had to go through that."

For a moment, he was silent. Then he pushed the drapes aside and looked out the nearest window. "Ashcroft got into his carriage a few minutes ago—he left in a hurry. A Magisterium coach is pulling out now, too. It appears we might not have even needed Silas."

Elisabeth took a few more steadying breaths, cautiously accepting their victory. Her plan had worked. What had happened was real. "Did you see the looks on everyone's faces? I think they truly . . ." She paused. "Nathaniel?"

He had steadied himself against the wall, blinking hard. She was about to ask whether he was all right when he set his glass down on the windowsill, sloshing champagne over the rim. She hadn't touched her own drink, wherever it had gone, but evidently he hadn't been as careful. Now that she looked more closely, she made out the darkness of his widened pupils. His color was high, his cravat disheveled.

"Nathaniel . . ."

"Will you come with me?" he asked quickly, as though he feared what she might say. "I'd like to show you something."

She hesitated, her chest tight. "What about Ashcroft?"

"I suspect that we might not need to worry about him any longer. Not tonight. Possibly not after tonight, either." He looked down, a muscle shifting in his jaw. "I just thought that we—"

The realization came upon Elisabeth swiftly, leaving her dizzy. If suspicion took hold against Ashcroft, everything would change, and soon. There would be no more evenings in Nathaniel's study, heads bent close together, sharing dinner by the fire. She would have to face her future, and her future might not have him in it.

"Yes." Before he could have second thoughts, she took his hand. Distantly, she observed that the music had turned sweet and sad. As though she had stepped outside her body, she watched him wrap her in his coat, exquisitely careful, and draw her out through the glass doors at the end of the hall.

The night air cooled her flushed cheeks. Their footsteps crunched along the path toward the gardens. Somewhere close by, a fountain splashed. Tall hedges enfolded them, perfumed with the wistful scent of blossoms past their prime, and Nathaniel's arm warmed her side. After her attack in the hallway, she felt drowsy and dreamy and strange, weighed down by the unsaid words between them.

At last they reached a gate, nearly hidden by the hedges. Nathaniel found a latch and let them inside.

Elisabeth's breath caught. Summer hadn't lost its hold on this secret place. Roses flourished in a hundred different shades of pearl and scarlet, their heady perfume drenching the cultivated paths. At the end of the walled garden stood a pavilion of white marble, shining in the moonlight, its balconies overgrown with vines. They walked forward arm in arm, passing beneath arbors that dripped with blooms, the paving stones carpeted in petals.

"How did you find out about this?" Elisabeth asked, as they climbed the pavilion's steps. She felt as though it might vanish beneath her feet at any moment, like an illusion.

"My parents used to bring me here when I was young. I thought it was the ruin of an ancient castle. Maximilian and I would play for hours." He paused. "I haven't been back here since. He would have been fourteen now—my brother."

Silence fell between them. They had reached the top. Over a balustrade twined with blossoming white roses, the view looked out across the gardens, back toward the palace. Its windows sparkled like diamonds in a stone setting, the towers framed by stars. They were too far away for Elisabeth to guess where the ballroom was amid all that light: a different world, one filled with music and dancing and laughter.

Sorrow constricted her throat. She considered Nathaniel, his pale features just as distant. She didn't know what to say or how to reach across the gulf between them. She couldn't bear the thought of leaving him, as everyone else had done, everyone but Silas, whose service came at such a terrible cost. The pain of it sang inside her like music, every note a wound.

"I'm sorry," Nathaniel said. "I didn't bring you here to tell you about my family."

"No." She shook her head. "Please. Never apologize to me for that."

"It's hardly an appropriate topic for a celebratory occasion."

She saw him drawing inward, preparing to lock himself away. "You aren't like Baltasar," she blurted out, realizing this might be her only chance to say it. "You know that, don't you?"

His face twisted. For a terrible moment, she thought he might laugh. Then he said, "There's something you have to know about me. When my father began researching the ritual, I knew exactly what he was planning. I never tried to stop him. I hoped that it would work. I wanted them back, Max and my mother. I would have done any evil thing to have them back."

"You were twelve years old," she said softly.

"Old enough to know right from wrong." Finally, he looked at her, his eyes bleak. "My father was a good man. All his life, he was good, except for the very end." His expression said, *So how can there be any hope for me?*

"You're good, Nathaniel," she said quietly. She placed a hand on his cheek. "You are."

Beneath her touch, a tremor ran through him. He looked at her as though he were drowning, as though she had been the one to push him, and he did not know what to do. "Elisabeth," he said, her name wrung from him as a plea.

Her heart stopped. His eyes were as dark and turbulent as a river in midwinter, and very close. She felt as though she stood on a precipice, and that if she leaned forward, she would fall. She would fall, and drown with him; she would never resurface for air.

She tilted toward him, and felt him do the same. Her head spun. Nothing could have prepared her for this: that she would experience her first kiss in moonlight, surrounded by roses, with a boy who summoned storms and commanded angels to spread their wings. It was like a dream. She readied herself for the shock and the plunge, for the quenching of this agony inside her, which strained her soul to breaking.

Their lips brushed, divinely soft; the barest touch, more intoxicating than the perfume of the roses. "You don't taste of champagne," she breathed out dizzily, wonderingly. "I thought you would taste of champagne."

This time, he did laugh. She felt it as a shiver of air across her cheek. "I didn't drink any. I thought I had better not."

"But—" She drew back, and looked at him. Had she imagined that moment in the parlor? The moment he had suddenly lost his balance, seemed disoriented, right after he'd looked outside and said . . .

The hair stood up on her arms.

"Is something the matter?" Nathaniel asked.

"I don't know." She glanced around. "If you didn't want to talk about your family, why did you bring me here?"

"I . . ." His brow furrowed. "Oddly enough, I can't precisely . . ."

He didn't know. He couldn't remember. Because he hadn't made the decision to bring her here—someone else had. She yanked up her skirt and drew Demonslayer, whirling to face the rest of the pavilion.

In the shadows, someone began to clap.

"You caught on more quickly than I anticipated, Miss Scrivener," Ashcroft said, stepping into the moonlight, poised in midclap.

Elisabeth could barely breathe. "You cast a spell on him," she whispered. Demonslayer trembled in her grasp.

"Now, there's no need to fight me," Ashcroft said. "I've only brought you two here to make a simple transaction."

He reached behind himself, and yanked. Iron chains rang out against the marble as a slim figure went sprawling at his feet. At first Elisabeth couldn't make sense of what she saw: long white hair, fanned unbound across the stone. A beautiful face contorted with suffering, sulfurous eyes downcast.

"Give me the girl," Ashcroft said to Nathaniel, "and I'll give you back your demon."

TWENTY-SIX

THE BLOOD DRAINED from Nathaniel's face. For an instant he looked years younger, a frightened boy on the verge of losing everything once more. "Silas?" he asked.

The chains shifted. Silas looked up at Nathaniel, his eyes clouded with pain. The effort of even that small motion seemed to overwhelm him. He subsided against the marble, his eyes sinking shut.

Nathaniel stared. Inch by inch, his expression hardened, like the portcullis of a vault winching down. When he was finished, he had no expression left at all. He took a step toward Ashcroft. "What do you want with Elisabeth?" he demanded, each syllable as sharp as glass.

"Haven't you figured it out? To reach Prendergast, naturally. I know Miss Scrivener can access him." Ashcroft smiled blandly at the horror on their faces. "You aren't the only ones with a scrying mirror, you know. You really should look into your household wards, Nathaniel. Some of those old spells haven't been updated in centuries. And you might want to tidy up your study as well."

Elisabeth's stomach roiled. As clearly as day, she saw the devices on the desk of Nathaniel's study, with their many lenses and mirrors. All those evenings she had thought herself safe by the fire—Ashcroft's presence now darkened those memories like a stain. She struggled to wrap her mind around the violation.

"You were just pretending in there," she realized aloud. "You wanted us to think that we had won."

"Not the most agreeable experience, granted, but it hardly matters. In a few days, no one's going to care about ballroom gossip."

Blood sang in Elisabeth's ears. Her grip on Demonslayer tightened. Without thinking, she moved.

"I wouldn't," Ashcroft warned, halting her in her tracks. He twisted the gryphon's head on his walking stick, and a sword slid free, brilliant in the moonlight. He placed the edge against Silas's white throat, where it sent up a curl of steam. Silas didn't move or make a sound, but his eyelashes fluttered, as if he were struggling to remain conscious.

"This one wasn't easy to subdue," Ashcroft went on, "even with a trap in place. I have half a mind to kill him, simply to rid myself of the trouble."

"Wait," Nathaniel said, his voice raw. Ashcroft looked up, expectant. The sword shifted minutely from Silas's neck. From a distance, Elisabeth heard Nathaniel finish, "I challenge you to a duel."

"A sorcerer's duel?" Ashcroft laughed. "Good gracious. You do know those were outlawed by the Reforms. Are you certain?"

Tightly, Nathaniel nodded.

"Oh, very well," Ashcroft said. "This should be novel."

"Nathaniel," Elisabeth whispered.

He met her eyes. Deliberately, he flicked his gaze toward

Silas. Then he pivoted on his heel. He strode all the way to the opposite end of the pavilion, where he turned to face them again, gazing at Ashcroft across the long expanse. His voice rang out as he rolled up his sleeves. "The rules of a duel are thus: we may not involve our demons. No weapons, aside from sorcery. Once we begin, we fight to the death. Do you accept?"

"On my honor," Ashcroft said. His ruby eye twinkled. He slipped his sword through his belt and strolled forward, placing himself opposite Nathaniel.

Ashcroft wasn't planning on playing fair. But neither was Nathaniel. The moment Elisabeth freed Silas, it would be three against one. She tensed, preparing herself. As Ashcroft and Nathaniel bowed to each other, the time between each heartbeat stretched to an eternity. Neither of them rose from the bow. She glanced between them, uncertain. Their eyes were shut in concentration; under their breath, they were both murmuring incantations.

Nathaniel was the first to finish. He straightened with a whip of emerald fire in his hand, its flames spitting green embers onto the marble. But when the whip lashed across the pavilion, Ashcroft sliced his hand through the air and harmlessly swatted it aside. A torn sleeve revealed that he had transformed his arm: the skin was armored in golden scales, his fingers tipped with claws. When he smiled, his canine teeth lengthened into fangs.

She didn't have time to watch what happened next. She dove for Silas, falling to her knees beside him. Her hands roved over the chains that bound his wrists behind his back, encircled his chest, his waist, his legs. Wherever they touched his bare skin, they left raw, steaming welts. He stirred beneath her touch, but didn't seem in full command of his senses. Her heart skipped a beat when his cuffs rode up, exposing blackened marks on both sides of his arms, as though they had been impaled on an iron spike.

No matter how frantically she searched, she couldn't find a weak spot, a join, or even a lock holding the links in place. It was as though the chains had wrapped themselves around his body and seamlessly fused together.

Silas drew in a labored breath. "Miss Scrivener," he rasped. "Behind you."

Elisabeth spun. An elegant figure was draped over the rail, leaning against an arbor lush with late-blooming roses. A stray beam of moonlight revealed leisurely fingers dangling from a knee, their lacquered claws the color of blood. The rest remained indistinct, veiled by blossoms and shadows, but Elisabeth knew who this was, even before she spoke.

"Do you take my master for a fool?" Lorelei's voice dripped with satisfaction. "He would not leave Silas unguarded. Though I confess, I enjoyed watching you struggle."

Elisabeth raised Demonslayer between them. Nearby there came the crack of Nathaniel's whip, and shortly afterward a choked-off cry of pain. She couldn't tell whether it had belonged to Ashcroft, or Nathaniel. She didn't dare take her eyes from Lorelei.

"Lay down your sword, darling," the demon said. "We don't have to fight. If you surrender yourself, my master will take you back. You've already had a taste of how well he treats his guests. New gowns every evening, chests full of jewels, and as many plum dumplings as your heart desires. Doesn't that sound tempting?"

"No," Elisabeth said. "He would use me to reach Prendergast, and then he would kill me."

Silk slithered against stone as Lorelei slid from the railing and emerged into the moonlight. She wore an obsidian dress that shone with jeweled undertones, like a starling's feathers. The flickering green of Nathaniel's sorcery, intertwined with the gold of Ashcroft's, reflected in the depths of her crimson eyes.

"Not now that he understands your value," she breathed, her gaze fixed hungrily on Elisabeth's face. "A girl who can resist magic—how special. Just imagine how useful you could be to him: able to see through any illusion, impervious to the influence of demons. That will be an advantage in the coming days." A smile curved her scarlet lips. "And if you stood at his side, he would reward you. I promise."

"What do you mean, the coming days?" Elisabeth shifted her hold on Demonslayer, and felt sweat slicking the pommel. "What does Ashcroft want from Prendergast?"

"Oh, dear." Lorelei's lips curved in an enigmatic smile. "Did I say too much?"

It was no use listening to demons, Elisabeth told herself. They were liars. Deceivers. Untrustworthy to the core.

Except when they weren't.

A scraping sound came from behind her: Silas attempting, in vain, to rise. She adjusted her stance, putting herself between him and Lorelei.

"What are you doing?" Lorelei's eyes narrowed, trying to puzzle out Elisabeth's actions. Shock registered on her face, followed by dawning delight. "You foolish girl! You care for him!"

Elisabeth answered not with words, but with her sword. Demonslayer's edge whistled through the air, passing within a hairsbreadth of Lorelei's stomach as she took a dancing step backward, her long black hair streaming around her.

"This is even better than I had imagined," she said, alight

with glee. "Silas doesn't return your tender feelings, you know. You will understand that one day."

Elisabeth swung again and again, relentlessly driving Lorelei back against the railing. The demon laughed, a tinkling, rapturous sound, as she dodged each strike. She was baiting Elisabeth, toying with her. But not for long. She underestimated the strength of Elisabeth's resolve—and the next moment she gasped, her hand flying to her cheek. She stood frozen, staring wide-eyed at Elisabeth. A single rivulet of blood trickled out from beneath her fingers. Demonslayer had cut her face.

And now, its point rested at the hollow of her throat.

From this angle, Elisabeth could see the other battle raging across the pavilion. Black streaks charred the marble where Nathaniel's whip had scored the ground. Both men were out of breath, but still standing. Relief flooded her. Although Nathaniel's sleeve had been sliced open, and his collar clung to his neck with sweat, he didn't appear injured. Above the unraveling cravat, his face was a mask: fixed with concentration, dark hair tangled, his eyes and the streak at his temple the same shade of lucent silver.

His whip snaked out again, the tongue of emerald flame licking toward Ashcroft, who struck the spell aside, then cried out and fell to one knee, catching himself with his demonic hand.

The strike had been a feint. While Ashcroft had been focused on Nathaniel's whip, the rose vines climbing across the balustrade had come to life and lashed themselves around his ankle. When he moved to tear through them with his claws, more vines snapped out, binding his wrist. The thorns squeezed tighter, pulling his arm taut. Grimly, Nathaniel advanced.

Demonslayer rested at Lorelei's throat, unfaltering. A heartbeat passed. And then, impossibly, Lorelei was no longer there.

Elisabeth stumbled forward. She whirled around. Lorelei

stood balanced on the railing several yards away, petals swirling in the breeze created by her preternatural speed. As Elisabeth watched with a sense of dawning horror, Lorelei brought her fingers to her lips and whistled.

An answering growl echoed across the pavilion. Elisabeth ducked just in time. The arbor exploded as though struck by a cannon, spraying torn blossoms and slivers of painted wood in every direction. A fiend hurtled past her and skidded to a stop on the marble, shaking loose the leaves tangled in its horns. Then it exhaled a steaming breath and fixed its red eyes on Elisabeth. Several more fiends loped up the stairs, bone and sinew rippling beneath their scales.

She spun, trying to anticipate which of the demons would attack first. She aimed Demonslayer first at one target, then another, the sword's point wavering with desperation. She couldn't face the fiends and Lorelei at the same time.

Seeing Elisabeth cornered, Nathaniel paled. He hesitated mid-incantation. This was the reaction Ashcroft had been waiting for.

Time seemed to slow as a seam of golden light appeared in the air in front of Ashcroft, and as he thrust himself into it, through it, vanishing from the place he had knelt to appear behind Nathaniel instead. The vines that had bound him unraveled to the ground like cut ropes.

Nathaniel turned. Elisabeth screamed. Ashcroft's clawed hand swept through the air, each talon as long as a knife. The blow struck with enough force to knock Nathaniel a step backward.

At first Nathaniel appeared unharmed, and Elisabeth entertained the mad hope that the blow had somehow missed him. He wore an expression of surprise, almost puzzlement. Then he stumbled back another step. He looked down, where spots had appeared here and there on his shirt, small at first, but spreading, blooming like poppies, soaking through the fabric until his entire chest was slick and red. The whip in his hand fizzled out. He dropped to his knees.

Elisabeth's vision blurred. She threw herself forward, striking blindly at the fiend that crouched between her and Ashcroft.

Iron bit into scales. The fiend howled as she yanked Demonslayer from its shoulder and struck again, and again, barely conscious of her body, the wild strength that filled her at the sight of Nathaniel stupefied and bleeding. With one last yelp, the fiend collapsed. Elisabeth leaped forward, using its toppling body as a springboard even before it struck the ground. For a moment, she seemed capable of flight. Demonslayer shone like liquid moonlight, wreathed in steam; Nathaniel's coat billowed out behind her, and the wind whistled in her ears.

But she never finished the leap. A weight slammed against her in midair, bowling her back to the ground. Her world dissolved into a jumble of rank breath, obsidian scales, a splatter of hot saliva across her neck. Demonslayer spun from her hand, striking sparks on the marble as it skittered out of sight. Just as she began to make sense of the second fiend's attack, a clawed foot pressed against her ribs, pinning her to the ground. Spots swam before her eyes as its weight crushed the air from her lungs.

At a ninety-degree angle, she watched Ashcroft draw his sword. Nathaniel was bent forward now, one hand braced on the ground, the other gripping his chest. Blood twisted in a stream down his wrist.

Hopelessness grayed her thoughts. She saw no way they could survive this. No, not *they*—for *she* would survive, stolen back to Ashcroft Manor as the Chancellor's prize. She realized, in despair, that she would rather die at Nathaniel's side.

"I must admit," Ashcroft said, "it's a shame to see you go. The final heir of the great House Thorn, cut down before his prime." He considered Nathaniel as he ran his thumb down the sword's edge, testing its sharpness. "Then again, you always were determined to be the last, weren't you? You would do anything to prevent another Baltasar—another Alistair."

Nathaniel's shoulders hitched. His other hand struck the ground, catching his weight, leaving a gory imprint as his fingers shifted. Ashcroft watched him pityingly.

"So I suppose," he said, raising his sword, "that in a way, I'm merely giving you what you've always wanted."

Nathaniel looked up, his eyes clear and cold. On the marble, using his blood, he had drawn an Enochian sigil. And it was beginning to glow with emerald light.

Ashcroft's expression went blank. *So that's what he looks like when he is truly taken by surprise,* Elisabeth thought. The sigil blazed brighter and brighter, and he fell back with a shout of pain, throwing an arm over his eyes. She squeezed her own shut, feeling the magical shock wave ripple over her as a rush of tingling sparks.

The ground heaved. Marble cracked and crumbled. When she opened her watering eyes, it was to the sight of the rose vines, now as thick around as tree trunks, shedding fragments of the balustrade. The pavilion had been imprisoned in a tangle of thorns, unearthly in the moonlight, like something from an old tale. The colossal spines pierced stone and demons alike. As she watched, the vines continued growing, curving and twining, wrapping the bodies of the fiends as their gleaming points stretched toward the starry sky.

She didn't smell blood, or charred flesh, or anything else foul. Only the sweet, wistful scent of the roses. The pressure on her chest had lifted, and when she looked over her shoulder, she saw the fiend that had attacked her being enveloped by vegetation. The light faded from its eyes as buds unfurled into leaves, hiding it from view.

Ashcroft staggered, disoriented and blinking. He bumped into the interlocking thorns that had grown around him like a cage. Elisabeth had eyes only for Nathaniel. As she watched, he swayed and passed out, collapsing in a pool of blood.

With a cry, she started forward. And in doing so, she stumbled straight into Lorelei's waiting arms.

The demon folded her in a cold, hard embrace. A glamour's numbing calm enveloped Elisabeth, forcing her thoughts to slow and her muscles to relax. She became an insect, caught in a spider's web.

"Relax now, darling," Lorelei murmured into her ear. "It's almost over. Once my master frees himself, he'll make short work of the Thorn boy. Do you hear his heartbeat fading? I do." Claws skimmed down the side of her face, over her ear, stroking her hair. The hands turned her around. "Watch him die."

That was a mistake. At the sight of Ashcroft smashing through the thorns to reach Nathaniel, Elisabeth felt everything at once: the sting of her cuts and bruises, the blood pumping through her veins, the night air filling her lungs, the breeze cooling her wet cheeks. Her surroundings grew sharp-edged and crystal clear as Lorelei's influence faded to cobwebs.

And there was Silas. At some point during the battle, he had managed to drag himself up into a crouch. Though agony fogged his yellow eyes, he watched her calmly, with meaningful intent. Demonslayer lay beside him, almost touching his bound hands. He looked at the sword and then back at her. He was waiting for her signal.

Elisabeth couldn't nod. Lorelei would see. Slowly, like a cat, she blinked.

Demonslayer slid across the marble. When it came within reach, Elisabeth stomped on the hilt, flipping the sword into the air. She ignored the bright slice of pain as she caught the naked blade in one hand and thrust it backward, deep into Lorelei's body.

There was less resistance than she expected. Lorelei choked, coughed. Her claws tightened convulsively on Elisabeth's arms. "You," she gritted out. "How dare you—"

And then she was gone. The death of a highborn demon was not like that of a fiend. No body remained, just tendrils of steam that wisped around Elisabeth, entangling her in a final embrace, smelling faintly of brimstone.

Without thinking, she staggered to Silas. She thrust Demonslayer through a link in the chains and twisted, levering the sword with all her might. Metal groaned. The link warped and split open.

Too late. Out of the corner of her eye, she saw Ashcroft raise his sword above Nathaniel's chest. She couldn't get there in time. And Silas, weakened—

The chains clattered to the ground, coiled empty on the flagstones.

Ashcroft's sword flashed in the moonlight, inscribing a downward arc.

And the point emerged red, protruding from Silas's back, where the weapon had speared him through the heart. In the span of a breath he had appeared between Ashcroft and Nathaniel, using his own body as a shield.

The world went still. Silence descended like frost. Silas's loose hair hung down, hiding his face. After a moment his pale hand rose to touch the length of iron that entered his chest, almost curiously, though in doing so, his claws sent up wisps of steam.

"I don't understand." Ashcroft spoke haltingly. "He didn't command you to do that."

Silas looked up at him. Their expressions could not have been more different. Silas was a carven saint, his marble countenance beautiful, impassive, untouched by emotion or pain. And Ashcroft was a mortal confronted, for the first time in his life, by something he couldn't comprehend.

"Had you let him die," Ashcroft said, "your bargain would have been fulfilled. The life he promised you—you would have received it. But now you've lost everything."

"Yes," whispered Silas. "I feel it. It is gone."

Ashcroft's eyes were wide. "Tell me why, demon! Tell me what you stood to gain—"

A trickle of blood ran from the corner of Silas's mouth, shockingly red against his white skin. He closed his eyes, seemingly in relief. Then, he vanished.

The moment Ashcroft's sword came free, Elisabeth was there to meet it. Iron clashed against iron as she forced the Chancellor back, sparing none of her strength. He managed a series of clumsy parries; then Demonslayer locked with his sword's hilt and wrenched the weapon from his grasp, sending it flying out of reach.

Panic flashed across his face. With a jolt, Elisabeth realized that both of his eyes were blue. Not only had his demonic mark vanished, his right sleeve hung in tatters over a normal arm. In Lorelei's absence, he was no longer a sorcerer, just an ordinary man.

Slowly, he lifted his empty hands in surrender.

"Are you going to kill me, Miss Scrivener?" he asked, his

face uncharacteristically solemn. "If you do, it will change you forever. It will set you down a path from which you cannot turn back. Believe me—I know."

Demonslayer drooped. In Elisabeth's moment of hesitation, Ashcroft's boots scuffed against stone. Moving faster than she could have predicted, he dodged between the vines and vaulted over the edge of the pavilion.

She dashed forward and caught herself against the crumbled balustrade, heart pounding, tensed to give chase. She could overtake him easily: he appeared to have twisted his ankle leaping down, for he stumbled as he fled through the tangle of roses. She could pursue him, and catch him, and end his plot for good.

Or she could run in the opposite direction, and find the help she needed to save Nathaniel's life.

TWENTY-SEVEN

THE REMAINDER OF the night passed in a blur. First there was the disorienting brightness of the palace, followed by the startled faces of the guests Elisabeth encountered in the halls. After that she recalled shouting, a flurry of action. A physician was summoned. Someone inquired after the wound on Elisabeth's hand, but she claimed that the blood was Nathaniel's, which got everyone outside in a hurry. The next thing she knew, she stood in the rose garden as two men carried Nathaniel's limp body into a carriage.

His condition was serious. She could tell that much by the physician's urgency, the cries that rang out for help. She tried to go to him, but hands held her back. They needed to know what had happened. *The Chancellor*, she said, and no one believed her. Not until a man called from the top of the pavilion and held up Ashcroft's sword, the gryphon on its pommel unmistakable in the moonlight.

Pandemonium. Lord Kicklighter's booming voice cut through the din. A guest helped her toward the carriage—and how strange everyone's finery looked, marked here and there with smears of Nathaniel's blood. Her own gown had been ruined beyond repair. Silas would not be pleased about that; they had spent an entire day together shopping, and he had patiently sat through several fittings, during which Elisabeth had had to stand very still, so that the seamstress did not stick her with pins. She could clearly picture his look of disapproval.

Then she remembered that Silas had been run through with a sword, and was gone.

She rode inside the carriage with Nathaniel and the physician. The wheels jostled over uneven ground, and once, Nathaniel groaned. Sweat beaded his forehead, but his hand felt freezing cold. She didn't remember taking hold of it. The physician was busy applying pressure to Nathaniel's chest. He glanced once at her injured palm, then at her face, and said nothing.

They pulled up outside Nathaniel's house, where a crowd had gathered. Half of the ballroom appeared to have followed them to Hemlock Park, now mixed with reporters and sorcerers wearing their nightclothes. Lights blazed in the homes all the way down the street, their windows flung open, people leaning out. Elisabeth barely noticed the commotion, because none of it was a fraction as strange as what was happening to Nathaniel's house.

All of the gargoyles had come to life. They prowled along the roofline and coiled themselves, snarling, around the corbels. The thorn bushes that grew in the unkempt gardens surrounding the house had stretched to tall, impenetrable hedges, rattling menacingly at anyone who drew near the iron fence. Dark clouds boiled overhead.

"The wards have activated," the physician told her. "The house recognizes that its heir is in danger, and will do anything to protect him from further harm. The difficulty is, there's no one else of his bloodline who can safely let us through. Miss Scrivener, does Nathaniel trust you?"

She watched the men lift Nathaniel from the carriage. In order to reach his wounds, the physician had removed his shirt. His skin, where it wasn't covered in blood, was as white as paper. His head lolled, and one of his arms dangled loose. His black hair fell like a spill of ink around his ashen face—black, without a hint of silver. The wrongness of it left her dazed.

"I don't know," she said. "Yes. I think so."

"It's unconventional, but we haven't much time. Try approaching the house. If anything threatens you, retreat quickly. I'd rather not end up with two patients tonight."

The hubbub quieted as Elisabeth stepped forward. Faces watched anxiously from the crowd. She recognized one of them as one of the girls who had gossiped about her in Ashcroft's conservatory, who looked stricken now, clutching a friend's hand.

During the carriage ride, Elisabeth hadn't let go of Demonslayer. It shone at her side as she crossed the threshold of the open gate, toward the thorn bushes, their crooked boughs looming above her. Instantly, their rattling ceased. A whisper ran through the hedge. Then the branches retreated, creating a path to the front door. One gargoyle sank down, and then another, lowering their heads like retainers welcoming the return of their queen.

Silence prevailed. She walked up the path and ascended the steps. When she reached for the doorknob, the bolt clicked on its own, and the door swung open without a touch.

Stunned, she stood aside to let the physician pass. He hurried up the path, giving instructions to the men carrying Nathaniel, his fingers on Nathaniel's pulse. A bespectacled young woman hurried alongside them, laden with bags and cases. Behind them, the branches closed back in, weaving together like threads on a loom, blocking out the crowd. The last thing Elisabeth saw before the thorns knit shut was a reporter gazing back at her. Wonder transformed his features, and his pencil had fallen to the ground, forgotten.

She followed the procession upstairs, unable to take her eyes from Nathaniel's unconscious face. There wasn't room for her in his bedroom, so she stood outside, flattening herself against the wall every time the physician's assistant passed with an ewer of water or an armful of blood-soaked linens.

No one said anything, but it was clear that Elisabeth was getting in the way. Numbly, she drifted back downstairs. She took off Nathaniel's coat and hung it on the coatrack. She noticed a few droplets of blood on the foyer's floor and used her gown to wipe them up, since its ivory silk was already ruined. Afterward she sat on the bottom step, her head buzzing with white noise. Dimly, from upstairs, she heard the scuffle of feet accompanied by a tense exchange of voices. The grandfather clock ticked in time with the beating of her heart.

As of this moment, Ashcroft was ruined. Everything would come out in the morning papers. The entire world would know him for who he truly was. But this didn't feel like a victory. Not with Silas lost, and Nathaniel bleeding upstairs. Not with Ashcroft still at large.

No—the fight wasn't over yet. It would be foolish to imagine otherwise. She sat for a moment longer, considering this, and then she rose and walked with purpose into Nathaniel's study, where she seized the magnifying device from his desk, flung it to the ground, and smashed it beneath her heel. She proceeded to the next room, where she found another mirror and tore it from the wall. She didn't stop there. A path of destruction marked her progress around the house. Glass cracked, shattered, exploded across carpets, bounced in glinting fragments down the furniture. No mirror was safe. She took Demonslayer's hilt to the one in the parlor, where she had spent so many hours studying grimoires, and watched her reflection splinter, then go tumbling to the floor. When she was finished downstairs, she made her way upward, leaving a trail of shards along the hallways.

It seemed as though she should feel something, but she did not. Her injured hand didn't hurt, even as blood ran freely down Demonslayer's pommel. The mirrors in their cumbersome frames yielded to her without effort. It was as though she were made of light and air, barely tethered to the physical world, at once unstoppable and in danger of coming apart, burning up, floating away.

At last, she reached her bedroom. She picked up the scrying mirror. She tried to explain what had happened to Katrien, who asked her a number of questions she couldn't answer, because at some point, words had stopped making sense. When they were finished talking, Elisabeth wrapped the mirror in a pillowcase and dropped it down the laundry chute. Ashcroft wouldn't be able to spy on her from there. Then she set about making the rest of the room safe, in the only way she knew how.

An incalculable amount of time later, she came back to herself, Demonslayer clenched in her good hand, surrounded by broken wood and glass. She thought, *Silas isn't going to like this.* Then she thought, *I will help him clean it up.*

The grief, when it came, struck her like a punch to the gut. She doubled over and sank to the floor, her breath coming in strangled gasps. She was not made of air or light. She was weakly, devastatingly human, and she did feel pain, more than she could bear. Silas was gone. She didn't know what Nathaniel was going to do, or how she was going to tell him, or whether she could endure the look on his face when she did. She didn't know if Nathaniel would wake again at all.

She wept until the world softened and blurred around her, and at last she knew nothing more.

When she next opened her swollen eyes, it was to the sight of an unfamiliar woman sitting on a chair in the corner. Afternoon light shone through the curtains. Elisabeth looked down at herself in bed, easily managed because she had been propped up on the pillows. A bandage swathed her injured hand. Demonslayer lay atop the covers on her other side, her fingers still clenched around the grip.

"Dr. Godfrey and I couldn't pry it from you, even after you fell asleep."

Elisabeth looked back at the woman. She wasn't unfamiliar, after all. She was the physician's assistant, thin and bespectacled, wearing a starched white pinafore. Dried blood streaked the front, but its presence didn't seem to bother her.

"My name is Beatrice," she said. "I'm the one who's been tending to you."

Elisabeth's heart skipped. She couldn't take her gaze from the stained pinafore. "Is Nathaniel—?"

"He's doing well. At least, as well as can be expected. Drink this." She brought a glass of water to Elisabeth's lips and watched her swallow some of it before she went on, speaking calmly, as if for her this was a perfectly ordinary morning, no different than a conversation over breakfast. "Magister Thorn lost a great deal of blood, but Dr. Godfrey is confident he will recover. Sorcerers can survive remarkable injuries with the help of their household wards. Even so, he shouldn't get out of bed until his chest has begun to heal."

Relief crashed over Elisabeth. She shoved herself upright, then froze, biting back a groan. Every inch of her body hurt. Even her bones ached. "There's a mirror in his room," she said. "I must—"

Beatrice laid a hand on her shoulder. "Dr. Godfrey and I have already seen to it." She added, more gently, "You told us what you had been doing last night, when we found you here on the floor. You don't remember that?"

Elisabeth didn't, and she preferred not to imagine the state in which they'd discovered her, but she was grateful they had taken her seriously. She looked down, gritting her teeth against her body's protests. "May I see Nathaniel?" she asked.

"If you'd like, though he won't wake for hours yet. When he does, he may not be quite himself. He's been given laudanum for the pain."

She helped Elisabeth into a dressing gown and walked her down the hall. Elisabeth wasn't sure she could have managed the journey on her own. While she tottered along like an old woman, Beatrice told her how lucky she was not to have broken anything. "Most people would have, after taking such hard blows." And then she looked askance at Demonslayer, still clutched in Elisabeth's hand.

When they reached Nathaniel's doorway, she could only stare. Nathaniel looked marooned in the broad expanse of his four-poster bed, with its carved pillars and dark brocade hangings. His face was turned to the side, and the angle of the sunlight cut across his sharp cheekbone, making a sculpture of his features. Beneath the open collar of his nightshirt, bandages wrapped his chest.

Somehow, it didn't feel right to see him this way. His breathing was so shallow that his chest barely rose and fell. His face was still: his brow smooth, his mouth slack. Blue shadows tinted the skin beneath his eyes. It seemed as though he would break if she touched him, as though he had transformed into a substance other than flesh and blood, as fragile as porcelain.

Beatrice assisted her into the armchair pulled up near him and turned to go. She paused at the doorway, her bedside manner parting slightly, like a curtain, to reveal a hint of wariness underneath. "Is it true Magister Thorn has no human servants?" she asked. "Only a demon?"

"Yes, but there's no need to be afraid. Silas—that's his name—he isn't here any longer. Even if he were, he wouldn't—" Elisabeth fought for words, gripped by an overpowering need to explain, to make Beatrice understand. It felt unacceptable that no one else knew who Silas was and what he had done. She finished with difficulty, "He sacrificed himself to save Nathaniel's life."

Beatrice frowned, gave a slight nod, and left, unmoved by the revelation. *She thinks he acted under Nathaniel's orders.* And as simply as that, Elisabeth realized no one would ever appreciate Silas's final act. It was not a story that anyone would believe. He had vanished from the world like mist, leaving nothing behind except rumors: the dreadful creature that had served House Thorn.

The injustice of it overwhelmed her, stung her eyes like needles. For a long time she sat in silence, her head bowed, blinking back tears.

Fabric rustled. Beside her, Nathaniel had stirred. She held her breath as his eyelashes fluttered, even though his movements appeared less a conscious effort to wake than a reaction to a dream. Impulsively, she reached over to brush a lock of hair from his forehead. The strands slid through her fingers, softer than silk. She had so little to give him, but at least she could let him know that he wasn't alone.

Nathaniel's eyes cracked open, bright and unfocused.

"Silas?" he whispered.

Elisabeth's heart crumpled. She finished tucking his hair behind his ear, and then she took his hand. She watched him slip, reassured, back to sleep.

The loss of his demonic mark told her that he'd gained back the two decades of life he had bargained to Silas. Yet it was impossible to be glad for him. She knew that given the choice, he would trade the years away again in a heartbeat to have Silas back.

Hours passed. Beatrice came and went, bringing a cold lunch scavenged from the kitchen. Afterward, Dr. Godfrey changed Nathaniel's bandages. Elisabeth sat gripping the chair's armrests as the stained cloth peeled away to reveal four jagged lines carved diagonally across Nathaniel's chest. They stretched from the bottom of his ribs on one side to his collarbone on the other, clamped together with sutures. She forced herself not to look away, remembering the sweep of Ashcroft's claws, the blank look on Nathaniel's face as he stumbled backward. She could tell that the wounds would leave fierce and permanent scars.

When Dr. Godfrey finished reapplying the bandages, he placed his palm on Nathaniel's forehead and frowned.

"What's wrong?" she blurted out.

"He's developing a fever. That's common with injuries of this nature. Wound fevers can be dangerous, but in his case, the wards should protect him from any serious harm." He paused. "Magister Thorn? Can you hear us?"

Weakly, from the bed, Nathaniel had coughed. Elisabeth balanced on the edge of her seat, every muscle tensed. Soon Nathaniel's eyes drifted open, the pale clear gray of quartz. He regarded her in silence, studying her face as though he had never seen it before, or as though he feared he had forgotten it while he slept. Finally he said, "You stayed with me." His voice was barely a sigh, a breath.

She nodded. Tears filled her eyes. She swallowed, but the words came out anyway, unstoppable. "I'm sorry. This is all my fault. It was my idea to confront Ashcroft at the ball. Without me, none of this would have happened."

A wrinkle appeared between his eyebrows. At first she thought he was having trouble remembering. Then he said, "No. The scrying mirror . . . you couldn't have known." He paused, collecting his strength. Even breathing seemed to hurt. "Ashcroft. Did you catch him?"

Tearfully, she shook her head. She didn't want to tell him the rest, but she had to. "Silas—" Her voice sounded high, odd, unlike itself. Her throat closed up. She couldn't finish.

The wrinkle deepened in confusion. She saw the moment he began to understand. His gaze didn't leave her face, but he went very still.

Silverware chimed in the hallway. Beatrice. She had gone downstairs to make tea.

Nathaniel went alert. Before Elisabeth could stop him, he heaved himself upright. He instantly went gray with pain and listed to one side, catching himself on his elbow, but he didn't make a sound. He stared at the door with such intensity, waiting, that when Beatrice came into view and saw him, she froze.

"If you'd like to sit up," Dr. Godfrey said, "we'll arrange the pillows for you. You mustn't strain yourself so soon."

Nathaniel didn't seem to hear him. A sense of impending doom hollowed Elisabeth's stomach. Beatrice was holding the same silver tray that Silas always used. Nathaniel's eyes were stark, wild, almost unseeing.

"Get out," he said quietly.

Beatrice and Dr. Godfrey traded a look.

"Both of you. Get out."

Beatrice came forward and set the tray on the nightstand, then stepped back, her hands folded against her pinafore. She had the manner of someone accustomed to dealing with difficult patients. But she didn't know that to Nathaniel, what she had done was unforgivable.

Her crime was simple. She had brought tea. She wasn't Silas.

Calmly, she began, "The laudanum may make you feel—"

Nathaniel surged out of bed, grabbed the tray, and flung it against the wall. Everyone flinched as the porcelain shattered, leaving a splash of tea dribbling down the wallpaper.

"OUT!" Nathaniel roared. "Get out of my house!"

His voice echoed from every direction, magnified. The walls shook and groaned ominously; a trickle of plaster dust fell from the ceiling onto the bed. He stood panting in his nightshirt and pajama trousers, his eyes ablaze with feverish light.

"Come along, Beatrice," Dr. Godfrey said, closing his leather case with a snap. He shot Nathaniel one last look as he ushered his assistant from the room. Footsteps creaked on the stairs. A moment later, the front door clicked shut.

Elisabeth glanced out the window. The sun hung low in the sky, winking redly through the thorn bushes. Their tangled branches unwound to let Dr. Godfrey and Beatrice pass, then laced back together again.

She turned back to Nathaniel, her mouth hanging open.

His rage had vanished, though not the febrile glitter in his eyes. "Come on, Scrivener," he said brightly. "We must go at once. Do you mind if I lean on you?"

"Wait," she protested. "You aren't supposed to be out of bed."

"Ah. That explains why my legs have stopped working." He gave Demonslayer an approving glance. "Good, you've come prepared."

"But—" As he slumped, she rushed to catch him before he struck the floor. He had gone so droopy that it required some effort to arrange his arm over her shoulders. "Where are we going?"

He laughed as though she had asked a completely nonsensical question. "We're summoning Silas, of course. We're getting him back."

Her eyes widened. She hadn't known bringing Silas back was possible. But just like that, she knew where to take them without Nathaniel having to say it out loud. The forbidden room. The one behind the locked door.

It took them an eternity to make their way down the hall, pausing every time he sagged against her, blinking his way back to consciousness. Surely this wasn't a good idea. If she had any sense, she would turn around and put him back to bed. He couldn't frighten her off like Beatrice and Dr. Godfrey; even if he could, he wouldn't be able to make it down the hallway by himself. But as soon as the thought occurred to her, her conscience revolted.

He would never forgive her for the betrayal. And she could not leave him alone, as he had been as a boy of twelve, with no one else in the world to depend on. Right now, she was the only person he had left.

When they reached the door, Nathaniel muttered an Enochian phrase under his breath and snapped his fingers. Nothing happened. He blinked, stared uncomprehendingly at the door-knob, and then swore. "Silas is the one who keeps track of all the keys. Ordinarily I just . . ." He snapped his fingers again, to no avail. His magic was gone. She saw in his face how much its absence shook him, as though he had put out his hand to steady himself and found nothing, only empty air. Now he didn't know what to do.

"Hold on." She raised Demonslayer and slammed its hilt against the doorknob. The first blow dented the knob. The sec-ond sent it clattering to the floor.

Nathaniel began shaking. She looked at him in concern, only to discover he was laughing. "Scrivener," he said.

She frowned. "What?"

"It's just—you're so—" He was laughing too hard to finish, gasping helplessly from the pain. He made a motion with his hand that suggested a hammer striking a nail.

"I think you've had too much laudanum," she said. She pushed open the unresisting door and drew him inside.

The stink of aetherial combustion almost choked her. As she looked around, the back of her neck prickled. The curtains were drawn, letting in only enough light for her to make out that the room appeared empty. A few small objects that she couldn't identify lay scattered across the center of the room, as though children had once lived there and left a few of their toys behind. For the first time in weeks, she felt the imaginary presence of the house's ghosts, of Nathaniel's dead. Moving carefully, she lowered him to the floor and crossed the room to yank open the curtains.

Dust swirled amid the sunlight that flooded in. Looking down, she jumped aside. An elaborate pentagram was carved into the floorboards beneath her feet, the grooves burnt black and caked with grime. Stains darkened the wood within and around it—bloodstains, some of them so large she wondered whether they marked places where people had died. The objects she had glimpsed turned out to be half-melted candles, anchored in pools of their own wax at each of the pentagram's five points. Two other items waited on the floor beside the circle. A matchbox and a dagger, the metal dulled by a patina of dust.

She remembered what Silas had said to her all those weeks ago. *You would not wish to see.* This was where he had been brought into the mortal realm, not once in the distant past, but time and time again.

Nathaniel fumbled with the matchbox, his fingers trembling too violently to withdraw a match. Elisabeth tucked Demonslayer under her arm and took it from him. "I want to help," she said. "How is this done?"

He looked up at her, so pale, the steeply angled light shining translucently through the thin fabric of his nightshirt, revealing the outline of his body beneath. He looked like a ghost himself. "Are you certain?"

This was worse than using the scrying mirror. Worse even than stealing from the Royal Library. On the first day of her apprenticeship, Elisabeth had vowed to protect the kingdom from demonic influences. If she participated in a summoning, and a rumor somehow got out, even a whisper of speculation, every Great Library would be closed to her. No warden would speak to her. She would become an outcast from the only world in which she had ever belonged.

But her oaths meant nothing if they asked her to forsake people she cared about in their greatest moment of need. If that was what being a warden required of her, then she wasn't meant to become one. She would have to decide for herself what was right and what was wrong.

Though she didn't speak, Nathaniel saw the answer written on her face. His hand curled into a fist against the floor. She thought that he might attempt to dissuade her, but then he said, "Light them in order, counterclockwise. Make sure you stay outside the circle. Don't cross the lines. That's important."

Elisabeth clumsily struck a match with her bandaged hand and moved around the pentagram. As each candle flared to life, it seemed to mark the immolation of something past and the beginning of something new. So many of her memories were characterized by flame. The gleam of candlelight on Demonslayer's garnets. Warden Finch, the ruddy glow of a torch playing across his face, asking her if she was consorting with demons. The Book of Eyes reduced to ashes on the wind.

As she shook out the final match, she looked up to find the dagger in Nathaniel's hand. Before she could react, he drew it along his bared wrist, beside the scar that twisted up his forearm. Only a shallow cut, but the sight of blood beading on his skin still made her heart skip with a fluttering anxiety she had never felt before on anyone else's behalf. When he was finished, the dagger fell from his weakened grip.

"Stand back," he said. He pressed his wrist to the edge of the circle, leaving a red smear on the floorboards. When he spoke again, his voice echoed with ancient power. "By the blood of House Thorn, I summon you, Silariathas."

Silariathas. Silas's true name. It did not slither from her mind like the other Enochian words she had heard Nathaniel speak, but stuck fast, smoldering, as if branded by fire onto the surface of her thoughts.

Outside, the sun sank behind the rooftops, plunging the

room into shadow. A breeze disturbed the stagnant air, snuffing out all five of the candles simultaneously. The curtain rings chimed as the drapes stirred. And a figure appeared at the center of the pentagram.

He wore nothing but a white cloth draped loosely around his waist. In his nakedness he appeared not just slender, as she had thought of him before, but thin, almost gaunt. Shadows traced his ribs, the bones of his wrist, the sharp edges of his shoulder blades, a form elegant in its spareness, as if everything unnecessary had been pared away. His unbound hair hung in a straight and silvery cascade that fell past his shoulders, hiding his downcast face. Where the sword had entered him, his chest was smooth. He looked different like this—more beautiful, more frightening. Less human than ever before.

He lifted his head and smiled. "Hello, Nathaniel."

TWENTY-EIGHT

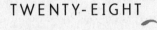

FOR A MOMENT, nothing happened. Gazing up at Silas from the floor, Nathaniel wore the expression of a man about to plunge into a battle that he knew he could win, but only at a terrible cost. Elisabeth didn't understand. She hadn't expected a joyful reunion to take place inside a blood-soaked pentagram, but this . . . it felt wrong. There was something so strange about Silas's smile.

"Silas," she said, stepping forward. "Are you all right?"

"Don't." Nathaniel's rough, urgent command struck her like a slap. His hand caught her wrist. "Don't touch the circle."

She could have easily shaken off Nathaniel's hold. Instead, it was Silas's look that stopped her in her tracks. His pupils were so dilated that his irises appeared black, circled by a thin yellow edge, like the sun during a full eclipse. His eyes held no trace of his usual self, no sign that he even recognized her.

"He can't cross the lines," Nathaniel said, "but the instant you touch them, he will claim your life. He'll kill you."

That made no sense. Yesterday morning, Silas had brought

her breakfast. He had helped her into her ball gown and clipped on her earrings. But Nathaniel wouldn't say something like that unless he meant it. "What's wrong with him?" she whispered.

Briefly, Nathaniel squeezed his eyes shut. Sweat glistened at his temples, pasting down a few curls of his hair. "He's hungry," he said after a long pause. "Usually, highborn demons are summoned directly after their previous master has died. When they're sated, they're easier to bargain with. But it's been six years since . . ."

Since the death of Alistair Thorn, Elisabeth thought. *Since Silas's last payment.*

"Silas isn't human," Nathaniel went on. "When he's like this, the time we've spent with him, the understandings we've reached—none of that matters any longer. The hunger is too great."

And Silas wasn't just hungry. He was starving. Slowly, he turned his unnerving gaze back to Nathaniel. If he cared that they were talking about him, or even heard them, he gave no sign.

"Silariathas," Nathaniel said, with a calmness Elisabeth couldn't fathom, though perhaps it was the laudanum, or the blood loss, or the simple fact that he had faced this version of Silas before. "I have summoned you to renew our bargain. I offer you twenty years of my life in exchange for your service."

"Thirty," Silas countered, in a soft, rasping voice.

Nathaniel answered immediately, without hesitation. "Twenty-five."

"You would offer me so little?" Silas looked down at Nathaniel as though he were a crawling insect. His whispered words pelted like sleet. "Remember who I am. Before House Thorn bound me to its service, I served emperors and kings. Rivers flowed red with the blood of mortals I slew at their bidding. You are just a boy, and I debase myself folding your clothing and fetching your tea. Thirty years, or I will find a new master, one who will reward me in proportion to my worth."

Nathaniel's eyelids fluttered. Grimacing, he put a hand to his chest and gripped the bandages through his shirt. When he let out a gasp, Elisabeth realized he was using the pain to keep himself conscious. He was fading, and any moment now, he would give in. He would do anything to get Silas back, even bargain away time that he might not have.

She couldn't bear it. Silas watched without pity, without even interest, the suffering of the boy who loved him, whose life he had gone to such lengths to save.

"Nathaniel's hurt, Silas!" she exclaimed. "Can't you see?"

Silas's gaze disengaged from Nathaniel, slowly, as though he found it difficult to look away, and fixed upon her instead. Her breath caught at the emptiness in his night-dark eyes, but she didn't waver.

"I know you still care," she said. "Just hours ago, you sacrificed yourself for him. Don't waste that by asking so much of him. What if he doesn't have thirty years to give?"

"Miss Scrivener," he whispered, and her skin crawled; so he did recognize her, after all. Somehow, that was worse. "You continue to mistake me. When I intercepted the Chancellor's blade, I did so knowing that I would be summoned again, this time for an even greater reward. You see sacrifice where there is only selfishness."

"That isn't true. I was there."

"If you wish to prove it," he said, "you need only step inside the circle."

She saw the truth, then: the strain gripping his muscles, the wretchedness struggling to break through his cold, hungry mask. If she stepped forward, he would kill her; he wouldn't be able to stop himself. But he did not want to hurt her. He didn't want to take three decades from Nathaniel, either. She believed that with her whole heart.

"Take the ten extra years from me," she said.

"Elisabeth," Nathaniel croaked. "No."

She forged on, "You said yourself that my life was like no other you'd ever seen. You would like to taste it, wouldn't you?"

Silas's lips parted. In his black eyes, a flicker. Whatever battle raged within him left the icy surface untouched. Finally he whispered, "Yes."

"Then take it. Let's end this."

She remembered the night that he had given her Demonslayer, when he had advanced on her and frightened her. It was like that again, watching some terrible light go out of him as his hunger retreated. His lashes lowered. Hooded, his gaze considered the floor. "You understand that I can only serve one mortal at a time. As long as I walk this realm, you will be marked. But you will receive nothing in return."

"I know."

"The same conditions as before, Master Thorn?"

Nathaniel was leaning on one arm, which trembled with the effort of holding him upright, and he didn't have the strength to look at either of them. The silence spun out. She felt him trying to summon the energy to resist, to argue, finding his will sapped and his last reserves spent. At last, miserably, he nodded.

Silas stepped out of the pentagram and knelt before them. He took Elisabeth's unbandaged hand and kissed it. As his lips brushed across her skin, a touch as silky as the petals of a rose, she felt the promise of the ten years she had pledged to him draw out of her body and into his—a dizzy, weakening sensation, like blood rushing from her head. Next, he took Nathaniel's hand and repeated the gesture. She watched the silver flow back into Nathaniel's hair, beginning at the roots, a trickle of mercury flowing through the strands.

"I am your devoted servant," Silas said to him. "Through me, you are conferred the art of sorcery. Any command that you give, I shall follow."

Exhaustion slurred Nathaniel's words. "You hate following commands. If I order you around, you always make me regret it."

A faint, beautiful smile illuminated Silas's face. "Even so."

Smoothly, he moved to stand, but he wasn't able to complete the motion. Nathaniel had thrown his arms around him and now held him fast. Silas wasn't accustomed to being embraced. That much was plain. He stood bent, frozen, his eyes wide, staring over the top of Nathaniel's head, as if he hoped his gaze might land by chance upon an excuse great enough to relieve him of his present difficulty. When no such excuse presented itself, he raised his hand and carefully placed it atop his master's tousled curls. They remained that way for a time, until Nathaniel's arms loosened, then slipped from Silas's waist. He had fallen unconscious.

Silas looked down at him and sighed. He arranged Nathaniel's limbs and lifted him as though he were a child who had drifted asleep by the fire, and now needed to be carried upstairs to bed. He performed the maneuver with such familiarity that Elisabeth understood he had done it many times before, though doubtless when Nathaniel was much smaller. Silas bore his master's weight easily, but the fact remained that fully grown, Nathaniel posed an awkward burden, to say the least.

"I will see Master Thorn settled." Silas paused to sniff the air beside Elisabeth. "Then, Miss Scrivener, I shall draw you a bath. I believe supper is also in order. And—has no one lit the lamps?" He looked aggrieved. "I have hardly been absent for twenty-four hours, and already the world has descended into ruin."

Life and order returned to the house. Light chased away the darkness that pressed against the windowpanes. Linens were stripped, beds tidied, the remainders of meals whisked away. The shards of mirror-glass vanished from every room. Finally, after running his index finger down a wall sconce and inspecting it for dust, Silas announced that he was going to put something on for dinner and vanished into the kitchen. Elisabeth sat for a few minutes alone with Nathaniel, watching him sleep. She was tempted to lay her head on the covers and join him. Instead, she forced herself to get up and head downstairs. She needed to talk to Silas.

She moved quietly through the house. Even so, when she neared the kitchen door, he spoke without turning around. "I have found the scrying mirror, Miss Scrivener." His tone was mild. "In the future, I advise against using the laundry chute to dispose of magical artifacts."

Abashed, she came inside and perched on a stool by the hearth. There were signs of Beatrice having made use of the kitchen: a cutting board with a loaf of bread beside it, the remains of diced vegetables. A pot simmered on the fire. When Nathaniel kicked her out, she had been making soup.

Silas was dressed impeccably in his servant's uniform once more, his hair tied back, surveying Beatrice's work with disdain. As she watched, he adjusted the cutting board so that it sat parallel to the edge of the counter. She searched inside herself for resentment, fear, anger toward him, and found nothing.

He had always been honest with her about what he was.

"What have you done with the mirror?" she asked.

"I have placed it in the attic, facing a portrait of Clothilde Thorn. Should the Chancellor happen to look through it, I trust he will receive an unpleasant surprise." Before Elisabeth could respond, he said, "Would you try that broth and tell me how it tastes?"

She found a ladle and dipped it into the pot. "It's good," she reported.

"But not exceptional?"

"I suppose not," she said, unsure whether there was such a thing as exceptional broth.

"I feared as much," he sighed. "I shall have to start over from the beginning."

Elisabeth watched him dice carrots and onions, hypnotized by the rhythmic tapping of the knife against the board. After last night, it seemed impossible that his alabaster hands should look so flawless. His burnt, steaming wounds flashed before her eyes, and she winced. "Silas," she said tentatively. "How did Ashcroft catch you?"

The knife paused. She couldn't tell if the hint of tension in his shoulders was real or imagined. "He used a device invented by the Collegium during the Reforms, designed to control rebellious sorcerers by capturing their servants. I did not expect it. I had not seen one since the days that I served Master Thorn's great-grandfather."

"I'm sorry." Guilt twisted her stomach. "If I hadn't asked you to go—"

"Do not apologize to me, Miss Scrivener." His voice sounded clipped, as close to anger as she had ever heard him. "It was my own carelessness at fault."

Elisabeth doubted that. Silas was never anything but meticulous. However, she received the impression that he wouldn't appreciate her saying so out loud.

Finally, he spoke again. "You came downstairs to ask about the life you bargained to me. You wished to know how it works."

She sat up in surprise. "Yes."

"But now you are having second thoughts."

"I'm wondering if—perhaps it would be better not to know." She hesitated. "I could still live to be seventy, or I could die tomorrow. If I knew—if you told me—I think that would change the way I lived. I would always be thinking about it, and I don't want that."

Silas continued chopping, aware she wasn't finished.

"But I would like to know . . . how it happens. Do you do it yourself? Or do we just . . . ?"

She imagined herself toppling over dead, her heart stopped in an instant. That wouldn't be so terrible, at least not for herself. The thought of Nathaniel dying that way—

"No," said Silas. "It is not like that." Now it was his turn to hesitate. He went on softly, "It is impossible to know how many years a human will live, or in what manner they will die. Life is like the oil within a lamp. It can be measured, but the pace at which it burns depends upon how the dial is turned day by day, how bright and fierce the flame. And there is no predicting whether the lamp might be knocked to the ground and shatter, when it could have blazed on a great while longer. Such is the unpredictability of life. It is good you do not have many questions; I do not have any answers. A portion of the fuel, the life force that once belonged to you and Master Thorn—I hold it now within myself. That is all I can tell you. The rest remains uncertain."

Thoughtfully, Elisabeth leaned back against the fireplace's warm stones. "I see." She found his explanation strangely comforting—the idea that she had no preordained number of years remaining, that even Silas didn't know her fate.

The warmth of the stones soothed her bruised and aching muscles. Her eyelids drooped. She felt as though she were half in the kitchen, listening to the quiet rattle of pots and pans, and half back in Summershall, dreaming of the apples in autumn, the market saturated in golden light. Eventually, she was roused by Silas setting the table in front of her. Her stomach growled at the rich aroma of thyme emanating from the pot on the fire. She blinked the rest of the way awake, watching him lift the pot's lid and glance inside.

She wondered how he could tell whether it was finished, finding the taste and presumably the smell unappetizing. "Did one of the servants teach you how to cook?" she asked drowsily.

"No, miss." He straightened to fetch a bowl. "The human servants did not speak to me, nor I to them. I learned through practice, as a matter of necessity. The appetite of a human boy of twelve is almost as frightening as that of a demon. And the lack of manners; I shudder to recall it."

Guiltily, she took the napkin and placed it on her lap, conscious of the look he had just sent her beneath his lashes. "So you didn't start until after Alistair died."

He nodded as he ladled soup into the bowl. "Initially, I didn't have the faintest idea how to care for Master Thorn. He came to me in poor condition; he had badly cut his arm drawing blood for the summoning—that is the scar, which I had not the knowledge to tend properly. . . ."

Silas's movements slowed, then stilled. His eyes were distant, gazing not at anything in the kitchen, but far into the past.

Firelight flickered across his youthful face, lending his alabaster features the illusion of color. Even that wasn't enough to make him look mortal. She was aware of the vast gulf between them: his unfathomable age, the inscrutable turning of his thoughts, like the cogs within a machine.

"First, I learned how to make tea," he said finally, speaking more to himself than to her. "When humans wish to help, they are forever offering each other tea."

Elisabeth's chest squeezed. She pictured the two different Silases: the one in the pentagram, eyes dark and empty with hunger, and the other in the pavilion's moonlight, a sword through his chest, his features etched with relief.

She said, "You love him."

Silas turned away. He set the pot's lid back in place.

"I didn't understand before," she went on quietly. Beneath the table, the napkin twisted in her hands. "Truthfully, I hadn't thought it possible. It wasn't until today, when I finally saw why—" *Why you had taken twenty years of Nathaniel's life.* She didn't finish.

Silas rose and set the bowl before her. "Enjoy your supper, Miss Scrivener," he said. "I will attend to Master Thorn, and see if I can persuade him to take some broth."

As he turned, his eyes caught on something near her face, and he paused. He reached toward her, his claws very close to her neck, and drew out a lock of her hair. Her heart skipped. Several of the strands shone silver against the chestnut tresses spilling over his hand. Silas's mark. It wasn't as noticeable as Nathaniel's, but she would still have to hide it—perhaps cut it off in order to avoid suspicion.

"I had nearly forgotten," Silas murmured, gazing at the silver as though mesmerized. "It is an extraordinary sign of trust for my master to have allowed you to hear my true name. You are the first person outside House Thorn to know it in centuries. Now, if you wish, you can summon me. But there is something else you must know. You also have the power to set me free."

Her mouth had gone dry, despite the soup sending up fragrant tendrils of steam. "What do you mean?"

His eyes shifted to her face. In the firelight they looked more gold than yellow. "Bound in servitude, I exist as a pale imitation of my true self, the greater part of my strength locked away. You saw a glimpse of what I truly am inside the pentagram—only a glimpse. Were you to free me, I would be unleashed upon this realm as a scourge, a cataclysm beyond reckoning."

A chill ran down Elisabeth's spine. Was he asking her to free him? Surely not. But she could think of no other reason why he would tell her this.

"As a child, Master Thorn once proposed the idea," Silas said, very softly. "He liked the thought of setting me free, of allowing us to be equals instead of master and servant. I told him not to. I give you the same warning now, though I don't believe you require it. Do not free me, Miss Scrivener, no matter what comes for us, no matter how unspeakable things become, because I assure you that I am worse."

He held her gaze a moment longer, then straightened and inclined his head in a bow. "Good night, miss," he said, and left her sitting petrified by the fire.

TWENTY-NINE

THE NEXT MORNING, Silas brought a copy of the *Brass-bridge Inquirer* inside from the stoop. A gargoyle had been gnawing on it, but it was still readable, and her pulse sped to a gallop as she smoothed it flat across the foot of Nathaniel's bed, pressing the torn strips back into place.

Ashcroft's name was everywhere. Her eyes skipped between the front page headlines, unable to decide where to settle first. There was the column on the left: DEADLY DUEL THROWS ROYAL BALL INTO CHAOS. And then on the right: MAGISTE-RIUM SCRAMBLES TO INSTATE NEW CHANCELLOR. But the bold text crowding the page's center was by far the most exciting: OBERON ASHCROFT, CHANCELLOR OF MAGIC, IMPLICATED IN GREAT LIBRARY SABOTAGE.

She bent over it and began to read. *"Due to his multiple attempts to silence Elisabeth Scrivener, a key witness in the Great Library investigation, Chancellor Ashcroft is believed to be connected to the recent string of attacks. He is wanted for attempted murder and the illegal summoning of lesser demons.*

The Magisterium has assembled a perimeter around his estate, where he is believed to be hiding, but as of yet have not been able to penetrate the wards. . . ."

She trailed off, remembering what Ashcroft had told her when she'd first arrived: his wards were powerful enough to repel an army. Perhaps the Magisterium hoped he would surrender, but Elisabeth couldn't see that happening. Ashcroft wouldn't go easily. And on the pavilion, he had almost spoken as though it no longer mattered whether people found out about him—that if his plan succeeded, its results would make all of this irrelevant.

Quietly, Nathaniel moaned. She looked up, but he hadn't woken. He was twisting in the throes of fever, his cheeks flushed, his hair damp with sweat. She watched him turn his head and mutter something inaudible against the pillow. His loose night-shirt clung to the lines of his body, but had slipped off one shoulder, revealing a glistening collarbone.

She rose and wrung out one of the cloths in the basin nearby. When she folded it and placed it on his forehead, she felt the heat radiating from his skin even before her hand drew near. He winced as though the wet cloth were painful. Tentatively, she stroked his damp curls, and at her touch, he sighed and went still. His breathing eased.

Something drew tight inside her, like a violin string awaiting the touch of a bow. Looking down at him, her heart ached with a song that did not have words or notes or form, but strained nonetheless to be given voice—a sensation that was not unlike suffering, for it seemed too great for her body to contain. It was much like how she had felt on the pavilion, when they had almost kissed.

She withdrew to the window, where she pressed her burning

cheeks against the cold panes. Outside, snowflakes fell glittering past the glass. The snow had begun overnight, shortly after Nathaniel had woken screaming and delirious from a nightmare, and then subsided shivering in Silas's arms. Unable to sleep afterward, Elisabeth had been awake to see the first flakes drift down. It had fallen steadily ever since. Now a thick coat blanketed the gargoyles, who shook themselves occasionally, sending up sparkling puffs of white. A shimmering layer of ice glazed the branches of the thorn bushes and the rooftops across the street. She gazed in wonder at the scene. She had never known a winter storm to arrive so early in the year.

With her face pressed to the window, she became aware of a distant noise, a sort of buzzing sound—shouting, she realized, distorted to a tinny vibration by the leaded glass. She frowned and squinted through the snow. The scene that resolved itself was so ridiculous that it made her blink, wondering whether her imagination had gotten the best of her.

A man was stuck in the hedge, his arms and legs tangled in thorn branches, shouting for help as a lion-shaped gargoyle prowled toward him. Her eyes widened when she saw that he was wearing a postman's uniform. She tightened her dressing gown and pelted down the stairs.

The front door sprang open without a touch. A blast of cold air struck her, flinging snowflakes into the foyer. She barely noticed the frigid shock as her bare feet sank deep into the snow.

"Don't hurt him!" she cried to the gargoyle, which was poised to spring, its stone tail lashing back and forth. The snarl fell from its whimsical face—apparently carved by someone who had never actually seen a lion—as she approached and laid a hand on its shoulder.

"Thank god you're here," the postman sputtered. "I didn't realize that blasted hedge would come alive. Sorcerers, I tell you. Why don't they use magic to collect their packages, and save us ordinary folk the trouble?"

"I don't think they're practical enough," she said as she helped him free his limbs from the branches. "The last time I saw Nathaniel conjure an object, it nearly fell on my head and killed me. Thank you." She turned the package he had handed her around, and her heart leaped at the name scrawled above the return address: Katrien Quillworthy.

The postman waved her off. He was already beating a hasty retreat through the passage that had opened in the hedge. "Just tell that sorcerer of yours to stop making it snow. It's falling over the entire city, you know, not just in Hemlock Park. At this rate, the river will freeze solid by nightfall. Half the houses on my route are snowed in, traffic's a nightmare. . . ."

She almost protested, but then she thought of the way Nathaniel had been muttering incoherently ever since his night-mare, shivering with violent bouts of chills. This wouldn't be the first time he'd cast spells in his sleep.

She looked up at the milk-white sky with a renewed sense of awe. Snowflakes spiraled downward, settling on her hair and eyelashes. Silence had enveloped the normally bustling street, the quiet so profound that she could almost hear the ice crystals chiming in the clouds: a high, chalky, clear ringing, as though someone were tapping the highest keys on a piano far above the rooftops. *Nathaniel did this,* she thought.

In her head, she repeated what the postman had called him. *That sorcerer of yours.* Was that what everyone thought now? Suddenly she felt oddly clumsy, like the world had shifted a few degrees on its axis. Clutching the package, she hurried back inside.

She tore off the wrappings in the study, and held her breath as she unfolded the beautifully drawn map of Austermeer within. She had forgotten it was on its way. Katrien had put it in the post almost two weeks ago, at the start of their meetings, after she had found it gathering dust in one of the Great Library's storage rooms. They had always planned to hang it above the fireplace.

Elisabeth stood on her toes and pinned it up. Standing back, she saw that Katrien had circled Ashcroft's attacks in red ink. Knockfeld. Summershall. Fettering. Frowning, she scavenged a pen and inkwell from the desk and circled Fairwater, too. With the four libraries marked off, Harrows represented the fifth and final target of a near complete, almost perfect circle around the kingdom.

Slowly, Elisabeth sat down. The pattern reminded her of something. A half-formed idea itched at the back of her mind, but it slipped away whenever she reached for it, always just outside her grasp. Her eyes traced the map over and over. Beside the Royal Library at the very center of the circle, Katrien had drawn a question mark. They had never figured out whether Ashcroft planned to target Brassbridge after Harrows.

For a moment her surroundings receded and she was back in Ashcroft Manor, raising her champagne glass in a toast. She heard her own voice alongside the other guests, reciting after Ashcroft, *To progress.* Ghostly laughter echoed in her ears. What was she missing? Frustrated, she dug her knuckles against her eyes until bursts of color filled her vision.

She shouldn't be sitting safely in Nathaniel's house. She should be out there doing something, fighting back against Ashcroft. But this wasn't a battle she could win alone. As the minutes ticked on, all she could do was wait.

• • •

Nathaniel's fever broke the next morning. When Silas changed his bandages, the strips of linen came away clean. The wounds beneath no longer looked raw and angry, but had healed overnight to the shiny, healthy pink of weeks-old scars.

"It is the doing of the wards," Silas explained, seeing Elisabeth's expression as he prepared to remove Nathaniel's stitches. "Magic has been laid down in the house's stones by Master Thorn's ancestors for hundreds of years. Spells of protection and healing, intended to guard each heir."

The snow tapered off to a fine glittering dust as the afternoon wore on, and none too soon; the drift on the windowsill was already eighteen inches deep, burying the gargoyle that had stationed itself on the roof outside. Quiet muffled the house, as though the walls had been stuffed with feather-down. Out of tasks to do, Silas transformed into a cat and slept curled up by Nathaniel's feet, his nose tucked beneath his tail. Elisabeth watched the two of them drowsily, surprised to discover that Silas did sleep. She had always imagined him staying awake through the night polishing the silver or prowling Brassbridge's streets on mysterious errands. Did he have his own room in the manor? She had never seen any sign of where he kept his clothes. Her eyelids drooped. One day, she would ask Nathaniel. . . .

She opened her eyes some time later to find that it had already grown dark. Flames crackled in the fireplace, and Silas had tucked a blanket over her legs. Her breath stopped when her gaze traveled to Nathaniel. He was awake. He had pulled himself up against the headboard and was staring into the shadows of the hall, one hand resting loosely on his bandaged chest, his gray eyes unreadable in the light of the candles arranged around the room. When she shifted, he looked at her and drew in a ragged breath. Anguish shone in his eyes.

"Ten years, Elisabeth." His voice cracked with emotion. "You shouldn't have done it. Not for me."

She had braced herself for this moment during the long hours of waiting, trying to imagine how he would react once he regained his senses enough to recall what had happened, but she still wasn't prepared for the intensity of his expression. She had thought he might be angry with her, or perhaps berate her for her foolishness. With his gaze upon her now so raw with despair, she saw that she couldn't have been more wrong. One by one, her rehearsed arguments fell away.

Quietly, she asked, "Would you have done the same for me? I think you would have."

"That is not—" But he couldn't finish, for his stricken look plainly said, *Of course; that and more. Anything. Everything.* He pressed his eyes shut before he could betray himself further, but she had already seen enough to leave her shaken. He continued evenly, "When Silas brought you back, I knew no good would come of an association between us. I wished daily that you would leave." He dragged a hand over his face. "I thought—I hoped— that after the battle, you might have come to your senses. That I would wake and find you gone."

The words were harsh. She held her breath, waiting for the rest.

"But you stayed with me. And selfishly, I was glad—I had never wanted anything more in my life. Damn you," he said. "You unmanageable, contrary creature. You have made me believe in something at last. It feels as wretched as I imagined."

She wiped at the wetness on her cheek. "You wouldn't like me if I were manageable," she said, and he laughed, a soft, tormented sound, as though she had slipped a knife between his ribs. She thought she understood what he was feeling, because she felt it too: a sort of joy and pain at once, an unbearable yearning of the heart.

"I'm sure you're right." He sounded hoarse. "Though I have to admit, I could have done without almost getting crushed by a bookcase the first time we met."

"That only happened once," she said. "There were extenuating circumstances."

This time his laugh was louder, surprised. His eyes locked with hers, and her breath caught. His longing for her was plain, as tangible a sensation as an invisible thread drawn tight between them. He tensed and looked away, his gaze landing on the window.

"It's been snowing?" he asked.

"You did that while you were asleep." At his expression of horror, her heart plunged, and she added quickly, "It's all right. You haven't hurt anyone. It's just snow." She stood and took his hand. "Come look."

Nathaniel appeared doubtful, but he stiffly climbed out of bed and allowed her to help him to the window seat. As they settled there, Silas opened one yellow eye. He regarded them for a moment, and then he leaped off the bed and padded from the room.

There was barely enough space for both her and Nathaniel on the window seat's cushions. A frosty chill penetrated the glass, but his body was warm from bed, and close, his bent leg pressing against hers.

Snow had transformed the city. Even in the blue twilight she could see impossibly far across the rooftops, their shingles etched in white, the view luminous and clear. Chimneys sent up wisps of smoke. Clouds parted to reveal a glittering sky.

Every glow was refracted: the warm burnishing shine of the streetlamps, the cold luster of the stars, banishing the darkness to almost nothing. Night would never truly fall in the presence of so much light.

She had expected the streets to be empty, and for the most part they were—of traffic, of shoppers. But people trooped nevertheless through the snow and the golden lamplight, some in groups, others in pairs holding hands, all traveling silently in the same direction. There was an almost sacred quality to the procession, like a vision of saints crossing from this life to the next.

"Where are they going?" she asked.

"To the river." Nathaniel's breath fogged the glass. Gradually, the tension bled from his shoulders. "When it freezes, everyone goes skating."

"Even in the dark?"

Slowly, as if caught in a dream, he nodded. "I haven't been in years—I used to go with my family. They light bonfires along the shore, and roast so many chestnuts you can find your way there by smell." He paused. "If you'd like, I'll take you there this winter."

There were an infinite number of reasons to turn him down. It was unlikely she'd be here come winter. She might not even be alive. A mere twenty minutes away by carriage, Ashcroft was in his manor, scheming.

But it seemed to Elisabeth that evil could not exist right now, in this place, not with all those people making their pilgrimage by lamplight to the river; there was too much beauty in the world for evil to possess any hope of victory.

"I would like that," she said.

"Are you sure? I'm already having second thoughts. I just

had an image of you speeding around with knives attached to your feet."

She frowned at him. He was grinning. She realized, with a pang, that she had missed his smile: the wicked look it gave him, the amusement that sparkled in his eyes like sunlight dancing across water. As they gazed at each other, and seconds passed, his grin began to fade.

"Don't stop," she said, but it was no use. He looked serious again.

Yet it was not the same seriousness as before. The air had changed between them. She grew keenly aware of every place their bodies touched, which now felt hot instead of merely warm, a heat that spread to her cheeks and tightened her stomach—a sweet, almost painful anticipation.

She swallowed. "I wanted to ask," she said, "about when we were on the pavilion—when we . . ." Nathaniel was looking at her in such a way that she nearly couldn't finish. "Was that you?" she asked. "Or was it Ashcroft's spell controlling you?"

He didn't answer with words. Instead he leaned forward and kissed her, his lips as soft as crushed velvet, his fingers tangling in her hair.

Afterward, he drew away. Disappointment flooded her, but he only moved far enough to rest his forehead against hers. "God, Elisabeth, I've been doomed since the moment I watched you smack a fiend off my carriage with a crowbar. How could you not tell? Silas has been rolling his eyes at me for weeks."

She laughed. In a dizzying rush, a great many of the things he had said and done suddenly made perfect sense. She felt transformed by the revelation. Nothing else existed but their mingled breath, the chill of the window against her side, the memory of the softness of Nathaniel's lips lingering on her own. It was her turn to lean forward.

"Wait," he said, forcing out the word with an effort. "This is—we shouldn't."

"Why not?"

"It wouldn't be fair to you. I can't offer you a decent future. Even as a child I gave up any hope of leading a good or normal life. To subject you to that, to drag you into the shadows with me—"

Tenderness swelled in her chest. Everything was always so complicated with him. She found his hand, resting on her cheek, and laced their fingers together.

"I'm already with you, and it suits me perfectly well," she said. "You're enough for me the way you are, Nathaniel Thorn. I want nothing more."

Then they were kissing again, with urgency. Back on the pavilion, she had been right; this did feel like drowning, a desperate, gasping, weightless plunge, Nathaniel's mouth as vital as air, the world receding far away as they sank together into a fathomless depth of sensation. She reached for him, wanting to feel him close against her, only to hear his breath catch. Too late, she remembered his bandaged chest. Before she could apologize, he pressed her down against the cushions.

Raised above her with his hands braced on either side, he took her in, his eyes dark and his lips flushed. His loose, rumpled hair cast blue shadows over the angular planes of his face; she thought distantly that he would need to have it cut soon, or start tying it back like Silas.

He leaned his weight onto one arm and reached for the belt of her dressing gown. With her heart in her throat, she nodded. She watched him slip the knot deftly, using just one hand, and part the garment with infinite care. Candlelight shimmered over the pale cream satin of her nightgown. She was aware of her quickened breath, her chest rising and falling, the tickle of the garment's lace edge and the cling of its sleek fabric.

"I fought the Book of Eyes in a nightgown," she told him, barely a whisper.

"In that case," he replied, "I expect I don't stand a chance."

She couldn't tell whether he was joking. His expression was almost one of agony. She took pity on him and placed her hands on his shoulders, nervousness quivering through her like a note of music as she pulled him down.

They kissed gently this time, shyly, now that the first heady rush was spent. Nathaniel cupped her face, caressing her hair, and then ran his hand down her side until he found her waist, his calloused fingers catching on the satin. Her skin had grown so sensitive to his touch that she surprised herself by shuddering in pleasure; the nightgown's slippery fabric melded with her body, and she barely felt as though she were wearing anything at all. Her focus narrowed to the heat of their lips and breath, the lush squeeze of his hand on her hip, the shifting muscles of his back as she skimmed her fingertips across his shoulders, marveling at how strong he felt, the way their bodies molded as though made to fit together. When she turned her head to let him press kisses to her neck, the chill air beside the window tasted of snow and starlight. The city's lights shimmered through patterns of frost.

Time seemed to slow. Reflected in the glass, the wavering flames of the candles stood still. Snowflakes hung sparkling in the air. She didn't know if it was Nathaniel's doing, or a different kind of magic entirely.

A fierce, urgent joy thrummed through her body. She felt as though she could leap out the window and take flight, soaring high above the rooftops, impervious to the cold. She closed her eyes and gripped Nathaniel's back, lost in the overwhelming sensation of his mouth against her skin.

A knock came on the door.

Heat scalded Elisabeth's cheeks as they both jerked upright. Minutes ago, the door had been open. Silas must have closed it at some point, and she could only imagine what he'd seen. "We're decent," she said, tugging the edges of her dressing gown into place.

The door creaked open. As usual, Silas's expression gave no indication of his thoughts. She instantly felt foolish for imagining that, after centuries of living among humans, he might have the capacity to be shocked by her and Nathaniel's behavior.

"Master," he said. "Miss Scrivener. I am sorry to disturb you, but you must come at once. Something is happening to the Codex Daemonicus."

For a split second, Elisabeth sat frozen, her ears ringing with Silas's words. Then she burst upright, almost bowling the armchair over in her haste to seize Demonslayer from the corner. Without a second thought, she charged outside.

Her eyes watered. She coughed. A haze hung over the hallway, and when she reached the stairwell, smoke billowed up from the foyer in oily clouds. The sour, unmistakable stench of burning leather choked her nostrils. Dimly, she was aware of Nathaniel and Silas following her as she flew down the stairs.

"Did anything spill on the Codex?" she shouted over her shoulder, mentally going over the precautions they had taken. Following the night that it had transformed into a Malefict, she had been careful not to set any candles nearby. But perhaps one of the potions in the study had exploded, or a magical artifact had acted up—

"No, miss," Silas replied. "Until a moment ago, all was well."

Elisabeth's stomach twisted. If the damage to the Codex hadn't happened on their end, that could only mean one thing.

Ashcroft had found a way inside.

THIRTY

WHEN ELISABETH REACHED the study, she drew up
short, squinting through the smoke that filled the room.
Her blood ran cold as she took in the scene. The Codex hovered several inches above Nathaniel's desk, its pages fanned out,
splayed at such a hideous angle that it risked breaking its own
spine. Embers danced along the edges of the pages, and the cover's leather bubbled like boiling tar.

Nathaniel appeared next to her, his shirt pulled over his nose
to block out the smoke. "It looks like it's being tortured."

That was precisely what Elisabeth feared. "I have to go in,"
she said, starting toward the grimoire.

He caught her arm. "Wait. We have no idea what's happening. You could get trapped in there."

His face was pale. Regret pierced her like a blade. She would
give anything to reverse time, to be back upstairs with him, her
troubles far away.

"You're right, but we have no other option. If Ashcroft is

torturing Prendergast, I must stop him, or at least try."

He opened his mouth to object, but she didn't hear what he said. She had already reached out and taken hold of the Codex, its cover searing her hand like a hot iron even through the bandages, and the world was spinning away.

She appeared in Prendergast's workshop with a stumble, almost slipping on the wet floorboards underfoot. The room looked as though it had been through an earthquake. The table lay overturned on its side; cracks splintered the ceiling beams. A tremor shook the dimension, and jars slid down the buckled shelves and shattered, spilling their slimy contents across the floor.

And this time, she hadn't come alone. Nathaniel's hand gripped her arm. Silas stood beside him, holding his wrist in turn. They exchanged looks. Either Prendergast had let them in on purpose, or he was no longer able to keep them out.

"Oh, wonderful," Prendergast said weakly. "More visitors. Forgive me for not getting up and offering you tea."

He lay crumpled on the floor between the leaning shelves, as though someone had thrown him there like a discarded rag. Elisabeth dove to his side. His complexion was the color of porridge, his face contorted with pain.

"What happened?" she asked. "Where's Ashcroft?"

Prendergast dissolved into a fit of coughing. When he recovered, he gasped, "You've just missed him. We had a delightful chat." Elisabeth bit back her frustration as more coughs wracked his thin frame. "Help me sit up, girl," he panted at last. "That's it. I want to see what he's done to my . . . oh." He fell silent. She followed his gaze. Across the room, embers smoldered along the broken edges of the floorboards, exactly like the Codex's pages. Ashes swirled away into the void.

"The dimension is collapsing," Nathaniel provided for Elisabeth's benefit, coming into view. "We can't stay here long. A few minutes at best."

Prendergast's eyes widened. "*You*. You're a Thorn." He turned to Elisabeth and spat, "Are you mad, bringing someone like him along? Have you any idea who he is?"

Nathaniel tensed. Reflexively, he ran a hand through his hair—trying to make the silver streak less visible, she realized. "You weren't a friend of Baltasar's, I take it."

Prendergast sneered. "Certainly not, demons take him. Those of us with any sense stayed as far away from him as we could. Even Cornelius wouldn't touch him. And you're the spitting image of him, boy."

Nathaniel looked sick. Elisabeth couldn't let this go on. "We need to know what happened," she interrupted. "Is Ashcroft coming back? I don't see why he would have left, unless . . ."

She trailed off. Prendergast wouldn't meet her eyes.

"Unless you told him your secret," she finished.

"In my defense," he said, "pain is considerably more persuasive when one hasn't felt it in hundreds of years." He shrank from Elisabeth's expression.

"What did you tell him? We need to know!"

"If you think I am going to allow the truth to fall into the hands of a Thorn—"

"It doesn't matter! It's over!" She resisted the urge to shake him until his teeth rattled. "All of this, everything you've done"—she waved at the workshop—"will have been for nothing if you don't help us. Nathaniel is here to stop Ashcroft. Whether you believe that or not, you're almost out of time. This is your last chance to make things right."

Prendergast's head hung. His mouth twisted into a grimace.

Several seconds passed, and then he seemed to come to a decision. "Watch closely," he instructed sourly. "I don't intend to repeat myself."

He yanked six rings from his gaunt fingers. While Elisabeth and Nathaniel watched, perplexed, he started arranging them on the ground. Understanding dawned as he set the final ring in place. The shape was as familiar to Elisabeth as the back of her own hand. One ring in the center, the five others spread around it to form an evenly spaced circle.

"What pattern have I made?" he asked.

"The Great Libraries," Elisabeth answered, at the same time Nathaniel said, with equal certainty, "A pentagram."

Silence fell.

Elisabeth looked again, more closely this time. In her mind's eye she drew lines between each of Prendergast's rings, connecting them to create a star inside the circle. The shape *was* a pentagram. But it was also a map of the Great Libraries. It was both.

Dread slammed into her, knocking the air from her lungs. "Counterclockwise," she whispered. When Nathaniel looked at her, she said, "Something has been bothering me all day, ever since Katrien's map arrived. I know what it is now. The attacks on the Great Libraries are occurring counterclockwise. Knockfeld, Summershall, Fettering, Fairwater. Then Harrows. The pattern reminded me of when I lit the candles for Silas's summoning."

"Go on, girl." Prendergast's dark eyes glittered. "You're almost there."

She turned to him and said, "Cornelius built the Great Libraries."

"Yes. He constructed them to form a summoning circle."

Elisabeth's mind reeled. She wondered, distantly, if she might be ill. She didn't want to believe Prendergast. If he was telling the truth, the Collegium had been founded on the darkest lie imaginable. Her own life, a lie. The magic that flowed through her veins, the beauty and majesty of the Great Libraries—could it all have been for this?

She spoke haltingly, stumbling onward. "The Maleficts— Ashcroft intended for them to be defeated, didn't he? That's the point of the sabotage. He's using them in place of candles."

Prendergast nodded. "A ritual this size calls for more than wick and wax. When a Malefict is destroyed, it unleashes a vast amount of demonic energy. Position a sacrifice of that nature at each point of a pentagram, and one ends up with sufficient power to breach the veil for a greater summoning."

Elisabeth's nails dug into her palms. Once more she felt the effort of driving Demonslayer into the Book of Eyes, saw the gouts of ink pour forth as she twisted the blade. A crucial part of Ashcroft's plan, carried out by her own hands.

"But *why*?" Nathaniel broke in. "Why create such a large circle? Ordinary pentagrams work perfectly well. There's no reason he could possibly . . ." He paused, his narrowed eyes boring into Prendergast. "Ashcroft needed something from you before he could complete the ritual. What was it?"

Prendergast returned Nathaniel's glare. Animosity darkened his features. "A name. That's what I've been guarding all these years."

"A name," Nathaniel echoed flatly.

"You know of lesser demons, fiends and goblins and so on, the lowest subjects of demonic society. And you know of the highborn demons who rule them, like your demon there. But the highborn are ruled by something else in turn. On the Otherworld's throne sits a being of almost limitless power—a creature called an Archon."

Both Nathaniel and Elisabeth turned to Silas. His face was as inscrutable as a marble carving, but his yellow eyes, fixed upon Prendergast, seemed to glow with a cold inner light. Almost imperceptibly, he nodded. Prendergast was telling the truth.

A humorless smile twisted Prendergast's mouth. "Cornelius and I were close friends, or so I thought. I told him of my travels in the Otherworld. We theorized that the Archon's true name could be used to summon it, supposing a sorcerer could assemble a ritual equal to the task, which I did not believe possible. For years, the matter never rose again between us. Then, one day, he asked me for the Archon's name. By then he had already begun building the Great Libraries. When I realized what he was planning, and refused to tell him, he flew into a rage. Until that moment, I believe he truly expected me to help him. He viewed the Archon as a resource, something that could be harnessed and controlled for the betterment of mankind. . . ."

"Progress," Elisabeth murmured. How ignorant she had been, they all had been, raising their glasses in praise of Ashcroft's plan.

"Arrogance," Prendergast corrected. "There is no controlling a being like the Archon. Yet Cornelius's heir is going to attempt the summoning. Tonight."

She looked to Silas. "What will happen if he succeeds?"

"If the Archon is permitted to enter your realm, its power will destroy the veil that separates our worlds." Silas's lips thinned. "Demons will run free, slaughtering your kind with abandon."

She stood so quickly that the blood rushed from her head. "We must stop him," she said, glancing to Nathaniel in appeal. The hopelessness she saw in his eyes sent a jolt through her stomach.

"Even the full strength of the Magisterium would take hours

to breach Ashcroft's wards. We don't have that much time. He'll have finished the ritual by then."

"Then you go directly to Harrows," Prendergast said, "and prevent the final sacrifice."

"But it's a three-day journey," Elisabeth protested.

"Not necessarily." Prendergast gripped the nearest shelf and wrenched himself to his feet. He staggered deeper between the broken shelves, trailing his fingers along the jars, skulls, and books that lay tumbled along them. Finally he dragged out a chain, on the end of which hung an onyx stone. No, not a stone—a round crystal vial, filled with blood.

"I alone discovered the means by which to travel between dimensions, to fold reality like a tapestry, joining one location to another. The magic lives on in my blood. Since I no longer possess a true physical form, this is the final sample remaining." Bitterness warped his mouth. "And here I am, about to hand it over to a Thorn."

Elisabeth couldn't stand the mistrust etched across his face. "Nathaniel isn't Baltasar," she blurted out. "I swear to you, he's different."

Prendergast gave her a sour look. "There is enough blood to transport the three of you to Harrows and back." He threw the vial to Nathaniel, who caught it one-handed, startled. "Use it carefully, boy. It will exact a toll."

As Nathaniel ducked his head through the chain, Prendergast limped away. He set a chair upright and then leveled a bleak stare at the overturned table. Elisabeth lifted it back into place for him, even knowing her efforts wouldn't do any good. The embers had eaten away another several feet of the floorboards. In minutes, the section they were standing on would be consumed, and the table would topple into the void.

Another tremor shook the workshop. Wood groaned, and more jars smashed around them. Prendergast's fingers spasmed on the chair's backrest.

"What about you?" she asked. "Can we take you with us?"

He shook his head. Slowly, as though every joint ached, he eased himself into the chair, facing the approaching darkness. "Go, girl," he said in a rough voice. "My time is finished. Pray that yours meets a better end."

THIRTY-ONE

ELISABETH FELL. IMAGES whipped past like scenes glimpsed through the window of a runaway carriage. Darkened hills. Trees silhouetted against the night sky. Countryside spread beneath a crescent moon. And stranger vistas, like a forest of gray, twisted branches shrouded in mist, and a ruin overgrown with luminous flowers. They were not hurtling through the mortal realm or the Otherworld, but somewhere in between.

She couldn't close her eyes. In this place of nothingness she felt no wind, no breath, only the pressure of Nathaniel's hand gripping her own, accompanied by the endless sensation of falling.

And then wind slammed against her body. It tore the breath from her lungs, whipped her hair around her face. Cold pierced to the marrow of her bones. The ground reeled beneath her as though she had been spinning in circles; the stars whirled overhead.

She staggered, only for her boot to meet empty air. An arm hooked around her waist and yanked her back. Stones tumbled from the lip of rock where she had stood a second before, plunging silently toward the trees far below. The three of them had materialized on a cliff's edge. Stunned, she took in the dizzying drop as Silas dragged them away from the precipice.

"We seem to be in the right place," he remarked, "but you may wish to take more care with your aim on the return journey, master."

Nathaniel laughed, a wild sound. Then he bent over and retched. Something dark spattered the pine needles underfoot.

"It is not his blood, Miss Scrivener," Silas said when she cried out in alarm. He steered Nathaniel toward a boulder and firmly sat him down before he fell over.

Of course. The vial hung half-empty against Nathaniel's chest, the upper portion of the crystal coated in a red slime. In order to harness Prendergast's magic, he had had to drink it. He'd explained the principles of the spell as they'd leaped from the disintegrating Codex back to his study, scrambling to tug their boots and coats on over their nightclothes. This was blood magic, strictly banned by the Reforms, which Elisabeth thought he had declared altogether too cheerfully as he'd raised the vial to his lips.

"Are you all right?" she asked, a twinge of nausea stealing through her relief.

Nathaniel grinned at her, even though he still looked slightly peaked. "Don't worry, I've swallowed far less wholesome substances. Once, for instance, I was permanently banned from a lord's estate for—"

"Let us save that story for another time, Master Thorn," Silas interrupted, ignoring Nathaniel's frown. "If memory serves, the Inkroad passes by this hill, and the Great Library lies less than a quarter mile onward. You will be able to reach it in a few minutes."

"Aren't you coming with us?" she asked.

"I am a demon, Miss Scrivener," he replied softly.

She looked down at her hands, which had curled into fists. Silas had fought back against Ashcroft as hard as any of them. But if he came with them, the wardens would attempt to kill him on sight. The injustice of it made her sick.

He paused, taking in her expression. "I will accompany you as far as the road. That should be safe enough, as long as I am not seen."

They recuperated for a few moments longer before Silas vanished into the trees. Elisabeth thought she glimpsed where he had gone: a trembling branch, and a flash of white that might have been a cat's fur. She helped Nathaniel back to his feet, shooting him a worried glance when he stumbled. Her own dizziness had worn off, but she had only experienced Prendergast's magic secondhand. Nathaniel shouldn't even be out of bed in the first place.

A springy mat of needles cushioned their steps as they picked their way down the hill, passing gnarled pines and stones that thrust from the earth like broken bones. Above them, the jagged range of the Elkenspine rose to soaring heights, the summits stark white and imposing against the night sky. Snow streamed from the peaks like pennants, blown loose by the wind. Elisabeth shivered. The wind tearing through the branches seemed to howl forth the landscape's loneliness and isolation; her ears had already begun to sting from the cold.

Lights glittered ahead, winking between the heaving boughs of fir trees. That was the first glimpse Elisabeth received of the Great Library. When they reached the road and the view opened up, they both trailed to a halt.

They had to tilt their heads back to see the entire structure. It rose skyward like a black citadel, carved straight from the base of the mountain. Lamplight glowered behind its tall, arched stained glass windows, their panes locked away behind iron grilles. Torches guttered along the rampart that circled it in front, so high that Elisabeth couldn't make out anyone patrolling the top, though she knew the wardens had to be up there, watching.

Warily, they pressed onward. Barricades had been erected on the road, studded with metal spikes facing outward. She and Nathaniel traded a look. The barricades weren't designed to keep grimoires in—they were made to keep people out. The library was equipped to withstand a siege.

As they finished winding through the barricades, the sound of their footsteps rebounded forbiddingly from the wall. Elisabeth saw no evidence of a gate or doorway in the riveted iron sheets that made up its exterior, towering high above them.

"Hello?" she called up. "Is anyone there?"

Her voice echoed, bouncing back and forth between the high crenellations, a thin and desolate sound. For a moment, all was silent. Then a rumbling, clanging, grinding cacophony answered her—the friction of gears, the awakening of some immense machinery buried within the wall. The ground trembled. A motion at the top of the rampart caught her eye: cannons, swiveling down to aim at them. On second thought, *cannons* seemed like an inadequate word. The mouth of each gun was wide enough for a person to crawl inside.

She tensed in horror. "They aren't going to fire on us, are they? Nathaniel?"

His eyes were closed, his face calm, lips moving soundlessly beneath the clamor of the gears. Her ears popped as the air grew heavy with damp. She looked up to see the sky above the Great Library boiling with clouds, their underbellies lit a menacing shade of green.

Figures leaped away from the cannons as a bolt of lightning forked over the rampart, barely missing them. The machinery ground to a halt. A slot slid open above their heads, and a pair of eyes glared down at them. A warden.

"Identify yourself, sorcerer!" he called down.

"Excellent," Nathaniel said cheerfully. "I've gotten your attention. I am Magister Nathaniel Thorn, and this is Miss Elisabeth Scrivener. No doubt our reputations have preceded us. We come with an urgent warning for the Director."

If their names had any effect on the warden, he showed no sign. In fact, he still looked as though he'd prefer killing them to talking to them. "No one's allowed in or out of the library. Magisters aren't an exception. Leave, or we'll fire."

"Wait." Elisabeth tugged on the chain around her neck and pulled out her greatkey, lifting it to the light. She thought back to the conversation she had overheard between Mistress Wick and the Royal Library's Director. "I promise Director Hyde will want to see us."

The warden's eyes widened at the sight of the greatkey, and even further at the mention of the Director's name. As she had guessed, that name was only known within a select circle. To most people, he was just "the Director." With luck, the warden would assume she was here on the Collegium's authority.

Before she could lose her nerve, she continued, "We know the saboteur plans to strike tonight. We've come to stop it from happening." Further inspiration struck. "I carry Demonslayer, the sword of the former Director of Summershall."

"Show it to me."

Elisabeth folded her coat aside, allowing the torchlight to glitter on Demonslayer's garnets. She hoped Irena would understand it being used this way.

The warden's eyes flicked between her and Nathaniel. Then the slot slammed shut. Gears began rumbling again. But this time, it wasn't the cannons that moved. A sheet of iron slid aside, revealing a portcullis hidden at the base of the rampart.

"Step inside," the warden's voice commanded.

After a hesitation, they obeyed. Colossal wheel-sized cogs churned behind them as the wall rolled back into place. Now they were trapped between the wall and the portcullis, in a sort of outdoor prison cell. The space reeked of machinery grease and was large enough to contain a coach and a full team of horses. Judging by the signs of wear on the flagstones, it often did so. Anyone entering or exiting the Great Library had to stop here first for an inspection.

Past the bars, torchlight lapped across a grim courtyard. The flagstones were crusted with a white rime of what she first mistook for frost, but then realized must be salt.

They waited for several minutes, shifting from foot to foot to stay warm. Finally, the warden appeared on the other side of the portcullis.

"The Director will see you. But there are conditions. No weapons, and you have to wear shackles." His eyes traveled to Nathaniel. He lifted up a clinking bundle of chains and cuffs. "Iron shackles."

Nathaniel grimaced. "They'll keep me from using sorcery," he explained to Elisabeth under his breath. More loudly he said, "Fine. We accept."

If Nathaniel was willing to bear having his magic taken away, she wasn't about to make a fuss about handing over Demonslayer. But she nevertheless experienced a purely physical resistance when she tried. At first her hand wouldn't release the blade, and the warden had to tug on it, sending a twinge of pain through her injured palm, before her fingers allowed it to slide free. He handed their belongings off to a second warden, who vanished into the shadows. Then Elisabeth and Nathaniel turned around and allowed him to put on the shackles, binding their hands behind their backs.

The portcullis rose with a squeal.

"Follow me," the warden said.

Their shackles' chains clinked as they passed between the two grim obsidian angels flanking the door. The wind cut off abruptly when they crossed the threshold, replaced by a dusty silence filled with papery groans and mutterings. A handful of oil lamps did little to dispel the library's oppressive gloom. Most of the light entered through high stained glass windows, decorated with scenes pieced together in doleful shades of gray and crimson, which cast splintered pools of moonlight on the tall black shelves. A dour-faced librarian glanced their way, then shuffled off into the warren of corridors, his stained robes flapping around his ankles. Elisabeth had heard rumors that librarians considered an assignment to Harrows more of a punishment than a privilege. Now, it wasn't difficult to see why.

There was no atmosphere of warmth or welcome to indicate the presence of friendly, well-treated grimoires. Instead a clammy sense of watchfulness prevailed, and the air stank of wood polish and mildew. Unlike the other Great Libraries, no grimoires sat out in the open; every bookcase was enclosed behind an iron grate. Hisses of fury rang out from the shelves as they passed. She felt as though they were walking through a darkened courtroom, enduring the censure of its unseen judges.

"No grimoires lower than a Class Four here," the warden explained, seeing Elisabeth's expression. "High-security texts only." He sounded proud.

Without warning, a shudder traveled through the marble tiles beneath their boots. More gears, she thought, until a muffled howl rose up from the floor—a sound that was neither human nor machine.

Nathaniel drew in a sharp breath. "What was that?"

"Captive Malefict in the dungeon. Class Eight." The warden gave him an unpleasant smile, clearly enjoying the rare opportunity to enlighten a sorcerer. "It guards the entrance to the vault. Sometimes, we use it for practice."

The remark disturbed Elisabeth, but she dared not offer her opinion. They ascended a narrow, spiraling stair, lightless and creaking, and emerged into a similarly narrow and dreary hall, at the end of which the warden rapped on a door, opened it, and stepped aside.

As they entered, the warden touched her arm. She tensed, but he only muttered, after a hostile glance at Nathaniel, "The Director is hard of hearing. Helps if he can read your lips."

He pitched the advice for her ears alone. It took her a moment to understand why. Nathaniel was a sorcerer, an outsider, untrustworthy. She couldn't explain the rush of anger she felt toward the warden in response. Not so long ago, she had believed the same as him. But she did not want to be this man's ally and confidant, even in his own mind, leaving Nathaniel the odd one out.

A fire burned low in the room ahead, gilding the heads of the deer, wolves, and boars mounted on the walls, their plaques taking up almost every available inch of space. The figure who stood facing the fire resembled a beast himself: tall and broad, with a thick fur draped over the shoulders of his warden's coat. Wind rattled the loose casement of his tower window, letting in drafts that ruffled the papers on his desk.

She and Nathaniel stood in the doorway like children summoned to a schoolmaster's office, waiting for Director Hyde to turn around. Nathaniel shifted, unable to conceal his impatience.

Finally, the Director spoke. His deep, rumbling voice reminded Elisabeth of a bear. "The Great Library of Harrows has never been breached, by man or by grimoire, in the three hundred years since it was first carved from the mountain. It has weathered tempests and broken every siege brought to its gates. You say there is going to be an attack tonight. How would you come to know such a thing, and why should I believe you?"

Before she could stop Nathaniel, he took one long stride toward the desk. "Sir, no doubt the warden has told you our names. Given the Chancellor's attempt on our lives, and Miss Scrivener's previous involvement—"

A floorboard squeaked as Director Hyde turned. Nathaniel fell silent, and Elisabeth froze. Hyde's face was more scar than skin, lacerated by brutal claw marks that Elisabeth would not have thought survivable. Peering out from this landscape of ravaged flesh, his eyes were bright, hard, and above all—suspicious. His gaze raked across Nathaniel's mouth. He had turned quickly enough to hear, or see, the end.

"What's this about the Chancellor of Magic?" he growled.

At first the question made no sense. Then, making a quick mental calculation, Elisabeth's heart sank. She turned to Nathaniel. "No wonder the warden didn't recognize our names," she said under her breath. "They haven't heard the news. The Collegium must have dispatched a rider to all the Great Libraries right away, but the message won't reach Harrows until later tonight." Uneasily, she looked back to Hyde. "They don't know about Ashcroft."

"Damn it all. I didn't think of that. If only we'd brought a newspaper with us . . ." Nathaniel cleared his throat and continued in a louder voice, "Director, allow me to explain. Chancellor Ashcroft is a traitor. The night before last, he was unmasked as the saboteur."

Hyde glanced back and forth, taking in the ease of their exchange. *We're being too familiar with each other*, she realized. No respectable librarian would ever speak to a sorcerer the way she had, much less a magister. As if he were a friend—an intimate. But surely that didn't matter as much as the news they carried. Surely Hyde was taking them seriously. . . .

At last he said, "Scrivener. I know your name. You're from the Great Library of Summershall."

She nodded, setting her jaw against a quaver of foreboding. "The Chancellor took me captive in his manor," she explained. "While I was there, I overheard his plans. The rest of the story is complicated. But Nath—Magister Thorn is telling the truth. A rider will arrive from the Collegium to verify everything."

"Everything, including the imminent attack on this library?"

Nathaniel shot Elisabeth a look before he answered. His expression had become increasingly guarded. "No, we discovered that ourselves and came directly. We didn't have time to alert the Collegium. The Chancellor is sacrificing the grimoires as part of a ritual. I assure you I'm not exaggerating when I say that the fate of the entire kingdom is at stake."

"Please, Director," she broke in. "Harrows is the final step in the Chancellor's plan. You already knew that the saboteur was likely to target this location next, given the pattern of his attacks. He could be infiltrating the library even now."

That seemed to be the wrong thing to say. Hyde stepped around the desk, the floor creaking beneath his weight. His shadow fell over her, as frigid as the draft from the window.

When he next spoke, his voice was dangerously quiet.

"And how is it that you've managed to reach Harrows more quickly than the Collegium's fastest riders? Not you, Magister Thorn. I want Scrivener to answer me."

She swallowed. "Magic," she said, her voice trembling only slightly. "We used magic."

His face darkened. "Are you saying you have dabbled in sorcery, Scrivener?"

She couldn't take it back. She raised her head, meeting his eyes. "Yes. And I would do it again if I had to."

His fist seized the front of her cloak, bunching the fabric in his huge, scarred fingers, and lifted her from the ground.

"Let go of her," Nathaniel snapped. There came a scuffle and a rattling of chains; he had lunged for Hyde, and the warden keeping watch had seized him.

The Director paid Nathaniel no mind. His eyes roved over Elisabeth's face from mere inches away, full of disgust. Shame burned within her—shame as real, as physically painful as the lash of a switch—but she didn't look away. The Collegium's teachings held power over her still; perhaps they always would. She had grown around them like a sapling around a nail, taking the foreign part into the core of herself, no matter how poisonous. But she had not been through everything she had, fought and suffered, to yield to this man's will like a chastened apprentice.

"You've been corrupted," he growled.

"If that's true," said Elisabeth, "then we're all corrupted, and have been from the start. You know that the libraries we serve were built by a sorcerer. Have you ever questioned why?"

A scowl answered her. Of course. This was not a man who asked questions. He'd followed orders his entire life until he'd eventually become the person giving them, one identical cog swapped out for another to keep the library's machinery running the exact same way it had for centuries.

Even so, she couldn't give up hope of breaking through to him. "Have you ever seen a summoning circle, Director?" she pressed. "No—I don't suppose you have, but surely you can imagine—"

"Silence!"

Spittle flecked her face. She choked on her words, stunned into obedience as his other hand came up, roughly, and seized a hank of her hair. Too late, she understood what he had been looking for, and what he had found. Silver gleamed between his scarred fingers.

"You bear a demon's mark," he snarled.

Silence. Hideous silence, in which she heard the rasp of the warden's indrawn breath.

"Director," Nathaniel interjected sharply, a note of real panic in his voice, "I speak on my honor when I say that Miss Scrivener's mind remains entirely her own, that this situation is far more complicated than you can possibly—" He stopped there with a grunt, as though the warden had kneed him in the stomach to shut him up.

Elisabeth barely heard. *Too late, too late, too late.* If only she had remembered to snip off the silver lock . . .

Hyde's features twisted in revulsion. With a great heave, he threw her to the floor, sending her sprawling. She landed poorly, and cried out when the shackles cracked against her spine.

"Elisabeth!"

"I will listen to none of your lies," the Director ground out. "You are a disgrace to the Collegium, girl. Corrupted. Tainted. Addled by demons." Each word struck her like a kick to the stomach.

"Have you gone completely mad?" Nathaniel roared. "She risked her life to come here! She's trying to *save* you, you imbecile!"

Hyde whirled on him. "And you, no doubt responsible for leading the girl into darkness. I have seen enough of this vile display." To the warden, he said, "Take them to the dungeon. They cannot be trusted. Only time will tell whether they are telling the truth, or are involved in the sabotage themselves."

Through a haze of misery, Elisabeth felt the warden wrestle her upright and march her out the door. Judging by the storm of invectives that followed, Nathaniel was being treated similarly. She had never heard him so angry. The air even held a faint tang of sorcery, as though his rage was nearly sufficient to overcome the iron.

They were taken back down the spiral stair and past the shelves, down a few more times, and soon she stumbled over the roughly hewn stones of a dungeon passage, averting her eyes from the sputtering torches. Metal clanked; then she was shoved forward into a cell, bare aside from a bucket in the corner and a scattering of straw on the ground. Nathaniel received such a hard push that he went down onto his knees, unable to catch himself with his hands bound. The cell door slammed shut.

The warden paused before he turned away. He regarded Elisabeth expressionlessly, his hand on the hilt of his sword.

"It isn't too late to stop this," she said, gathering her strength. "There's still time—"

"I don't speak to traitors," he interrupted. Then he left without another word, his boots echoing down the corridor into silence.

THIRTY-TWO

FOR A MOMENT Elisabeth stood frozen, too shocked to react. Then she threw herself against the bars. She spun around and felt at them with her bound hands, scrabbling for a loose piece of metal, crumbling mortar, a rusty hinge—anything she could use to break them out of the cell. She was stronger than an ordinary person. If only she could find a weak spot—

"Elisabeth, stop."

Nathaniel might as well have spoken a different language. She gritted her teeth and yanked harder, even though doing so sent a spike of pain through her injured hand. A wildness filled her, taking over her body, the same as when she had struck down the fiend on the pavilion, or the time she had destroyed all the mirrors in Nathaniel's house.

After tonight, she would never be able to enter a Great Library again. But that wouldn't matter if Ashcroft succeeded, and there were no libraries left to speak of. She didn't know who made her more furious in that moment, Ashcroft or Director Hyde. To think that the world could fall to ruin due to the decisions of a single small-minded man in charge—that that was all it took to doom everyone—

"Elisabeth!" Nathaniel exclaimed.

She whirled on him, suddenly remembering, with glorious clarity, that the warden hadn't confiscated Prendergast's vial. "Can you use that to free us?" she demanded.

He was breathing hard, staring at her. It took him a moment to grasp the object of her question. "No," he said. "Not while I'm wearing iron. Listen," he went on, but she cut him off, turning back to the bars.

"It was after midnight when we fought Ashcroft," she said. "The Collegium couldn't have sent someone any earlier than that. The rider won't get here for hours." *We'll be stuck in a dungeon as the kingdom goes up in flames.*

"Elisabeth. You're hurting yourself."

"No, I'm not." After that first stab of pain, she'd felt fine.

Nathaniel pushed himself between her and the bars before she could start again. "Look at your hands," he said, his expression strange.

She twisted to look over her shoulder, raising her hands as best she could within the confines of the shackles. The dim light of the torch down the hall traced over her skin, and she saw that Nathaniel was right. Blood darkened the bandage on her palm. She had torn two of her fingernails nearly off.

"Sit down." His shoulder pressed against hers, herding her toward the back of the cell. "Take a moment to rest."

She stumbled along reluctantly. "We never discovered how Ashcroft is carrying out the attacks. If he's working with someone, or—" She stopped, disturbed by how little they actually knew. "We have to be prepared for anything."

"And you won't be if you hurt yourself trying to wrestle a cell door. Honestly, Scrivener. We don't need to escape on our own. Silas will come rescue us."

Silas. She had forgotten. "But how will he know we need help?"

"He'll just know. He always senses when I've gotten myself into trouble." Nathaniel grimaced as he eased himself down the wall, sitting awkwardly with his bound hands, his shoulder tipped against the stone. "Sometimes I wonder whether he simply assumes I get into trouble by default when he isn't around to keep me out of it, but I prefer to credit his supernatural intuition."

Guilt sank claws into her body. Nathaniel should be the one resting, not her. Distressed, she crouched beside him. A moment later, he slid sideways a few inches until his shoulder rested against hers.

The frenzied energy drained from her muscles, leaving her weary and cold. Their breathing was the only noise in the dungeon's subterranean silence. She remembered the silence well from Summershall—the oppressiveness of it, the way it played tricks on the mind. She couldn't imagine how much worse being imprisoned alone in this place would feel, knowing that the kingdom's highest security vault lurked somewhere nearby within the labyrinth of stone, its slumbering inhabitants powerful enough to destroy entire cities if released. . . .

Her breath stopped.

"What's wrong?" Nathaniel asked.

She turned to him. "The grimoire Baltasar wrote—is it called the Chronicles of the Dead?"

He stiffened. His face looked spectral, his eyes dark pools in the feeble torchlight. For a moment, she thought he might not respond. Then, finally, he nodded.

Elisabeth didn't want to tell him, but she had to. "It's here. Here in Harrows. They transferred it in secret the night I stole the Codex."

Nathaniel exploded to his feet. "Why didn't you say anything?"

"I forgot. There was so much going on at the time." Unhappiness wrung her heart as she watched Nathaniel turn away, pacing across the cell. She hesitated, then asked, "How much do you know about the Chronicles?"

Nathaniel drew up short, gazing out into the passageway. When he spoke, his voice sounded clipped. "It contains the spell Baltasar used to raise his army, among other necromantic rituals. As to what powers it would manifest as a Malefict, that's a librarian's area of study, not mine." She sat in silence, waiting. He was holding something back. At last he leaned his forehead against the bars and went on, "My . . . my father read it. To prepare. He wasn't quite the same when he returned. I was never able to decide exactly what was different about him. Sometimes, I thought it felt like he had brought something back with him. Other times, it was as though he had left a piece of himself behind."

She studied Nathaniel's face, the stark lines of his profile. "I'm sorry."

"What for?"

Everything, she thought. "I dragged you into this," she said. "You wouldn't be here if it weren't for me."

"You're right. I would be alone in my study, utterly miserable, spending my final hours unaware that demons were about to overrun the world." He returned and slumped beside her, tipping his head back against the stone. "I like this version better. The one with you in it."

"Even if we die?"

Briefly, he shut his eyes. "The last month has been the happiest time of my life that I can remember since I was twelve, the fiends and the blood drinking and the imminent threat of a demonic apocalypse notwithstanding. I think—I think I was a bit dead already, before you came along." He turned his head, taking her in. "It's an honor to fight by your side, Elisabeth, for however long it lasts. You've reminded me to live. That's worth having something to lose."

Elisabeth swallowed. She did not have anything to say; she could only think how intolerable it seemed that she had once found his face so cruel. Impulsively, she folded herself up and tucked her head against his chest. After a pause, he rested his chin on her hair. She sat listening to his heartbeat in the dark.

The moment stretched on, the passage of time impossible to calculate, and her thoughts stretched with it, casting outward. She pictured the Great Library from above, its guttering torches and soaring black towers rising above the wilderness.

How long would it take Silas to find them? She wasn't certain that she shared Nathaniel's confidence. The defenses here were like nothing she had seen before. Even if Silas could scale the sheer wall encircling the building, it was clad in iron and patrolled by wardens. And that was just the beginning; next, he would have to sneak through the library and get past the countless locked iron gates leading to the dungeon.

After waiting for what felt like hours, she sat up. "You don't think Silas has been caught, do you?" she asked.

"I should think not," answered a whispering voice from the corridor, sounding faintly injured. "I am not an amateur."

"Silas!" they both exclaimed, rushing to the bars.

He sighed as he stepped into view. "Not so loudly, if you please."

Nathaniel grinned irrepressibly at the sight of him, unearthly in the torchlight, but pristine and unruffled, no different than he looked on a regular evening at home. "You weren't hurt?"

Silas waved a hand, dismissing the question as beneath him. "I see the pair of you have wasted no time getting yourselves thrown into prison." He bent to inspect the door, then drew a warden's key ring from his pocket, holding the iron carefully within a wadded-up handkerchief. "What is this, master—the third time I've broken you out of a jail cell?"

Nathaniel coughed. "Minor misunderstandings, on both previous occasions," he assured Elisabeth.

Silas detached one of the keys from the ring and used it to unlock Nathaniel's shackles. While Nathaniel got to work on Elisabeth's, Silas selected a second key and tried it on the door. He spoke mildly, his lashes shading his eyes. "At least you're wearing clothes this time, master."

"I'll have you know," Nathaniel said, "that that was an accident, and the public certainly didn't mind. One woman even sent me flowers." To Elisabeth, he added, "Don't worry. She was forty years old, and her name was Mildred."

Silas snatched his hand back as the door swung open, dropping the keys with a hiss. A tendril of steam rose from his fingers. He moved to step away, but was arrested in midstride by Elisabeth, who seized him in an embrace, followed by Nathaniel, who hugged him from the other side. He froze, completely rigid, enduring their affection in the manner of a purebred house cat being squeezed by a toddler. When he twitched, they finally released him.

"We shall never speak of that," he warned, brushing off his sleeves. "Miss Scrivener, if you would follow me, I believe your sword has been taken to the armory."

She scooped up the key ring. The three of them crept through the dungeon's passageways in single file, retreating into the shadows whenever a patrol's torch came near. Fortunately Silas knew exactly where to go, and after several minutes they reached an iron-banded door, which Elisabeth was able to open with one of the keys. She gasped at the room beyond. Torchlight flickered not just over swords, but a bristling collection of axes, spears, crossbows, and even a spiked weapon she tentatively identified as a morning star. After recovering Demonslayer from an arms rack, she seized a belt and tightened it around her waist. As Nathaniel watched, amused by her enthusiasm, she stuffed its pouches full of salt rounds.

"What now?" he asked.

Elisabeth squeezed in a final salt round. "We need to find the vault. All we have to do is stop whoever's come here from getting inside. Silas, did you pass it on your way to the dungeon?"

Silas had been strolling through the aisles, his hands clasped behind his back, gazing at the weapons with an unreadable expression. He'd stopped in front of an ancient, cruel-looking device hanging from the ceiling, which resembled a giant cage filled with rusty spikes. Elisabeth's heart skipped a beat, her eyes darting from the spikes to his wrists.

"No," he said, turning away, "but I can sense the psychic emanations of the grimoires. I will take you there."

He showed no sign of whether the device was the same variety Ashcroft had used to trap him. She cast the room another look as they left, seeing the racks of weaponry anew. For Silas, this place was a torture chamber.

When they snuck back into the passage, the ground shook with the force of a familiar-sounding howl.

"We must be near the Malefict," Nathaniel said.

Silas inclined his head. "There is no way around it. All routes to the vault travel through this hall."

Cautiously, they made their way around the corner. At the end, the passageway opened into a cavern, a space so large that its ceiling disappeared in a haze of smoke and shadow. Stalactites hung like teeth from the substanceless dark above. Below them, lit by fires in charred, smoking braziers, a sort of pit arena had been carved into the stone. Their boots clanged softly on the metal walkway that encircled it, bounded by railings. A ladder—one of several—descended to the sawdust-covered floor far below, which was marked by scuffs and grooves, as of those made by a restless, pacing animal.

Or a monster.

As they watched, the Malefict lumbered into view. It was the size of a small house, powerfully but crudely built, its bear-like form missing ears, a nose, and even eyes, the leather of its muzzle crisscrossed with badly stitched seams. A heavy chain dragged behind it, each link large enough to yoke an ox, the other end attached to a system of gears and pulleys fixed to the cavern's wall. It wagged its head back and forth, disoriented by the pain of the iron collar around its neck. Ink wept from open sores, gleaming wet down its shoulders, and old scars scored its leather-bound hide. Nathaniel gazed down at it with a troubled expression. Feeling sick to her stomach, Elisabeth recalled the warden's explanation upstairs.

"This is wrong," she said. "It isn't a practice dummy, to be beaten with weapons while it suffers in chains."

Silas stopped beside her, his face impassive. "Do you not believe it an evil creature, Miss Scrivener?"

Her hand clenched around Demonslayer's hilt. She was beginning to understand that evil wasn't so simple a concept as she had once imagined. Perhaps it wasn't wrong for Malefics to want to hurt humans—the humans who had created them, imprisoned them, tormented them with salt and iron—and ultimately, consigned them to their twisted forms.

"None of this is its fault," she said at last. "It didn't choose to be a monster."

If Silas had an opinion on the matter, he didn't offer it. Nathaniel said, pointing, "Look. There's the vault."

On the opposite side of the arena, on the ground floor, there was a portcullis recessed into the stone. Anyone who climbed down and attempted to reach it would get slaughtered by the pacing Malefict. Unless they managed to put the monster out of its misery first.

Impulsively, she drew Demonslayer and started for the ladder. Nathaniel grabbed her arm. Before she could object, he spun her around and trapped her against the stone. Her thoughts took a moment to catch up. Nathaniel was rigid with tension, his body drawn tight as a bowstring, but he hadn't been seized by a sudden, passionate desire to kiss her against a dungeon wall. Rather, he was using his dark coat to shield them both from view.

They weren't alone. At first she heard only the Malefict's labored snorts and grunts. But then footfalls rattled the walkway nearby. Out of the corner of her eye, she watched Director Hyde step onto the path through the passage they had just left behind. She held her breath until he turned, scowling, in the opposite direction, his suspicious gaze failing to detect their hiding spot just a few feet away. They sagged in relief as he set off, unsuspecting.

The feeling was short-lived. Hyde must have been on patrol, heading down to inspect the vault. No matter what he had said in his office, he was too vigilant a man to hear a warning like theirs and completely disregard it. Yet in coming down here, he was putting himself, and his keys, precisely where Ashcroft needed them.

An earsplitting metallic squeal echoed through the cavern. Hyde had used his Director's key to activate the pulley. Gears churned, winching the chain upward link by heavy link. The Malefict bellowed, straining against its collar, a futile effort; no matter how hard it struggled, the machinery dragged it inexorably through the sawdust. When the winch clanged to a stop, the chain had been tightened so much that the Malefict's front end hung off the ground. It dangled there like a bull waiting to be slaughtered, head low, dripping ink from reopened sores.

Hyde climbed down the nearest ladder and set off across the arena without so much as a backward glance. He unlocked the portcullis, entered, and shut it behind himself.

The machinery rumbled back to life. Slowly, the pulley began lowering the Malefict to the ground. With a jolt of alarm, Elisabeth realized that they had only moments to cross the arena.

"We have to follow Hyde," she said, starting for the ladder. "Where's Silas?"

Nathaniel nodded upward. Elisabeth followed his look, and wished she hadn't. Silas had evaded Hyde's attention by climbing straight up the cavern wall, and now he clung there like a spider, gazing down at them with inhuman yellow eyes.

"He'll catch up," Nathaniel said. "Let's go."

Seconds later, Elisabeth's boots struck sawdust. When Nathaniel landed beside her, the Malefict turned its stitched, weeping face in their direction. The pulley's wheel groaned as the monster plodded forward, stretching the chain to its limit, snuffling blindly at the air. Nathaniel gave the ancient machinery a critical once-over. He grabbed Elisabeth's wrist, hastening them onward.

They were halfway across the arena, running side by side, when there came a deafening, shrieking crash that shook the cavern, and an object bounced past them in a spray of sawdust: the pulley wheel.

There wasn't time to react. They could only run. Elisabeth felt across the key ring, selecting the largest key by touch. That should be the key restricted to wardens. The problem was, she didn't know for certain whether it would open this portcullis. Depending on how close they were to the vault, it might respond only to the Director's personal key. And if that were the case, there would be no time left to turn and make a stand; the Malefict would be upon them, and it would crush them in an instant.

The portcullis drew closer and closer. The Malefict's shadow stretched across them, the earth shuddering with its bounding strides. She raised the key. Her hand remained steady as she inserted it into the lock, but the Malefict was too fast. Its shadow plunged them into darkness—

And vanished, the ruddy light of the braziers flooding back in. Astonished, she looked over her shoulder. The Malefict lay sprawled on the ground some distance away, insensible, and Silas stood interposed between them, one hand raised in the attitude of a concluded slap across the face. Ink dripped from his claws.

Forcing her mouth shut, Elisabeth turned the key. A mechanism thumped inside the wall, and the portcullis's teeth lifted from the ground. Silas did not move. Nathaniel seized the back of his coat and dragged him into the passageway.

For a terrible moment Elisabeth thought that Silas had been hurt, but then she saw he was merely gazing down at his soiled hand in disgust. She offered him a corner of her coat. Without comment, he used it to wipe off his claws.

Of Hyde there was no sign, not even a glimmer of his torch in the deep darkness ahead. Nathaniel conjured a green flame in his hand, illuminating a stair leading downward, its steps glistening with moisture. Water dripped nearby, unseen. Elisabeth's eyes widened at the tunnel's unexpected beauty. The stone was the pure black of obsidian, veined with sparkling mineral bands.

"Silas, can you tell if anyone else is down here with us?" She kept her voice low, but if the Director was hard enough of hearing that he hadn't doubled back already, she doubted talking would make a difference.

Silas finished inspecting his nails and glanced down the stairwell. "This mountain is full of pyrite; I expect the vault's location was chosen for that very reason. The presence of so much iron inhibits my senses. I'm afraid I cannot say for certain."

"If it helps," Nathaniel said, "there wasn't any trace of magic back in the arena. I don't think anyone's gotten past the Malefict ahead of Hyde."

"Unless Ashcroft knows a secret way into the library," Elisabeth pointed out. "Cornelius planned this from the very beginning. He could have had a hidden corridor built into the mountain—something only he knew about."

"Is it possible for something like that to remain undiscovered for so long?"

"I think so. I found all kinds of secret passageways in Summershall, and the senior librarians didn't have a clue."

They fell silent as they stole forward. Nathaniel extinguished his flame when the reddish glow of Hyde's torch reappeared ahead, outlining the fur draped over his shoulders. While they snuck after him, his purposeful stride rang from the naked stone. He held the torch high in one hand, the other clasping his sword, never pausing to look behind him.

Elisabeth held her breath. Any moment now . . . any moment . . .

Her heart leaped to her throat when the torchlight poured over an irregularity on the ground: a pair of boots protruding from an adjoining tunnel. Staring straight ahead, Hyde didn't seem to notice. He kept walking.

The three of them paused, allowing Hyde to gain a few steps as they took in the sight of the warden lying collapsed in the tunnel. A woman, still armed, sprawled loosely on the ground. Her torch had fallen into a puddle and gone out. The dim, shifting light made it impossible to tell whether she was still breathing.

"She lives," Silas whispered. "There is no injury. She is merely asleep."

They looked at each other. *The sleeping spell*. The attack had already begun. And yet Hyde was nearly at the vault, and they had seen no sign of the attacker.

The truth struck her like lightning.

Elisabeth abandoned every pretense of stealth. "Stop him!" she cried, lunging after Hyde. "Stop him from getting inside the vault!"

Too late. The portcullis at the end of the passage slammed down, separating Hyde on the other side. She skidded to a halt.

He turned to face them through the grille. A smile spread across his face, grotesquely stretching his scars. The expression looked wholly unnatural on his features, yet there was something familiar about it all the same. It was a smile she had seen many times before: in the gilded halls of Ashcroft Manor, in the palace ballroom, on the rose pavilion by moonlight.

It belonged not to Hyde, but to Chancellor Ashcroft.

THIRTY-THREE

"**I** SEE YOU'VE FIGURED it out, Miss Scrivener," Ashcroft said, his cultured voice uncanny on Hyde's scarred lips. "Quite honestly, I'm surprised it took you so long. After all, you've met the Book of Eyes."

The Book of Eyes.

At once, the missing pieces snapped into place. When Elisabeth had battled the Malefict in Summershall, it had taunted her with the truth of who had killed the Director. Irena herself had described the spells it contained: magic that allowed sorcerers to reach into people's minds, read their thoughts, and even control them. How had the Book of Eyes known the saboteur's identity? The answer was simple—it had encountered him before. Given his status, Ashcroft would have been one of the rare few trusted to study such a dangerous grimoire.

To carry out his plans, he hadn't needed to work with an accomplice, or even leave the comfort of his manor.

"You've been possessing the Directors," she said numbly.

"You've been forcing them to perform the sabotage with their own hands."

"Beg pardon?" Ashcroft leaned closer to the bars and frowned, rubbing Hyde's ear. "You know, I can barely hear what you're saying. Quite inconvenient, really. But no matter. I won't have to wear this body for long." Spinning the key ring jauntily on his finger, he turned and strolled deeper into the vault.

Blood roared in Elisabeth's ears. Nothing felt real. She took in the vault as though she were dreaming: an immense natural cavern, the walls glittering with pyrite. Towering angel statues stood vigil along the walls, carved from obsidian, streams of molten iron pouring from their cupped hands to the floor below. A circular channel conducted the liquid metal around the room's circumference like a moat. Ashcroft stepped Hyde's body over a narrow black stone bridge, the edges of his coat wavering from the heat distortion. His movements were oddly clumsy, and once he even jerked sideways, barely regaining his footing before he pitched over the edge.

"Hyde is still in there," Elisabeth realized in shock. "He's battling for control." And then she thought, *This is what happened to Irena.*

Without warning, a blast of emerald fire exploded past her, singeing the tips of her ears. It funneled through the grille and twisted after Ashcroft like a cyclone. But as it neared him, it fizzled out in a shower of green sparks.

Nathaniel dropped his arm and swore. "Too much iron."

Moving in awful fits and jerks, Ashcroft flicked a residual ember from Hyde's fur. "I know what you're thinking, Miss Scrivener," he said without turning. He had succeeded in crossing the bridge. "You're wondering what it was like for dear, beautiful Irena when I entered her mind and forced her to betray everything that she loved. Poor woman—she never suspected anything. I cast the spell on her years ago in the reading room at Summershall. When you're the Chancellor of Magic, it's no trouble arranging a private meeting with a Director. My magic lived inside her for nearly a decade, waiting for me to activate it."

Elisabeth sucked in a breath. As though it had happened yesterday, she recalled the choking smell of aetherial combustion that clung to the reading room's armchair: the permanent residue of some old, powerful spell. Distantly, she was aware of Nathaniel steadying her.

"Irena struggled, too, of course. She was strong-willed, just like you. She was there with me the entire time, all the way to the vault, up until the very moment the Book of Eyes struck her down."

A sound escaped Elisabeth, something between a scream and a sob. Ashcroft wasn't paying attention. He had nearly reached the middle of the room.

A trio of massive obsidian columns dominated the vault's center, stretching unbroken to the ceiling. A crossed key and quill had been carved into the floor between them. Ashcroft stepped on the symbol as he approached, raising Hyde's torch. "Magnificent, is it not?"

At first she wasn't certain what he was referring to. Then light flooded the nearest column. Vapors swirled inside the translucent stone, wreathing a shape that hung suspended in chains. As though agitated by Hyde's proximity, the mist began to boil, and lightning flashed within its depths. Each flicker illuminated a grimoire's cover, bound in glossy black scales edged with silver. The cover inflated and deflated steadily, as though the grimoire were breathing.

The columns weren't meant to hold up the ceiling. Instead, they contained Class Tens.

"The Librum Draconum," Ashcroft said, a hint of true awe softening his voice. "Created using the hide of a Lindwurm— the last dragon in Austermeer, hunted to extinction in the fourteenth century. The spells inside can summon cataclysmic storms and earthquakes, invoke natural disasters on a world-altering scale. . . ."

He moved on to the next column, bringing the torch close. He released a wistful sigh. Within the chains hung—nothing. No . . . there was something there, reflective and shifting, mirrorlike, its surface flowing like water. Trying to focus on it made Elisabeth's head hurt.

"The Oraculis," Ashcroft murmured. "Provenance unknown. Its spells allow one to see the future, or so the theories suggest, but everyone who's read it has immediately taken their own life. A shame. I dearly would have liked to study it."

He approached the third case. Through the translucent obsidian, the torch revealed the slick, pulsing skin of a beating heart. It clung to the grimoire's cover like some hideous growth, its veins wrapped around the leather, sealing the pages shut. The veins bulged rhythmically, as though pumping blood—but the green glow that animated them was pure sorcery, the magic of House Thorn. Necromancy, keeping the long-dead heart alive.

"Ah. The Chronicles of the Dead." Ashcroft tapped on the case, and smiled pensively when the heart spasmed in response. "Those who try to open it instantly succumb to its magic. Except for you, Nathaniel. This book is yours. It calls out to you, no doubt. How would you like to meet your ancestor's work?"

"Don't," Nathaniel croaked. He gripped the bars, his fingers bled white.

Elisabeth's senses came flooding back on a tide of fury. "It won't work!" she shouted through the portcullis. "You won't be able to control the Archon! It's going to tear the world apart. When you summon it, you'll be the first to die!"

Ashcroft paused, peering at them, a hand cupped behind his ear. "I confess I've never been any good at reading lips," he said finally. He gave a rueful laugh. "You're asking me to stop, aren't you? Ah, Miss Scrivener, you do not understand. You cannot understand. This is the purpose handed down to me by my father, and his father before him, stretching back three hundred years. I am part of something far greater than myself." He tilted his head back, gazing up at the column. "With the Archon's power at my disposal, humanity will be transformed. No more sickness, or poverty, or war. It will be a marvel—a glorious era in which all is possible, and every dream made real. . . ."

He trailed off. Emotion shimmered in his eyes. Even wearing Hyde's form, something of Ashcroft's natural light and magnetism shone through.

He really believes what he's saying, Elisabeth thought, horrified. In his heart of hearts, he viewed himself not as the villain, but as the hero.

Ashcroft cleared his throat. "Let's see." He paced in a circle, inspecting the Collegium sigil on the floor. "Cornelius faced somewhat of a problem with this library's construction. How does one free a grimoire from an iron-filled vault several hundred feet beneath a mountain? Fortunately, the Collegium's own technology provided the solution."

He moved to draw Hyde's sword from its sheath, and stopped abruptly. Hyde's hand had clamped around the hilt, muscles bulging with resistance. His face purpled as the two minds fought for control. Hope filled Elisabeth's chest like a breath in the midst of drowning.

"The iron must be weakening Ashcroft's spell." She turned to Nathaniel, who was white as a sheet, staring at the Chronicles. She didn't think he would hear her if she spoke to him. Instead, she asked Silas, "Is there any way for you to get inside?"

Silas stood several paces back, a ghost in the darkness of the passageway. He stepped forward, reaching for the portcullis. Alarm clamored through her, but his hand stopped a hairsbreadth from touching the thick bands of reinforced iron.

"I fear not," he said. "This gate was designed to prevent beings such as I from entering. Even if I could, I would not be at my full strength inside the vault."

No wonder Silas had been hanging back. In the infernal red glow of the molten iron, he looked washed out, almost ill.

A ring of metal against stone yanked her attention back to Ashcroft. He had managed to free Hyde's sword, though in doing so he had lurched forward, nearly dropping the weapon. As she watched in dismay, he dragged the blade, scraping, until it stood vertically above the Collegium sigil, his weight bearing down upon it. And then, like a key fitting into a lock, the sword's point slid inside a hidden mechanism in the sigil. Sweating and trembling with effort, Ashcroft twisted it to the right.

For a moment, nothing happened. Then a clank echoed through the cavern. The floor shook, gears churning unseen as the Great Library's machinery awakened. A jagged crack raced across the ceiling. On the far side of the vault, one of the giant obsidian angels began to turn, not by sorcery but by the will of the cogs, its face motionless and serene. The stream of molten iron cascading from its hands slowed to a drip. Angled sideways, it created a blockage in the channel, and the moat slowly drained away at its feet.

In the place where the angel had once stood, a passageway now yawned. But Elisabeth had eyes only for the ceiling, where the crack had snaked across the cavern and split the rock above the portcullis. When she seized the bars and shook them, she felt a slight give.

Ashcroft was bent over now, Hyde's face writhing grotesquely. He staggered to the Chronicles' pillar and caught himself against it with a hand that clenched repeatedly into a fist. Using the other hand, he unsteadily raised his Director's key toward a slot in the column.

There was still time. Ashcroft missed once, twice, the key glancing from the stone. Elisabeth threw herself against the portcullis. Metal groaned as it pushed outward an inch on one side, the grille flexing against her shoulder.

With his lips peeled back from his teeth, Ashcroft at last forced the key into place. When he turned it, a panel slid open. Green-tinted mist flowed out of it, pouring down, lapping over Hyde's boots.

Thump-thump. Thump-thump. Thump-thump. The convulsions of the dead, ancient heart filled the cavern, thudding inside Elisabeth's bones. The stench nearly brought her to her knees. It was like standing at the entrance to a crypt, breathing in rot and stone and ancient magic, the smell of skulls crawling with beetles, of moss speckling crumbled tombs.

The portcullis screeched as she wedged her shoulder into the gap, using the passage's wall as leverage. But she was too late.

Too late to stop Ashcroft as he reached inside, and plunged his fingers into the beating heart.

THIRTY-FOUR

THE HEART'S VEINS pulsed with emerald light. They began to spread, to grow, twining rootlike along the chains, sending branching tendrils outward. Elisabeth's paralyzed thoughts fixed on the illustration of a nervous system that she remembered from one of Master Hargrove's anatomical texts. The Chronicles was growing into a Malefict, beginning with its heart.

Within seconds, the Malefict's expanding form crowded the inside of the column. Clawed fingers curled over the lip of the opening, their exposed tendons dripping ink. She remembered the shadows of those claws stretching across the Royal Library, reaching for the wardens as they wheeled its cage along the hall.

Ashcroft stumbled back, clutching his hand to his chest. Wild-eyed, he dove for the sword lying discarded beside the sigil. Not Ashcroft any longer—Hyde. Ashcroft had finished his work and relinquished his hold on the body, leaving Hyde at the mercy of the Chronicles of the Dead, just as he must have done to Irena after releasing the Book of Eyes.

The Malefict's hand shot out. Metal rattled as it jerked to

a halt mere inches from Hyde, reaching the limits of the chain wrapped around its wrist. The links warped under the strain as the claws stretched closer, grasping for him.

Determination hardened Hyde's face. He hefted his sword. "Not on my watch," he growled. "Not while I still live, abomination."

"*Then die,*" the Malefict whispered, in a voice like wind rushing from a sepulcher. One of the claws straightened and touched Hyde's cheek.

Hyde's face emptied. Green light flowed up the veins in his neck, rippled through his cheek, and traveled into the Malefict's claw. He blinked once. Then he toppled over dead, striking the floor as a blanched and withered corpse. His body exploded into dust upon impact, as though it had lain desiccating in a mausoleum for centuries.

The Malefict's hand shuddered as the stolen life pulsed up its wrist. Cracks spiraled around the column. That was the only warning before the pillar burst, sending chunks of obsidian flying. A tall, gaunt shape unfolded from the wreckage, obscured by swirls of dust. Broken chains dangled from its wrists, and a pair of antlers crowned its brow.

Elisabeth had seen that shape before, during the night she had spent with Nathaniel in the Blackwald. The grimoire's heart—Baltasar had torn it from one of the moss folk. A giver of life, transformed into a taker of it; she couldn't imagine anything more profane.

As though sensing her thoughts, the Malefict's head snapped around. Its green eyes burned through the dust. It stared at them for a long moment, perfectly still. Though it wasn't much taller than the Book of Eyes, its presence exuded an ancient, festering malevolence that sent terror washing over her skin in frigid waves. Her instincts screamed at her to reach for Demonslayer, but she couldn't move.

After a few more seconds, the monster appeared to lose interest. It turned and made for the passageway, stepping through the dry section of the channel before it disappeared into the darkness beyond.

The key ring jingled in Elisabeth's pocket. She was shaking as though she had spent a night outdoors in midwinter. Even so, she wiped her palms on her coat and redoubled her efforts to push open the portcullis. If the Malefict were allowed to escape, countless people would die. After what she had just seen, she wasn't certain if the wardens could stop it. What if it followed the Inkroad all the way to Brassbridge, sucking the life from entire towns as it went, leaving only dust behind?

Out of the corner of her eye, she saw Nathaniel staring after the Malefict. "Nathaniel," she gritted through her teeth. "Help me."

He didn't tear his gaze from the passageway. "Didn't you hear that?" he asked.

His voice sounded strange, almost dreamy. She paused, taking in his expression. He looked far calmer now than he had a moment before. But his eyes were bright, as they had been on the laudanum. Even the reddish glow of the vault failed to mask his pallor.

"The voice," he went on. "It was speaking . . . it wanted . . . you didn't hear what it said?"

A chill ran down Elisabeth's spine. She glanced at Silas, who gave a slight shake of his head—he hadn't heard anything, either. Carefully, he placed a hand on Nathaniel's arm. "Master," he said.

Nathaniel's brow furrowed. He scraped a hand through his

hair. "Sorry," he said, sounding much more like himself. "I don't know what came over me. Of course I would be happy to join you in a life-endangering act of heroism, Scrivener. You must only say the word."

Nathaniel braced his hands against the bars, and they pushed together. With one last agonized groan, the portcullis bent outward enough for them to squeeze through sideways. Silas leaped after them in the form of a cat, balancing on Nathaniel's shoulder. His tail lashed as they ran across the bridge, the heat of the still-steaming channel gusting over them like a forge.

Elisabeth forced herself not to look down when they passed Hyde's empty uniform, or to lift her gaze to the other Class Ten grimoires, roused from their stupor by the Chronicles' escape. Lightning crackled through the Librum Draconum's pillar, and a faint music emanated from the Oraculis, like chimes blowing in a distant breeze.

She reached the passageway first, and drew up short. The Malefict's stink of rot and stone hung about the entrance. Every fiber of her body rebelled at the thought of entering, but she clenched her jaw, drew Demonslayer, and pushed onward. A moment later a green flame ignited in Nathaniel's hand, illuminating the sheen of sweat on his forehead. He shot her a grin as he dashed beside her, but she knew it was only a front. He had to be even more frightened than she was. He was about to face the stuff of his nightmares. But the way he had looked a minute ago, almost peaceful . . .

Unease gripped her. "What did you hear the Chronicles say?" she asked.

He glanced at her quickly, and then away, fixing his gaze ahead. "I think I must have imagined it." He laughed unconvincingly, then forced out, "It wanted us to come—to go with it.

Join it. But that doesn't make any sense. Why on earth would it want that?"

Elisabeth hesitated. The Chronicles had spoken to Nathaniel alone. She doubted its invitation had been meant for all of them. "If it speaks to you again," she said, "promise me you won't listen. That you'll do anything you can to block it out."

Nathaniel's throat bobbed as he swallowed. "I will," he said.

Grimly, she hoped that would be enough.

The Malefict wasn't lying in wait for them; it had gone ahead. As the tunnel sloped upward, the first thing she heard was the Great Library's warning bell tolling mournfully through the stone, a sound that poured courage through her veins like fire. If the wardens had rallied in time, hope still remained.

The passageway ended in a steep flight of stairs. At the top, it looked as though the Malefict had burst through the remaining earth by force, creating a shattered opening filled with a circle of night sky. As they clambered over the erupted flagstones, they emerged into the chaos of a battle.

Cold struck Elisabeth like a slap across the face. Cannons boomed, red flashes lighting up the Great Library's salt-encrusted courtyard. A tang of gunpowder filled the air. Wardens pounded past, too engaged to spare her and Nathaniel a glance. Between each cannon blast, screams tore through the ringing in Elisabeth's ears. Ahead, a section of the wall had been breached, its machinery a smoking ruin. As she stared around, trying to get her bearings, a warden staggered back through the breach, grayness creeping across his features like frost. When he had almost reached the library's doors, he collapsed into dust.

The next cannon barrage illuminated a figure rearing above the rampart, the tines of its antlers stretching toward the moon.

With a sideways slash, the antlers took out a cannon, tossing it aside in a spray of masonry.

Elisabeth took a faltering step backward. It didn't seem possible, but— "It's gotten huge," she shouted over the din.

"It's drawing strength from each life it takes," Nathaniel shouted back. "It will only keep growing larger and more powerful."

She turned to him, the wind tangling her hair around her face. "We have to stop it."

Nathaniel's gray eyes lingered on hers. Then he nodded. He bowed his head, his lips moving. Clouds swept over the moon and engulfed the stars. For a moment, the wind stilled completely. An eerie calm descended over the courtyard as the cannons ceased firing, unable to spot their target in the dark. Even the tolling of the bell sounded muffled. In the sudden quiet, Nathaniel's incantation seemed to grow louder, the Enochian syllables echoing from the walls.

"It's the sorcerer," a warden called out. "There he is!"

Elisabeth had been afraid of this. With no evidence of Ashcroft's involvement, Nathaniel appeared to be responsible for the Chronicles' escape. As wardens pelted in their direction, she stepped in front of him, Demonslayer at the ready. Silas leaped from his shoulder, human again before he struck the ground.

Demonslayer clashed against the closest warden's sword, the vibration shuddering up her arm. He had the advantage of skill, but she was taller and stronger. Parrying recklessly, she managed to block his strikes until their blades locked.

"He isn't the saboteur!" she shouted over their crossed weapons.

The warden didn't listen. Veins stood out in his face as he

pushed against her, his sword screeching dangerously along Demonslayer's edge. Her stomach turned when she realized she might have to start fighting him in earnest—perhaps even risk killing him. She couldn't hold him off for much longer without one of them getting hurt.

Nearby, Silas neatly sidestepped another warden's swing, appearing behind him in the same breath. He seized the man's wrist and twisted. There came a sickening crack, and the warden yelled and dropped his sword. Before the weapon fell, Silas had already moved on to the next attacker in a blur of movement. One by one, wardens dropped like chess pieces around Nathaniel, left moaning and cradling their broken limbs.

Wind sliced across the courtyard. Nathaniel raised his head, his hair wild, his eyes rimmed with an emerald glow. Fire danced along his fingertips. He looked like a demon himself. Through bared teeth, he uttered the final syllables of the incantation.

Elisabeth gasped when she lifted from the ground, the toes of her boots weightlessly brushing the flagstones. Electricity snapped through the air, crackling over her clothes and standing her hair on end. The energy built and built until she thought her eardrums would burst—only to release in a rush that pulsed through her body, accompanied by a boom of thunder that felt as though the sky had plunged down to slam against the earth. Gravity yanked her back to the ground as a bolt of lightning flashed on the opposite side of the wall. It struck once, twice, three times, and kept going, each blinding, sizzling blast twisting between the Malefict's antlers and coursing down its body in rivers of green light.

When the lightning finally ceased, her vision was too full of smoke and blotched purple afterimages to see what had happened. But she was able to venture a guess when a tremor ran through the courtyard, as though something heavy had fallen, and a cheer rose from the ramparts.

With a great shove, Elisabeth heaved the warden away. He stumbled, appearing uncertain. More wardens had arrived on the scene, but they hung back, staring at Nathaniel.

His chest heaved. Sparks flickered over his body; miniature bolts of lightning crackled between the tips of his fingers and the flagstones. As if that weren't enough, he was grinning.

One of the wardens started forward.

"Stand down," snapped a voice from above. A stocky woman with close-cropped hair stood on one of the stairways that zigzagged up the inner side of the rampart, watching them. She vaulted over the railing and landed beside Elisabeth. "The battle isn't over yet," she said in a tone of authority, "and these two aren't our enemies. Those of you who can still walk, clear a position for the sorcerer on the rampart. He's a magister. We need him." When none of the wardens reacted, she shouted, "Move!"

Before Elisabeth could respond, she found herself hastened alongside Nathaniel toward the stairway. The warden in charge watched them askance. "You had better not make me regret this. Have either of you seen the Director?"

"The Malefict killed him," Elisabeth said hoarsely.

She looked grim, but unsurprised. "I suppose that means I'm the Director now." She paused, glancing at Silas before her eyes flicked to Nathaniel. "That's your demon, I take it?"

"Ah," Nathaniel said, shaking a few last sparks from his fingertips. Deliberately, he avoided looking at the injured wardens still rolling around in the courtyard, clutching their broken legs. "I'm afraid so, Director."

The warden—the new Director—was frowning. Elisabeth

braced herself for disaster. But all she said was, "He's a bit small," and turned back ahead.

Their boots clattered on the metal grating. When they reached the top, smoke billowed over them in rancid clouds. Amid the haze, the wardens toiling over the cannons were little more than dark smudges picked out by the glow of torches. Elisabeth rushed to the crenellations and looked down. A smoldering mass lay crumpled at the base of the wall, surrounded by toppled barricades, whose spikes combed the smoke as it streaked away in the wind. But the fallen Malefict wasn't disintegrating into ash.

"It isn't dead," she shouted back.

"I would be greatly obliged if you could make it dead, Magister," the Director said. "As quickly as possible, for all our sakes."

Veiled in smoke, Nathaniel and Elisabeth exchanged a look. She knew the truth: there was no way to contain a monster this dangerous. Ashcroft hadn't given them a choice. She imagined the Chronicles getting loose and rampaging through Brassbridge, smashing towers with its claws, leaving a trail of dead and dying in its wake. How would that compare to an invasion of demons? How many casualties, how much destruction? She did not know. It was as though she stood behind a scale, blindfolded, and it was her responsibility to weigh one disaster against another, to choose the way in which the world would end. As she and Nathaniel gazed into each other's eyes, the fate of thousands hovered in the air between them, and there was no time to speak or even think—only to act.

"Yes," she said, each word an agony. "Do it."

"I doubt more lightning will work," Nathaniel said, turning back to the Director. "I'll have to try something else. Give me a moment." He closed his eyes.

Elisabeth's free hand clenched as she stepped back beside

Silas. He was gazing out over the rampart, expressionless, the wind stirring his hair, which was beginning to come loose from its ribbon. She grasped at one last hope. "Isn't there anything you can do?" she asked him.

"I am not capable of miracles, Miss Scrivener." His lips barely moved, as though he were truly carved from alabaster. "I cannot fight the creature; it is the creation of my former master. Baltasar's orders forbid me, even centuries after his death."

She hesitated as an idea occurred to her. Silas's claim wasn't entirely true. If she freed him from his bonds, he would no longer be constrained by Baltasar's orders—by anything. He could stop this from happening. He would have the power to save them all.

"But I would not," he murmured. "You know that I would not."

His tone stopped her cold. "I'm sorry," she said, though she wasn't certain what she was sorry for, precisely—for the thought she had had, or for the hunger in Silas's eyes.

He inclined his head. Then, suddenly, his eyes widened. "Down," he spat. "Down!"

It was the first time she had ever heard him raise his voice. Everything turned sideways as he seized her and Nathaniel and flung them to the ground. The Malefict rose up over the rampart, smoke pouring from its mouth and slitted nostrils, eyes fulminating a foul, necromantic green. Silas pressed them flat as a colossal arm swept over the crenellations. Wind howled over Elisabeth, battering her senses, tearing at her clothes. A horrible sucking grayness dimmed her consciousness; she felt as though her life were a guttering candle being buffeted by a gale. Her hearing faded, and her vision dimmed. There came an eruption of green flame before the world split apart, shattering like a kaleidoscope.

Fragments of sound. Motion. A voice. "Elisabeth." The voice belonged to Nathaniel, tight with barely controlled emotion. "Elisabeth, can you hear me?"

His face hovered over her, a pale, blurry smear against the dark. Soot marked his cheek, and green embers swirled through the night behind him. He was cradling her with one arm, the other gripping her hand, squeezing it desperately. Her breath caught when she saw her fingers, shriveled and leached of color. But as she watched, the Malefict's touch receded. Sensation returned to her hand in a rush of pins and needles.

Nathaniel helped her up when she struggled to stand. Around them, devastation. Emerald flames licked over the battlements and danced along the empty uniforms scattered across the rampart. A lone cannon boomed, and a shriek reverberated through her ears—the Malefict. Nearby, the Director was barking orders, trying to rally the remaining wardens.

"I'm all right," Elisabeth said, adjusting her grip on Demonslayer. "I'm ready."

Nathaniel had a peculiar look on his face. He glanced meaningfully at Silas, then took a step backward. A protest rose to her lips even before he spoke. "I'm going to draw it away—"

"No."

"I have to. I'm the only person who isn't affected by its magic."

"Wait," she said. "You shouldn't. The voice—you might not be able to resist it."

"Don't worry. I have an idea. There isn't time to explain, but . . ." He was already turning, a fiery whip unraveling between his hands, its light transforming him into a tall, slim silhouette. The last thing she saw was a hint of a smile. "Trust me."

Ahead of him, the Malefict finished raking its claws through a tower and turned, chunks of masonry tumbling down its shoulders. Though it resembled the moss spirit they had seen in the Blackwald, the bark that made up its hide was darkened and decayed, split in places to reveal an inner green glow. Nathaniel looked impossibly small walking toward it, his whip a mere thread of light.

Elisabeth wasn't going to stand by and watch. She shoved Demonslayer through her belt and dashed toward the nearest cannon, its previous operator nothing but a uniform and a pile of dust. Sweeping the remains aside, she climbed onto the gunner's seat.

The device was a far cry from the medieval-style cannons she had read about in books. Like the rest of the Great Library's mechanisms, it was a complex instrument riddled with gears and pistons. She seized a wheel and experimentally wrenched it to the left, its metallic chill biting into her fingers. Machinery rumbled to life, shaking the seat so violently that only her grip on the wheel prevented her from being flung off. With a protesting groan, the cannon's barrel swung several feet to the left. Now, up. She heaved on an adjacent wheel, and the barrel rose. All that remained was a lever beside her hip. That had to be what fired the cannon.

Nathaniel's whip spun out, readying to strike. But he didn't follow through. He stood still, gazing upward as the Malefict stooped over him. Her heart skipped a beat, remembering the transfixed expression on his face in the vault. *Move,* she urged. *Fight.*

In the silence, the forest exhaled a breath. Wind swirled over the rampart, fetid with decay, as though issued from the mouth of a corpse. Boughs bent. Branches creaked. And a voice whispered, *"Thorn . . ."*

"Don't listen to it!" Elisabeth screamed. Her pulse throbbed against the collar of her coat as she rammed the lever down.

A rattling sound came from within, like chain links winching upward. The barrel shuddered, its mouth glowing red-hot. Then the cannon bucked in recoil, rattling her teeth and numbing her arm to the elbow. Somehow, she didn't let go.

There came a thin, high whistling, and then a thud. She stood, clutching the wheel for balance. Green light roiled around a metal ball embedded in the Malefict's chest. Elisabeth knew the cannonball must be huge, but against the monster's colossal frame, it appeared no larger than a marble.

The Malefict had barely reacted. She began to wonder whether this had been a foolish idea. Then, the cannonball exploded.

The Malefict shrieked as splinters of its barklike skin went flying. A white cloud puffed around the crater left behind—*salt*. The cannonball was an iron-coated salt round.

Far below, Nathaniel shook his head as though trying to clear it of cobwebs. His shoulders tensed, and he swept his whip through the air, the flame sizzling as it wrapped around one of the Malefict's wrists. Jerking the monster off balance, he raised his other hand, which let loose a volcanic blast of green fire. Thrown back, the Malefict caught itself by clamping its claws down on a battlement. As the smoldering embers fell, it regarded Nathaniel at eye level, near enough to reach out and seize him.

"*I know you,*" it whispered instead. "*Son of House Thorn, master of death.*"

"No," Nathaniel croaked, stepping back.

"*Why do you hide your nature? Deny the call in your blood?*"

Terror lanced through Elisabeth's chest. "Nathaniel!" she shouted. He didn't react, didn't even seem to hear her.

"*I see,*" the Malefict said. "*You wish to spare the girl you love.*"

But you know the truth of magic. The greatest power springs only from suffering." It drew closer to him, its spindle-toothed mouth seeping smoke. "*Join me,*" it whispered. "*Master of death, become the darkness that haunts you. Kill the girl.*"

Nathaniel's arm drifted to his side, the whip fizzling out. Slowly, he turned. Elisabeth didn't recognize the expression on his face. His coat was torn, and his eyes were rimmed in red.

Mouth dry, she spun the wheels, angling the cannon into a new position. She slammed the lever down again. As Nathaniel strode toward her, flames rippled over his shoulders and down his arms like the blossoming of some strange, translucent flower.

The cannon coughed. Stone sprayed several yards in front of the Malefict, a miss. She couldn't aim directly at its head without risking hitting Nathaniel.

Green flashes lit the rampart. The sky above them roiled, a violent, churning mass of storm clouds. Surrounded by a corona of fire, he looked barely human, untouchable.

Elisabeth's hands trembled on the controls. "Nathaniel, stop!"

He wasn't listening. As he continued to advance, lightning streaked through the sky, arcing between the peaks of the mountains. The earth rumbled as snow cascaded down a nearby peak, the avalanche boiling over the trees that dotted the slope with enough force to level a village. Elisabeth had never seen such raw destruction. Worse, Nathaniel didn't appear to even be aware that he was doing it.

A terrible thought struck her. She could adjust the cannon's aim. The cannonballs were made of iron; he wouldn't be able to stop one if she fired it at him. If that was what it took—if that was the only way to end this, to keep him from becoming another Baltasar—

A cool touch stayed her hand. "Wait," Silas said. His hair

had come free, flowing in the wind. She didn't understand how he could look so calm.

Nathaniel was almost upon them. Sorcery glazed his eyes. Flames rolled off his body like a cloak. In a moment, it would be too late to stop him.

"Elisabeth." His voice echoed unrecognizably with power. He held out his hand. The fire billowed back, away from his sleeve, so she could take it.

Trust me, he had said.

She remembered the day that they had met, when he had offered her his hand, and she had hesitated, certain he would hurt her. But the horrors she had imagined, those evil deeds—he had never been capable of them. Not Nathaniel, her Nathaniel, who was tortured by the darkness within him only because he was so good.

The Malefict's words repeated in her mind. *The girl you love.* The truth of it rang through her like the tolling of a bell.

Slowly, she climbed down from the cannon. Heat shimmered in the air, but she felt no pain. It was as though she had donned a suit of armor, become invincible. She stepped toward the emerald flames, and they parted around her, curving away from her body like cresting waves. Nathaniel's hand waited, outstretched.

Their fingers met. He closed his eyes. That was when she saw it: Prendergast's vial hung empty at his chest.

The Malefict howled in fury, sensing the trick too late. It surged toward them, mouth agape, its head looming closer and closer, fetid breath washing over them, as the magic seized them and Harrows spun away.

THIRTY-FIVE

ELISABETH, NATHANIEL, AND Silas materialized in an unfamiliar parlor, in the middle of a group of women enjoying their evening tea. At least they *were* enjoying it, until the severed head of the Chronicles landed on their coffee table.

It arrived with a crash that flattened the table's claw-foot legs and rattled the porcelain in the parlor's mirrored cabinets. Decapitated at the neck, its antlers shorn off, it looked like a boulder-sized lump of charcoal. Staring at it in shock, Elisabeth supposed that it had come near enough Nathaniel to get seized by the spell. But evidently Prendergast's magic hadn't been able to transport something as large as the Malefict's entire body between dimensions—only the head had come along with them. As its muscles relaxed, its tongue lolled from its mouth, glistening on the carpet like a giant slug.

A teaspoon dropped. The women sat stunned, ink splattered across the fronts of their silk dresses. None of them said a word as the head began to disintegrate, spouting embers onto the wainscoting.

"Excuse me, ladies," said Nathaniel. He bowed, which dislodged a trickle of soot from his hair. Then his eyes rolled up, and he collapsed face-first onto the floor.

Shrieks filled the air. Teacups went flying. As the women fled from the room, tripping over the carpet's fringe, Elisabeth dropped to her knees at Nathaniel's side and rolled him over onto her lap. Soot blackened every inch of his exposed skin. His charred coat was still lightly smoking, and the fire had singed his eyebrows. At some point he had gotten a cut on his forehead—she didn't know when, or how, but it had covered his face in blood. She pressed her fingers to his throat, and relaxed when she felt the steady rhythm of his pulse.

"*That* was his plan?" she asked Silas, pointing at the Malefict's head. As though being pointed at were the last straw, it slumped into a pile of ashes.

Gazing down at Nathaniel, Silas sighed. "Truth be told, miss, I suspect he did not possess a plan, and was simply making it up as he went along."

"Ugh. Where are we? Has anyone a clue?" Nathaniel opened one gray eye, startlingly pale against his soot- and blood-covered face. He looked around dubiously, as though he wasn't sure whether he wanted to wake up yet, and then slowly opened the other, focusing on Elisabeth's face. "Hello, you menace."

She laughed, weak with relief. As she stroked his hair back from his sticky forehead, an unbearable tenderness filled her. "I love you, too," she said.

Nathaniel's brow furrowed. He turned his face to the side and blinked several times. "Thank god," he said finally. "I don't think unrequited love would have suited me. I might have started writing poetry."

Elisabeth continued stroking his hair. "That doesn't sound so bad."

"I assure you, it would have proven more unpleasant for everyone than necromancy."

She laughed again, helplessly. A weightless, sparkling joy filled her, like the sunlight of a spring morning after the rain had stopped and the clouds went scudding away, and the world felt new and clean and bright, transformed into a better version of itself, heartbreaking in its beauty. The immensity of the feeling made her ribs hurt. She swiped her knuckles across her cheek, conscious of Silas watching them.

Nathaniel looked at her sidelong. "Scrivener, I know I cut a devilishly handsome figure lying here on the floor all covered in blood—which I hear some girls find quite appealing, strangely enough, and if you're one of them I'm not going to judge—but please stop crying. It's only a flesh wound. I'll be back to fighting evil any moment now."

She sniffed loudly. "I'm not crying. My eyes are watering. You smell awful."

"What? I never smell awful. I smell like sandalwood and masculine allure." He lifted his head to smell himself, and gagged. "Never mind."

"Perhaps you might consider not setting yourself on fire next time, master," Silas said, pointedly.

A clatter came from the hall. A pair of footmen crowded the doorway, one of them clutching an antique sword that looked as though it had been torn down from a mantelpiece, and was now trembling violently in his hands. "Surrender peacefully, sorcerer," he declared, after an encouraging look from the other, "and we won't hurt you."

Nathaniel squinted at him. "You look familiar. Are we in Lady Ingram's town house?"

I hope so, Elisabeth thought. The ink stain on the carpet looked permanent.

"Er," said the footman with the sword, uncertainly.

"Excellent." Before Elisabeth could stop him, Nathaniel hoisted himself to his feet and cast around, wobbling alarmingly. She took one of his arms, and Silas the other. Not seeming to notice that he couldn't stand on his own, he started for the doorway, explaining, "I aimed the spell to let us out near the Royal Library. We're only a few blocks away."

Elisabeth recalled the map of Austermeer, where Katrien had drawn a question mark beside the Royal Library at the center. "That's where Ashcroft is going to finish his summoning," she realized aloud. "It's the middle of the pentagram."

"Precisely. I'm hoping that I've managed to botch the ritual by taking part of the Chronicles with us. But it was so large, there might have still been enough demonic energy released back in Harrows."

"Then we can't waste any time." A grandfather clock ticked in the corner. With a sense of unreality, she saw that it was only eight thirty in the evening. What had felt like years in Harrows had only been a couple of hours.

As they approached, the footman halfheartedly menaced them with his sword. He looked relieved when Elisabeth grabbed it by the blade and plucked it from his hand. She examined the weapon—useless—and stuck it in an umbrella stand on their way out the door.

They emerged into a midwinter's dream. Laughter filled the night as a family trooped past, bundled in mittens and scarves, ice skates dangling from their fingers. A lone carriage sailed by in the opposite direction, the horse's hooves muffled to near-silence by the snow. Candles lit the windows of the houses along the street, affording glimpses of the scenes within: a woman placing a baby into a bassinet, a hound dozing in front of a fireplace beside his master's slippers. Elisabeth's breath puffed white in the air.

The peacefulness of it came as a shock. For a disorienting moment, she felt as though she had hallucinated everything that had happened to them since leaving Brassbridge.

Then, light touched the tops of the nearby towers. She shielded her eyes as it ignited the statue of a rearing pegasus, dazzling against the dark sky, like a bronze sequin sewn onto velvet. The towers' windows flamed gold and pink as the light poured downward. When it struck the street, it swept across the snow, transforming it into a wash of diamonds, glittering blindingly from the icy branches of the trees. Her breath caught. She thought instinctively, *The sun is rising*. But it wasn't—it couldn't be.

The horse drawing the carriage snorted and shied from the glare, its reins jingling. The family who had passed them turned around, exclaiming in wonder. Doors opened up and down the street; heads poked out, hands shading eyes, throwing long shadows across the snow.

"Look!" someone cried. "Magic!"

Luminous gold ribbons danced through the sky, shimmering and rippling, reminding Elisabeth of a description she had once read of the polar lights. It was breathtaking. Spectacular. A sunrise at the end of the world.

"What is that?" she asked. Nathaniel's muscles had tensed.

"Aetherial combustion. Matter from the Otherworld burning as it comes into contact with our realm's air." He hesitated. "I've never seen such a powerful reaction—only read about it."

Silas slipped out from beneath Nathaniel's arm and stepped off the curb, raising his face toward the light. It washed out his features and diluted his yellow eyes. His expression was almost one of yearning, like an angel gazing up at heaven, knowing he would never set foot in it again. He said simply, "The Archon is here."

Elisabeth and Nathaniel exchanged a glance. Then they set off at a run, skidding and stumbling in the snow. For a sickening heartbeat Elisabeth worried that Silas might remain behind, transfixed, but then he was at their side again, effortlessly catching Nathaniel's elbow before he slipped on a patch of ice.

"Its presence has opened a rift into the Otherworld," he told them. "When it is loosed from its summoning circle, the veil between worlds will rupture beyond repair."

"But that hasn't happened yet?" Nathaniel pressed.

Silas shook his head, the slightest motion.

"Then we can still stop it," Elisabeth said.

Silas's gaze lingered on her face, then flicked away. He watched Nathaniel beneath his lashes, expression inscrutable, and she wondered what he was thinking. "We shall try, Miss Scrivener."

Pedestrians clogged the street that passed in front of the Royal Library—skaters returning from the river, their cheeks flushed and their scarves crusted with snow. Everyone was staring at the dome above the atrium. The brilliant light had faded to a dull glow swirling inside the glass, casting the block into watery twilight. Golden wisps still danced around the building, flowing past its marble statues and carved scrolls, but they were growing fainter by the moment, eliciting wistful sighs from the crowd.

Elisabeth's stomach clenched. The sight was undeniably beautiful. And the timing couldn't have been worse. By the looks of it, these people thought it had been a magic show put on for their enjoyment.

"You have to go," she shouted, shouldering through them toward the library. "All of you, run! You're in danger!"

Heads turned, confusion written across their faces; most of them hadn't been able to hear her over the hubbub. And there was another, louder sound, drowning out everything else. A sound like grasshoppers shrilling in a field, swelling as it cascaded toward them. Screams.

At last, people began to run. But they weren't moving fast enough. They scattered in every direction as a fiend bounded into the crowd, snapping and snarling, its teeth flashing in the unearthly light. At the corner of her vision, Elisabeth saw a child trip over a dropped skating boot and fall, the motion tracked by the demon's red eyes. She let go of Nathaniel and leaped forward without a thought, slicing Demonslayer through the air.

The demon swung around to meet her, only to falter when her blade carved through one of its horns and kept going, separating bone and sinew like butter, and only stopped when it rang against the cobblestones, trailing steam. Elisabeth staggered back, readying herself to parry the demon's counterattack, but none came. Its body collapsed to the street, lifeless. She had nearly cleaved it in two.

There, another fiend, standing over a screaming woman—but it dropped before she could act, the crimson light fading from its eyes. She didn't understand what had happened to it until a pale blur streaked past, and a third demon fell limply to the ground. Silas wove through the crowd like a dancer, astonished faces turning as he flashed by. His claws gleamed, flicking out, slitting fiends' throats before they even saw him coming. Awe shivered through her, chased by an instinctive prickle of fear. This was a glimpse of the Silas of old, set loose on an ancient battlefield, surrounded by spears and pennants, transforming the front into a merciless waltz of death. Only back then, it would have been humans bleeding out with each stroke of his claws.

As though sensing Elisabeth's gaze, he paused long enough to nod at her. Her breath stopped. Then she nodded back and turned away, confident that he would take care of any fiends she couldn't reach.

Emerald light flared; Nathaniel's whip had spun out beside her. He staggered on his feet, but sent her a reckless grin, his teeth flashing white against his sooty face. An objection died on her lips when his whip snapped toward a fiend threatening a group of people. Crackling and spitting embers, it yanked the fiend away, directly into the path of Elisabeth's sword.

Conviction coursed through her as she struck the demon down. Her pulse thundered in her ears. After what she and Nathaniel had faced in Harrows, this felt like child's play. Nothing could stop them now.

They cut a swath toward the library, slowly gaining ground. The countless blows numbed Elisabeth's arms and left her blood singing. Every time a fiend leaped toward her, Nathaniel's whip slashed it aside. And whenever one charged at him, Elisabeth was there to meet it with her sword. Dozens fell at their feet.

But it wasn't enough. More kept coming, pouring endlessly down the Royal Library's steps, hurdling from its windows in glinting explosions of stained glass. Between the three of them, they were holding the demons at bay, but they couldn't push inside without letting fiends loose into the city.

Nathaniel's breath rushed hot across her ear. "Buy me time."

Once, she wouldn't have understood the request. Now she spun without hesitation, blocking the fiend that lunged for him as he dropped to one knee, splaying a hand on the cobbles. His hair tumbled over his forehead, hiding everything but the sharp slashes of his cheekbones and his crooked mouth, twisted into a grimace of concentration.

Sorcery snapped through the air. Elisabeth dealt a blow to the fiend that sent it toppling down at her feet. With her view now unobstructed, she saw the moment Nathaniel's spell took hold.

A row of hooded librarians were carved in bas-relief from one end of the library's facade to the other. As she watched, their heads lifted, and their grips tightened on the stone lanterns in their hands. Marble crumbled as they tore free from the building and stepped forward, marching in a faceless regiment toward the fray. They chanted as they went, a solemn dirge that rumbled through her bones like the turning of a millstone.

Above them, angel statues stretched and sighed and unfurled their wings. Their serene faces turned to appraise the battlefield. One climbed down from her perch and bodily flung a fiend aside. Another emotionlessly seized the corner of a sculpted cornice and wrenched it from the library, then hurled it down with enough force to squash a demon flat. Saints and friars joined the battle, swinging everything from marble incense burners to petrified scrolls. Gargoyles clambered from their timeworn posts to meet the fiends head on.

Howls of pain filled the night as the battle's tide turned. This was like the spell Nathaniel had used in Summershall, but magnified a hundredfold. He hadn't just made the Royal Library's statues come alive; he had created an army to fight at his command.

Gaping openmouthed, Elisabeth almost didn't notice the fiend barreling toward them until it was too late. She clumsily deflected its snapping jaws, only to see its claws swiping toward her from the other direction. Then a gonglike peal rang in her ears, and the fiend was swept away, trampled beneath the flashing bronze hooves of the pegasus from atop the tower. Victoriously, it tossed its mane and reared. The ground shook when it crashed back down, sending cracks spiderwebbing through the cobblestones.

"That should keep them occupied," Nathaniel said. He climbed to his feet. Then the color drained from his face, leaving him ghastly white.

Elisabeth caught him before he collapsed. Heat radiated from his body, even through his coat, as though he were back in the throes of a fever.

"Too much magic," he slurred, his eyelids drooping. "I'll be all right in a moment."

Her chest twisted into a knot. Just hours ago, he'd barely been able to get out of bed. Since then he had transported them across the kingdom not once, but twice. He had called forth fire and lightning, and awakened an army of stone. It was a miracle he'd remained standing for this long to begin with. "Can you go on?"

"Of course I can." He gave her arm a feeble pat of reassurance. "I may be useless, but my good looks might prove critical for morale. Silas?"

Appearing out of nowhere, Silas shifted into a cat and sprang onto Nathaniel's shoulder. Nathaniel took a fortifying breath and straightened, suddenly looking much improved.

"Silas is the conduit to my sorcery," he explained, grinning. "At times like this, he's able to lend me some of his strength."

Elisabeth could have kissed Silas, but the look in his yellow eyes suggested that no one had ever dared that and survived. Once she was sure Nathaniel could stand on his own, she took the steps two at a time, dodging a fiend tumbling down in the other direction. The battle had lost them precious minutes. She didn't allow herself to consider that they might already be too late.

The sight that awaited her at the top of the stairs drew her up short. A grand hallway led to the atrium, lined with floor-to-ceiling bookcases that reflected on the polished tiles. But at the end, where the archway should have been, there lay instead an expanse of cobalt sky spangled with stars. Displaced books floated weightlessly around the edges of the portal, which looked as though it had been slashed across the library with a knife. As she watched, a green-scaled imp clawed its way through and skittered up the shelves, peering down at them with glistening onyx eyes.

"That's a rift into the Otherworld, isn't it?"

"Most likely one of many," Nathaniel panted, reaching her side. "We need to find another way in."

"There isn't another way. Not without a senior librarian's key." The keys from Harrows still jangling in her pocket wouldn't match the Royal Library's inner doors. She glanced around, taking in the adjoining hallways that stretched to their left and right. Those merely led to study chambers, meeting rooms, the storage closets from which she had fetched her mop and bucket every morning. . . .

She sucked in a breath. "I know where to go. Follow me." She plunged around the corner without a backward glance.

Nathaniel was close on her heels. "If you're going to smash through another bookcase, make sure I'm out of the way first."

"I won't have to," she said. "I'm going to ask it nicely."

Ignoring his look of bemusement, she cast around for a familiar set of shelves. If only she had been paying more attention that day. Where exactly had she and Gertrude been when it happened? She pressed onward, racing past more rifts, which twisted across the corridor's walls and ceiling like gashes left by an invisible monster's claws. Everywhere, the Otherworld's influence seeped into the library. Busts of old Directors had lifted from their pedestals, floating at surreal angles. Candles hung in midair, and curtains billowed in an unfelt wind. She tried not to think about why the library's bell wasn't ringing, why the halls were empty of people; it was too easy to imagine the librarians drawn into the Otherworld's starry vastness, never to be seen again.

There. That was where the shelves had sprung open, revealing a secret passageway. Unsure whether there had been any specific action on her part that had triggered it, she flattened her palm across the grimoires and pressed her forehead to the spines.

"Please," she gasped. "Let me in."

Warmth pulsed through the leather touching her skin. A rustle ran through the grimoires, as though they were whispering to each other, carrying a message outward. She stepped back, and the panel swung open.

Nathaniel laughed in amazement. When she looked at him, she found him watching her, his eyes shining. It was the same way he had looked at her at the ball, when he had seen her in her gown for the first time.

"What is it?" she asked.

"I knew you talked to books. I didn't realize they listened."

"They do more than just listen." The floorboards creaked as Elisabeth stepped inside. She breathed in and out, tasting the dust in the air, then closed her eyes, envisioning the Royal Library as though it were her own body, its lofty vaults, its secret rooms and countless mysteries, the magic flowing through its halls.

"We're here to stop Ashcroft from summoning the Archon," she declared to the walls around her, feeling far less foolish than she'd expected. She knew, somehow, that something was listening. "What he's doing—it will destroy all of us. I know it's already tearing you apart. Can you take us to him?"

She had never tried that before: speaking not to just one book but to all of them, petitioning the library itself for aid. She had no idea if it would work. A breeze wafted past, stirring a cobweb against her cheek like the caress of an insubstantial hand. And then—

A shiver ran through the floor. Her eyes flew open as the wood of the passageway creaked and groaned. Around them, the boards rippled like pressed-on piano keys, warping the shape of the walls. The transformation swept forward, dislodging clouds of dust, opening a path that hadn't been there before. The passage was rearranging itself. Showing them the way.

She set off at a run. "Come on!"

Beside her, Nathaniel conjured a weak flame to light their steps. Worry lanced through her at the flame's feeble appearance, but other than that, Nathaniel seemed fine. Whatever Silas was doing was working.

The passageway reconstructed its shape continuously before them, sending them careening around so many corners that Elisabeth couldn't guess where they were headed. She wasn't certain if it was her imagination making her feel as though the library's magic coursed through her body, too, propelling her steps and expanding her lungs, an exhilarating sensation, as though she had become something more than human.

Finally, they reached what appeared to be a dead end—but she kept barreling forward, and sure enough, the wall swung outward before she collided with it, opening the way. It was the back of a bookcase; they had reached the passageway's other side.

They stumbled out into mist and silence. Dimmed lanterns made hazy blobs around them, like dozens of moons glowing through a thick fog. It took Elisabeth a moment to figure out where they were. The bookcase that had opened for them groaned as it swung back shut, a deep, quavering, almost subterranean sound, ending in a click that echoed from the high ceiling. Whispers scattered after it, scurrying through the mist.

"We're in the restricted archives," she said, surprised. Though the mist pressed against her face like a veil, somehow she knew which direction to go. "This way."

"Why would the"—she heard Nathaniel struggling to wrap his mind around what had just happened—"the library let us out here?"

"I'm not certain." It would have been much faster to take them directly to the atrium instead of leading them through the Northwest Wing. She forced herself not to reach for Demonslayer's hilt as she stepped forward. Despite the malevolence of this place, she was certain the library didn't wish them any harm.

Toward the middle of the corridor, the vapor thinned. The bookcases became visible, towering around them, mist lapping against their lower shelves like fog breaking against seaside bluffs. They seemed to be far deeper in the archives than she had ventured last time.

Without warning, a huge, white shape reared into the lamplight high above her, and she lurched back in alarm—but it was only a whale's skull, its skeleton suspended from the ceiling by thousands of wires, stretching far into shadow. She again had the unsettling feeling that the archives wasn't as straight a corridor as it appeared. That a person could get lost here, turned around inexplicably, wandering into sections of the hall that hadn't existed a moment before.

As they moved on, Nathaniel's question continued to nag her. Why *had* the library let them out here? Around them, the grimoires were silent. It felt as though they were listening, waiting. Holding their breath. As though they expected something to happen . . .

Her steps faltered at a flutter of motion nearby. The mist, eddying in a draft.

"Watch out for illusions," she said over her shoulder. Nathaniel jerked at the sound of her voice; he had been frowning at a book whose cover was inlaid with human teeth. "The grimoires might try to trick us."

"Not you, dear . . ."

Elisabeth whirled around. The voice had slithered from the mist, its source impossible to identify. She scanned the shelves, but saw no hint of which grimoire had spoken.

From the opposite direction, a different voice said: *"And I suppose we can make an exception for the other humans—"*

"Special circumstances, you see," whispered another.

"We won't harm a hair on their heads. We promise."

"Well? Aren't you going to get on with it, girl? We're waiting."

Helplessly, Elisabeth spun from one bookcase to another, chasing the speakers in vain. "What do you mean?" she appealed. "What do you want from me?"

But the voices had fallen silent.

Nathaniel stepped forward, reaching out as though to touch her shoulder until he stopped himself, uncertain. It was obvious he hadn't heard the grimoires. "Elisabeth?"

She shook her head. "It's nothing."

Frustration gripped her as they started forward again, the

shelves flowing past. It wasn't nothing. They had been brought to the archives for a reason. But she didn't see what could be more important than reaching Ashcroft and stopping his ritual as quickly as possible. If they even *could* stop him, just the three of them, with Nathaniel's magic spent—

Oh. The answer dawned more beautifully than a sunrise. Without a second thought, she turned on her heel and rushed toward the shelves.

Nathaniel sounded dismayed. "What are you—Elisabeth?"

The grimoires didn't hiss or rattle or spit ink at her approach. They merely waited, expectant. She stood on her toes to unhook the chain running across the nearest shelf. She yanked it free, then turned to him, its end dangling from her hand as the books unfolded their pages behind her, rising up. "The library wants to fight back."

THIRTY-SIX

NATHANIEL FOLLOWED HER as she dashed from shelf to shelf, throwing open cages, tearing chains away. This went against everything she had ever been taught. But she felt no guilt, no shame, no hesitation. She felt as though a dam had burst inside her, the waters roaring forth to overcome every uncertainty in their path.

Cries of jubilation filled the air. Grimoires that hadn't tasted freedom in centuries unfurled wings of parchment and took flight. Others toppled from the shelves and scuttled across the floor, joyfully riffling their pages. The corridor's somber gloom gave way to chaos.

"Wait," Nathaniel said. "Are you sure you should be doing this? The library was built by Cornelius. It was meant to summon the Archon from the very beginning." He sidestepped as a grimoire went flopping past his boots. "What if this is some kind of . . ."

He trailed off, but she knew what he meant to say. A trick. A trap. She didn't blame him. But at last, she understood.

The library no more belonged to Ashcroft and his plot than Elisabeth belonged to the unknown parents who had brought her into this world. It possessed a life of its own, had become something greater than Cornelius had ever intended. For these were not ordinary books the libraries kept. They were knowledge, given life. Wisdom, given voice. They sang when starlight streamed through the library's windows. They felt pain and suffered heartbreak. Sometimes they were sinister, grotesque— but so was the world outside. And that made the world no less worth fighting for, because wherever there was darkness, there was also so much light.

This was Elisabeth's purpose. Not to become a warden in the hopes of proving herself to people who would never understand. She wasn't a wielder of chains; she was a breaker of them. She was the library's will made flesh.

She felt it, now—the library's consciousnesses sweeping past her, through her, like a swift-flowing current. Hundreds of thousands of grimoires, coming together as one.

She didn't have words to explain any of this to Nathaniel. Not yet. Instead she looked into his eyes, and said, "Trust me."

Whatever he saw in her face drew him up short. He nodded. And then, as though he could hardly believe what he was doing, he turned to the shelf behind him and began to unhook the chain.

Together they ran down the hall, freeing as many grimoires as they could reach. With every chain she tore down, her courage blazed brighter. Ashcroft had made a mistake. He had come to her library. *Her* home. This time, he wouldn't escape the consequences.

She reached a familiar cage and halted, momentarily forgetting the noise, the paper flying through the air. A withered face floated in the dark, its needle-tipped ribbon glimmering amid the shadows.

"Will you help us?" Elisabeth asked.

The many-toned voice sounded amused. *"Is he handsome, this Ashcroft?"*

"Very."

"How delightful. Just show us the way, dear."

She didn't have a key that would open the cage, but she didn't need one. She wedged Demonslayer between its bars and twisted, bending the old, brittle iron until it curved enough for the grimoire to flutter free. Then she snatched up the Illusarium's glass ball and ran onward. An illusion ghosted to life at her side: the Director, Irena, her molten red hair flowing into the mist. Pride illuminated her wan features as she gave Elisabeth the faintest of smiles. Before Elisabeth could call out to her, she was gone, subsiding back into vapor.

Nathaniel made a choked-off sound. At first she thought he had seen Irena, too. But when she looked at him, his head was turned toward a different spot in the mist, where the figures of a smiling woman and a small, grave boy in a suit were swirling away. Silas gazed in the same direction, his eyes as bright as gemstones. The Illusarium had shown Nathaniel something else—his family. She freed one of her hands and sought his. Their fingers intertwined, squeezing tightly.

Moments later, they burst through the gate. A tidal wave of grimoires swept after them, tumbling into the Northwest Wing at their heels. Leading the expanding swell of parchment and leather, they flew past the skeletal angels carved into the archway and careened around the corner, straight into an army of demons.

Her heart nearly stopped. Scales and horns and wattles filled every inch of the atrium. Rifts spiraled up the tiered bookshelves, rising toward the dome, whose indigo glass had begun to shatter, the suspended shards glinting against the Otherworld's sky. More fiends leaped from the rifts every second. Imps scampered across the railings, and goblins loped along the balconies on all fours. There were hundreds of demons. Possibly even thousands of them.

But Ashcroft's forces were still outnumbered.

An imp stopped gnawing on a bookshelf to glance in their direction. Then, slowly, it looked up. Its black eyes widened, reflecting a swarm of specks, each shape growing larger by the second. A shadow stretched across the atrium as the grimoires came crashing down.

Elisabeth braced herself. An instant later, her world dissolved into a maelstrom of pages. She and Nathaniel stood hand in hand, their hair whipped by the wind, Silas digging his claws into Nathaniel's coat, everything blocked out by a seemingly endless cyclone of parchment that battered them like thousands of wings. The smell of ink and magic and dust choked her nostrils. For a moment, she couldn't breathe. And then, as abruptly as a flock of birds whirling past, the torrent ceased and their surroundings cleared.

For every demon, there were a dozen grimoires. A goblin keeled over, engulfed by a throng of books that surged over its body like a school of piranhas, gnashing and snapping their teeth. An imp squawked as pages snapped shut on its long ears, lifting it into the air. Nearby, a withered face rose above a pair of fiends, evaluating them like a professional seamstress. A needle whipped expertly between them, and they toppled to the floor, laced together with thread. Across the atrium, demons foundered, howling at paper cuts and blinded by wads of ink.

Rallied to action, grimoires cascaded from the balconies in waterfalls of gilt and multicolored leather. Dust clouds rose as they spilled onto the tiles from three, four, even five stories up. A flash of peacock feathers came from the direction of the catalogue room, and Madame Bouchard's operatic wail sent fiends writhing and pawing at their ears.

"We need to find Ashcroft!" Elisabeth yelled. Her voice sounded like a mosquito's whine, barely audible through the din. "He has to be here somewhere!"

Nathaniel caught her shoulder and pointed. Shards of the dome had begun to funnel downward toward the center of the atrium, siphoned by some unseen force. They exchanged a glance, then looked back to the chaos in front of them. The grimoires were winning—but they needed to be winning faster.

Struck by inspiration, Elisabeth set the Illusarium on the floor and brought Demonslayer's hilt down on its orb, splintering the glass. Mist gushed from the cracks, enveloping her in a damp, clinging grayness. When the vapor finished pouring out, the container rolled over, empty. She stared at it in shock. Had there been anything inside?

"*Ahhhhhhh,*" a ghostly voice breathed, emanating from nowhere and everywhere at once. Mist boiled across the atrium, reducing the combatants to shadows in the fog. Fiends lunged toward figures that rose from the mist, only to slump back down and tauntingly reappear behind them. Taking advantage of their distraction, the grimoires set upon them in earnest. Elisabeth watched a goblin attempt to dive out of the mist, then get dragged back in by an unseen force, leaving a silent ripple in the vapors. Yelps and whimpers followed. Then the sounds cut off abruptly, and an eerie stillness fell.

She and Nathaniel dashed forward as the mist began to

shred away, catching on the prone, scattered bodies of demons. She could barely believe it. None had been left standing.

"Look," Nathaniel said. "What are they doing?"

Pages whispered. One by one, grimoires were lifting from the mist. They came together in groups and rose upward toward the balconies in spiraling streams, like flocks of birds taking flight in slow motion. Elisabeth's eyes widened when she saw where they were headed. Each stream was flowing toward a rift.

Her first stunned thought was that the rifts were drawing them in, attempting to destroy them. But the grimoires weren't struggling. They were ascending peacefully, purposefully. Every time a book touched the surface of a rift, it flashed and disintegrated to ashes—and the rift's edges shrank inward ever so slightly, like wounds beginning to heal. Singing echoed throughout the fractured dome: high, clear notes, as pure and silver as starlight.

"They're trying to close the rifts." Elisabeth's heart squeezed like a fist. "They're sacrificing themselves to save the library."

There went Madame Bouchard. And there, falling in a rain of ash, the Class Four who had spat ink at the apprentices every morning. Each of those books possessed a soul. Many were centuries old, irreplaceable. And some of them had just now tasted freedom for the first time since they had been created—only minutes of it, after a lifetime of imprisonment. Still they sang as they gave their lives.

Tears stung Elisabeth's eyes. She couldn't let their sacrifice be in vain.

The mist was almost gone now; the pall was brightening. As the last few wisps swirled away, she and Nathaniel stumbled into the middle of the atrium, into Ashcroft's summoning.

A figure stood ahead, shards of glass circling it like planets orbiting a sun. It was taller than a man, slender and luminous, but even when Elisabeth squinted directly at it, she couldn't make out its features. She had the strange thought that it was like sunlight reflected by a mirror: shifting and intangible, a mere specter of something far greater, radiant and terrible to behold.

Head bent, it regarded the human standing at its feet.

Ashcroft.

He gazed up at the Archon, entranced, bathed in its glow, seemingly oblivious to the battle that had raged around him. Its radiance transformed his features. He looked a decade younger, his expression one of almost innocent yearning. Blood twined down his left wrist, clasped beneath his other hand. A dagger lay forgotten nearby.

Hope leaped within Elisabeth. He hadn't finished the ritual. The Archon was still inside its circle—a circle formed by the map of the library patterned on the floor in tile, which she had walked over dozens of times, never suspecting its purpose.

"Do you see Ashcroft's eyes?" Nathaniel murmured. "His mark is gone. He hasn't summoned Lorelei back."

Then he can't use magic to fight us, she thought. Heartened, she raised Demonslayer over her shoulder. The glint of light on its blade caught Ashcroft's attention. As though he had been expecting them, he spread his arms and gave them a boyish smile.

"Miss Scrivener," he called out. "Nathaniel! I was hoping you would come. You've played such an important part in this, I wanted you to see. Isn't it splendid?"

Behind him, a section of balcony disintegrated, the shattered railings and bookshelves floating in midair around the rift. The grimoires were slowing the destruction, but they couldn't overcome the Archon's power.

"You have to stop the ritual!" she shouted back.

He laughed. "*Stop* the ritual?"

"You're going to destroy everything. The library is falling apart!" She thrust Demonslayer at the slivers of Otherworldly sky twisting above them. "If this is what the Archon is doing already, what do you think is going to happen when you let it out?"

"Oh, Miss Scrivener. If only you understood." His blue eyes shone with sincerity. "Watch." He unclasped his wounded wrist and tilted it until a droplet of blood splattered onto the tile. The blood vanished instantly, as though it had never existed. He extended his arm, showing her that the cut on his wrist had healed, leaving the skin unscarred.

"Do you see now?" he urged. "Once I've bound it, leashed it to my command, anything will be possible. I will change the world."

There was no reasoning with him. Nathaniel seemed to have had the same thought. His whip snapped out, the flame crackling and sputtering. Silas crouched lower on his shoulder and closed his eyes, as though concentrating on lending Nathaniel all of his strength.

Ashcroft laughed again. This time, there was a hint of mania to the sound. He swept his arm through the air, and an arc of light sliced toward them, growing wider as it came.

Impossible. How—?

She didn't have time to think. She threw herself down on one knee in front of Nathaniel, raising Demonslayer above her head. The sword hummed as it sheared through the light. When she rose, its blade glowed red-hot, the leather grip uncomfortably warm and sticky in her grasp, as though it had begun to melt. Shaken, she realized it might shatter if she tried blocking another spell.

A second arc of light flew toward them. They dropped to the floor, watching the beam pass inches above their noses, near enough to slice several fine white hairs from Silas's tail. It sailed all the way across the atrium before it sizzled out of existence. For a moment Elisabeth thought it hadn't struck anything. Then a statue slid sideways and crashed to the floor, severed cleanly at the ankles.

To create the spell, Ashcroft hadn't even spoken an incantation.

"How is he doing this?" Elisabeth cried.

Nathaniel's jaw was clenched, his face glistening with sweat. "The Archon's power must be bleeding into him. Even without a bargain, it's overflowing like a fountain."

And before long, it will drown him.

They rolled apart, barely avoiding another arc as it carved a hissing groove through the floor between them, parting the marble as smoothly as a knife slicing into a pat of soft butter. Then another, sending them scrambling back. Nathaniel didn't have time to cast a spell, even if he had the strength for it. The attacks came without pause, too relentless for them to do anything but react.

"Silas—" she began, but the look in his yellow eyes silenced her. He couldn't transform without leaving Nathaniel helpless. One of these arcs, dodged a fraction too slowly, would leave Nathaniel dead before he struck the ground.

It was up to her, then.

Within the circle, the Archon's light had grown brighter, spilling out over the tiles. It seemed to have grown several feet taller. And its outline was clearer, now: she could make out the shape of wings, and a corona around its head that might have been a crown. More debris drifted toward its orbit, fragments of bronze and marble from the balconies joining the sparkling river of glass that encircled its body. Piece by piece, the library was coming apart.

Heedless of it all, Ashcroft wore a blissful expression, his eyes clouded by a glowing white haze. The light seemed to burn within him, blazing from the inside out. When Elisabeth ducked beneath his latest attack and sprang upright, her face hard with resolve, he smiled—not at her, at the Archon—and raised his arms in a gesture of supplication.

She started forward. Beams of light shot from above like falling stars, splashing on the tiles around her feet. The missiles darted down as swiftly as arrows, too quick to follow, impossible to dodge. She could only keep running. For a moment she felt breathless, invincible. Then, behind her, a sound that made her heart stop: a cry of pain. *Nathaniel.*

"Keep going!" he shouted.

His whip licked past her and wrapped around one of Ashcroft's wrists, wrenching him off-balance. She slammed into Ashcroft a split second later, knocking him to the floor so forcefully that his head cracked against the tile. Before he could regain his senses, she shoved him onto his stomach and yanked his arms behind his back. Remembering the shackles Nathaniel had worn in Harrows, she drew her greatkey's thick-linked iron chain over her head and knotted it around his wrists, tightly, without any consideration for his hands, which would redden and swell in moments. Then she hoisted him up by his collar, pressing Demonslayer to his throat.

He shuddered as the glow faded from his eyes. Then he blinked, dazed, trying to focus. "You cannot kill me, Miss Scrivener."

"This time, I will." She barely recognized her own voice,

thick with fury. Nathaniel's cry still rang in her ears. "If I have to—if that's what it takes."

"Ah, that isn't what I meant, I'm afraid." His eyes rolled up toward the disintegrating dome. "Unless I bind it, we're all going to die together."

Automatically, she looked to Nathaniel. Her mouth went dry at the sight of him sprawled on the tile, clutching his knee, his teeth bared in a grimace. Blood darkened his trouser leg. Silas had returned to human form, and had yanked off his own cravat to tie it as a tourniquet around Nathaniel's thigh, but there was something about his movements—the way his fingers paused, and his gaze lingered on Nathaniel's face—almost as though he knew. . . .

No. "What is he saying?" Her heart threw itself against her ribs, frantic, painful, again and again. She turned back to Ashcroft. "What do you mean?"

"The Archon's summoning can't be revoked. Not upon my death—not by anyone. It isn't an ordinary demon; there is no going back. Now do you understand? You must let me finish. You *must* allow me to bind it."

No. That couldn't be true. He had to be lying.

Because if he wasn't—

She remembered the way Silas had looked at Nathaniel as they'd run toward the Royal Library. *We shall try*, he had said. She wondered if he had known—known that their cause was hopeless since the moment the summoning began. Her gaze shifted back to Silas, and their eyes locked. He had never looked more ancient or more stricken with regret.

"I am sorry, Miss Scrivener," he said.

The Archon's light pulsed. Discordant, inhuman laughter reverberated through Elisabeth's mind, driving splinters through her thoughts. Cracks erupted across the floor and split the tiles. The highest tier of balconies—the only one left now—sagged like an unraveling ribbon, its railing and ladders lifting away. Above them, the Otherworld's constellations had engulfed the dome, but grimoires still ascended in endless streams, committing themselves to ashes. So much loss, so much sacrifice. How could this be the end?

Her mind reeled. When Ashcroft wrenched in her grasp, her numb fingers released him. As though from a great distance, she watched him heave himself toward the circle, awkward on his knees, and raise his face to the light.

"At last, it is time. Great One, I would make a bargain with you."

Another peal of laughter shook the library. The Archon blazed higher, stretching above the second story balconies. Elisabeth was no longer certain that the corona of spikes around its head was a crown. Now, those shapes were beginning to look more like horns.

Ashcroft groaned and slumped forward, shaking his head to clear it of the awful sound. A hint of confusion clouded his face as he looked up again. "I don't understand. Do you speak to me, Great One? I cannot hear your voice."

"You will never hear it, Chancellor," Silas whispered. He sat clasping Nathaniel's limp hand. "You are but an ant, striving for the surface of the sun. To hear its voice would burn your ears to cinders, and turn your mind to ash."

Ashcroft never took his eyes from the Archon. "No. I am different—this is my birthright. For three hundred years, this has been my destiny. My father, and his father—we have devoted ourselves to nothing else. I am worthy—" He grew hoarse.

The Archon tilted its unearthly horned head this way and

that, inspecting the confines of the circle, not paying him any attention whatsoever. Grayness stole over Ashcroft's features. He looked down at the circle, at the tiles that had cracked, breaking its pattern.

A giant luminous hand pressed against the air, and pushed. A stench of burning metal filled the atrium as the claws warped, coming up against an invisible membrane, and then drove through, reaching outside the circle. Ashcroft rocked back, eclipsed by the light stretching above him. When the palm descended, he didn't try to move, only sat gazing up, waiting for the end, and Elisabeth had to admit she wouldn't mind it, watching Ashcroft get swatted like a fly.

Instead the hand came crashing down on emptiness; she had seized him by the arm and dragged him away. As though he were a bundle of rubbish, she tossed him aside.

"Why?" he asked, rolling over, looking at her standing over him much as he had the Archon an instant before. "Why did you—?"

"I wanted to see your face when you realized you were wrong," she said. "That everything you've done, all the people you've hurt and killed, was for nothing."

Behind him, the Archon's claws raked through the marble. Its light stretched higher, almost touching the dome, blotting out half the atrium as it spread its wings. Dwarfed by its immensity, Ashcroft looked impossibly small. Sweat had broken across his brow; his throat worked. "Are you satisfied, Miss Scrivener?"

Elisabeth had desired this moment so greatly: his confidence shattered, his power stripped away. But now that she had it, she realized it was worth nothing to her at all.

"No," she said, and turned.

His face contorted. He scrabbled after her, collapsing to a

crawl, his eyes blank and unseeing. "You must believe me. I need you to understand. Everything that I did, I did for the good of the kingdom. Please—"

She kicked him, and he went sprawling with an anguished cry.

Not caring what happened to him next, she went to Nathaniel. His eyelashes fluttered at her approach, but he didn't wake. She crouched, taking his hand, and saw that Silas still held the other, clasped between his own as though it were spun from glass.

Light spilled over Nathaniel, reflecting brighter and brighter from the floor around him. She supposed the Archon would kill them at any moment, but all she could think was that his hand felt terribly cold. "Is he in any pain?"

Silas spoke without looking away from Nathaniel's face. "No. The end, when it comes, will be swift for you both. I imagined it would be better this way—for you to fight together, and to fall quickly, rather than enduring the death of your world without hope." He paused to smooth the lapel of Nathaniel's coat, then to carefully straighten his collar. As though it were an ordinary evening, Elisabeth thought, making him presentable to step outside. "I apologize for taking such a liberty."

Tears flooded her eyes, and her throat tightened. "What will happen to you?"

He betrayed himself with the slightest hesitation. Finally he said, "It matters not, miss."

"It does." She reached out to cup Silas's cheek. The evening's trials had left her hand filthy, hideous against his remote perfection. But he held very still, and allowed her to touch him, and she was surprised to discover that he felt human, not like a statue carved from alabaster.

A strange serenity came over her. There was one thing left

that she could do. This was the end of the world, and they had nothing left to lose. "Thank you. I just wanted to say that, before . . ."

His eyes flicked to her beneath his lashes. She saw the moment that he understood. She had thought him still before, but now he turned to stone. Though his expression didn't seem to change, there welled up in his eyes both wretchedness and hope, and a hunger so bottomless she could feel it yawning beneath his skin, like the devouring dark of a night without stars. The light had grown blinding; the Archon was almost upon them now.

"Silariathas." The Enochian name poured up her throat and rolled over her tongue like fire. "Silariathas," she said, her voice raw with power, "I free you from your bonds of servitude."

His pupils swelled, black swallowing up the gold. That was all she had a chance to see before the light grew so bright that she had to avert her eyes. A pulse traveled through the library, stirring her hair, as though a stone had been dropped onto the surface of reality, its ripples flowing outward. She gripped Nathaniel's hand, waiting to die. But a second passed, and then another—and she felt nothing.

Nathaniel's eyelids cracked open. The silver had bled from his hair. Groggily, he tried to focus. "Silas?" he managed.

Slowly, Elisabeth looked up. For a heartbeat she thought she had died after all, and was dreaming. Silas stood over them, one arm raised, blocking the Archon's light. *Not Silas. Silariathas.* Horns curled from his scalp, white as porcelain, their spirals ending in wicked points. The angles of his face had grown unsettling and cruel, their delicate beauty filed to inhuman sharpness. His ears were pointed; his claws had lengthened, thin and razor sharp.

He did not seem to have noticed the Archon. He was staring

down at Nathaniel, black-eyed and starving. "You dare address me so?" he hissed. With a contemptuous jerk of his arm, he flung the Archon's hand away. Then he rounded on Nathaniel, bending over him. He was shaking; his hair trembled. He said in a horrible rasping whisper, "Are you aware of what I am—what I will do to your world, as its people flee screaming across the broken earth?"

Nathaniel didn't look afraid. Perhaps he was too insensible to feel fear, which would explain what he did next: he took Silariathas's clawed hand and stroked it clumsily, as though Silariathas were the one in need of comfort, in all his immortal glory, and not the other way around. "It's all right, Silas," he said.

"Do not speak to me, insect," Silariathas spat, wrenching free of Nathaniel's touch. His fingers snapped around Nathaniel's neck, his claws pricking the tender skin as they squeezed. When a bead of blood appeared, he was the one who reacted, not Nathaniel—a shudder ran through him, all the way down his spine. Nathaniel weakly attempted a smile.

"If you kill me, it's all right."

Silariathas froze. His fingers slackened. "You are a fool," he grated, through lips that barely moved.

Nathaniel didn't seem to have heard. He was losing consciousness too rapidly. "It's all right," he repeated. "I know it hurts. I know." And as he slipped away, he mumbled, "I forgive you."

The silence afterward was so profound that Elisabeth heard nothing but the silvery lament of the grimoires, rising above them in streams. Even the Archon had gone still; it gazed down, head tilted, as though this was something even it had never seen before.

Silariathas looked up. Elisabeth followed his gaze and saw a grimoire she recognized passing over them, a withered face, the glint of a needle. They watched without speaking as it ascended to burn itself to ashes—a gruesome, tortured, deadly thing, monstrous but not beyond love, capable in the end of this final act of redemption. What Silariathas thought of it, Elisabeth could not tell. There was nothing in his devouring black eyes that she recognized. It wasn't until he looked back to Nathaniel that she glimpsed a hint of his other self: the being who had watched over Nathaniel as he grew from a boy to a young man, who had put him to bed and tended his wounds and made him tea, fixed his cravat, held his hand through every nightmare. Silas shone through the cold, cruel mask like light flaring behind a glass.

He bent over Nathaniel. Elisabeth swallowed. But he only brought Nathaniel's hand to his lips and kissed it, just as he had done after his summoning, even though agony wracked his face to do so, the hunger struggling every second for control. Then he put Nathaniel's hand down. He stood and faced the Archon.

"Silas," Elisabeth whispered.

Pain rippled across his features at the sound of her voice. He closed his eyes, driving the hunger away. "I am not its equal," he rasped. "I cannot fight it and win." Every word seemed to strain him. "But I have strength enough to end the ritual, and force it back to the Otherworld."

She couldn't breathe. Her lungs felt tight as a drum, locked around an unvoiced cry. She saw again the sword through Silas's heart. Demons could not die in the human realm. But if he went into the circle, and left them—

"What will Nathaniel do?" she choked.

Silas paused even longer. Finally he said, in a voice almost like his own, "I fear he must learn to put his clothes on the right side out. He will have twenty more years now to master the art. Let us hope that time is sufficient." He took a step forward. "Take care of him, Elisabeth."

Tears streamed down her cheeks. She jerked her chin in a nod. Somehow, Silas looked calm now, his face transformed by relief. Faintly, he was smiling. She remembered what she had thought upon seeing Silas smile for the first time: she had never seen anyone so beautiful. She had never known such beauty was possible.

Understanding at last what Silas meant to do, the Archon blazed to greater heights, sweeping its wings through the wreckage. Fragments of marble rained down around them. Tiles shattered, and the dome's glass sparkled like snow as it fell. But she saw only Silas's face, radiant, as he walked into the light.

EPILOGUE

ELISABETH FIDGETED IN her seat. Under different circumstances, the wait would be making her sleepy. Sun poured in through the window, glancing from the Collegium's bronze spires, casting a warm rectangle across her chair. Snores issued from a grimoire resting open on a stand in the corner, who occasionally woke up and wheezed dyspeptically before lapsing back into slumber. The room smelled of parchment and beeswax. But this office belonged to Mistress Petronella Wick, and Elisabeth was wound as tightly as a spring.

She nearly leaped from her skin when a loud, sucking *whoosh* broke the near silence, followed by a thump and a rattle. Just a delivery via the system of pneumatic tubes, arriving in the office from somewhere else in the Royal Library. Even so, her knuckles turned white. If she kept gripping the armrests like this, her fingers would go numb.

"Are you all right?" Katrien asked.

Elisabeth jerked her head up and down in what she hoped passed for a nod.

"If they'd brought us here to clap us in irons," Katrien said, "I'm fairly certain they would have done it already."

Elisabeth glanced at her friend. Katrien was wearing a set of pale blue apprentice's robes, her greatkey hanging against her chest. She was short enough that the chair's edge hit her below the knee, forcing her legs to stick out in front of her, a pose that made her look uncharacteristically innocent.

"But it never hurts to come prepared," she went on, craning her neck to inspect the desk's contents with interest. She was particularly fascinated by Mistress Wick's paperwork, which wasn't written in ink or regular script, but rather embossed with rows of bumpy-looking dots. "I snuck in a set of lock picks and a metal file just in case. They're in my left stocking."

"Katrien! What if someone finds them?"

"Then I suppose we'll have to resort to the second file. But I have to warn you, that one will be less pleasant for you to retrieve if I'm incapacitated. It's in my—"

Katrien clapped her mouth shut as the doorknob turned. Mistress Wick entered, resplendent in her deep indigo robes. The sunlight glinted on her key-and-quill pin as she took a seat opposite them behind her desk. Though her eyes never shifted in their direction, Elisabeth nevertheless experienced the same sensation of scrutiny as last time.

Last time, when she had sat in this office and lied.

"Elisabeth Scrivener. Katrien Quillworthy. I thought it would be most efficient to deal with both of you at the same time."

What did that mean? Elisabeth shot Katrien a look of pure terror, which was met with a shrug.

"First," Mistress Wick said, "I would like to update you on the situation with the scrying mirror. I appreciate your candor, Scrivener, in bringing the artifact to the Collegium's attention."

In the aftermath of the Archon's summoning, Elisabeth had been too exhausted to do anything but babble out the truth—all of it—in one long, barely interrupted stream to the wardens who had dug her out of the atrium's rubble. Shortly thereafter, the scrying mirror had been confiscated from Nathaniel's attic. Now a stab of panic set her heart pounding. For the first time, she realized that her honesty might have gotten Katrien in trouble, too.

Relief flooded her as Mistress Wick went on, "Based on my strong recommendation, the Preceptors' Committee has decided to omit the mirror from both of your records. There are some in the Collegium who would not look kindly on your use of a forbidden magical artifact, even in pursuit of saving the kingdom. I would prefer the information to never fall into their hands." She turned her head slightly. "Now, Quillworthy."

Katrien sat up straighter. "Yes, Mistress Wick?" she said, with a politeness that instinctively caused Elisabeth to brace herself, as that particular tone, coming from Katrien, had once preceded a firecracker going off in Warden Finch's face. This time, however, it seemed as though Katrien meant it sincerely.

"I'm pleased to share that the Committee has also approved the transfer of your apprenticeship from Summershall to Brass-bridge, also on my recommendation. Once this meeting has finished, you will be shown to your new accommodations in the Royal Library."

Elisabeth barely kept herself from laughing out loud in delight. She and Katrien shared a grin. From now on, they would only be a fifteen-minute walk away.

"My suggestion to the Committee was influenced not only by your efforts against Ashcroft," Mistress Wick continued, "but also your bravery in exposing ex-Director Finch's crimes. Had you not investigated his activities, it is possible he would never have been caught."

Their grins broadened. As it turned out, Finch had been using his new privileges as Director to illegally smuggle grimoires into the hands of private buyers. The entire time Katrien had been helping them with Ashcroft, she had also been plotting to rescue Summershall from his tyranny.

"You did excellent work, Quillworthy. I look forward to watching your career advance, and of course, providing any references that you require. Speaking of which—Scrivener."

A flush spread across Elisabeth's face. She was so convinced of her impending humiliation that she found that she couldn't speak. She looked down at her lap instead.

"Firstly," Mistress Wick said, "I knew who you were the moment you set foot in the Royal Library. Had I objected to the situation, I wouldn't have allowed the steward to hire you."

"Oh." Elisabeth paused. Blinked. "How did you know?"

"Most prospective maidservants are not quite so sanguine about books that bite off people's fingers. The steward was very impressed. Now, I have something here to give you." She removed a parcel from her robes and passed it across the desk. "It will not bite off your fingers," she said dryly, when Elisabeth hesitated to take it.

Uncertain, she accepted the parcel with trembling hands. She undid the string, folded the blue paper aside—and stopped breathing. From within, a newly forged greatkey gleamed up at her. Most of the Great Libraries' keys were tarnished from age and use, but this one was brand new, shining as brightly as gold.

"I know you likely would have preferred your old one back, but we were unable to recover it from the wreckage."

Mistress Wick's voice faded out. For a moment Elisabeth was back there, feeling the atrium quake, watching it collapse around her. After Silas had entered the circle, the dome had caved in, leaving her, Nathaniel, and Ashcroft buried under tons of debris. Long minutes of silence had followed as she waited for help to arrive. Pinned alone beneath the rubble, she'd had no idea whether Nathaniel had survived.

She blinked, and just like that, she was back in the sunlit office. She carefully touched her arms, but the last of her bruises had faded weeks ago.

"It's all right," she said, looking up from the greatkey. "I think I'm ready for a new one. But does this mean . . . ?"

Mistress Wick nodded. "Your apprenticeship has been officially reinstated—if you choose to accept it. I will be honest: there are those on the Committee who did not wish to allow your return. But they are outnumbered by those who regard you as a hero. There is no doubt in my mind that you will be accepted for warden's training should you decide to pursue it."

Elisabeth paused. "I'm no longer certain that I . . . want to be a warden." Nothing compared to the relief of speaking those words out loud. "In truth," she said, growing bolder, "I don't know what I want to do any longer, or who I want to be." She looked up from the greatkey and offered, "The world is so much bigger than I once thought."

Mistress Wick looked thoughtful. "I know that your view of the Collegium has changed. But do not forget that the Collegium, too, can change. It simply needs the right people to change it. There are a number of other, equally important posts in the Great Library in which you could make a difference. Wardens tend to forget that not all battles are fought with swords." Her voice gentled. "But you do not need to make a choice now. This key is a promise that whatever you decide, or don't decide, you are always welcome in the Great Libraries."

Elisabeth did miss wearing her apprentice's robes; the long sleeves were useful when there wasn't a handkerchief around. She tried not to sniff too loudly as she wiped her cheeks.

"Finally," Mistress Wick said, turning to both girls, "I must ask you to keep Cornelius Ashcroft's purpose for the Great Libraries a secret—for now. At the moment, only a handful of people know what actually transpired that day. The truth will get out eventually, but the preceptors wish to ensure that when it does, the Collegium is prepared to weather the storm."

And what a storm it would be. As Elisabeth exited the office a minute later, she wondered what kinds of gatherings robed officials were holding in dusty rooms, discussing the revelation that the Great Libraries had been created to summon the Archon. Soon, the news would tear the Collegium apart. And oddly enough, she thought that might be a good thing. It was about time that the old gears got ripped out and replaced with something new.

She and Katrien turned a corner. Deep in her thoughts, Elisabeth almost collided with a boy wearing the robes of a junior librarian.

"Hullo," he said, brightening at the sight of them. He turned from Elisabeth to Katrien. "Are you Katrien Quillworthy? My name's Parsifal. I'm the one who's supposed to show you to your room, and then give you a tour of the library." He swiveled back to Elisabeth, beaming. "And you must be Elisabeth Scrivener."

"Pleased to meet you," she said, sticking out her hand.

He gave it a conspiratorial shake. He also, possibly, attempted to wink—either that, or a piece of dust had flown past his spectacles and gotten in his eye. She couldn't tell which.

It had been a relief to discover that he was still alive. Contrary to her expectations, few librarians had perished during the summoning. When Ashcroft arrived with an army of demons to begin his ritual, they had barricaded themselves here in the offices of the Northeast Wing. Surprisingly, after the atrium collapsed, Parsifal himself had borrowed an axe from the armory to break them out.

Elisabeth prepared herself to walk on alone. Before they went their separate ways, Katrien caught her arm. "How are you doing—truly?" she whispered under her breath.

Elisabeth attempted a smile. "I'm all right."

Katrien's expression grew serious. "I know you cared about him. He meant a lot to you."

She nodded, her throat tight. "It's been . . . difficult. But things are getting better." Hoping she wasn't changing the topic too obviously, she glanced at Parsifal. "You'll like Parsifal. He's kind. Smart. And—er, gullible."

"Oh, perfect," Katrien said.

"Don't get him into too much trouble." She had a strong feeling that Parsifal was going to replace Stefan as Katrien's unwitting collaborator.

She grinned. "I will, but I'll get him out of it afterward. I promise."

Elisabeth spirits lifted as she crossed the atrium. The sound of workmen hammering echoed throughout the space, nearly drowning out the friendly rustling of pages. The sorcerers were long finished by now, but she had been there to watch them work as they raised the shattered balconies, mended pillars, made the bookshelves whole again, like a marvel at the dawning of the world. The atrium wasn't quite as it once was; half the shelves stood empty, and the map in the tiles hadn't been replaced. But beams of sapphire light still filtered through the newly repaired dome, and the air still smelled of parchment dust and magic. Every time she closed her eyes, she felt a stirring, a whisper—a ghost of the consciousness that had woken to rouse the library to battle, now lapsed into a long and peaceful slumber.

When she slipped past a group of librarians out the front doors, the chill in the air startled her. It was so warm inside, she had briefly forgotten that it was already winter.

A tall, slim shadow was leaning against one of the statues flanking the entry. As she made her way down the steps, the shadow detached, limping into the light with the help of a cane. Her heart leaped. After spending all those hours trapped in the wreckage, uncertain of Nathaniel's fate, she still experienced a moment of joy every time she saw him.

The emerald cloak was a thing of the past. In its place, he wore a dark overcoat with its collar turned up against the cold. It looked especially striking against his pale, angular features, with the breeze tousling his pitch-black hair; by now, she had gotten used to the way it looked without the silver streak. Another difference was the cane, which never left his side. As it turned out, there were some wounds even his household wards couldn't heal, especially after spending hours awaiting rescue in a library's rubble.

It was a miracle that they had survived. Hundreds of tons of stone and glass, and it had happened to fall in such a way that both of them had been spared. A miracle, people said, but Elisabeth knew the truth. It had been the library's doing, watching out for them until the very end.

"You're smiling," he observed, his gray eyes sparkling. "How did it go?"

She reached into her pocket and showed him her shiny new

greatkey. "I haven't made a decision yet. But it went—well. Far better than I expected." She sounded surprised even to her own ears.

"I'm glad," he said, with feeling. "It's about time something wonderful happened to you."

"Something already has, according to the papers. His name is Magister Thorn, Austermeer's most eligible bachelor."

"Ah, you know how they exaggerate. Just last week, they were still claiming that I planned to run for Chancellor." As they stepped down onto the sidewalk, he made a stifled noise of pain.

She shot him a concerned look, taking his arm in hers, which promptly bore a considerable portion of his weight. "Did Dr. Godfrey give you permission to walk all the way here?"

"No. He's going to have some choice words for me tomorrow. But as it appears the injury is going to be permanent, I'm of the opinion that I might as well begin getting used to limping around." Thoughtfully, he tapped his cane. "Do you think I should get one with a sword inside, like Ashcroft's?"

She shuddered. "Please don't." Her shudder turned into a shiver as a flurry of snowflakes whirled past. She squinted upward, astonished to see that the sky, which had been blue just minutes ago, was now filling with soft winter clouds. White flakes spiraled downward, spinning past the Royal Library's dome, swirling around the bronze pegasus atop its spire, which she was convinced now reared in a slightly different position than before.

Nathaniel had also stopped to take in the view. "Do you remember the last time it snowed in Hemlock Park?"

"Of course." Blood rushed to her cheeks at the look he was giving her. How could she forget? The frost and the candlelight, the way time had seemed to stop when they kissed, and how he had parted her dressing gown so carefully, with only one hand—

She wasn't sure which of them leaned in first. For a moment nothing existed outside the brush of their lips, tentative at first, and then the heat of their mouths, all-consuming.

"I seem to recall," Nathaniel murmured as she twined a hand into his hair, "that this"—another kiss—"is a public street."

"The street wouldn't exist without us," she replied. "The public wouldn't, either."

The kiss went on, blissful, until someone whistled nearby.

They laughed as they parted, their lips flushed and their breath clouding the air between them. Suddenly, the snowfall struck Elisabeth as very conveniently timed. "This isn't your doing, is it?" she asked, catching a few flakes on her palm.

She realized her mistake as soon as she spoke. But this time, his eyes barely darkened. He merely snapped his fingers, demonstrating the lack of a green spark. "Alas, my days of controlling the weather are over. To some people's relief, no doubt."

She ducked her head as they continued onward toward Hemlock Park. "Have you thought any more about—you know?"

He gave a considering pause. "I miss doing magic, but it wouldn't feel right, summoning another demon," he said finally. "The Magisterium offered to hand over a name from their records, but they aren't exerting as much pressure as I anticipated. Now that the Chronicles of the Dead has been destroyed, and Baltasar's spells along with it, there's no great urgency to have a Thorn waiting in the wings."

"That's good," Elisabeth said. Her chest ached a little. Just days ago, Nathaniel wouldn't have had the heart to carry on this conversation.

"It is. And I'll have time for other things."

"Like what?" she asked.

"Let's see. I've always wanted to take up fencing. What do you think? I'd look awfully dashing with a rapier."

She made a face.

"You're right—swords are your area, not mine. What about cheese making? Flower arrangement? There are so many possibilities, it's hard to know where to begin." He paused in thought. "Perhaps I should start with something simpler. Would you still like to go ice-skating?"

"Yes!" she burst out. "But—" She tried not to glance down at his injured leg.

A grin tugged at his mouth. "We saved the world, Scrivener. We'll figure out a way."

She relaxed. He was right. They *would* figure out a way.

"Even if you have to pull me on a sled," Nathaniel went on.

"I am not pulling you on a sled!"

"Why not? I dare say you're strong enough."

She sputtered. "It would get into the papers."

"I hope so. I'd want to save a clipping. I could put it in my scrapbook, next to all the articles about Ashcroft spending the rest of his life in a stinking, rat-infested dungeon."

She smiled the rest of the way home, admiring the snow beginning to dust the rooftops of Hemlock Park, causing the occasional gargoyle to flick its ear in irritation. Wreaths and garlands decorated the houses in preparation for the winter holidays. Carriages clattered past, flakes coating their roofs like powdered sugar. Meanwhile passersby paused to nod in Elisabeth and Nathaniel's direction, taking off their hats or even stopping to bow, their faces solemn. No one knew the entire story, but the battle in front of the Royal Library, their recovery from the rubble, and Ashcroft's subsequent confession had painted

Elisabeth and Nathaniel as saviors of the city.

Every once in a while, a witness to the battle would pause to ask if there had been a third person there that day. Someone else who had fought with them on the library's steps, as slight and pale as a ghost, there one moment and gone the next. They looked puzzled when they asked it, as though recalling a half-remembered dream.

Elisabeth answered them, but they didn't believe her, and she suspected that they never would. Not the whole story—that it was Silas who had truly saved them all.

As soon as they reached home, Nathaniel vanished into his study, complaining about paperwork. He had volunteered to help with identifying the magical artifacts salvaged from Ashcroft Manor, which was in the process of being renovated into a new state-of-the-art hospital. Surprisingly, Lord Kicklighter himself had taken up the initiative with all the enthusiasm of a general charging into battle. Having shut down Leadgate, he was now eyeing the other institutions that Ashcroft had funded.

Weariness descended over Elisabeth as she stood in the foyer. Strange, how many memories could exist together in a single place. There was the armchair Silas had put her in, when he'd argued with Nathaniel to let her stay. There was where they fought the Codex after it turned into a Malefict. Where she had wiped Nathaniel's blood from the floor after the Royal Ball, and sat waiting, not once but twice, to hear from Dr. Godfrey whether he would live or die. And where, her first morning here, Silas had brushed his gloved fingers over the empty space on the wall . . .

Some days, the memories hung over her like a weight. Each was light enough to bear on its own, but combined, they could make it difficult to even walk up the stairs. And yet, she wouldn't trade them away for anything. Their existence made this house, this life, a place she had fought for and won. A place where she belonged.

"Excuse me, miss!" Mercy called out, sweeping past with a mop, broom, and bucket all balanced in her arms at the same time. Elisabeth lurched forward to help, but Mercy waved her off with a laugh.

She was the first servant Nathaniel had agreed to hire. During those initial grueling days he had refused to consider anyone, until Elisabeth had tracked Mercy down using the records from Leadgate Hospital and brought her straight into his sickroom, where Mercy had declared stoutly, "I'm no stranger to people screaming in the night. And I'm not going to judge you for it neither." She had moved in by the end of the day.

"Please, call me Elisabeth!" Elisabeth shouted at Mercy's back, before she vanished around the corner. She kept trying to explain that it felt strange to be called "miss" by someone her own age. Yet, privately, that was only part of the reason why it made her uncomfortable. In truth, being addressed that way reminded her far too much of Silas.

Instead of returning directly to her bedroom, she wandered farther down the hall and around the corner, where the once-locked door of the summoning room stood ajar. She poked her head in, gazing around at the boxes and furniture that had accumulated inside. On a whim, she pushed aside two chairs and a rolled-up rug to uncover the pentagram.

She and Nathaniel had spent countless nights in here during his recovery, when he couldn't walk more than a few steps at a time but still insisted on making the journey down the hall. Together, over and over, they had lit the candles. Night after night, they had spoken Silas's true name.

And each time no unearthly breeze had answered them, no stirring of the curtains or ruffling of the flames.

They had never admitted out loud that Silas was gone. She supposed that was something that would come later. But one day Mercy had needed to move some boxes, and in her usual practical manner had happened to put them in here. More boxes had joined them, followed by other odds and ends. Weeks had somehow passed without Elisabeth noticing how drastically the room had changed.

Was that what it meant to lose someone? The pain never went away. It just got . . . covered up.

Meditatively, she moved the half-burnt, toppled over candles back into their proper positions. Her fingertips traced over the pentagram's grooves. It still hurt that Silas had no memorial, no grave. This carving on the floor was all she had left to remember him by. In some ways it was as though he had never existed at all.

She would have to talk to Nathaniel about that. Perhaps they could come up with something together. It would help Nathaniel, she thought, to have a place to visit, and perhaps leave flowers from time to time.

For now, for her, this would have to suffice.

She lit the candles, doing so in counterclockwise order out of habit. A strange sort of remembrance this was, holding a wake by herself in a room full of spare furniture. What would Silas think if he could see her? The ceremony wouldn't be up to his usual standards. But she doubted he would mind, even if he pretended to.

After she'd lit the final candle and shook out the match, she paused. An idea had stolen into her mind like an errant draft, elusive and unexpected.

No . . . of course that wouldn't work. Even so, she found the thought impossible to shake.

Moving slowly, she pricked her finger on the knife, and touched the blood to the circle. She sat back on her heels. Every time they had attempted to summon Silas, they had used his Enochian name. But what if—?

He had defied the Archon to save them. He had betrayed his own kind. The version of him that had won out in the end hadn't been Silariathas, ruthless and cold. It had been his other side that had fought and emerged victorious, proven true.

What if . . . what if?

She steadied herself, trying to calm the furious pounding of her heart. Into the silence, she said simply, "Silas."

At first, nothing. Then the hair hanging in front of her face stirred, as though moved by a breath. A sourceless breeze fluttered the fringe of the rolled-up carpet. A paper blew across the room, fetching up against the wall.

And all five candles snuffed out at once.

ACKNOWLEDGMENTS

The sophomore novel can be notoriously difficult to write, and my experience was no exception. I'm eternally grateful to my agent, Sara Megibow, and my editor, Karen Wojtyla, for their support as I struggled to write this second book. Without their understanding and patience, I would never have had the opportunity to find this story.

I owe a huge thanks to my entire publishing team at McElderry Books. Thank you, Nicole Fiorica, for answering my ridiculous questions so kindly. Thank you also to Bridget Madsen, Lisa Moraleda, Sonia Chaghatzbanian, Beth Parker, Justin Chanda, Anne Zafian, Chrissy Noh, and Ellen Winkler for helping this book become the best it could be, inside and out. And I owe my soul to Charlie Bowater, whose beautiful cover illustrations still leave me in awe every time I look at them.

Next, I would like to apologize to my parents, who put up with a great deal of bizarre, stress-induced behavior while I finished this book, and also made sure I didn't starve to death. "Thank you" doesn't begin to cover it. I'm also grateful to my big brother, Jon Rogerson, and my honorary sister, Kate Frasca; and Denise Frasca, for supporting my work so enthusiastically.

Jessica Stoops and Rachel Boughton: you already know how much you mean to me, and that I wouldn't be the same writer or person without the two of you. Thank you. And thank you to my dear friends Jamie Brinkman, Kristi Rudie, Erin Phelps, Nicole Stamper, Liz Fiacco, Jessica Kernan, Katy Kania, and Desiree Wilson for being the best group of people I could ever hope to know.

Fellow authors Katherine Arden, Jessica Cluess, Stephanie Garber, Heather Fawcett, Emily Duncan, Isabel Ibañez Davis, Ashley Poston, and Laura Weymouth—thank you for your wisdom and friendship and incredible books; this journey would be lonely without you.

Last but never least, I'm grateful beyond measure to the independent booksellers who have championed my work, including Allison Senecal, Nicole Brinkley, Sarah True, Cristina Russell, and Rachel Strolle. Thank you so much. You rock.

TURN THE PAGE FOR A SNEAK PEEK AT

AN ENCHANTMENT OF RAVENS

MY PARLOR smelled of linseed oil and spike lavender, and a dab of lead tin yellow glistened on my canvas. I had nearly perfected the color of Gadfly's silk jacket.

The trick with Gadfly was persuading him to wear the same clothes for every session. Oil paint needs days to dry between layers, and he had trouble understanding I couldn't just swap his entire outfit for another he liked better. He was astonishingly vain even by fair folk standards, which is like saying a pond is unusually wet, or a bear surprisingly hairy. All in all, it was a disarming quality for a creature who could murder me without rescheduling his tea.

"I might have some silver embroidery done about the wrists," he said. "What do you think? You could add that, couldn't you?"

"Of course."

"And if I chose a different cravat . . ."

Inwardly, I rolled my eyes. Outwardly, my face ached with the polite smile I'd maintained for the past two and a half hours. Rudeness was not an affordable mistake. "I could alter your cravat, as long as it's more or less the same size, but I'd need another session to finish it."

"You truly are a wonder. Much better than the previous portrait artist—that fellow we had the other day. What was his name? Sebastian Manywarts? Oh, I didn't like him, he always smelled a bit strange."

It took me a moment to realize Gadfly was referring to Silas Merryweather, a master of the Craft who died over three hundred years ago. "Thank you," I said. "What a thoughtful compliment."

"How engaging it is to see the Craft change over time." Barely listening, he selected one of the cakes from the tray beside the settee. He didn't eat it immediately, but rather sat staring at it, as an entomologist might having discovered a beetle with its head on backward. "One thinks one has seen the best humans have to offer, and suddenly there's a new method of glazing china, or these fantastic little cakes with lemon curd inside."

By now I was used to fair folk mannerisms. I didn't look away from his left sleeve, and kept dabbing on the silk's glossy yellow shine. However, I remembered a time in which the fair folk's behavior had unsettled me. They moved differently than humans: smoothly, precisely, with a peculiar stiffness to their posture, and never put so much as a finger out of place. They could remain still for hours without blinking, or they could move with such fearsome swiftness as to be upon you before you could even gasp in surprise.

I sat back, brush in hand, and took in the portrait in its entirety. It was nearly finished. There lay Gadfly's petrified likeness, as unchanging as he was. Why the fair folk so desired portraits was beyond me. I supposed it had something to do with vanity, and their insatiable thirst to surround themselves with human Craft. They would never reflect on their youth, because they knew nothing else, and by the time they died, if they even did, their portraits would be long rotted away to nothing.

Gadfly appeared to be a man in his middle thirties. Like every example of his kind he was tall, slim, and beautiful. His eyes were the clear crystal blue of the sky after rain has washed away the summer heat, his complexion as pale and flawless as porcelain, and his hair the radiant silver-gold of dew illuminated by a sunrise. I know it sounds ridiculous, but fair folk require such comparisons. There's simply no other way to describe them. Once, a Whimsical poet died of despair after finding himself unequal to the task of capturing a fair one's beauty in simile. I think it more likely he died of arsenic poisoning, but so the story goes.

You must keep in mind, of course, that all of this is only a glamour, not what they really look like underneath.

Fair folk are talented dissemblers, but they can't lie outright. Their glamour always has a flaw. Gadfly's flaw was his fingers; they were far too long to be human and sometimes appeared oddly jointed. If someone looked at his hands too long he would lace them together or scurry them under a napkin like a pair of spiders to put them out of sight. He was the most personable fair one I knew, far more relaxed about manners than the rest of them, but staring was never a good idea—unless, like me, you had a good reason to.

Finally, Gadfly ate the cake. I didn't see him chew before he swallowed.

"We're just about finished for the day," I told him. I wiped my brush on a rag, then dropped it into the jar of linseed oil beside my easel. "Would you like to take a look?"

"Need you even ask? Isobel, you know I'd never pass up the opportunity to admire your Craft."

Before I knew it Gadfly stood leaning over my shoulder. He kept a courteous space between us, but his inhuman scent enveloped me: a ferny green fragrance of spring leaves, the sweet perfume of wildflowers. Beneath that, something wild—something that had roamed the forest for millennia, and had long spidery fingers that could crush a human's throat while its owner wore a cordial smile.

My heart skipped a beat. *I am safe in this house,* I reminded myself.

"I believe I do like this cravat best after all," he said. "Exquisite work, as always. Now, what am I paying you, again?"

I stole a glance at his elegant profile. A strand of hair had slipped from the blue ribbon at the nape of his neck as if by accident. I wondered why he'd arranged it that way. "We agreed on an enchantment for our hens," I reminded him. "Each of them will lay six good eggs per week for the rest of their lives, and they must not die early for any reason."

"So practical." He sighed at the tragedy. "You are the most admired Crafter of this age. Imagine all the things I could give you! I could make pearls drop from your eyes in place of tears. I could lend you a smile that enslaves men's hearts, or a dress that once beheld is never forgotten. And yet you request eggs."

"I quite like eggs," I replied firmly, well aware that the

enchantments he described would all turn strange and sour, even deadly, in the end. Besides, what on earth would I do with men's hearts? I couldn't make an omelette out of them.

"Oh, very well, if you insist. You'll find the enchantment in effect beginning tomorrow. With that I'm afraid I must be off—I've the embroidery to ask after."

I stood with a creak of my chair and dropped him a curtsy as he paused at the door. He gave an elegant bow in response. Like most fair folk he was adept at pretending he returned the courtesy by choice, not a strict compulsion that was, to him, as necessary as breathing.

"Aha," he added, straightening, "I'd nearly forgotten. We've had gossip in the spring court that the autumn prince is going to pay you a visit. Imagine that! I look forward to hearing whether he manages to sit through an entire session, or hares off after the Wild Hunt as soon as he's arrived."

I wasn't able to school my expression at the news. I stood gaping at Gadfly until a puzzled smile crossed his lips and he extended his pale hand in my direction, perhaps trying to determine whether I'd died standing up, not an unreasonable concern, as to him humans no doubt seemed to expire at the slightest provocation.

"The autumn—" My voice came out rough. I closed my mouth and cleared my throat. "Are you quite certain? I was under the impression the autumn prince did not visit Whimsy. No one has seen him in hundreds . . ." Words failed me.

"I assure you, he is alive and well. Why, I saw him at a ball just yesterday. Or was it last month? In any event, he shall be here tomorrow. Do pass on my regards."

"It—it will be an honor," I stammered, mentally cringing

at my uncharacteristic loss of composure. Suddenly in need of fresh air, I crossed the room to open the door. I showed Gadfly out and stood gazing across the field of summer wheat as his figure receded up the path.

A cloud passed beneath the sun, and a shadow fell across my house. The season never changed in Whimsy, but as first one leaf dropped from the tree in the lane, and then another, I couldn't help but feel some transformation was afoot. Whether or not I approved of it remained to be seen.

DISCOVER NEW YA READS

READ BOOKS FOR FREE

WIN NEW & UPCOMING RELEASES

RIVETED

YA FICTION IS OUR ADDICTION

JOIN THE COMMUNITY

DISCUSS WITH THE COMMUNITY

WRITE FOR THE COMMUNITY

CONNECT WITH US ON RIVETEDLIT.COM

AND @RIVETEDLIT

Isobel knows that every enchantment has a price.

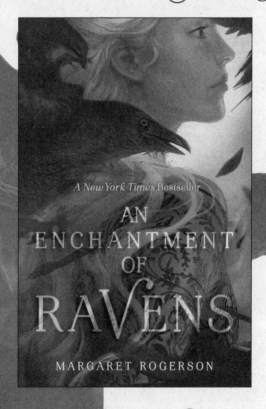

A *New York Times* Bestseller

AN
ENCHANTMENT
OF
RAVENS

MARGARET ROGERSON

Will it cost her her life
when she defies the
ancient power of the fairy
courts and falls in love
with one of the fair folk?

PRINT AND EBOOK EDITIONS AVAILABLE
From Margaret K. McElderry Books simonandschuster.com/teen

Once, a WITCH
MADE A PACT
WITH A DEVIL.

The story says they loved each other, but can the story be trusted at all? Find out in this lush, atmospheric fantasy novel that entwines love, lies, and sacrifice.

"You won't want to leave the beautiful and eerie world Gratton has created."

–Justina Ireland, *New York Times* bestselling author of *Dread Nation*

"Horrifying, heartbreaking, and heartwarming, a lush fairy tale rooted in a moral quandary."

–*Kirkus Reviews*, starred review

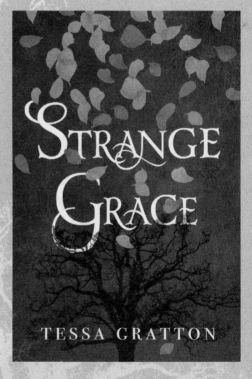

PRINT AND EBOOK EDITIONS AVAILABLE
From Margaret K. McElderry Books
simonandschuster.com/teen

In Alys's village, fear of the soul eaters rules village life.

So Alys must hide her gifts, in case she's called a witch too. And when disaster strikes, Alys must embark on a journey to save her world, a journey through the darkest parts of the fforest—and into the depths of her own heart and soul.

THE
BEAST
IS
AN
ANIMAL
Peternelle van Arsdale

PRINT AND EBOOK EDITIONS AVAILABLE

From Margaret K. McElderry Books   simonandschuster.com/teen

HEY CHOSE HER TO BE QUEEN.
THEY CHOSE WRONG.

PRAISE FOR *THE IMPOSTOR QUEEN*

"Readers will find conspiracy, magic, war, romance, prophecy, corruption, and the truth that there are multiple sides to every story. . . . Recommend to readers who enjoy magical fantasy with a little romance mixed in—especially to fans of Victoria Aveyard's *Red Queen*."　　　　　*—School Library Journal*

"Scorching and chilling. . . . Full of passion, fire, and ice."
　　　　　　　　　　　　　　　　—Kirkus Reviews

PRINT AND EBOOK EDITIONS AVAILABLE

From Margaret K. McElderry Books

simonandschuster.com/teen